PRAISE FOR
WHERE THE DEAD SLEEP

"With *Where the Dead Sleep*, Joshua Moehling solidifies his place as one of the best new voices in the mystery genre. Moehling nails the spirit of small-town life in Minnesota's unique North Country. His understanding of the darkness that can haunt the human spirit twists his story in wonderfully unpredictable ways. Fans of Walt Longmire or Joe Pickett or my own Cork O'Connor have reason to celebrate and look forward to a long life for Moehling's series and its fresh, vibrant protagonist Ben Packard."

—William Kent Krueger, *New York Times* bestselling author of the Cork O'Connor series

"Small town secrets have never been so deadly in this compelling thriller featuring my new favorite deputy, Ben Packard. The plot will grab you; the characters keep you coming back for more."

—Lisa Gardner, *New York Times* bestselling author of *One Step Too Far*

"In *Where the Dead Sleep*, Joshua Moehling continues the compelling journey of tough as nails and conflicted Deputy Ben Packard as he patrols his old stomping grounds of Sandy Lake, Minnesota. Exploding with secrets, this novel has everything you want in a riveting mystery: a brutal crime, fast-paced action, expertly drawn characters that thrust the story from the page, and a jaw-dropping ending that you won't see coming. Looking for a new favorite hero to root for? You've found him in Moehling's Ben Packard."

—Heather Gudenkauf, *New York Times* bestselling author of *The Overnight Guest*

"Evocative and charming with a deadpan wit, Joshua Moehling's *Where the Dead Sleep* is a richly satisfying mystery with fully-drawn characters— especially the winning and deeply human protagonist, Sheriff Ben Packard.

Joshua Moehling's skill as a writer and storyteller is evident on every page. I can't wait to read the next installment in this excellent series!"

—Nick Petrie, bestselling author of *The Runaway*

"Observant and authentic (and funny, too), *Where the Dead Sleep* is a perfect mystery, the literary descendant of *Fargo* and *Mare of Easttown* and an exploration of all the nooks and shadows that make Sandy Lake, MN, an ideal place to spend a summer and a chilling place to pass a winter. I'd highly recommended it to every fan of crime fiction but especially those reading in a lake house just after sunset."

—Adam White, bestselling author of *The Midcoast*

"Joshua Moehling has quickly become one of my favorite must-read authors, and *Where the Dead Sleep* shows exactly why. The characters are rich, and the small-town setting, where everyone has a secret and everyone is a potential suspect or victim, is brought vividly to life. This is a suspenseful, gut-wrenching page-turner of the highest order. Not to be missed!"

—David Bell, *New York Times* bestselling author of *Try Not to Breathe* and *She's Gone*

"*Where the Dead Sleep* is a beautifully written mystery that had me on the edge of my seat. Joshua Moehling has created unforgettable characters in a story that kept me guessing the whole way through. *Where the Dead Sleep* is not to be missed."

—R. J. Jacobs, author of *This Is How We End Things*

"When a diabolically wealthy family pits themselves against each other, it's hard to know who to believe, unless you're Deputy Benjamin Packard. Josh Moehling lays out a deliciously complex plot and turns sleepy Sandy Lake into anything but."

—John McMahon, author of *The Good Detective*

PRAISE FOR
AND THERE HE KEPT HER

"A dark and complex mystery that will consume you, starring a protagonist who is equal parts quirky Milhone and steady Gamache."

—Julie Clark, *New York Times* bestselling author of *The Last Flight*

"Joshua Moehling is a fresh, powerful new voice in crime fiction. His debut novel is a twisted ride with a detective you won't soon forget. This book isn't just unputdownable, it's the definition of the word."

—Samantha Downing, international bestselling author of *For Your Own Good*

"When Deputy Sheriff Ben Packard investigates the disappearance of two teenagers in Sandy Lake, Minnesota, he exposes the seamy underbelly of a small American town. *And There He Kept Her* is a sharp, intense thriller combining a dark plot with a relentless pace. An absorbing, impressive debut."

—A. J. Banner, #1 Amazon, *USA Today*, and
Publishers Weekly bestselling author

"There's a terrific new voice in crime fiction, and it belongs to Joshua Moehling. *And There He Kept Her* is a taut, beautifully written thriller reminiscent of Karin Slaughter. A novel with heart, its protagonist, Deputy Sheriff Ben Packard, is the kind of hero we need today, a man wrestling with his sexual identity as he searches for missing teens in a small Minnesota town guarding secrets of its own."

—Jonathan Santlofer, author of *The Last Mona Lisa*

ALSO BY JOSHUA MOEHLING

And There He Kept Her

WHERE THE DEAD SLEEP

JOSHUA MOEHLING

Poisoned Pen
PRESS

Published by Poisoned Pen Press, an imprint of Sourcebooks
P.O. Box 4410, Naperville, Illinois 60567-4410
(630) 961-3900
sourcebooks.com

Library of Congress Cataloging-in-Publication Data

Names: Moehling, Joshua, author.
Title: Where the dead sleep / Joshua Moehling.
Description: Naperville, Illinois : Poisoned Pen Press, [2023] | Series:
  Ben Packard ; book 2
Identifiers: LCCN 2022061914 (print) | LCCN 2022061915 (ebook) | (hardcover) | (epub)
Subjects: LCGFT: Detective and mystery fiction. | Novels.
Classification: LCC PS3613.O3344 W54 2023 (print) | LCC PS3613.O3344
  (ebook) | DDC 813/.6--dc23/eng/20230106
LC record available at https://lccn.loc.gov/2022061914
LC ebook record available at https://lccn.loc.gov/2022061915

Printed and bound in the United States of America.
VP 10 9 8 7 6 5 4 3 2 1

For my mom and dad

CHAPTER ONE

THE DOG WAS INCONSOLABLE.

He had spent the night pacing the house, lumbering on three legs, wheezing and thumping like a jug band, all thudding footsteps and panting breaths and tinkling tags. Occasionally, overcome by some canine emotion, he would topple sideways as if there was no point in going on, only to find the strength to rise again once that spot on the floor got too warm.

Back in the bedroom, the dog watched his sleeping human, yawned, then whimpered and nudged the bed until Ben Packard lifted his bleary face out of the pillow.

Packard touched his phone to check the time—not yet 5:00 a.m.—and reached down to pet Frank. At Packard's touch, the corgi got on his hind legs and put his single front paw on the side of the mattress, looking for some help to get the rest of the way up.

"No, go lie down," Packard whispered. "There's no room for you."

In Frank's spot on the bed was a naked man breathing low and deep whose name Packard couldn't remember.

Don or Dan.

Dave?

The day prior was the Sandy Lake Labor Day festival. Packard had walked the length of Main Street through a crowd dressed in shorts and sunglasses soaking up the sunshine on the last official weekend of summer. It felt nice not to be stuck at his desk or investigating anything for once. His only job was to say hi to people and make sure everyone was having a good time.

Vendors under tailgating tents lined both sides of the street and fanned themselves behind tables set up with soaps and candles and local honey. There was Adirondack furniture for sale, and wooden signs painted with rules for the cabin and every saying imaginable involving the words *mama* and *wine*.

Gary Bushwright was there, advertising his dog shelter and kenneling services. A black Lab mix and a long-haired dachshund panted in the shade. Gary was dressed in cargo shorts and flip-flops. His enormous beard obscured most of the Gary's Kids logo on his T-shirt. He twiddled his fingers in Packard's direction and beckoned him under the tent as he talked to the mom of the two blond girls petting the dogs. "Deputy Packard got his dog from Gary's Kids, didn't you?"

Packard took off his sunglasses. He was tall, in his early forties, with a swimmer's build that made even the department's bland uniform look good. He had a neat, trimmed beard and dark hair, slightly receded at the temples, that he kept military short. "I got most of my dog from Gary. He only came with three legs."

One of the girls looked unconvinced. "Dogs have four legs," she instructed.

Packard took out his phone and pulled up a photo of Frank. "See, only three feet. Gary gave me a discount, but he also said he'd order a new foot. I'm still waiting."

"Why don't you get the foot?" the younger girl asked Gary.

"Honey, he's teasing you. The deputy is very happy with his dog as is, and he's going to pay extra next time he wants him kenneled."

Packard gave the girls deputy stickers and made his way to the park where St. Stephen's Catholic Church was hosting a bake sale and a dunk tank. A soggy old man in jean shorts and a white tank top sat suspended over the water, egging on a ten-year-old boy throwing left-handed.

Stan Shaw, the current elected sheriff of Sandy Lake County, and his wife, Marilyn, were sitting on folding chairs in the shade of a tall arborvitae. Stan looked gray and gaunt. The back of his hands and his arms were spotted and badly bruised from every time he'd been stuck with a needle. An oxygen tube went under his nose and connected to a tank between his feet.

"I got a report about some trouble over here," Packard said.

Marilyn put the last bite of a brownie in her mouth, stood up, and hugged him. "The only trouble over here is me not fitting into my pants after working this bake sale all day," she said.

Stan gave Packard a slight smile and held out his hand. "It's a beautiful day," he said, looking genuinely pleased to be outside. Cancer had withered his body and weakened his voice. If Packard hadn't been making regular visits to see his boss for the past several months, he didn't think he'd recognize the man whose hand he was shaking.

"Great to see everyone enjoying themselves," Packard said.

There was a crash from the dunk tank as the old man dropped into the soup. The boy throwing the balls looked at his parents with surprise.

"I bet you took a few dips in that tank," Packard said to Stan. He and Marilyn were longtime members of St. Stephen's.

"Fewer than you might think," Stan said. His voice was barely more than a whisper. "I reminded people I knew their license plate numbers and where they lived."

On the far side of the park, firefighters and deputies helped kids in and out of a fire engine and a patrol car that had its emergency lights flashing. Another thrower dunked the old man.

"Benjamin, there's pan-banging chocolate chip cookies over there," Marilyn said. She was brushing crumbs from her blouse with one hand and holding

Stan's hand across the gap between their chairs with the other. "They're crinkly and have crunchy salt on top. Make sure you try one."

Packard adjusted his belt. "All right then. I'm going to keep moving. I'll stop by the house after the budget meeting with the council later this week."

At this point in his cancer battle, Packard knew Stan Shaw cared about the department budget like he cared about thirty-year mortgage rates. Keeping him in the loop was a game they played, more for Packard's benefit than Stan's. "Keep up the good work, Sheriff," Stan said.

Packard didn't think he'd ever get used to Stan calling him that. Technically, Packard was the acting sheriff. Even that felt like a title he hadn't earned, didn't deserve. There was no point protesting. Stan felt otherwise.

From the park, Packard wandered over to the fenced area behind the stage where the bands playing later that night were waiting their turn to sound check. He said hi to the high school band director and the brother-and-sister acoustic duo, then navigated a maze of folding chairs and tables to where three others were sitting.

"You guys must be the headliners."

"We're three of the six," said a man in a sleeveless T-shirt with drumsticks in one hand. He stood up to shake Packard's hand, said his name. Dylan? Dale? Mid- to late thirties. Blond hair swept back from his forehead and buzzed short on the sides. Arms and shoulders like grapefruits packed into a tube sock. He introduced the other two. "The rest are on their way."

"What's the name of your band again?"

"Maneater," the drummer said with a raised eyebrow. "After the Hall & Oates song."

They were based in St. Cloud and billed themselves as a yacht-rock cover band. They played songs by Michael McDonald, Christopher Cross, and other light rock artists from the '70s and '80s.

"Are you coming to see us tonight?"

"Planning on it," Packard said. "I'll be off duty in a few hours."

"I'll look for you," the drummer said. He lifted the front of his shirt to wipe his forehead, showing off a flat stomach and the colorful waistband from a pair of designer underwear.

Packard looked and the drummer caught him looking and smiled.

———

When they took the stage later that night, the members of Maneater all wore white captain's hats with gold embroidered anchors. The lead guitar player took the costuming to the next level with a white officer's uniform, open at the throat to reveal his hairy chest and gold chains. He traded off singing duties with a young woman with thick, curled hair and a voice fit for church or a blues bar. Rounding out the band were a keyboardist, a bass player, and a fat man in a Hawaiian shirt who provided the requisite '80s saxophone solos.

The drummer had changed into tight white pants and a striped shirt that made him look like he was in the French navy. The shirt was a size too small and stretched taut as a sail.

As the sun set, the band played "Right Down the Line" and "Ride Like the Wind" and "Sara Smile." The crowd knew every word to every song. The band played "Islands in the Stream" and "Silly Love Songs" and "Love Will Keep Us Together." Small kids wearing glow-in-the-dark necklaces practiced their dance moves with their parents in front of the stage. More people filled in behind them. A trio of intoxicated women off to one side clung to each other and danced in circles and smoked cigarettes as they sang along.

The drummer played a solo during Chaka Khan's "Ain't Nobody." He looked good up there, sweating under the low-hanging stage lights, bouncing and swiveling as he rolled over the top of everything in his kit. He had forearms like Christmas hams.

The band played their last song—"Lonesome Loser"—and thanked everyone for coming out. As they broke down their equipment, fireworks shot up behind the old water tower. Packard watched the upturned faces in the crowd change colors as explosions echoed down Main Street. Labor Day meant another summer in Sandy Lake had come and gone. Fall would be too short. Winter loomed.

When the final shower of sparks winked out, the crowd began to disperse. Packard talked to people he knew, never wandering far from the stage. He was stalling. He couldn't say exactly what he was expecting with regard to the drummer, but he wanted to create the opportunity for something to happen. The end of another season—more than birthdays or New Year's Eve—made him feel the passing of time. A person only had so many summers in his life.

He was looking at his phone when the drummer suddenly appeared at his side. "How'd you like the show?"

"That's the most bulletproof set list I've ever heard," Packard said.

"People love the yacht rock. We could play a gig every day of the week if we wanted to."

"I believe it."

"Are we too late for a beer?"

Packard checked the time on his phone. "Last call at the beer tent was ten minutes ago."

"Where can we still get a drink?"

"Bob's is right there." Packard nodded at the hole-in-the-wall bar at the end of Main Street, where yellow light and the noise of a crowd spilled from the open door.

"What about your place?" the drummer asked.

Packard turned and really looked at this guy, trying to be certain that the proposition meant what he thought it meant. The drummer gave him a sideways grin and a raised eyebrow. Packard remembered the flash of flat belly and designer underwear he'd seen earlier.

It meant what he thought it meant.

Packard closed the distance between them by a step. "You want to go to my place?"

"I do."

"Then let's go."

They walked to the end of the street and then across the park. People were disappearing into the dark, carrying kids and lawn chairs. "I'm the red Ford truck," Packard said.

"I'll follow you."

At his house, the beers Packard opened were barely touched, forgotten in a flurry of mouths and hands under shirts and the *jingle thunk* of pants with phones and keys in the pockets hitting the floor. Frank barked and danced around their ankles for a minute, then found a rawhide that was more interesting and left them alone.

There was no getting back to sleep. Packard slid out of bed and grabbed his phone. Frank followed him out to the living room, where Packard opened the sliding glass patio door to see if the dog wanted to go out. Cold morning air swirled in, making them both dance from foot to foot. Frank looked up at Packard like he was out of his mind for even suggesting such a thing.

Packard closed the door and stood naked in front of the glass. Fog lurked in the low spots and on the lake behind his house. It had been a long summer of tying up loose ends from the Emmett Burr case. They'd found three women buried on Emmett's property and still only knew the identities of two of them. Jenny Wheeler, the daughter of Packard's cousin, had been held captive by Emmett and nearly became his fourth victim. Between that case, the extra duties of being the acting sheriff, and coming home to a house in a permanent state of construction, Packard felt like a rope being twisted tighter and tighter.

But today was his day off. Nowhere to go, no need to get out of bed if he and the drummer decided not to. A strange, elusive feeling came over him in the moment. *Contentment* was too strong a word. A touch of peace maybe. A temporary madness.

Then his phone vibrated in his hand and the screen said DEPUTY REYNOLDS, and Packard's satisfied feeling took flight and left him behind.

"Sorry to call you so early, Sheriff, but you're up to catch the next case according to Deputy Thielen."

Packard had the irrational thought that his deputy could see him naked in the window, so he stepped back from the glass into the darkness of the living room with Frank at his heels.

Last night at the dance, he'd promised Thielen he'd take the next case, no matter what it was, because she was overwhelmed with work. He'd failed to stipulate that he meant after his day off.

"What's going on, Reynolds?"

"We've got a male victim. Multiple GSWs. Someone came through a sliding glass door, shot this guy in his bed, and fled. Wife called it in. She's unharmed. We've got the location secured and crime scene has been called."

"Who is it?"

"The victim is William Sandersen."

"The wife's name?"

"Carolyn Walbach."

The names didn't mean anything to Packard. "Send me the address. I'll be there as soon as I can."

Before going back to the bedroom he googled *Maneater band MN*. The About Us page on the band's website listed Maneater's drummer as Brad Ruble.

Brad?

That didn't sound right. He could have sworn it started with a *D*. Doug or Drew?

Whoever he was, he was awake when Packard came back to the bedroom.

"I heard you talking. Work?"

Packard nodded and turned on the lamp by the bed.

"Must be serious for them to call you this early."

Packard said yeah but didn't elaborate. "Listen Brad, I hate to do this to you, but I'm needed at the scene and I can't leave you here. No offense. It's just..."

Brad sat up and rubbed his face. "I get it. Wouldn't hurt to get back to

St. Cloud and get my gear unloaded before it gets hot again." He fell back and pulled away the bedsheet so Packard could see all of him, stretched out and naked. "How much of a hurry are you in?"

Packard looked at the drummer, then looked at the time on his phone. "I should… I should get going."

"You need to shower, though, right?"

"I do."

"Want company?"

"A quick shower," Packard said.

"I can be quick," Brad said and stuck out his hand.

Packard put down the phone and hauled the drummer out of his bed.

––––––––

The sky was turning from purple to gray with the coming dawn as Packard poured coffee into his travel mug. He handed Brad his in a to-go cup with a lid.

"That's some bathroom you've got," Brad said. Every other room in the house was still in a state of construction, but the main bathroom was an oasis with its infrared sauna, two-person shower, and heated floor. "Like something out of a hotel," he said.

"That was the idea," Packard said as he herded him toward the door. "It was great meeting you, Brad. I enjoyed it."

"Likewise," Brad said. He smiled but looked like he had something else he wanted to say. *Nothing can get in the way of a long Minnesota goodbye*, Packard thought. *Even between two strangers. Even when there's a dead body waiting.*

Brad reached for his wallet and took out a card. "My numbers. Stay in touch."

Packard looked at the card. "Wait, your name is Dave?"

CHAPTER TWO

PACKARD FOLLOWED DAVE BACK toward town and when they came to the highway, Dave went one way and Packard went the other. The name thing was embarrassing but not mortally so. Dave said Brad was the band's old drummer, who had quit after his wife had twins. Dave had been drumming with them for six months, and no one had gotten around to updating the website. They both had a good laugh about it. Dave's business card was from his day job as an insurance inspector. He told Packard to call if he found himself in St. Cloud.

The hazy glow of a good lay made up for the early hour. Packard drove and grinned as he recalled things they'd said and done. There was no shortage of comedy in the male nude or the slip slide of unfamiliar bodies. *Enjoy this feeling,* he reminded himself. It would burn off as soon as he came face-to-face with the dead man.

The nav system in the sheriff's SUV took him east on a two-lane highway into the rising sun, past the turnoff for Blank Township. Blank was all of five blocks by five blocks. It had streets named after trees that ran north–south, and numbered avenues that ran east–west. Two baseball diamonds marked one end of town, a one-stall fire station the other.

Packard headed north and up a slight rise that slowly revealed two sheriff's cars and an ambulance with lights going. The crime-scene van hadn't arrived yet, not unexpected since it was early on a Sunday morning. It would take time to round up the team. All the emergency vehicles were parked in a row, blocking one lane of the road. No one parked on the gravel shoulder in case the shooter had parked there. Part of the investigation would be to go up and down both sides of the road, looking for signs of a stopped vehicle.

Packard parked in the line and got out. Yellow tape twisted and flapped across the driveway of a split-level house with a two-car garage. Behind the house, Packard saw the blue-black water of a small lake. From where he stood, it looked like no other houses shared the water.

Deputy Reynolds, the department's newest hire, was standing at the door. He was a pink-faced local kid just out of college with a criminal science degree. He looked like he shaved once a month. Had a wife and a baby already. "Tell me again who we've got," Packard said.

"The victim is William Sandersen. His wife is Carrie Walbach."

"Different last names?"

"Yeah. Second marriage for both. Deputy Baker is inside with Ms. Walbach. I've been out here standing where I was told."

"Anybody else in the house at the time? Kids?"

Reynolds shook his head.

"Who's in the other squad?"

"Deputy Shepard is around back."

Packard grunted, like he did every time Shepard's name came up.

Through the door, a short set of stairs went up to a living area and another set went down to a lower-level walkout. Carolyn Walbach was sitting on a sectional sofa with her back to the front windows, dressed in a thick white robe and light-blue slippers. Her eyes were red. She looked exhausted and frightened. Deputy Baker—black hair, early forties, graying goatee—sat next to her and was writing in a notebook.

The sight of another officer was enough to bring fresh tears from Carolyn. She pressed a tissue to her nose and lowered her head.

"Carolyn, I'm Ben Packard. I'm the acting sheriff and a detective with the Sandy Lake County Sheriff's Department. I'm sorry for your loss."

Carolyn nodded and he let her cry for a minute. She looked to be midforties, with a thin face and straight brown hair that came down to her shoulders.

He asked Baker if they had consent to search and Baker nodded. "Carolyn, I'm going to look around, and then I'll want to ask you some questions," he said. "I'll be right back."

Packard noted signs of money spent everywhere he looked. The living room had hardwood floors with inlays around the perimeter. The furniture was new and looked vaguely uncomfortable. Walls had been taken down and a beam put in to open the upper level so you could stand in one place and take in the high-end kitchen, the French doors that opened to a deck overlooking the lake, and a dining area where an expensive light fixture sprouted Edison bulbs in all directions over a sleek wooden table. Down a short hallway were a guest bedroom, a bathroom, and a master suite. Packard did a double take at the unmade bed and the absence of a dead body.

He went downstairs and found a carpeted great room with a pool table and leather recliners in front of a movie screen. A large gun safe was tucked into a corner. There were three doors—one led to laundry and a bathroom, one to another guest room, and the final one to yet another bedroom, this one with a dead man in the bed and the smell of blood in the air. A sliding glass door was half-open. Packard could see Shepard in the backyard, staring at his phone.

Packard stayed out of the room and shined his flashlight on the body in the bed. It was turned away from the door. There was blood on the wall behind the bed and on the sheets. Packard spent a minute imagining the door sliding open in the middle of the night and someone shooting Bill Sandersen in his sleep. The door didn't look forced from where Packard stood. Unlocked doors weren't as common as they used to be but not unheard of either. Could be someone left it unlocked to let the killer in, or the killer came in a different way and only exited through the sliding door.

Back up the stairs to the living room. Through the large front window behind Carolyn, Packard saw the crime-scene van pull up behind his vehicle. A man and a woman in black shirts got out. There was nothing but farmland across the road from the house. Not the most rural location, but no neighbors within half a mile, at least.

Packard took a chair from the dining room table and set it in front of the couch. He started by asking Carolyn to state her full name, date of birth, and relationship to the victim. He asked her what she did for work.

"I'm the CEO of the Gherlick Family Trust. It was started by my father thirty years ago. The trust makes annual grants to organizations across Minnesota that are trying to address issues associated with child poverty."

Packard nodded, made some notes in his notebook. "Carolyn, I know Deputy Baker has been taking your statement about what happened, but I'd like to hear it for myself before we let you try to get some rest."

Carolyn took a deep, hitching breath. Her shoulders twitched involuntarily, a sign of someone who'd been up all night. She looked like she wanted nothing more than to slowly tip to the side and close her eyes. "I was asleep in my room—"

"Back up," Packard interrupted. "Tell me what you and your husband did last night."

"I spent the evening visiting my mother. She's in the early stages of dementia. I stop in and see her every other evening or so. Bill went out to meet his friend Roger."

"What's Roger's last name?"

"Freeman," Carolyn said.

"What time did you get home? What time did Bill get home?"

"Me around ten. Bill later. Probably around midnight."

Packard was waiting for Carolyn to look him in the eye when she answered. So far she'd only stared at her hands in her lap. "Did you see him or talk to him when he got home?" he asked.

"No. I was in bed already," Carolyn said.

"Did you hear him come in?"

"Yes."

"Then what?" Packard asked.

"He went to bed, I guess."

"You and your husband have separate bedrooms."

Now Carolyn looked at him. "Yes. Bill uses a CPAP machine for sleep apnea," she said and used her hand to cover her nose and mouth. "He snores terribly. It's better for us both to have our own rooms."

"How long have you been married?"

"A little over two years."

"Children?"

"I have two grown children from my first marriage. Twins. Rebecca and Ryan. They're both graduated from college. Rebecca lives in Duluth, Ryan in Minneapolis. Bill never had any kids."

The two crime-scene investigators came through the door at that point, led by Deputy Reynolds. The woman carried a plastic storage bin with a lid. The man had a metal clipboard and a camera. Both were already wearing black gloves and cotton booties over their shoes.

"Where should we start?" asked the woman.

"Downstairs bedroom on the right," Packard said.

"Was the intruder anywhere else in the house that you know?"

Packard looked at Carolyn. She closed her eyes and ran her fingers through her hair and tucked it behind her ear. "Just in the lower master as far as I know." She didn't seem entirely sure.

"Have you noticed if anything was stolen or is missing from anywhere in the house?" Packard asked.

"I haven't really looked," Carolyn said. "I've barely been off this couch since the police first arrived."

The investigators disappeared down the stairs. Packard resumed his questions.

"Okay... Grown kids from your first marriage. Your ex-husband is who?"

Her ex-husband was Jerod Walbach. Current address was Sandy Lake.

They'd been divorced since the kids were small. Jerod was remarried and had grown kids with his second wife. Everyone was on friendly enough terms.

"So no one here last night other than you and your husband. You were home for an hour and a half or two hours before he got home. You go to bed in different rooms at different times."

Carolyn inhaled through her nose and nodded.

"And then what happened?"

"I think I fell asleep around twelve thirty or so," she said. "And then there was a loud bang. It woke me up."

"Did you know what it was?"

"No. My first thought was that something large had fallen downstairs."

"What did you do?" Packard asked.

"Put on my robe and went to the top of the stairs. I called Bill's name a couple of times to see if he was up. Then I thought if he was wearing his CPAP he probably wouldn't hear me, so I went down to his room to see if he was okay."

"Did you have a reason to think he wasn't okay?"

"Just the loud sound and the fact that he wasn't up same as me."

"And then what?"

"I kept calling his name and getting no response. I opened the door to his bedroom, and the first thing I noticed was the sliding door was open. I thought he'd gone outside to see what made the noise. Then I turned on the light and I saw him and...blood..."

She broke down at that point. Deputy Baker hadn't written anything else down, meaning he already had all this info in his notes.

"Did you go to your husband or try to help him?" Packard asked. She said she put her robe on before going downstairs. It was white and Packard didn't see a drop of blood on her anywhere.

"No, he wasn't moving and his eyes were open. I was terrified. I didn't know if someone was still in the house hiding somewhere. I turned off the light and ran for my phone and locked myself in the bathroom."

"Did you see any car lights or hear anything outside before or after you went downstairs?"

She stopped to think. "No, nothing."

"There's a gun safe downstairs. Do you have the combination to that?"

"Yes."

"Are there guns in it?"

"A lot of guns," Carolyn said.

"Are there other guns in the house?"

"There's a handgun in a holster in the nightstand beside my bed."

"When's the last time you fired it?" Packard asked.

"Bill took me to the gun range maybe six months ago. Not since then."

Baker got up and called downstairs for one of the investigators to bring him an evidence bag. "We're going to have to take the gun in your bedroom and all the other guns," Packard said. "We'll give you a receipt for everything."

Carolyn nodded. Packard told her the ambulance waiting outside could take her into town to get checked out if she wanted. She said she wasn't hurt and didn't want to go. She didn't want to talk to a counselor.

Packard told her she'd need to be out of the house for the next several days. Carolyn said she could stay with her mother. She stood up and said she wanted to change clothes and put some things together.

"Stay seated for now. I need to talk to the investigators before you do anything."

Carolyn sat again, looking like she didn't appreciate being told she couldn't move freely in her own home.

"Just give me a minute. I can't have you in that room alone with an unsecured weapon. Standard procedure," Packard explained.

Packard met the female investigator at the bottom of the stairs. Her name was Becky. "There's a gun in the nightstand upstairs. I want everything Carolyn is wearing bagged. I also want a GSR swab on her." He had no reason to believe Carolyn had shot her husband. He had no reason not to believe it. Swabbing her for gunshot residue and checking her clothes would provide data that could point him in one direction or another.

Becky nodded, grabbed several paper bags out of her storage container, and went upstairs.

Erik, the other tech, was taking photos of Bill Sandersen's body.

"Murder weapon?" Packard asked.

"Not that we've found yet. No shells either, though I suppose we may find one tangled in the bedding somewhere. He was shot twice."

"Twice? His wife only heard one shot."

"There's definitely two holes in this guy, and I can tell you he wasn't asleep when it happened. Bullet nicked a finger going in. He got a defensive hand up."

Packard looked at the pale, frozen face of Bill Sandersen. Goatee, heavy-set, with pale skin around the eyes and lines at the temples from being outside wearing sunglasses. His hair was cut short in a straight line across his forehead. He had blood on his face. The T-shirt he was wearing over a pair of white briefs was dark with it.

Packard went upstairs and out the front door. The sun was up. A light breeze made ripples across the pond behind the house. It was going to be a beautiful Sunday unless you or your husband had been shot by an intruder the night before.

Deputy Howard Shepard was standing out back, playing a slot machine game on his phone. He was everything Packard thought a deputy shouldn't be: physically unfit, a chain smoker, unobservant. The two of them had butted heads nonstop since Stan Shaw had appointed Packard as acting sheriff.

"You know this guy?" Packard asked, pointing back at the house.

Shepard pocketed his phone. "A little bit. Bill Sandersen. Works at Sandy Lake Auto. I bought a truck from him. Used to see him at the casino with his old wife."

"Who was she?"

"Sherrilyn Sandersen. Maiden name Gherlick. Goes by Sherri."

Something was echoing in Packard's head. "His current wife is Carolyn or Carrie. And his old wife was Sherrilyn or Sherri?"

Shepard raised his eyebrows a couple of times, waiting for Packard to figure it out.

"Sisters?" Packard asked.

"Bingo."

"He divorced his wife and married her sister?"

Shepard made a gun with his fingers and pointed it at Packard. "Nice job, Detective."

If being a good deputy required no more than smoking cigarettes and having an encyclopedic knowledge of town gossip, Shepard would have been top ranked. He knew more about some folks than their internet search history did.

"Carolyn said they hadn't been married long. Why'd he divorce Sherri and marry her?"

"Word is that he spent all Sherri's money so he moved on to a sister who still had some left."

"Where'd the money come from?"

"Family money. They're Gherlicks. Their old man was John Gherlick. His brother was Jack Gherlick. John owned the local bank. Jack got into the construction and building supply business. You know his son Danny from the goings-on last spring. Together they couldn't be underbid. They both made huge fortunes."

The goings-on last spring referred to Danny Gherlick's son, Sam, a small-time drug dealer who died when his car came down on top of him while he was working under it. Connecting Sam to the missing teenagers had eventually led Packard to Emmett Burr.

Shepard's knowledge of the sisters and their common husband was useful information. It would take Packard a lifetime to meet all the people in Sandy Lake and coax out their histories and secrets.

Packard checked the time on his phone. Shepard's overnight shift was just about up. "Thanks for the info, Shepard. You can take off. I'll drive Carolyn to her mother's. Reynolds and Baker can stay behind until the next shift comes on."

Shepard gave a sarcastic salute and shook out a cigarette as he made his way around the house. Packard bit his tongue about the cigarette. It was too early in the day to let Shepard push his buttons.

Carolyn sat beside Packard in the sheriff's SUV. A change of clothes seemed to have temporarily refreshed her. She was wearing jeans and a pink blouse and a light jacket. She smelled like laundry detergent and hand lotion. A suitcase with clothes and shoes was in the back seat of Packard's vehicle.

She'd declined his offer to stop for coffee or food on the way to her mother's. She wanted to know what was going to happen to Bill's body. Packard explained it would stay in the house until the crime-scene team had documented everything, then be picked up and transported for an autopsy. He told her it might be a week or more before the body was ready for burial.

Carolyn took all this in without a word. She stared out her window as they drove on rural roads, past flashes of water, scrub trees, and manufactured homes on empty acres. She had the blank, stunned look of someone who'd been hit between the eyes.

"Carolyn, who would come into your home and shoot your husband in his bed?"

She didn't respond right away. Packard drove and watched her out of the corner of his eye. She was mindlessly spinning her wedding ring on her finger. "I don't have any idea," she whispered. "I can't imagine even knowing someone who would do such a thing."

Packard thought about the fact that the killer only shot Bill. There was no attempt—as far as they knew—to penetrate the house further to try to kill Carolyn, too. Would it have been different if they had shared a bed? She might have been shot to eliminate a witness had she been lying next to him. It made Packard wonder if the killer knew about the sleeping arrangements.

"You and Bill have only been married a couple of years. Tell me how you met."

"It's no secret that Bill is my sister's ex-husband. You're bound to find that out soon enough."

"Already did," Packard admitted.

Carolyn gave him a surprised look that quickly turned to resignation, as if she should have known. "I was in love with Bill long before my sister entered the picture. We were boyfriend and girlfriend in high school. He was my first boyfriend. Two years older than me. He was cute and he had a car. My mother was old-fashioned and thought teenage girls had no business owning cars, driving cars, being in cars. Bill could take me places, but I had to constantly reassure my mother that I wasn't in the back seat with my skirt up. Her big fear was that I would get pregnant and shame the family." Carolyn shook her head at the ridiculousness of it all.

"What happened between you and Bill back then?"

"What happened was that my father set up trusts for us girls that we'd come into when we turned twenty-one. Then he stepped off a five-gallon bucket and hung himself in the garage. Sherri is almost four years older than me. She came into her money and wanted to party. So did Bill."

Packard waited for her to go on, but she seemed to think that explained everything. "They ended up getting married. And were married for a long time, right?"

"Yes."

"Why did they get divorced?" Packard asked.

"He said it wasn't fun anymore. They fought constantly. My sister drinks full time so you can imagine how old that can get."

Packard nodded. "And what made you want to marry Bill all these years later?"

Carolyn stared at him so long he had to take his eyes off the road to meet her gaze. "Have you ever been lonely, Detective?"

Packard looked away. He was alone most of the time. Lonely rarely but sometimes deeply. He thought of loneliness as existential, but being a loner was not something he wanted to build an identity around the way he'd seen others do. He'd decided, and reaffirmed again after moving to Sandy Lake, that the key to being alone but not lonely was to make the most of what he had and not romanticize what he didn't. That thinking had worked for him so far. He would continue to believe it until it didn't.

Carolyn was probably looking for a simpler answer.

"I have been lonely," he admitted.

"I'd been divorced from my first husband for a long time. The kids were grown and moved out. And here comes Bill making me feel like a high school girl again."

"What's your relationship with your sister now? What was Bill's?"

"My sister and I only talk about our mother and her needs now that she's got dementia. Any other topic is full of land mines. As far as her and Bill...I assume the only person she hates more than me is him."

"Do you think your sister killed Bill?"

"I think my sister is capable of anything, given her circumstances. I also think if my sister came to my house to kill Bill, she wouldn't have stopped there."

They were getting close to where Carolyn's mother lived on Spirit Lake. Carolyn told him to turn left, turn right, follow the curve. They came up to a brick-red rambler, likely built in the late seventies. It would have been an expensive home at the time. It looked small and dated compared to what people were building now. If it came on the market, the land alone would be worth half a million. The house would be a teardown.

Packard stopped by the curb. There was a white Toyota sedan parked in the driveway. "I'm going to need a list of Bill's friends, acquaintances, and interests."

"He had a whole life of his own before we married a couple of years ago. People I don't know. He and Sherri liked to drink, go to bars, gamble. I never told him he had to cut off all his old friends, but I made it clear I wasn't interested in any of that. We spent most of our time just the two of us, or us and his sister and her family."

"Give me some names of people Bill would hang out with."

"I mentioned Bill was with Roger Freeman last night. The two of them are trying to get the money together to get their business idea off the ground. I think things have been tense between them lately."

"What's the business?" Packard asked.

"They want to open a bar. A place with beers on tap, TVs, and chicken wings. Like Buffalo Wild Wings but smaller and local."

"Why the tension?"

She said she didn't know for sure. She said Roger had shown up at the house about a few weeks ago, and from the living room window she could tell they were almost yelling at each other across the bed of his truck. Roger had looked furious. She assumed it was about money. "Bill asked me if I would put fifty thousand dollars from my trust into his bar. I told him no."

Packard noted the way she said *my* trust and *his* bar. He didn't blame her. If Shepard was right, Bill had helped spend Sherri's money until it was gone. Two years into his new marriage—to his ex-wife's sister with her own trust fund—he was asking her to put up the money for him to open a bar. Packard had a feeling Bill would have been the place's best customer.

"Where does Roger live?"

"His folks run a dairy farm west of Sandy Lake. Twelve, fifteen miles out on Highway 18. White farmhouse with the concrete silo missing its top."

"Who else?"

"Bill likes playing poker at the casino." Another reason not to give him $50K of her money, Packard thought. "The only name I know among his poker buddies is Ronnie Winder."

"Is Ronnie Winder the guy who owns Winder Marine and Powersports?"

"That's him."

Finally, something he knew about someone in this town without having to learn it from Shepard.

Packard got Sherri's address from Carolyn and asked her not to call her sister and tell her about Bill. "I'm very happy to let you handle that," Carolyn said. "I'll warn you, if you show up before noon she'll likely be passed out in bed still."

A Black woman in purple scrubs and a hijab came out the front door and looked their way with her hand shading her eyes. "That's Zeinab, one of Mom's caretakers. I can't imagine what she's thinking, seeing me sitting in a police car."

Packard gave Carolyn one of his cards from the console between them. "Call me if you need anything or think of something else I should know. Someone from the sheriff's department will contact you when you can return to your house."

Carolyn gathered her things and walked up to the house. Zeinab held the door open for her and the two of them disappeared inside.

Packard reached into his pocket for his phone and found the business card Dave the drummer/insurance inspector had given him that morning. They could have still been in bed if Bill Sandersen hadn't gotten himself shot.

Packard raked the card against his knuckles as he pondered his next move. He had two sisters, a family fortune, a shared husband, and an angry best friend. The mind reeled with possibilities.

And it wasn't even 8:00 a.m.

CHAPTER THREE

IF CAROLYN WAS RIGHT and her sister, Sherri, was still crocked this early in the morning, it made sense to talk to Roger Freeman first. The guy was a dairy farmer. He was probably up before Packard took the first call about Bill at 4:30 a.m.

The sun was out, the sky clear blue. The chill he had attributed to the early hours seemed to linger, a promise of things to come.

Packard turned off the highway onto a long dirt drive with a shelter belt on one side that separated the dairy operation from the field beside it. He saw a small farmhouse painted bright white but still looking like it was sagging under the weight of time. Behind it was a mobile home on blocks and a long clothesline. Past the house were a large barn and various other outbuildings, a crumbling brick silo, a newer steel one, and two storage tanks.

A stooped old man in a feed cap and a flannel jacket watched from the open end of the wide barn as Packard rolled up and stopped past the house. He started rocking toward Packard on hips that didn't flex and knees that didn't bend.

Packard introduced himself and shook the old man's hand. "I'm looking for Roger," he said.

The old man scratched his stubbly face with fingers stiff and swollen with arthritis. "He in trouble?"

"Not that I know of. I need to ask him some questions about his friend Bill Sandersen."

"Bill in trouble?"

"Bill's dead," Packard said.

The old man didn't seem surprised or moved by the news. "Roger's in there feeding cows," he said and then continued on to the house.

Packard walked up to the barn and saw a tractor pulling a round, blue feed mixer down the center aisle. Ground silage spilled from the side in front of a line of hungry heifers with their heads poked through the bars of the feed front. A lazy breeze spun the blades of the box fans hanging overhead but couldn't push out the eye-watering smell of wet manure and the yeasty odor of the fermented feed.

The driver gave Packard a nod and raised his hand to indicate he needed a minute. He backed up the tractor to the beginning of the aisle and passed in front of the cows again, doubling the size of the pile in front of them.

The man who climbed out was tall with a slab of fat that clung to the front of him like a child with its legs wrapped around his hips. He had tired eyes and a beard going gray at the chin. When he took his hat off to scratch his head, Packard saw his hair was shaved down to stubble.

Packard introduced himself and was glad when Roger led the way out of the barn into fresher air.

"I just came from Bill Sandersen's house," Packard said as they stood in the gravel that surrounded the barn. "Someone shot Bill in his bed last night. He's dead."

"Aww...what?" Roger's face collapsed. He leaned forward with his hands on his thighs, stood up, and walked in a circle. "Bill's dead?"

Packard nodded, watching Roger closely. He looked genuinely distraught. "Any idea who would have it in for Bill like that?"

Roger stood with his hands on his hips. "No idea. None. The guy's my best friend. He can be an asshole sometimes, but who isn't?"

"What can you tell me about Bill?"

"We've been friends our whole lives." Roger had stop to get control of himself. He took off his hat and turned his back for a minute. "Went to school together, graduated the same year. We drifted apart a bit through our twenties. He married Sherri and I moved down to the Cities because I said I'd be goddamned if I was going to be a dairy farmer like my parents and grandparents before them." He laughed sourly.

"What did you do down in the Cities?"

"Worked as a bouncer, a bartender, drove a cab. I always felt like if I found the right job I'd find where I fit in down there, but it never happened. I lived in a string of shitty apartments, had girlfriends come and go. Started dealing coke to make extra money but knew I was headed for trouble."

"What brought you home?"

Roger shifted on his feet and took a deep breath. Dealing with the news that his best friend was dead and having to tell his life story seemed to twist his insides. "I had an uncle who was Dad's partner in all this." He waved a hand in the direction of the barn. "He dropped dead of a heart attack shoveling snow at the age of sixty. My aunt wanted out of Minnesota and out of the dairy business so my dad paid her for my uncle's share. Put him in a big hole at a time when he was slowing down himself. Eventually it became clear to me I was never going to be happy in Minneapolis, and if I stayed on the path I was on, I was going to end up in jail or dead. I thought if I came home and put in a hard day's work on the farm I'd see the reward."

"How long ago was that?"

"About ten years ago," Roger said.

"And you and Bill started hanging out again?"

"Yep, just like old times. Hanging out at the lake, drinking beer all day. Snowmobile rides and ice fishing in the winter." Roger smiled at the memories. "Bill and Sherri lived a nonstop party. Neither had to work because of her money."

Cows mooed in the barn behind them as a gust of wind kicked up a cloud of dirt before calming down again.

"I heard from Carolyn about the trust funds they got when they turned twenty-one," Packard said.

"Bill told me them girls had over a million bucks each. That was thirty years ago."

"Did Sherri and Bill think a million bucks was going to last them the rest of their lives?"

Roger reached back and hiked up his pants. "I don't think those two thought past the plan for next weekend. If even one of them had a job, that plus four percent interest off a million bucks—forty grand—could have been a comfortable lifestyle around these parts. When the money got low, they stopped having fun. Bill's only in if things are fun."

"What did you think when he turned around and married the sister?"

Roger shook his head. He took off his cap and scratched his forehead. "Carrie and Sherri couldn't be more different. I've been on more three-day benders with Bill and Sherri than I can count. We'd drink and putt around in a pontoon and drive from bar to bar until closing time. Sherri will party until she can't hold her head up. Carrie hasn't had me over for so much as a meal. When I go by the house, she sends Bill outside 'cause she's worried my boots might have cow shit on 'em. They're night and day, those two. I couldn't tell you one thing they have in common."

"Money," Packard said.

Roger shrugged. "Maybe good pussy runs in the family."

Packard opened his mouth, closed it. There weren't too many topics of conversation that could shut him down, but the inheritable characteristics of female genitals was one of them. He shrugged noncommittally. It was the best he could do.

"Carolyn said you and Bill were planning to go into business together."

Roger groaned and hitched up his sagging pants again. "Can we walk? My feet hurt when I stand too long."

He and Packard put their backs to the sun and slowly walked the dirt paths that connected the farm's buildings. Roger told him the bar was Bill's idea. Bill was looking for a way to make his own money. He'd gotten a job selling cars at Sandy Lake Auto after the divorce, and he hated it. What he liked was drinking and gambling and being the life of the party. He and Roger came up with the bar's concept—beer and wings. Simple menu. Popular with the locals and out-of-towners. Add a bunch of TVs and sports channels and pull-tabs, and they thought the money would roll in.

The problem was they needed money to make money. If they could find an existing building that was already configured for a restaurant, they figured they'd need $100,000 to get started. The plan was to come up with half on their own, then try to get loans for the rest. Bill registered an LLC with the State of Minnesota and opened a business account at the bank with both their names on it. Roger put in $20,000—everything he'd managed to save in his life. Bill said he'd put in $20,000, too.

"His first deposit was $6,000," Roger said. "A month or two later he put in $2,800. Then $900. At that rate, it was going to take years to come up with the first $50,000."

They came to a fence surrounding a muddy pen off the far end of the cow barn. Roger put his foot on the bottom brace and leaned against it. Cows moved in and out of the barn freely. Their bellies and udders hung heavy, pulling their hides tight. From behind, the bones of their pelvises looked like defiant fists punching skyward.

"Carolyn said things had been tense between you and Bill recently. Was it about the money?"

"It was about him taking twenty thousand dollars out of our account when he'd barely put ten thousand of it in himself."

"What did he do with the money?"

"I don't know. He wouldn't tell me. Now the sonofabitch is dead."

"How'd you find out he'd taken the money?"

"When I got the statement. This was a few weeks ago. I went to his place and he said he'd invested it. I said in what, the casino? He liked playing poker, if you didn't know. Thought he was better than he was. He said, *Nah, nah. Trust me. I got a plan. It's going to come back big time. I promise.*"

Bill had a plan. That was as much as Roger knew about where his money had gone.

"I'm sure this makes me look like a prime suspect, but I'm telling you I wouldn't put up everything I own to start a business with Bill, then turn around and kill him. I trusted the guy. Even after he wouldn't tell me what he did with the money I still had faith in him. That probably makes me sound like a fool. I can't help it. I'm a dairy farmer. Optimism is in our blood. When you work as hard as we do for almost nothing in return, optimism and hope for better days are all that keep you going."

Roger made a sound like *gah* and turned his head away and wiped a thumb across his eyes.

Packard gave him a minute and watched the cows. His gut told him Roger was telling the truth. The confrontation between them was weeks old. The time for Roger to kill Bill over the missing money would have been in the heat of the moment, not almost a month later.

"Roger, someone was mad enough at Bill to shoot him in his bed in the middle of the night. Who do you think that was?"

"I really have no idea. I didn't know Bill to be hated by anyone like that."

"Not even Sherri?" Packard asked.

"No. I think Sherri still misses him. Maybe she just misses the good times. She's been in a bad way since the divorce. She's had so many DWIs that she can't drive anymore. Every patrol deputy knows she's got a suspended license. She's got a waitressing job that puts her around more booze than is good for her. I think she's pretty lonely."

Packard was running out of questions. He told Roger he'd never been on a dairy farm before, and Roger said he'd be happy to show him around. They went back through the barn, where the cows moved about on the wet concrete floor. They had open pens lined with sand where many of them sat chewing their cud. Roger moved through the animals with ease. Their size and number felt menacing to Packard, and he'd been locked in a garage with a seven-foot black bear before. He couldn't help but think how an unexpected kick or a crushing hoof might alter the course of his life.

The herd numbered over two hundred heads. About two-thirds of them were giving milk at a time. The others were dry because they were late into a pregnancy or recovering from one. Roger showed Packard the milking parlor off the side of the barn, where the cows were led into two rows of twelve milking stations. He introduced Packard to their hired man, Ricardo, who used a rotating brush to clean the cows' teats before attaching a set of floppy nozzles. It took three or four minutes to milk each cow. It had to be done three times a day.

"We're getting a little over twelve dollars per hundred pounds of milk currently. It costs about thirteen dollars to make it," Roger said. "I'm going to work today from 4:30 a.m. 'til about 10:30 tonight for negative dollars."

"What's driving the price?" Packard asked.

"Too much milk on the market, too few people buying it. Everywhere you look, it's almond milk and oat milk and whatever the hell else. What about you? You buy milk by the gallon anymore?"

Packard dodged the question because he did not. "I eat a lot of Greek yogurt," he offered.

"That's good. But even that market has started to shrink. People are moving on to the next thing. Meanwhile, the cost of everything else goes up and the price we get for our milk goes down. I don't know how much longer we can keep going at these margins."

They walked outside, past long rows of hay kept dry under vast sheets of white plastic, then by hutches where the baby calves were bottle-fed. The males would get sold to other farmers to be raised for meat. The females would join Roger's herd or also get sold to keep a lid on the numbers.

They made their way back to the house. "Tell me what you did last night," Packard said.

"Worked. I was taking care of cows and doing paperwork until about ten thirty. Me and Ricardo stay in the trailer during the summer." He pointed to a mobile home behind the main house with its own wooden deck and a satellite dish on the roof. "The main house gets crowded with four of us. Ricardo does other work in the winter, and I move into the house when it gets too cold in the trailer. Ricardo and I watched Jimmy Fallon and went to bed."

"Interesting," Packard said.

"Not together. We didn't go to bed together," Roger clarified. He looked desperate to be understood on that point.

Packard shook his head. "I mean interesting because Carolyn said Bill was with you last night."

Roger stopped in his tracks. "She told you we were together last night?"

Packard nodded. "She told me that Bill told her he was meeting you last night."

Roger shook his head. "No, sir. That's not true!" He seemed almost panicked. "I don't know why he would tell her that. Any other time, if that's what he told her and he wanted me to cover for him, I would. But not when there's been a murder. I haven't even talked to Bill in about a week, let alone seen him. I don't know where he was last night, but he wasn't here."

"Hmmm," Packard said.

"Maybe he was up at the casino and didn't want her to know."

"Maybe," Packard agreed.

Roger's phone rang then. He took it off the clip on his belt. "It's Sherri," he said.

"Don't answer if you don't mind. I asked Carolyn not to call her about Bill. I told her I'd give her sister the news."

Bill nodded and put the phone back on his belt. A few seconds later, it dinged with a text message. Then another. And another. He looked at the screen and turned it toward Packard.

"You're too late. She already knows."

CHAPTER FOUR

HAD HE REALLY EXPECTED to get to Sherri before the news about her ex-husband did? Sandy Lake, like every other small town, had a mycelial information network whose roots went deeper and reacted faster than any social media. Between all the people with police scanners and the drive-by gawkers, awareness of the murder would be almost instantaneous. Packard couldn't imagine being the kind of person who would call or text someone with news about a dead family member, but then he couldn't imagine himself doing a lot of things he saw people do every day while he was on the job.

He could see the back side of the condos where Sherri lived from the road. It was one of four buildings, five units each, with gray siding and steep-pitched roofs.

Packard found the address by matching the numbers on the end of the buildings, then parking in the driveway for Unit 7. Next to the garage was a semi-enclosed front patio. Sherri was sitting at a glass-topped table, yellow with tree pollen, in front of the kitchen window. She was petite, the size of an adolescent with the lined, sun-damaged face of a woman in her fifties. Black yoga pants, a Twins T-shirt, and dark hair pulled back through the opening in a camouflage baseball cap. Packard thought she looked familiar but wasn't sure why. Might have been the resemblance to her sister.

Before he could introduce himself, she stabbed out the cigarette she was smoking and said, "I didn't do it."

Packard paused and looked around. There was an identical building facing this one. He imagined every window in the complex cracking open the second the sheriff's SUV pulled in and all the people hanging back in the shadows, watching.

"Are you okay if we go inside and talk?" he asked.

Sherri grabbed her cigarettes and led the way. The front door was set further back from the patio, dead leaves blown into the corners. It was dark inside the house. The living room furniture was too big for the space, like it came from a different house. Out the back she had a view of what some might generously call a water feature and others would call a drainage ditch. A sprayer in the middle shot water into the air to keep it from also being a mosquito hatchery.

Packard couldn't help comparing Sherri's place with Carrie's. One was open and light and airy. The other closed and cramped and dark. One lived on a lake. The other next to a pool of stormwater runoff.

Packard declined the offer of a drink. Sherri poured herself a glass of white wine from a bottle in the fridge and drank it standing at the counter. Packard went around and sat at a barstool underneath a narrow countertop peninsula.

"You've obviously heard about Bill," he said. "I'm sorry if this is hard for you."

Sherri didn't say anything as she lit another cigarette.

Packard took out a pen and the notebook that fit in his shirt pocket. "Tell me where you were last night."

"I was at the band downtown with some girlfriends. I saw you there."

Packard tried to remember details from the previous evening that didn't involve Dave the Drummer. Kids and families, a crowded beer tent surrounded by orange snow fencing. Fireworks.

"We were up front dancing," she said. "Me and two girlfriends."

She was one of the three drunk women near the stage. That's why she looked familiar.

"I remember. You ladies looked like you were having a good time."

"We had fun. What about you? I saw you talking to the drummer at the end of the night." Sherri gave him a raised eyebrow that he ignored. He should have known all eyes would have been on him. He was a known entity to everyone because of his job or because of the gossip about him. He'd hoped his status as the town unicorn would have worn off by now. At the same time he was starting to realize it wasn't his being gay that people found interesting—it was who he might be being gay with.

"What did you do after the band?" he asked.

Sherri took her cigarette and her wine and left the kitchen and walked to the sliding door that opened onto the back patio. Packard swiveled on his stool to keep her in sight. "Went to Bob's Bar," she said. "I'm practically a part owner considering how much money I've spent there."

"Your girlfriends still with you at this point?"

Sherri pushed the door open a crack and held her cigarette outside. "One of 'em. We kept drinking until almost midnight I guess."

"How'd you get home?"

"She drove," she said.

"What shape were you in when you got home?"

"Hammered." She said it the way someone else would say *tired* or *hungry*.

Packard had no way of knowing whether that was true or not. Or whether she could hold her liquor well enough to still get in the car, drive to her sister's, shoot her ex-husband where he slept, and make it home without causing an accident or otherwise calling attention to herself.

"Have you had any contact with your ex-husband recently?"

Sherri smoked, shook her head, and tried to blow the smoke outside. "What would I say to him? He spent all my money, left, and married my sister."

"How did you feel about him marrying Carrie?"

Sherri gave him a look like he was a fool for asking such a question. "Did you ever hear the story of the wedding?"

Packard shook his head. Shepard probably had.

"I wasn't invited, obviously. They got married at the golf club. What a joke that was. Have you ever seen Bill hit a golf ball? Shank! Slice! They rented a big banquet room, but it turns out not a lot of people want to attend an awkward wedding between a woman and her sister's ex-husband. And that was before I showed up and made everything uncomfortable."

She was enjoying retelling the story, staring beyond him into the past, the location of her last success. "My girlfriend, Kristie, and me just decided we were going to crash it. We sat at a table with some of Bill's coworkers and ate the chicken dinner along with everyone else. People were too afraid to say or do anything. Mom came up to me while I was at the bar. Said I better behave or leave. She didn't mean a word of it. Mom loved that I was there. She hated Bill and was against their relationship, the wedding, all of it. Carrie sat at the head table, mad as a wet cat, while Bill just sat there with his mouth open. Everyone else in the place acted like they were strapped to their chairs and couldn't turn their necks."

Packard had no trouble picturing the scene Sherri had caused. He imagined fifty people in a room with a gas leak, watching a crazy woman waving a lighter.

"The first people left thirty minutes after dinner ended. They didn't even wait for the cake to be cut. After that, it was a steady rush for the exits. People couldn't wait to get out of there. Kristie and I drank about three hundred dollars' worth of booze that my sister paid for, danced to the DJ she paid for, ate big pieces of her wedding cake, and had a blast. By eight you could count on one hand how many guests were still there. The best part was that I didn't have to flip a table or throw a drink on anybody. I ruined it just by having a great time."

Sherri smiled at Packard and raised her wineglass like they were toasting. He circled the word *mom* in his notes. "You said your mom is no fan of Bill's."

"My mom hates Bill. She also has dementia and wears a diaper. She didn't kill Bill, if that's what you're thinking."

Sherri finished her cigarette, then flopped down on the giant sectional sofa with her empty glass.

Packard said, "I'm going to ask you the same question I asked your sister and Roger. Who do you think would come to Bill's house in the middle of the night and shoot him in his bed?"

Sherri put her feet on the coffee table and bounced her knee. Packard had the sense that she was trying not to get up and pour herself another glass of wine. She took off her hat and ran her hand through her hair. It had been dyed almost black but had an inch of gray at the roots now. "Are you sure Carrie didn't do it?" she asked.

"I'm not sure of anything at this point," Packard said.

"Yeah, but it's always the spouse, isn't it?"

"Often it is. Who's your second guess after your sister?"

Sherri turned away from him and stared out the sliding glass door at the fountain spraying drainage water into the air. Packard thought he saw her chest hitch like she was choking back a sob. She picked at the skin on her thumb and shook her head. "I don't have a second guess. I don't know what Bill was up to anymore," she said. She sounded more rueful than uncertain. "He didn't have any enemies when we were married. Who knows who he's pissed off since then?"

Packard got a few more details out of her. She worked part time as the condo manager for a discount on her rent. She dealt with tenant complaints and hired subs when someone needed a toilet snaked or a broken window replaced. She also worked as a waitress at the Silver Dollar Saloon, where her friend Kristie was a bartender. They always had to work the same shifts because Kristie was her ride. Her next shift started at four.

Sherri stood up and walked with him to the door while looking at her phone. Packard remembered the texts she'd sent Roger. "How did you find out about Bill?" he asked.

Sherri bit her lip and shook her head. "I shouldn't say."

"Was it your sister? I asked her not to call you."

"No," Sherri said. "If she'd done something she wasn't supposed to, I'd rat that bitch out in a minute." She looked undecided but touched her phone screen, then turned it so Packard could see it.

At first he just saw a blue bubble that said **Call me. Something's happened to Bill.**

At the top of the screen was the name of the sender in her contacts: **Dep Shep.**

Packard felt his blood start to boil.

Fucking Shepard.

CHAPTER FIVE

BACK TO CARRIE'S.

Packard drove by a deputy fifty yards up from the house making impressions of tire tracks where a turnoff bridged the ditch and led into the cornfield. It looked to be the nearest place for the killer to park that wasn't in the driveway or on the side of the road.

The crime-scene van, two patrol cars, and a vehicle from the local funeral home were parked in front of Carrie's house. Another deputy was standing outside.

Packard's anger toward Shepard was still white-hot. He'd taken photos of Sherri's phone displaying the text from Dep Shep and the record of her four-minute phone call with him. When confronted, Shepard would claim all he'd done was notify the deceased's family. The problem for him was that it wasn't his job to do so. He'd also violated department policy by doing it via text and a phone call. It was Packard's investigation, and everyone working on it was supposed to follow his orders. Shepard had jumped at the chance to put himself in the middle of someone else's misfortune because it was gossip gold.

Packard walked around to the back of the house and found the funeral-home driver sitting at the patio table. A collapsible gurney was standing by.

"They're almost ready to move the body," he said. Like many of the smaller counties in Minnesota, Sandy Lake had a contract with the medical examiner's office in Saint Paul to handle autopsies when required by law. The funeral home would get paid for transporting the body back and forth.

Packard put on a pair of black gloves before stepping through the sliding door into Bill's bedroom. The two crime-scene techs—Becky and Erik—were still there. Becky was in the process of removing the bedroom's door handle to take back to the lab for fingerprinting. The plate around the light switch had already been bagged. Erik was photographing blood splatter on the wall behind the bed. Bill was still on the mattress.

"What else do you know?" Packard asked as he leaned closer to Bill to see his wounds.

Erik lowered his camera and stepped back from the bed. "Shot twice, as I said this morning, but from two different directions, it appears."

They'd found 9mm brass casings from both shots. Erik described the shot that hit Bill in the finger before taking out a chunk of his neck. The second shot hit Bill on the opposite side of the body, in the right shoulder. "He got it coming and going. There's blood splatter in two different directions. I'd say the first shot came from the doorway, the second one from the direction of the sliding door."

"Two shots is twice the noise," Packard said.

"Maybe the killer was more concerned about making sure this guy was dead."

There was a cell phone on the nightstand. No password. Packard scrolled through the recent calls and text messages. The last few texts were between Bill and Roger.

Bill 9:53 PM where are u?

Roger 9:55 PM where u think?

Bill 10:01 PM I'll pick you up in 15 min

Roger 10:03 PM ok lover

Packard pulled the phone closer, unable to believe what he was reading. Had Roger lied to him about not seeing Bill last night? Packard went to the list of contacts on Bill's phone to see if there were any other Rogers listed. No. He scrolled through the rest of their text string, which only went back thirty days. Their exchanges were all variations on the most recent. **Where are you? You free tonight? I'll be there soon.**

Before moving to Sandy Lake, Packard had dated another cop back in Minneapolis named Marcus. Their texts to each other in the beginning had been much the same. Just enough details to arrange a hookup. They were only together for thirteen months when Marcus was killed responding to a domestic disturbance call. His death and the emptiness Packard felt afterward had prompted the move to Sandy Lake.

But Roger and Bill? Business partners and lovers? Or was the lover response a joke? Roger had been desperate that Packard not think that he and Ricardo were buggering each other in the trailer back at the farm. Trying to imagine the bowlegged dairy farmer he'd interviewed call the dead man in the bed "lover" was a bridge too far even for Packard. He couldn't see it.

He wrote down the phone number. It was different than the number he had for Roger, and it didn't match any of the other numbers he'd collected so far that day. When he tried calling it from his phone, it rang and rang. No answer. No voicemail.

Packard asked Erik to log the cell phone, then sealed it in a Faraday bag so it couldn't be remotely wiped. He eased past Becky dismantling the bedroom door and looked at the lower living area.

"Have either of you looked at the gun safe at all?" he asked the two techs.

They both said no. Carrie had told him that morning that it was full of guns. Surprisingly, Packard found it unlocked. He eased the heavy door open and called Erik over to photograph the inside before he touched anything.

There were four smaller handguns on the top shelf, all in nylon holsters. None that would fire a 9mm round. One side of the safe held half a dozen shotguns and rifles. The other side was divided by shelves holding knives and boxes of ammunition, a digital camera with different lenses, photo albums.

Packard knelt down to pull out the accordion folders in the very bottom. Something sharp stabbed him in the knee.

"Get a shot of this," he said to Erik. It was a diamond earring, all but invisible in the gray carpet. No sign of a jewelry box in the safe. Packard took out his flashlight and shined it on the empty second shelf where he could see residue left behind by four rubber feet on the wood's finish.

"Looks like there used to be something sitting here. Let's look around for a jewelry box or something that fits these marks."

Did the killer come to rob the place or to kill Bill? The blood splatter said the shooter got past Bill, at least initially, and shot him from the bedroom door. Why come all the way in if the goal was just to shoot Bill? The killer could have slid open the patio door and shot him twice from there. Did the killer get to the safe? Was it unlocked already or did Bill unlock it for him before being marched back to bed and shot while he raised his hand in defense?

Packard remembered the look on Carrie's face when asked whether the killer had been anywhere else in the house. She wasn't sure of the answer. She claimed not to know if anything had been stolen. If it was a habit to leave the safe unlocked, Packard could see that being the first thing she would check after calling 911. He could also see her being frightened and not wanting to be downstairs with a dead man and no idea where the killer was.

Erik said he had all he needed from Bill's body as far as photos and measurements. Packard left him to help the funeral-home driver bag it and load it on the gurney while he went upstairs.

In Carrie's bedroom he found that she'd made her bed at some point, probably while changing her clothes. The attached bathroom was clean, the countertops bare. On the dresser by her bed he saw a framed photo of each of her two kids. He pulled open the top drawer and found two stacks of neatly folded shirts. No sign of a jewelry box. No evidence that anything was out of place. It reminded him of a bedroom set in a showroom, not a place where someone actually lived.

There was nothing else to see here. Packard got in his truck and drove to the spot where the deputy was casting the tire tracks in the turnoff.

"Tracks look like they're from a truck," he said. "Interesting thing is that they don't continue on to the other side of fence. Definitely someone pulled in and then out." He said he'd know more about the tires' make and size once they could match the tread and measurements with others in their database.

Packard thanked him and headed back to town.

Sunday of Labor Day weekend was a quiet time at the station. Dispatch was fully staffed, but everyone else was off or out on patrol. The front desk where the department's administrator, Kelly Phelps, sat was dark. She had flown to Palm Springs to meet girlfriends and see Barry Manilow in concert. Kelly was the world's biggest fanilow. She traveled the country to see Barry in concert and recently had followed him to four different cities in the UK. More than a hundred was the answer when anyone asked her how many of his concerts she'd been to.

Packard hummed "Weekend in New England" as he went back to his office and spent the next hour writing down his notes from his conversations with Carrie, Roger, and Sherri. He noted Erik's initial blood splatter findings and the texts on Bill's phone from Roger. It felt like laying out the pieces of a puzzle and turning them all right side up. In his mind, the puzzle was a picture of Bill dead in his bed. He didn't have all the pieces yet. When he did, he'd know who killed Bill—and why.

———————

Later that night, after stopping at home to pick up Frank and a six-pack, Packard and Jill Thielen sat at the table on her back deck eating chips and salsa while her husband, Tim, flipped burgers.

Jill Thielen was the other detective in the department. Blond, five feet tall in shoes. She had the body of a triathlete and was fighting hard to not let turning forty in the coming year slow her down. Tim was older, already in his fifties, long and lanky with knobby knees, wearing dark socks and sandals and a Boundary Waters Canoe Area T-shirt. He had a dark beard and gray hair that curled out over his ears and behind his neck. He was the opposite of Thielen in every way. Soft where she was hard. Relaxed where she was taut.

The two of them had become Packard's closest friends since he moved to Sandy Lake. Making new friends made him feel like he was putting down the roots necessary to have the life he wanted in their small, rural community.

"So what happened with you and the guy from the band last night?" Thielen asked.

The evening sun was in their faces and they all wore sunglasses. Packard drank his beer and stared off into the distance. A creek cut through the back of the property. Earlier in the summer the three of them had put kayaks in and floated a couple of miles down to a campground where there was a run-down bar with pull-tabs and pickled eggs.

"What are you talking about?" Packard asked.

"Come on, we saw the two of you leave together."

Packard tried to look innocent. "I was walking in the same direction as someone else so you assume we left together?"

Thielen put her hand on his and lowered her sunglasses. "It didn't take a mind reader to know what you two were thinking. I could see the cock in your walk from a mile away."

"You're insane," Packard said, pulling his hand away. "Tim, you're a psychologist. What's wrong with your wife?"

Tim turned from the grill, greasy spatula in hand. "Sorry, buddy. I saw it, too."

Packard shook his head and laughed into his beer. "You're not totally wrong," he admitted.

"I knew it," Thielen said and clinked her beer against his. "Tell me everything."

"I'm going to tell you nothing."

They ate bacon cheeseburgers and chips and broccoli slaw with sesame dressing. Dessert was wedges of watermelon drizzled with honey and lime. Frank and the Thielens' old yellow Lab sat nearby waiting for table scraps. As the sun set, the humans put on jackets and moved to seats around a firepit. The six-pack was gone. Tim made them a round of Wisconsin-style old-fashioneds with brandy and 7Up.

Packard let Frank up in his lap as he told Thielen about his interviews with Carrie, Roger, and Sherri. Thielen had lived in the area a lot longer than Packard but didn't know the saga of the two sisters and their common husband.

"You know the names of the men in that Gherlick family—the brothers John and Jack that took the family money and made two fortunes out of it," Thielen said as she leaned forward in her Adirondack and sprayed mosquito repellent on her bare legs. "You know Danny and his brothers because they own the building and supply business. But the Gherlick women end up marrying and giving up their name and fading into the background. It's sexist."

Thielen had kept her last name when she married Tim. In the moment, Packard couldn't even think of what Tim's last name was. He always thought of them as the Thielens.

"So who do you like for the pulling the trigger?" Thielen asked.

"None of 'em, to be honest," Packard said.

"Not even Carolyn? It's always the spouse."

"I don't disagree. If she was the one dead in bed and Bill had made the 911 call, there'd be four of us with a finger in his ass and a fifth shining a light up it."

"It could be someone you haven't identified yet."

"Or somebody is a good liar," Packard said. "Actually, I think all three of them are lying to me about one thing or another. Maybe not as it relates to Bill getting shot but about tangential things." He told her about the jarring text messages between Bill and Roger. The one that said **Ok lover**.

Tim poked at the fire with a long stick from where he sat. "I know it's hard to imagine a man with two wives having homosexual inclinations, but it's not unheard of. I've had multiple clients who married and then struggled with the shame they felt about their authentic selves," he said.

Thielen shook her head. "I'm not arguing with what you're saying, honey, but I call bullshit on that being the case with those two. I know at least two women in this town who have had their clock punched by that dairy farmer. He doesn't have a gay bone in his body."

Packard's phone buzzed in his pocket right then. MARILYN SHAW was the name on the screen. He had a sudden thought about phones and names and the mental image he had when he saw the words *Marilyn Shaw*. It was then Packard realized what was going on with Bill and Roger. "It's someone else's number," he said to Thielen. "He programmed it as Roger in case Carrie ever got a glimpse at his phone."

He held up a finger for Thielen to hold the thought, then swiped to take the call. "Marilyn, how are you?"

"Benjamin, it's over," she said. "Stan died an hour ago."

Six months after hiring Packard, Stan Shaw was diagnosed with colon cancer. Doctors pulled out enough of his entrails that he needed a colostomy bag when they were done. Stan came back to work, but before long the cancer returned. It was at that point that Stan appointed Packard acting sheriff over the objections of the county board and others under his command.

The call with Marilyn was short. Just long enough for her to tell Packard that Stan had finally let go and there was nothing she needed. She wanted him to let the rest of the department know. She was too tired for a bunch of phone calls. "I'll take care of it, Marilyn," he said. "I'm with Thielen now. We're both heartbroken. We're going to miss him."

They went inside while Packard called dispatch and asked them to start communicating the news. He called Kelly in California. She had worked for

Stan for all sixteen years he was sheriff, and eight years for the guy before him. Everyone knew Kelly was the real boss you needed to keep happy. She'd never forgive Packard if she heard about Stan via a text blast.

"Packard, we're in an Uber on the way to dinner before night two of Barry Manilow. This better be important."

Maybe a text would have been better. "Marilyn just called. Stan's gone."

He heard her gasp. "Goddamnit," Kelly said.

"What happened?" someone in the car with her said.

"Oh hell," Kelly said.

Packard could already hear the tears in her voice. "I'm sorry to spoil your night," he said. "I'm going to have dispatch do an end-of-watch call at 1930— about twenty minutes from now. Call me back if you want to listen."

He used Thielen's computer to log into his work email and send a short statement to everyone in the department. He had a group text on his phone that he used to get out the same message.

At seven thirty, with Kelly and her girlfriends listening via speakerphone, Packard and Thielen and Tim stood around the dining room table with Thielen's police radio in front of them.

Cheryl in dispatch started by calling out Stan's badge number three times and waiting for a response. "Sandy Lake one eight nine… Sandy Lake one eight nine… Sandy Lake one eight nine… Sheriff Stan Shaw, a twenty-four-year veteran of the Sandy Lake County Sheriff's Department, died of complications from cancer earlier today, September 4. He led a life of service both on and off the job. Sheriff Shaw, you are a hero in this community and will be missed by all who knew you. God bless you and your family. Rest in peace, Sheriff. You are clear to go 10–7. We have the watch from here."

The dispatch tone sounded and the message was broadcast again. Thielen held Tim's hand, crying. Packard felt numb. The last EOW he'd heard was Marcus's when they replayed it at his funeral. Packard had been just another face in a sea of blue, no place of honor for the man who'd had a secret relationship with the fallen officer.

In Stan's case, they'd all known this was coming. Packard had a draft press release from the sheriff's department ready to go. Still, knowing this day was inevitable was not the same as doing the real work of anticipating what would follow. Packard never wanted the job of acting sheriff. He'd said yes as a favor to Stan, who had given him a job when he needed to put distance between himself and Marcus's death, who had intuited what Packard's boundaries were and hadn't asked a lot of questions Packard didn't want to answer. Stan had trusted him, and Packard wanted to repay that trust in whatever way he could.

But acting sheriff was a temporary title. A badge made of ice. Somehow, even while writing a press release announcing Stan's death, Packard had imagined the sheriff would come back, tell Packard to get his shit out of his office, and start hollering at Kelly from the back instead of using the computer to message her.

The uncertainty of what came next was unsettling.

Packard turned off the radio and said goodbye to Kelly on the phone. Thielen had her arms around Tim, her wet face in his side. Packard saw her staring at him like she wanted to say something. She didn't need to. He was already asking himself the same question.

Now what?

CHAPTER SIX

LABOR DAY WAS A shit time to try to get any work done.

Packard swam laps in the lake behind his house, then dressed and drove to where Bill Sandersen worked at Sandy Lake Auto only to find it closed for the holiday. What kind of car dealership was closed on Labor Day, he wondered as he waited for his turn to pull out of the lot. A steady stream of traffic was headed south out of town. Trucks pulled boats and trailered Jet Skis. There was still beautiful weather to come, but a lot of the vacationers used the long weekend to get a jump on shutting things down for the season.

He drove aimlessly for a while until he spotted the sign for the Peavey-McGill Funeral Home and pulled in on the off chance they might already have some of the details for the sheriff's funeral. As he approached the door, a woman sitting in the only other car in the lot said, "They're closed."

Packard tried the locked door anyway. "I should have known," he said.

The woman was red-faced and had obviously been crying. "Who died?" he asked her.

"My brother Bill."

"Sandersen?"

The woman looked surprised and nodded.

"Can we go somewhere so I can ask you some questions?"

———————

The woman's name was Wendy, and Bill was her older brother. She and Packard sat at a metal table in the sunshine in front of the Cup O Java. Wendy was short and plump, wearing a blue T-shirt and stretch jeans. Her eyes were still red, but she was out of tears.

"Carrie texted me that my brother was dead—murdered—and asked me to make the arrangements. Said she was too upset to think clearly. When I tried to call her, she didn't answer. I went to the house but she's not there. A deputy told me that Bill had been shot and that's all they knew so far. I have one day off this weekend, and the funeral home being closed was the last straw." She looked like she was about to cry again.

Packard confirmed the briefest details about Bill's death for her and explained she still had plenty of time to make arrangements since Bill's body would be in Saint Paul for a while.

"Is finding out via text from Carrie that your brother had been killed what you would expect from her?"

Wendy sipped her frothy iced drink through a straw as she thought about it. "I mean… I'm so mad at her right now, I don't know what to say. I want to call bullshit on her grief being bigger than mine. He's my brother!" She used her straw to mix up her drink. "I don't know. Mostly she's been fine to be around since she and Bill got married. We didn't see them a lot—my kids' birthdays, Thanksgiving, etc. She played along, but you could tell it was an effort for her. Her sister was the one who attended these things with Bill in the past, which I'm sure was never far from Carrie's mind. Honestly, it was awkward for all of us."

"Was Bill happy being married to her?"

"I think so. We didn't really talk about it. I asked him in the beginning if he wasn't worried that people were going to think he was a gold digger. He said he loved Carrie. That they'd reconnected after all these years and still felt something for each other." Wendy sipped her drink and shrugged, indicating she was open to the possibility, but her raised eyebrow betrayed that she thought the idea was probably bullshit.

"Here's an interesting thing about his divorce from Sherri, though," she added. "They were fighting a lot about money, drinking too much. Typical for those two. A divorce was probably inevitable, but Bill told me Margaret— Sherri and Carrie's mom—forced Sherri into it. Sherri was broke and needed money just to pay the bills. Margaret said she'd only give Sherri an allowance if she got divorced from Bill. She said she wasn't supporting two deadbeats."

Packard made a few notes. Sherri had already told him her mother hated Bill. Using her checkbook as a lever to pry them apart was the sign of a woman who didn't take no for an answer. She must have been less affected by her dementia back then.

"What else was going on in Bill's life? Where should I be looking for a killer or a reason to kill him?"

"His gambling was an issue. I'm guessing a big chunk of Sherri's money went to the casino. Both of them had problems. He liked to play poker. She could smoke cigarettes and sit in front of a slot machine for hours like it was showing a movie."

"Did Bill owe anyone money that you know of?"

Wendy said she had no idea. The only time Bill asked her for money was when he asked her to invest in the chicken wings restaurant. "My husband and I argued about it a lot. I work in the bakery department at MarketFoods, and he teaches history and coaches football at the high school. We aren't exactly sitting on a pile of reserve cash."

Packard nodded. There was a lot of money to be found in various parts of the county. Multimillion-dollar mansions surrounded the best lakeshore. The people in those homes didn't make their living in Sandy Lake. Many of the county's residents were just getting by. Others weren't even doing that.

"I had five thousand dollars sitting in a savings account that I got when our mother died a while back. I gave it to Bill because it was originally Mom's money. I thought if this was something he and Roger were doing together, it was less likely the money would be turned into poker chips."

Packard told her about the shared account Bill and Roger had opened together. "Roger put twenty grand into that account. Bill put in a total of $9,700."

"Five thousand of that was mine," Wendy said.

"Bill recently took twenty thousand out, and Roger has no idea what he did with it."

Wendy's face fell. "I knew better and I gave it to him anyway. Talk about gambling," she said. "Maybe we're the problem—the people giving him easy access to money he didn't earn. It kept him from working for it. It kept him from being a better person."

Later that afternoon, Packard was back in his office. He wrote up his conversation with Wendy. He looked up the most recent annual report for the Gherlick Family Trust, where Carrie was the CEO. The fund had almost $300 million in assets. Carrie made just shy of two hundred thousand dollars a year in salary. The five other board members made about half that.

A database search of the phone number Bill had texted the night he died showed a carrier but no customer information. Packard had a feeling he was looking at a burner phone or a phony number generated by a burner app that allowed a user to send and receive texts on their primary phone while keeping their actual number private. Tracing it from the carrier to the app creator to an Apple ID or something similar could take weeks.

Packard's own phone rang. The name on the screen was JIM WOLF, the chair of the county board of commissioners. "I heard about Stan," Jim said when Packard answered. "Terrible news but not unexpected, I guess."

"It's a big loss for everyone who knew him," Packard said. He knew Jim wasn't calling to express his condolences. He wasn't that kind of guy. "What can I do for you, Jim?"

"Listen, I know it's Labor Day, but we still have a regularly scheduled board meeting tomorrow."

"I'm supposed to present the numbers for next year's budget. I haven't forgotten."

"Yeah, that's still on the agenda. I've been talking to the other board members about what's next for the sheriff. By that I mean the next sheriff. Stan got sick not long after winning his last election. You've been doing his job for almost a year now. Sheriff isn't on the ballot for the election coming up in November, but the board thinks it should be."

Packard said nothing. The board was basically giving interested parties less than two months to register and campaign for the job. On one hand, Packard thought it was the perfect amount of time. Election campaigns—at every level of government—went on too long, generating nothing but noise and nonsense. On the other hand, it was really no time at all. Stan had started campaigning hard a year in advance. He was always a shoo-in—the voters of Sandy Lake County would have reelected him sheriff until the oceans dried up—but he never took that for granted.

"We need to make the announcement immediately so people have time to file before the ballots are printed," Jim said.

Sometimes during interviews with suspects Packard liked to keep quiet and just let the person continue to fill the silence on their own until they got to the nut of things. He turned in his chair and looked out the window at the blue sky hanging over what should have been his day off. He could have taken Frank out in the kayak. He could have driven to St. Cloud and banged the drummer again.

"You'll have to run if you plan on keeping the job," Jim said.

There it was. Jim made it sound like Packard was playing a game of keep-away and the board wanted its ball back.

Despite the number of times he mentioned the board, Jim Wolf was the one who wanted the election. He'd protested Stan's decision to appoint Packard, had even tried to float the idea of letting the board take the necessary time to review potential candidates and make the decision while Stan focused on his health. Stan reminded Jim that the board had no authority to make decisions within the department. Their approval was a formality, nothing more.

"Anything you want me to do or say about this at the meeting tomorrow night?" Packard asked.

"No, no. Just thought you should know."

"Now I know," Packard said. "Kelly sent the budget slides last week before she went on vacation. Shouldn't be any surprises."

"I saw them. See you tomorrow night."

Packard hung up. He didn't particularly care that Jim didn't want him in the job. Didn't particularly care that Jim and others wanted a new sheriff elected as soon as possible now that Stan had died. Nothing unreasonable about that.

Two things had to be true if you wanted to be sheriff: you had to want the job and you had to be electable. Packard was questionable about the first one and doubtful about the second. Why would anyone vote for the new guy in town? The new gay guy, more specifically. And why would he want to give up being a detective and take on the bureaucratic job of sheriff full time? Meetings and budgets and personnel issues, your future employment tied to the whims of the voting public.

No thanks.

So why did Jim's call piss him off so much?

CHAPTER SEVEN

SOMEONE WAS TRYING TO get into the house.

Carrie sat tall at the sound of the handle turning and someone pushing their weight against the locked front door. Not Zeinab—she wasn't scheduled to come until later. Carrie got up from the dining table, heart racing. When she heard keys jangle and saw through the window who it was, she sighed and went back to where she and Margaret had been eating lunch.

Sherri came barging in like a deer through a plate-glass window. She was wearing cutoff shorts and a black tank top. She had big sunglasses and a huge purse and was already talking before the door closed behind her. "What the fuck? Why don't you answer your fucking phone?" she asked.

"Because I don't want to talk to you or anyone else right now," Carrie said. She took a bite of her sandwich and studied its layers like she'd never seen one before. "How'd you get out here? I thought your license was suspended."

Sherri took off her sunglasses and dropped her purse on the kitchen counter. "It is and I can't drive my car because it's the only red Mercedes in town and every goddamn cop around knows I don't have my license. I borrowed a car from a girl who just moved into the condos. Traded her some weed for her keys."

"Charming," Carrie said. She reached across the table and nudged Margaret's plate closer to her. "Mom, finish your fruit."

Margaret bit into a piece of sliced apple. She'd been dressed for the day in brown slacks and a red sweater. Her hair hadn't been done and looked flat in the back.

"So why are you here?" Carrie asked over her shoulder.

"I don't know. I thought maybe you could tell me what the fuck happened to my ex-husband."

"Somebody shot him. He's dead. You can leave now," Carrie said.

"Shut up. I'll leave when I'm ready," Sherri said. She went to the refrigerator and opened both doors. "Is there anything to drink in this house?"

"Yes, we have a fully stocked bar on the premises for Mom and her nurses and all the day drinking that goes on around here," Carrie said.

Sherri opened and closed cupboards until she found a few random liquor bottles covered in grease and dust in the cabinet over the stove hood. A bottle of cheap Canadian whisky had half an inch left in the bottom. Sherri got herself a glass with ice and emptied the bottle into it.

"Those breasts make you look like a whore," Margaret said suddenly.

"Mom, give it a rest," Sherri said. She stuck her thumbs under the straps of her tank top and adjusted herself. "This boob job is fifteen years old. You've seen them a thousand times."

"Whores walk around with their breasts out like that," Margaret said.

Carrie turned her chair around sideways and smiled at her sister like a snake. Sherri sipped the whisky. "You don't look too upset, considering your husband has been murdered."

"I don't know what people expect of me," Carrie said. "What's the appropriate amount of upset I should be when my idiot husband got mixed up with the wrong people and got himself killed?"

"What people?"

"I don't know what people. The ones who killed him. Friends of yours, probably."

"Oh sure, all the murderers I'm friends with," Sherri said.

Carrie ignored her. "What I should be upset about is that he drew those people right to my house. I could have been killed, too. For no reason."

"You didn't see anything or anyone?"

"No," Carrie said.

"Then for all you know it could have been me," Sherri said. "Couldn't take the thought of you two together anymore."

Carrie got up from the table and took her and Margaret's empty plates to the sink. "I told the detective it wasn't you because you wouldn't have stopped with Bill. That said, I'd be surprised if you weren't involved somehow."

"Involved in what? Why would I want to kill Bill?"

"You tell me," Carrie said close to Sherri's ear as she walked by. She helped their mother up from the table and walked her over to a recliner in front of the TV. There was a pad in the seat in case of accidents.

Sherri fished an ice cube from the glass and sucked the whisky off it. "So where's the money Bill took from Roger?"

"I didn't know he had taken money from Roger."

"Twenty grand," Sherri said.

"How did you know about it?"

"From Roger."

Carrie gave her sister the stink eye. "So Bill's dead and there's twenty grand missing and you wonder why I think you might have had something to do with it."

"And I'm wondering if you didn't have something to do with it."

Carrie shrugged, sat on the couch, and picked up the TV remote. "I'm not the one who needs twenty grand. I have my own money. You, on the other hand, are a broke bitch. When's the last time you had your hair done, Roots?"

Sherri stared into her empty glass like she was trying to think of a come-back or trying to make more whisky appear out of thin air. Carrie watched her, then turned back to the TV. Sherri was never the smart one. She was the saucy one as a child, the sexy one when she was old enough to attract boys. She threw herself into situations regardless of the consequences. She was exactly the kind of person who could be talked into murdering her ex-husband for a meager amount of money.

Sherri sucked the last of the liquid from the bottom of the glass, then dumped the ice in the sink. "How long are you going to stay here?" she asked.

"Until the police tell me I can have my house back. Maybe longer," Carrie said. "I don't know if I can live there again. Bill ruined it for me."

Sherri shouldered her purse and put on her sunglasses. "Typical. Bill's dead and all you can think about is how you've been inconvenienced. My advice— work on your grieving widow act if you don't want people to recognize you for the monster you are," she said.

Carrie dropped her head and took a deep breath. When she looked up, her eyes were wet. "I loved Bill. I don't know what I'm going to do without him." She blinked and tears ran down. "Like that, you mean?"

Sherri looked disgusted. "You remind me of Mom when we were kids. Crazy bitch," she said.

"Alcoholic whore."

Margaret was picking crumbs off her sweater. "Girls, be nice," she said.

––––––––––––

After Sherri left, Carrie moved to the end of the couch closest to her mother's chair. She'd hoped that cutting back the hours of the home health aides and spending time alone, just the two of them, might help clear Margaret's mind. The aides agitated her. She angered easily and was prone to tantrums. Having strangers in her house—especially Muslims and Mexicans—was particularly upsetting. Why couldn't Carrie hire real people to help her, Margaret asked, meaning where were all the white people who wanted to bathe her and change her diapers. Carrie explained to her that the aides were trained professionals who cared about her and wanted to help. If she couldn't be happy with the home health aides, the alternative was moving to the nursing home. Margaret still had enough of her marbles to know she didn't want that.

Now that Sherri was gone and it was quiet again, Margaret looked around her with the curious, unknowing gaze of a child.

Carrie put her hand on Margaret's arm. "Mom, do you remember when you gave me all your jewelry?"

Margaret looked at her but didn't say anything. Her tongue was working on something behind her teeth.

"Do you remember the hummingbird pin?"

Margaret nodded. "With the rubies and the diamonds," she said.

"That's the one. Where did you get it?"

"From your father."

"Was there anything special about it?"

"About what?"

"The hummingbird pin," Carrie said.

Margaret stuck out her tongue and picked something off the end of it that she rubbed between her fingers. "I'm tired," she said.

Carrie sighed and guided her mother's hand to the button on the side of the recliner that extended the footrest. A minute later Margaret was lightly snoring.

The killer had asked Bill specifically about the hummingbird pin before he shot him. *Where's the hummingbird pin? It's not here.*

It wasn't with the rest of Carrie's jewelry because it was something she actually wore, pinned to her coat in the front closet. If she could go home again, she'd bring it back with her. Maybe something tactile would thin the logjam in her mother's mind and let memories flow.

How had the killer known about the pin? What was special about the pin?

CHAPTER EIGHT

THINGS STARTED TO RETURN to normal on Tuesday. The town was still swollen with people whose long weekend was overflowing into the week. Yellow school buses moved against the tide, dragging the unwilling up a slope into the volcano of a new school year.

Packard drove by Sandy Lake Auto again and found it open this time. Brightly colored pennant flags flapped over the lot. The sun blazed on dozens of windshields.

Packard pushed through the tinted doors into a heavily air-conditioned office area. No cars inside, just several small cubicles, a few offices on the back wall, and a separate waiting area for people getting their cars serviced. It smelled like burned coffee and printer toner.

A smiling salesman came at Packard from the right. "Morning, Deputy, can I help you with something?" Another man in a suit and tie was standing in the doorway of an office in back.

"Are you here about Bill?" he called.

"I am," Packard said.

"Come on back."

Packard nodded at the salesman and walked back to the guy in the suit, who introduced himself as Stephen Carter. He was tall with a bushy mustache and a ring of dark hair around a shiny pate. He closed the door, then sat behind the desk.

"I was surprised you guys were closed yesterday," Packard said. "Isn't Labor Day a big day for selling cars?"

"It can be if you own a dealership and have promotions and numbers you're obligated to. All of our cars are used. Most of our inventory are former rental cars and lease returns that we buy at auction. It's my business so I decide when we're open and closed. No one wants to work on the last day of summer."

"Can't disagree with that."

"I've only heard gossip so far about what happened to Bill," Stephen admitted. "I've been trying to contact Carrie, but she hasn't been answering her phone. Understandable, given the circumstances."

Packard confirmed that Bill was dead, not by his own hand, and identified himself as the lead investigator on the case. "How long has Bill worked here?"

"Two years, maybe a little longer. He and I went to high school together. He asked about a job around the time one of my guys was retiring. I admit I was surprised to see him. He and Sherri's lifestyle was legendary. A lot of us looked at them and thought it must be nice to have all that money and not a care in the world."

"What made you hire him?"

"He needed a job. He had divorced Sherri and was marrying Carrie. I think his exact words were it was time to start pulling his own weight. He didn't have any experience in sales, but our stuff mostly sells itself. It's not a high-pressure, high-commission operation."

Stephen told him how the cars were labeled with the price. There was no negotiating. Take it or leave it. The sales guys (they were all guys) could make extra by selling oil-change packages or extended warranties. The whole business operated on a profit-sharing basis—everyone from the admins to the mechanics to the sales guys earned a bonus when the business did well.

Packard asked if he had an employee file on Bill. Stephen picked up the phone and asked someone to print Bill's file. "It'll be just a few minutes," he said, hanging up.

"What kind of employee was Bill?"

Stephen leaned back in his chair and smoothed his tie down his front. "Bill was a master bullshitter. Some people like that and others don't. He liked to sit in here and talk about our high school days. Football games, girls, parties. He was pretty nostalgic for the old times. Hell, I get it. We're both in our fifties. We got more years behind us than ahead of us. Our lives are what they're going to be at this point."

"Did he talk to you about his idea to open a restaurant with Roger Freeman?"

Stephen looked surprised. "No. Not a word. I know Roger from back in the day, too."

It made sense that Bill wouldn't want to tell his current boss that he was making plans to go into business for himself.

"Anything about money problems or gambling losses?" Packard asked.

"Nope."

"I want to talk to the people he hung out with at work."

Stephen said he'd take him out to the garage. There were two mechanics Bill spent more time with than others. "He told me he was trying to quit smoking for Carrie, but he was lighting up with these guys pretty regularly behind the building."

They left the office and stopped at a cubicle where a young woman with white plastic glasses and bright lipstick gave Packard a manila folder with Bill's HR records in it. Stephen led him through the waiting area and through a door into the service bay where he had three lifts and half a dozen guys working. They all wore gray short-sleeved shirts that had an embroidered patch with their name on it. Packard stood by the door and waited while Stephen tapped two guys on the shoulder, then motioned for Packard to follow them through a steel door that opened onto the back lot.

"Detective Packard, this is Paul and Ryan, two of my mechanics," Stephen said unnecessarily since their names were on their shirts and their fingers were black with engine grime. They both nodded instead of shaking hands. Stephen jingled his keys in his pockets while he waited for the questioning to start.

Packard said, "I need a few minutes alone with these guys, Stephen. I'll stop in your office before I leave."

Stephen looked put out but nodded and left them alone. When he was gone, Packard said, "Smoke 'em if you got 'em. I don't mind."

Both Paul and Ryan lit up. Ryan was the younger of the two—mid- to late-twenties. Black hair buzzed to the skin on the sides and around the back, longer on top and slicked back. Heavily tattooed arms. Looked like a weight lifter.

Paul was older, over fifty. Lines around his eyes. Gray hair. He had the remnants of his good-looking younger self, but he also looked like he'd lived hard and was mostly cigarette ash and greasy food on the inside.

Packard gave them the bare minimum on what had happened to Bill. They'd both already heard he was dead, and they'd both last seen him on Friday. "We stood right here just like we are now, talking about the weekend," Ryan said. He seemed nervous. He stood with a hand wrapped around a giant bicep. He had a wrench tattooed down the length of his forearm.

"What did he have planned?" Packard asked.

"Nothing," Ryan said.

"I saw him in the afternoon and he told me the same thing," said Paul. "No plans. He seemed pretty bummed about having a three-day weekend and nothing to do."

"What else did you guys talk about when you met?" Packard asked. "What was Bill like?"

Ryan looked at Paul like he wanted him to go first, or to say something so he didn't have to. Paul just shook his head. Ryan said, "He always wanted to know what was up with me and my girl. His favorite thing to say was if he knew what he knew now when he was my age, he would've done a lot of things different. He was always warning me not to let my current piece of ass blind me to all my options. I laughed along a couple of times, but I finally had to tell him not to disrespect my girl like that." Ryan puffed on his cigarette and blew the smoke sideways. "Mostly we just talked about sports and work and shit like that."

"He ever talk about his wife?"

"Not with me," Ryan said. "I couldn't even tell you her name."

There was a generation gap that even gossip had a hard time bridging. People Bill's age—maybe his parents' age, too—were familiar with the scandal he caused marrying two sisters. But go a generation or two in the other direction, and they had no idea who these people were. They were too busy trying to be known for their own transgressions.

Ryan ground his cigarette out on the bottom of his boot and put the butt in the receptacle by the door. "I should get back to work. Sucks what happened to the guy, but I didn't know him that well. I thought he was a dick, to be honest."

Packard let him go after getting his full name and a number where he could reach him if he had more questions.

Paul decided to have a second cigarette. "Bill liked to gamble," he said, as he shielded the cigarette and flicked the lighter. Packard caught a glimpse of dice tattooed on the palm of his hand.

"I've heard he and his ex-wife were regulars at the casino," Packard said.

"It was more than that, though. He was after high stakes recently. He found out about a game run out of someone's house."

"Did he go?"

"He went," Paul said.

"And?"

Paul blew smoke out. "He said he walked out with what he went in with. But if you know gamblers, you know they brag about the wins and lie about the losses. So..."

"Where was the game?"

"I don't know. Some rich guy's house on a lake. Sounded like he had to jump through all kinds of hoops to get invited. Ronnie Winder was the one who helped him out."

Winder Marine and Powersports was practically across the street from the dealership. Bill could have easily walked there during lunch or on his breaks when he wasn't smoking cigarettes with Ryan and Paul.

Bill told Roger he had taken the money out of their shared account because he had a plan. Was that a euphemism for the poker game?

A sparkling wet Honda CRV pulled out of the car-wash bay beside them and pulled up to the vacuum station. A young woman in tight white shorts and a pink tank got out and fed quarters into the machine.

Paul didn't know anything else about the high-stakes game. Couldn't pinpoint in his memory when Bill had gone. A month ago. Two months ago. He was distracted by the girl bent over, vacuuming out the back hatch of her car.

"I get Ryan not being a fan of Bill's. What did you think of him?" Packard asked.

Paul shrugged, not taking his eyes off the girl. "You could bullshit with the guy, no problem, but he definitely acted like he was better than you. He made it clear that working for a living was for suckers. He was only slumming with us clock punchers until he could get set up for himself. He wanted to start a business. He didn't want to talk about it because he didn't want anyone stealing his idea."

"His top secret chicken wings and beer restaurant."

"Was that it? Maybe I will steal it now that he's dead," Paul said.

"Any guesses who would want to put a bullet in Bill?" Packard asked.

Paul shook his head. "None at all," he said and fed his cigarette butt into the stand by the door. "But like Ryan said, he was kind of an asshole so there could be a list."

———

Packard went back to Stephen's office and asked if Bill had his own desk or computer. Stephen told him that the sales staff used desks out in the open with shared terminals for closing deals and completing paperwork with customers. They had cubes for when they weren't on the floor.

Bill's cube had a sport coat over the back of the chair and a Styrofoam cup with a skin on the surface of last Friday's coffee. No personal effects. Just a laptop and a spiral notebook.

The same woman with white glasses who had given him Bill's HR folder—her name was Katherine—came over and keyed in Bill's employee ID and password. Packard opened up the email application and found hundreds of unread messages from Stephen, the service department, and other Sandy Lake Auto email addresses. Bill either didn't know the first thing about email or he couldn't be bothered.

Katherine showed him an application where he could see Bill's sales for the last year.

"How were his numbers?"

"Fair," she said. "The cars sell themselves for the most part." She leaned over his shoulder with her hand on the back of his chair and clicked the screen. She smelled like orange blossoms. "He wasn't good at the upsell," she said and pointed her finger at a column of numbers. "Frequently missed his numbers there."

Packard opened the notebook and found a small number of pages with last names, phone numbers, dollar amounts, things underlined or boxed. A lot of ink that felt like it added up to nothing.

Packard stood up and scanned the dealership over the walls of the cube. He imagined Bill in the same sport coat every day, loitering in the customer lounge, smelling of cigarettes and coffee, waiting for his chance to step up to customers when it was his turn at bat.

Katherine was standing in the cube with him, maybe one inch into his personal space. She smiled.

"Did you know him well?" he asked her.

"No. He'd stop by and flirt when he first started working here, but I shut that down." She stepped closer and lowered her voice. "I have an app on my computer that I can make call my desk phone with a keystroke when I need to get rid of someone," she confessed. "I always got a call whenever Bill stopped by to talk about anything other than his check or his time off."

"You didn't happen to go to his house and shoot him Saturday night, did you?"

"Detective, if I shot every annoying man who crossed my path, there'd be dead bodies from here to the tip of Florida."

Packard asked her to write down Bill's user ID and password on the inside cover of his notebook, then went out to his vehicle to get an evidence receipt for the laptop. She blushed when he shook her hand and thanked her for her help.

Winder Marine was just across the street and down the road a bit so Packard decided to walk. He tossed the laptop into the passenger seat. Something loose slid out of the notebook.

It was Katherine's business card. She'd written her cell phone number on the back and the words *Call me!* with a smiley face.

Packard laughed and wondered if it was possible that there were people in Sandy Lake who hadn't heard the gossip about him yet.

———————

Paul, the older mechanic, had been the second person to mention Ronnie Winder in connection with Bill. Carrie had identified him as one of Bill's friends as well. Packard knew Ronnie only vaguely as one of the sponsors for the ice-fishing festival held every year on Lake Redwing. Stan Shaw had been a big supporter of the festival, encouraging his deputies to get involved either on or off the clock. The festival had been canceled last year because of an abnormally warm winter.

At Winder Marine a giant END-OF-SEASON CLEARANCE banner was strung up in the parking lot. Trailered boats baked in the afternoon sun. Hiding in the shade of the building were rows of ATVs and vaguely militaristic-looking UTVs. Inside, Ronnie had a mix of fishing boats, lake toys, and snowmobiles on display. He was standing behind the counter in a pale-blue polo shirt, a gaunt man whose thinness made him look older than he was. His hair was parted down the middle and brushed back on the sides, likely the same haircut he'd had since he was eight years old. Packard could tell by the expression on his face that Ronnie was expecting him.

"I figured someone from the sheriff's department would be here before long," he said. "Fucking Bill."

"Tell me about him," Packard said.

"I played a lot of poker with him up at the casino," Ronnie said, scratching the side of his nose. He looked to be in his midforties. He had a pointed face that made him look vaguely like a rat. "He was a pretty good customer of this place back when he and his old lady had money."

"When did you last see him or talk to him?"

"It's been a few weeks."

"Was it when you set him up with the high-stakes game?"

Ronnie looked like Packard had just thrown a punch at him. "Who told you about that?"

"Someone Bill told about it."

"Listen, I did everything I could to talk him out of that game. Bill had a poor accounting of himself as a player. It's one thing to sit at a five-dollar table at the casino and play for hours. He had enough money that the losses didn't matter and the wins were all he remembered. I told him that when he started asking about the game. I've only played in it once. I'm a better player than Bill, and I knew in a hurry I was out of my league with those guys."

"What guys?"

"I can't tell you that. These guys have more money than you can imagine. Some of them are very good customers of mine."

"Tell me about the game then. When is it?"

"It's infrequent. All the guys have to be up here at the same time. They're all big shots from the Twin Cities or Milwaukee or Michigan. They're longtime friends of the main guy or they live near him on the lake."

"What's the buy-in?"

"Ten grand cash just to sit at the table. The way these guys play, you can lose that much in a single hand."

"How'd you do when you played?"

"Walked away with four thousand of my twenty-thousand-dollar buy-in. It was a lesson in humility."

"Bill never had a chance, did he?"

"Zero. Like I said, it's one thing to keep your cool in a low-stakes game at the casino. But when every raise is hundreds or thousands of dollars, you start to sweat. It's like blood in the water to these guys. Any one of them could have ten grand fall out of his pocket and not miss it."

"Any chance Bill walked out of there owing somebody money?"

"Maybe. I don't see these guys taking an IOU from a small fish like Bill. He was an idiot, but I'm pretty sure he would have recognized he was done when he lost his buy-in."

"So give me the name of the host."

"Come on, Packard. Don't put me in this spot. It'll hurt my business."

"I'm investigating a murder, Ronnie."

"Why do you think the poker game had anything to do with Bill getting himself killed?"

"I'm not saying it did, but I have to know about it so I can rule it out."

Ronnie picked at something on his elbow while he considered his options. "Let me do this. Let me call the guy and have him call you. That way it's not on me for giving you his name."

"He needs to call me by the end of the day. If I don't get a call, I'm coming back to you with a subpoena for your billing records. I'll find out who your biggest customers are and start calling them myself. Understand?"

"Yeah, I got it. But I think you're wasting your time. Bill was nothing to these guys. A fly. What could Bill do to them that would be worth risking everything they have to kill him?"

"I don't know, but how many times have you swatted an annoying fly?"

Ronnie sighed. "Lots."

———

It was lunchtime by the time Packard left Winder Marine. He grabbed a sandwich in town and then made it to the station for the first time that day. Kelly was at her desk, trying to eat a salad out of view of anyone coming in. Her frosted hair was pulled back with big bangs in the front. Her eyes were red. Just the sight of Packard made her put her hand over her mouth and blink away the tears.

"Come on, Kelly. No crying."

Packard used his card to get through the secured door and went around to her desk. Kelly got out of her chair and hugged him. It was the first time she'd ever done so. Most of the time she treated him like a child she wanted out of her sight. She was old enough to be his mother.

"I wouldn't have gone to Palm Springs if I'd thought this was the weekend he would go," she said, keeping her head turned so as not to get makeup all over the front of him.

"I saw him at the festival with Marilyn on Saturday," Packard said. "He didn't look great, but he didn't look like he was going to die within twenty-four hours either."

Kelly got a tissue and used it to dab under her lashes before she sat again. "Gah. I've got so much catching up to do after a long weekend and now a funeral to plan on top of it."

"Do you know when it is?"

"Thursday at ten thirty at St. Stephen's. You're speaking about Stan as a public servant and a law enforcement officer."

"I can do that. I've been working on something."

"Send me a copy. I'll tell you if it's good enough."

"Yes, sir."

Kelly gave him a look like he'd better watch himself. "New subject," she said. "I heard that the election for sheriff is on the agenda for the board meeting tonight."

Of course, she had. Kelly knew everyone in every department in the county government building. If Shepard had a corner on town gossip, Kelly had the inside track on the real news of how things worked and got done in Sandy Lake.

"If you wanted to make a motion that the board are a bunch of ungrateful assholes and that you should keep the job until the current term is up, I would second it."

"I'm not sure I get to make motions," Packard said.

Kelly looked disappointed in his lack of imagination. "I assume you're going to run."

"I don't think so. I came here to be a detective. I like doing investigations. I only took on the sheriff job as a favor to Stan. Putting myself out there in an election feels like it would be unpleasant and a waste of time."

"Sounds like a lot of excuses to me. You should run."

Packard shrugged noncommittally. "It'll be interesting to see who does run."

"That's what I'm worried about," Kelly said. "Anyway, do you want me at the meeting tonight as backup for the budget slides?"

"No, I got it covered. You've got enough on your plate. Keep me posted on the details about the funeral."

Kelly nodded and turned in her chair, dismissing him. "Sorry for hugging you," she said without turning around. "Don't take it the wrong way and think I like you or anything."

"The thought never crossed my mind," Packard said.

———————

Packard spent the rest of the afternoon writing down the notes from his interviews with the guys at Sandy Lake Auto and Ronnie Winder. He paged through the notebook from Bill's desk again and found nothing. Bill's laptop went into the evidence locker and Packard sent an email about it to Suresh, the department's digital forensics expert.

At five o'clock he drove home, walked Frank, and made dinner: grilled chicken breast, corn on the cob, and a salad. He reviewed the budget slides one last time as he ate.

He was back in town, one floor up from the sheriff's department, for the county board meeting by seven. Everyone sitting at the curved table at the head of the room looked like they'd rather be anywhere but there. Same for the few people scattered in the gallery.

The first order of business was to acknowledge the passing of Stan Shaw. One of the commissioners made a motion that they should observe a moment of silence in honor of the sheriff, it was seconded and then approved, and then everyone was asked to lower their head. Packard thought it was ridiculous how much talking it took to get everyone to shut up.

After the moment passed, Jim Wolf, the chair of the board, said, "Speaking of Stan, I've spoken to the other commissioners and I would like to make a motion that we hold a special election in November for the office of sheriff."

"Seconded," said Wally Shafley, Jim's closest ally on the board.

Commissioner Janelle White, whose territory covered the townships in the northern part of the county, asked whether there wouldn't be a benefit, financial or otherwise, to allowing Deputy Packard to finish out Stan's term.

"We'd be paying a full-time sheriff's salary to the new person after the election," Janelle said. "We'd save money by continuing to pay Deputy Packard to do the job part time for the next two years."

It was true. The board had given him a 20 percent raise to serve as acting sheriff, which still hadn't brought him up to the lower end of the sheriff's pay range. He'd miss the bump when it was gone, but he'd gotten by on his regular salary before. It just meant the home renovations would take longer.

"Two more years with someone acting as sheriff in a limited capacity is too long," Jim Wolf said. "Now's the time to fill the position. The ballots haven't been printed yet. There's time for anyone who wants to run to get their hundred signatures and file an application by the deadline, which I propose be one week from this Friday."

The motion regarding the election passed. Commissioner White then made a motion that the board should officially thank Deputy Packard for his service to the county in his role as acting sheriff.

She paused for a second. Jim Wolf looked around. Wally looked at Jim. Another commissioner, who'd been looking at his phone in his lap, looked up, realized the noise he'd heard in the background was Janelle making a motion that needed a second, so he seconded whatever it was she'd said. Motion passed.

Packard kept his expression neutral. He looked around and made eye contact with a guy to his right who'd been staring at him throughout the entire election conversation. Packard folded and unfolded the printout of his slides. That the sheriff had to kowtow to these circus clowns year after year to get the money needed to fund the department was another reason he wasn't interested in the job.

When it was time, he gave his presentation about the proposed budget. There were no questions. He then sat through the rest of a meeting he had no interest in. The guy in the audience who'd been watching him stood up with another guy—cousins, it turned out—and presented their business plan and application requesting to construct a microbrewery at a location on the edge of town alongside the Sandy River. The board was very enthusiastic about the idea and gave unanimous approval for their application.

After the meeting, the cousins stopped to talk to Packard on their way out. "Sheriff," said the one who'd been staring at him all night as they shook hands.

"Ben," Packard corrected.

"I'm Kyle. This is my cousin Mark." They were both wearing suits that they looked like they couldn't wait to get out of. Kyle had short black hair thick enough to stand up on its own and a five-o'clock shadow that made Packard think of sandpaper. A scar that ran through his top lip gave him a crooked smile.

"You should come by and check out the site," Kyle said. "We've already got the building up. We'll start moving in equipment in a few days. Tonight was more of a formality than anything."

"I've noticed your building," Packard said. "I'll stop by."

He shook hands again with both of them again and wished them luck.

It felt like Kyle held his grip and his gaze a microsecond longer than necessary.

Packard's phone rang with a call from a blocked number on the drive home.

"Ronnie Winder told me you wanted to speak to me, Detective."

"You're the host of the poker game," Packard said.

"I am."

"We need to meet," Packard said. "I need to know about the game Bill Sandersen played in."

"I'd prefer to talk about it now. Over the phone. I'm happy to tell you whatever you want to know. I really don't want to get involved in a murder investigation."

"You're already involved. I need to know your name. I need to know who else played that night. I need to know what Bill did and said and what everyone else did and said."

"You put me in an awkward spot, Detective."

"I haven't done anything," Packard said. "Bill put you in an awkward spot by getting himself killed. You put yourself in an awkward spot by letting him play in your game. I don't know who you are, but it'll take me two phone calls or less to find out. It's going to be more pleasant for all involved if you don't make me work for this."

There was silence on the other end. "I'll call you back," the man said.

Packard had changed into track pants and a T-shirt and was trying to wrestle a chew toy away from Frank when he got the call back.

"All right, Detective. I am Leon Chen. I live at 800 Silver Creek Lane."

Packard knew the neighborhood—multimillion-dollar mansions on the east side of Lake Redwing.

"I'm having another game tomorrow night. I needed to confirm everyone was okay with you coming. Everyone who played the night Bill did will be there. Come by and you can talk to all at once. 8:00 p.m."

"Who's going to be there?" Packard asked.

Leon Chen read off a list of names, several of which made Packard's eyebrows go up.

"See you tomorrow," Packard said.

CHAPTER NINE

WEDNESDAY MORNING STARTED WITH a swim and a call from a number with a 651 area code as he was sitting in the sauna afterward. "This is Ashley from the Ramsey County Medical Examiner's Office. I've got preliminary results on your gunshot victim."

She confirmed Bill's manner of death was homicide from multiple gunshot wounds. One to the neck and one to the chest that penetrated his lung, superior vena cava, and aorta.

"I also found evidence your guy was sexually active in the hours before his death. There were traces of semen on his genitals and inner thigh."

Packard thought about the texts between Bill and "Roger" he'd found on the phone. I'll pick you up in 15 min. ok lover. Sex seemed implied. Not between Bill and Roger. He still didn't believe that at all.

"Can you tell if someone else was involved or whether he might have…you know…taken care of himself?" Packard asked.

"You can say 'masturbated,' Detective."

"I'd rather not."

"It's my opinion that intercourse was involved," Ashley said. "I found traces of other bodily fluids with a pH different than that from the semen. I also found pubic hairs from another source tangled with the deceased's."

"How do you separate pubic hairs?" Packard wanted to know.

"Comb the area, then compare the loose ones with samples from the body. I found several that were coarser and shorter than the others. Under a microscope I found evidence of hair dye. The hair shaft was dark in color but gray at the base."

Another strike against Roger. The bowlegged dairy farmer didn't seem the type to dye his pubes.

Sherri, Bill's ex-wife, had dark hair with gray showing at the roots.

Packard talked to Ashley for a few more minutes. The full toxicology report would take a couple of weeks to run and write up the results. She told Packard he could arrange to have the body transported back to Sandy Lake whenever he was ready. They had all the samples they needed.

Packard showered and shaved, dressed, and ate breakfast. He looked over his notes from his first interview with Sherri. She told him she had ended the night at Bob's Bar the night Bill was killed and that she'd spent a fortune there over the years. When Bill texted "Roger" to find out where he was, the response was **where u think?**

Bill would have known Sherri meant Bob's Bar. He'd likely sat on a barstool beside her the whole time they were married.

Add dyed pubes and it all made sense.

It was almost 9:30 a.m. when Packard parked in front of Sherri's condo. He hadn't bothered to call ahead. If she was sleeping off another late night, too damn bad.

After several heavy presses on the doorbell, she answered wearing a pair of men's boxer shorts and a Corona T-shirt with the sleeves cut off. Her hair looked like she'd been rubbing a balloon against her head.

"Christ, man. What the hell?" she said.

"Why didn't you tell me you had sex with Bill the night he was killed? You were probably the last person to see him alive."

Sherri stared down at her bare feet. She looked tired and not ready to admit the truth.

"I found your texts on his phone. Bill had your number listed as Roger. Probably in case Carrie was ever nearby," Packard said. "It's not the number you gave me so I'm guessing you have a burner phone or an app you used just in case Carrie ever looked too closely."

"Fuck," Sherri said. She grabbed a handful of her hair and moved it from one side of her head to the other. "Just wait here a minute. Let me get my cigarettes and a coffee and we'll talk."

"Let me in. I'll start the coffee while you do what you need to do."

———

Her coffee maker was a Keurig. He made her cup in a mug that said Don't Talk to Me Before I've Had My Coffee. Or After. Ten minutes later they were sitting on the front patio, Sherri smoking a cigarette and trying to wave the smoke away from Packard's direction.

"Tell me the truth about Saturday night," he said.

"I was out with friends watching the band. You saw me. We went to Bob's Bar after. Bill texted me while I was at the bar. He was off the leash and wanted to meet."

"This is something you two did regularly?"

Sherri shrugged and sucked on her cigarette.

"The two of you have been divorced for several years, but you still have an intimate relationship. Explain that to me."

"We had to get a divorce. We ran out of money. My mom said she'd give me an allowance—enough to cover the rent on this place—but the condition was Bill had to go."

"I'm surprised you agreed."

"It wasn't that hard. A lot of the fun had gone out of our marriage when the money was gone. I wanted Mom's allowance, and I wanted Bill to get a job and start figuring out the rest of his life. The only way to get both was for us to split."

"And then he married your sister."

A dark cloud passed over Sherri's face. She looked like she wanted to bite the filter off her cigarette. "That wasn't part of the plan," she said.

"What was the plan?"

"There wasn't a plan. Just that somehow, some way, I hoped we'd get back to the good times."

"You needed money for that. Maybe Bill's plan was to get your sister's money."

"If Bill got even five dollars out of my sister, it was by keeping the change after she sent him to the store for milk. That bitch is tight with a dollar. I would have told him that ahead of time if I'd known about the wedding before it happened."

Packard wondered if Sherri and Bill were running an elaborate con on her sister or if he had three people on his hands who were incredibly foolish when it came to love and money. He was leaning toward the latter.

"So Bill texted you Saturday night. What happened?"

"He picked me up downtown. We drove around for a while. He gave me shit about drinking too much. Then we parked and fucked in his truck."

Packard kept what he knew about the evidence of their coupling to himself. The less time he and Sherri spent discussing her pubic hair the better.

"Were you still in love with him?"

Sherri slumped in her chair. "Come on, don't ask me that," she said and leaned her head back and blew smoke up in the air.

"Well?"

"I don't know. Maybe."

"And you didn't think I should know any of this after Bill ended up murdered in his bed just hours later? About your relationship or the fact that you were the last person to see him alive."

Sherri leaned forward and stubbed out her cigarette. "I didn't see how it mattered. I didn't kill him. And I don't know who killed him or why." She sat back in her chair and exhaled the last smoke from her nostrils. "Also, I don't want my sister finding out I've been fucking her husband all this time from you or anyone else. She'll find out from me when it twists the knife the most."

"What is it between the two of you? I don't get it," Packard said.

"Just good old-fashioned sibling rivalry," she said.

Sherri promised there wasn't anything else she wasn't telling him. Packard believed her like he believed in Bigfoot. He asked her if she needed a ride anywhere and she said no, she needed to go back to bed. Packard left her there, smoking another cigarette, with a warning that he'd better not find out that she was still holding out on him.

At the station, Packard made a quick loop, saying hi to the dispatch operators and anyone sitting at a desk. He ran into Suresh making tea in the break room and asked what he'd found on Bill's phone. "Almost nothing," Suresh said in his heavily accented English. He was a young man, but his rapidly thinning hair and bushy mustache made him look older than he was. "This man has no online presence that I've been able to find."

Packard had hired Suresh a year ago on an H1-B visa after a fruitless local search for someone with the skills the digital forensics position demanded. Even ads he ran in the Twin Cities market hadn't turned up a candidate willing to move to Sandy Lake for the salary the job offered. Suresh and his wife, Prachi, were from Bangalore. She was currently pregnant with their first child.

Suresh stirred milk into his cup of tea. "He has no social media apps on his phone. He's got some poker and slot machine apps. He got texts and phone calls from just a few people. One person is called Princess Kay of the Milky Way. What is meant by that?"

"Did you track the number?" Packard asked.

"Yes, to a Roger Freeman."

Packard laughed. "Princess Kay is the title given to the winner of the statewide dairy princess pageant. Roger is a dairy farmer. It's a joke."

"I see," Suresh said, looking confused.

Packard followed Suresh back to his office. "Have you gotten to his computer yet?"

"No. I've been busy with some other work for Detective Thielen."

"Suresh, my stuff is always more important than hers."

"Oh? She told me the opposite. Come back tomorrow. I'll have more info," Suresh said.

Packard thanked him and asked him how much longer until the baby arrived. "Only six weeks," Suresh said, beaming. "We are so very excited."

Packard spent the rest of the afternoon following up on other parts of the investigation. The gunshot residue tests on Carrie's hands and clothing came back clean. GSR was fairly easy to wash or rub off, and there'd be none if she had changed clothes before calling 911. The absence of evidence wasn't the same as evidence.

He'd had a diver and a deputy in a sheriff's boat on the pond behind her house for the last two days looking for anything the killer might have wanted to get rid of in a hurry. The metal detector found a tire rim and several fishing rigs but nothing else. No gun. The diver said the water was weedy and murky. Their chances of finding anything were small.

Packard went over the list of items collected and bagged by the crime-scene crew. Bill's wallet, including $42, his driver's license, several credit cards, and a casino loyalty card were on the list.

Packard picked up the phone and called his contact at the casino. Raymond Pike was the head of customer loyalty and was often willing to answer Packard's questions about goings-on at the casino with a minimal amount of hassle. It helped having someone on the inside when matters of jurisdiction and authority between tribal police, who ruled on the reservation where the casino was located, and the county clashed.

"You only call when you want something," Pike said by way of a greeting.

"This time is no different. One of your customers was murdered recently. He has a player's card there. I'm wondering if I can come up and get some basic info without a warrant."

"I'm not even going to make you come up here," Pike said. "Read me the number on the back of the card."

"I don't have the card. It's in evidence. His name is Bill Sandersen. S-E-N at the end. I have a DOB if there's more than one."

"I found him. What do you want to know?"

"When was he there last?"

"He last used his card here on June 17. He made a two-hundred-dollar buy-in at poker table number four, averaged ten-dollar bets, and played for ninety minutes."

"Do you track who was at the table with him?"

"That I can't tell you."

"Can't or won't?" Packard asked.

"Next question," Pike said. There were limits to what he could share, and he had no problem letting Packard know when he got too close to the line.

"What other information do you have about him?"

"His membership level has dropped from our highest tier eight years ago to our lowest, meaning he doesn't come or spend as often. I have his name, address, phone, email. His room preferences. His drink of choice is a Jack seven."

"Does the card have any cash value? Can you load money onto it?"

"No. It tracks points, but the points themselves have no cash value. They can only be redeemed for goods and services."

Packard tried to think of what else about Bill's casino habits might be useful. "Is there a joint name or anyone else on the card?"

"Cards can't be shared. Even among spouses. Each player has to have their own card."

"If he came up there and didn't use his card, would there be a record of that?"

"We'd have him on five hundred different security cameras. But to see that you would need a warrant."

Packard thanked Pike and hung up just as Kelly came to his back to his office and knocked on the doorframe. "Funeral is tomorrow. I emailed you the schedule," she said.

"I saw it. Thanks for cleaning up my eulogy."

Kelly shrugged. "What happened at the board meeting last night?" she asked.

"They approved the motion to put the sheriff on the ballot. No one asked any questions about the budget slides."

"Well, no shit. I got that from reading the minutes. I mean what did you say when they talked about the election?"

Packard leaned back in his chair. "I don't agree with Jim Wolf on much, but I agree that two more years is too long to go with an acting sheriff. The job needs someone to do it full time."

"Want me to get your application filled out?"

"I told you I'm not running."

Kelly crossed her arms and gave him a look that would have made a weaker man shuffle his feet or check his zipper. Packard had practiced steeling himself against it.

"I'm not running. I'm a detective. Not a politician."

Kelly kept giving him the look.

"Put your eye daggers away. I'm not running."

"That's what you think," she said.

He tried changing the subject. "What do you know about the brewery that's opening up in that spot by the river?"

"I know a lot about it. It's two of my nephews opening it. They're cousins. Mark grew up here. He tried to get a spot going down by the Cities, but they weren't in a great location and couldn't rise above the competition. His cousin Kyle is the brewer. They're both moving back here and hoping the location and a lack of competing breweries will give them a shot. I'm not a beer drinker, but others say their stuff is pretty damn good."

"Be a nice place to sit outside by the river when the weather's nice."

Kelly mm-hmm'd and turned on her heel. "Let me know when you change your mind about that application," she called back.

"I'm not changing my mind."

———————

Packard worked through the evening. Dinner was a microwaved meal he kept in the freezer in the break room. When it was time to leave for the poker game, he went out through the sally port and found Shepard smoking a cigarette before heading out on patrol for the night shift. It was the first he'd seen Shepard since dismissing him from the scene at Carrie's house.

"We need to have a word, Sergeant," Packard said, making sure the door was shut behind him.

"What about, Boss?"

"You texted and phoned Sherri Sandersen about her ex-husband's murder practically from the scene."

Shepard flushed red. "I just… I was notifying next of kin."

"She's not his kin. She's his ex-wife and a potential suspect until I decide she isn't. I don't understand what goes through your head, Shepard. I was the last person you talked to at the scene, and your first inclination after walking away was to text someone who could be a suspect."

"I didn't think of her as a suspect. I used to know her, and Bill to a lesser degree. I just thought she'd want to know right away that something happened."

Packard shook his head. "The policy says the deputy assigned to the investigation—that's me, not you—makes the next-of-kin notifications in person, not via text."

"Well, I misspoke," Shepard said. "I wasn't notifying next of kin. I was letting a friend—"

"I'd stop talking if I were you," Packard warned. "You're supposed to keep confidential information revealed to you in your official capacity secret unless revelation is necessary in the performance of your duty. It wasn't your duty to tell Sherri about Bill. You're not supposed to let personal feelings or friendships influence your decisions. Any of this ringing a bell? It's page one of our code of conduct."

Shepard regarded the end of his cigarette and said nothing.

There'd been plenty of time for Packard to get over his fury toward Shepard. What remained was weary resignation. He had nothing left to offer Shepard in the way of second chances, favors, or warnings. Things like this had been going on for too long.

"I've filed an incident report on this including the evidence from Sherri's phone. You violated policy and compromised my investigation," Packard said.

Shepard knew findings from an incident investigation would mean disciplinary actions coming his way. He shook his head. "You've had it in for me since the sheriff handed you the reins."

"That's bullshit, Shepard. I don't expect any more from you than I do from everyone else. Do your job. That's it. And don't interfere with my job. We're supposed to be on the same goddamn team."

Shepard fumed. His face was red. He ground his cigarette out on the bottom of his shoe and tossed it in the ash can. "Am I suspended?"

"You're not suspended. This is an internal matter for now. I'm recusing myself from any decision-making about this since I'm both the acting sheriff and the lead investigator on the case you potentially compromised. The city attorney will review the facts and make a recommendation about what to do."

Shepard looked like he had more to say. He looked like he was working something up in his mouth. He got in his vehicle and slammed the door, taking his anger out on the seat belt and the gearshift. Packard watched his deputy pull out and drive off in a fury to serve and protect the people of Sandy Lake.

———————

He went home, let the dog out, and changed out of his uniform into dark pants, a short-sleeve shirt, and a sheriff's department windbreaker. He wore his gun on his hip.

He took his time driving to the poker game, taking the long way around the lake, window down. The sun had set half an hour earlier. Homework and early bedtimes had emptied the late evening shadows of summer kids. He smelled firepits and cooling lake water and late-season fireworks. A lot of the cabins were dark, no cars in front.

He drove and thought about Shepard. He felt no satisfaction in disciplining the deputy. If there was an easy fix for the animosity between them that didn't require Packard to lower his standards, he'd have taken it. Every time he was thankful to see Shepard doing more than the bare minimum, there were two times when Shepard put his foot in it. He needed discipline or he needed to go. He'd been doing the job too long to change on his own.

The houses got bigger and farther apart as Packard made his way around the lake. It had only taken a few generations for the family cabins that had once been here to be sold, the lots consolidated, and mansions built in their place, then torn down and rebuilt with more contemporary designs. Locals called this stretch of Lake Redwing the Gold Coast. Even the local wealthy families—like the Gherlicks and Jim Henkel, the science-fiction writer—didn't have homes here or like this. The money on the Gold Coast was from out of state or out of the country.

800 Silver Creek Lane looked like rectangular glass boxes set side by side and stacked at ninety-degree angles three stories high. Black siding broke up some of the glass, but you could see right through much of the house.

Leon Chen was waiting with the giant front door wide open as Packard got out of his vehicle. Chen had a glass of bourbon in his hand. "Saw you coming on the monitor," he said. "Welcome."

They shook hands. Leon Chen was Chinese, in his late fifties with black hair that had receded and was turning gray. He was dressed in linen pants and a blue blazer over a white button-down shirt.

Chen closed the door. "Detective, your shoes please."

Packard stared at his feet, confused, then noticed Chen was offering him a pair of black slippers that matched his own. There were several other pairs of shoes just inside the door. Packard squatted, untied his shoes, and pulled on the slippers.

He followed Chen up a set of floating stairs the color of green sea glass. The wall was textured wallpaper.

He'd run Chen through the databases and came up with nothing. Google told him Chen owned an architectural firm with offices in the Twin Cities, Chicago, and Milwaukee. They did mostly commercial designs but also homes for high-end clients. His bio said his father had been a shop owner in San Francisco, his mother a waitress.

At the top of the stairs, a double-wide doorway opened into a room filled with white couches and floor lamps with long, arching necks. Three sides of the room were glass. Accordion doors at the far end were closed, but Packard could see they opened onto a wide deck overlooking the lake.

A poker table was set up behind the couches, and a buffet of food and drinks was laid out at the wet bar. An Anishinaabe man dressed in black and white with his hair pulled back in a long braid sat in the dealer's spot. Four other men were already seated at the table. One of them was Jim Wolf, the chair of the county commissioners. He didn't look particularly happy to see Packard.

"I don't know that I've ever seen you out of uniform, Packard," Wolf said. "You look almost human."

"I've never seen you not sitting," Packard responded. "Do you have legs or are you just a torso propped in a chair?"

Jim Wolf slowly stood up. He was five inches shorter than Packard, who turned and ignored him as Chen offered food, a drink. A woman dressed the same as the dealer stood by ready to serve him. "No thanks. I just have a few questions."

"Have a seat," Chen said, indicating at the poker table. "Play a few hands with us while you ask your questions."

"I can't afford this game," Packard said.

"Yes," Chen said. He moved a stack of red chips from his pile in front of the empty seat next to him. "Please, it's just for fun."

Chen introduced him to others at the table. "You know Jim Wolf. Next to you is Alan. He lives two houses down. Next to him is Richard. Also has a home here on the lake. And I'm sure you know Tim O'Reilly." Packard nodded at the retired former Twins pitcher who at one time had one of the biggest contracts in Minnesota sports history.

Packard could feel the money in the room. He sensed everyone's eyes on him, sizing him up, not just as a player but as an object with inherent value. Judgment was written on their faces. Bill must have felt like the kid who sat at the wrong lunch table. This was not his crowd. They would have let him know it before the first card was dealt.

The dealer's name was Arnold. The game was Hold 'em. The ante was five hundred dollars, or a single red chip. Packard broke his stack in two. He had twenty thousand dollars in front of him.

He folded after the ante on the first few hands, watching how the other players bet, played with their chips, and drank. He asked his questions as the hands went by. Only Jim Wolf knew who Bill Sandersen was before he showed up to play that night.

"I know the family, obviously," Wolf said.

"What do you mean 'obviously'?" Packard asked.

"He married two of the Gherlick girls. I knew their old man a little bit. Carrie and her mom have contributed to my campaigns in the past."

What he really meant was that he was rich and the Gherlicks were rich and rich people know each other. Jim Wolf was a Realtor who dealt exclusively in luxury estates. He also had a property development business, which was a fancy way of saying he flipped houses. His role on the board of commissioners gave him access to all kinds of inside information, but his cozy relationship with the county attorney meant there wasn't a conflict of interest he couldn't find his way around.

"Are you the one who told him about the game?" Packard asked Wolf.

"Not me. I'm guessing he heard about it at the casino. Leon pays these guys from the casino"—he waved dismissively at the dealer—"to deal for us. I'm sure word gets around."

Arnold kept his eyes on the table and remained expressionless.

"Why did you let him play?" Packard asked Chen.

Chen shrugged, peeked at his cards again, then tossed them at the dealer. "I get tired of taking these guys' money. I thought some new blood might make things more interesting."

"Was it interesting?"

"What was interesting was how mediocre he was," Chen said. "He had the money, but he didn't have the skills."

"How much did he lose?"

"All of it," Chen said. "He walked out of here with nothing."

Packard took the next two hands, building the pile of chips in front of him. He'd played a fair amount of poker with friends in college and later when he was going through the police academy in Minneapolis.

"How did Bill react when he started losing?"

"Desperate," said Tim, the retired Twins pitcher. "He started playing more erratically. Betting on hands he should have folded. He couldn't read us if our cards were stuck to our foreheads."

On the next hand Alan, Richard, and Jim Wolf built a big pot between the three of them. Alan was a vice president at a large health insurance company based in the Twin Cities. Richard had worked for a medical device manufacturer before going on his own and starting a company that made heart ablation equipment.

When the river card turned, Jim raised and Richard folded. Alan shuffled his chips, then finally called. Jim took the hand with a three of a kind. Alan tossed his cards showing a low pair.

Packard had had enough poker. He decided the next hand was going to be his last. Leon and Alan folded after the hole cards were dealt. Packard was holding an ace and an eight of clubs. The flop was an ace of diamonds, an eight of hearts, and three of clubs, giving Packard two pairs, aces and eights.

Jim came out with a two-thousand-dollar bet. Richard checked. Packard raised to five thousand.

Jim eyed the flop, eyed Packard. He leaned back in his chair. Fiddled with his chips. "How much you got in your pile?" he asked.

Packard broke his chips into even piles of five thousand dollars each. "Thirty-one thousand five hundred," he said.

Jim thought about it. "All in," he said.

Richard folded.

Packard pushed his chips in to the pot without looking at Leon.

Jim was holding pocket kings to Packard's two pair. "Goddamnit," he said, standing up. Packard said nothing.

The dealer burned the top card. The turn was king of clubs. "Yes!" Jim said, making a fist. He leaned on the table in anticipation of the next card. Packard sat forward. Arnold burned the top card.

"You need a three or an eight, Packard, or you're fucked," Jim said.

The river was a ten of clubs.

"I'll take a club," Packard said.

Jim Wolf blanched as he counted the clubs on the table. He'd been so busy watching for a full house that he missed the potential flush Packard was holding. "Sonofabitch," he said.

Everyone but Chen and Packard got up from the table while Arnold cleaned up the chips and the cards. Packard's haul was just shy of seventy-five thousand dollars. He'd taken half of it right out of Jim Wolf's pocket, knowledge that gave Packard more satisfaction than the money itself. He tipped two thousand dollars of Leon Chen's money to Arnold to split with his coworker and told Chen he was done.

"I'll send you a check for your winnings minus the twenty thousand dollars I fronted," Chen said.

"No, thanks," Packard said. "I'm here on official business. It wouldn't look good if I took fifty thousand dollars from a group of guys I was questioning about a murder. Especially if it turns out one of you killed Bill Sandersen."

"Nobody here killed Bill fucking Sandersen," Jim Wolf said from over by the wet bar. He stirred his rum and Coke with a stick that he sucked the end of, then dropped in the garbage. "He came here, lost all his money, and left. None of us have a motive for killing a nobody like Bill. What would possibly be the reason? I'd have been happy to take his money from him anytime he wanted to play again. You can't beat a dead man at cards."

He had a point, as much as Packard was loath to admit it. He pulled everyone aside one at a time during the break, starting with Arnold and his coworker, Marissa. Marissa hadn't been present the night Bill played. Arnold confirmed what the others had already said about Bill's erratic play. "I felt bad for the guy. He was blood in the water and these guys were the sharks."

"Did you know Bill from the casino?"

"I've seen him play. I'm sure I've dealt to him. I don't know him personally."

Richard hadn't started his Labor Day weekend until Monday and had been two hundred miles away on Saturday. Saturday night, Jim Wolf had been volunteering in the beer tent downtown while the band played. He'd gone home and gone to bed after.

Leon Chen had been in town since Friday. He lived alone and had no verifiable alibi for Saturday. He said he'd taken a few work calls with international clients on the other side of the world, then gone to bed early.

"How do you live in a glass house like this?" Packard asked. They were standing in front of the folding doors that opened to the deck. There were no visible blinds or curtains. He could see wind in the trees closest to the house. The landscape lighting was pointed toward them, the lake invisible in the dark beyond. "What do you do when you want privacy?"

Leon grinned and raised a finger. "Siri, set family room privacy to one hundred percent."

Instantly, all the windows turned opaque. Packard resisted the urge to touch the glass. "How does that work?"

"Liquid crystal film sandwiched between two layers of glass. An electric charge turns it opaque," Leon said. "Made in China," he added proudly.

Just then there was a bang and Packard felt the painless laceration of flying glass. He lunged for Leon, knowing the sound of a gunshot when he heard one. A second shot caused the entire window to collapse in a wave of shattered safety glass.

"Everyone get on the floor!" Packard yelled.

"What in the hell is going on?" Jim Wolf said.

"Quiet!" Packard was listening to what sounded like a boat accelerating away. "Can you kill the lights?" he asked Leon.

Leon had Siri turn off all the interior lights plus all the landscape lighting. Blood was running from Packard's cuts into his left eye. He went out to the deck through the shattered doorway. With all the lights off and only one good eye, he couldn't see the boat at all, just the chop in the water left behind.

"Leon, do you have the boat keys?"

Leon nodded and went to a drawer where he'd left his keys, wallet, and phone before the game started.

"Come with me," Packard said to Leon. To Jim Wolf, he added, "Call 911. Tell them about the shooting. Tell them I've gone after the boat."

He and Leon ran down the stairs in their black slippers to the yard below and all the way to the end of the dock. It was pitch-dark. Packard could hear a boat motor far in the distance.

Leon showed him the right key and how to start the boat. It was a thirty-foot Sea Ray with dual 250 Mercs on the back. A hundred and fifty grand if it was a dollar.

Packard got behind the wheel and the motors turned over after a few cranks. "Stay here," he said to Leon and put the boat into reverse, then made a tight turn and headed out from the bay.

Packard flicked on the boat's lights, which helped him be seen but did nothing for his visibility. He came out of the bay, went to the right for a bit, cut the other direction, heading farther from the house. He saw lights on the water ahead of him and eased off the throttle as a pontoon materialized from the dark. A couple was snuggled under a blanket on the back bench. Packard could smell weed in the air.

"'I'm with the sheriff's department. Did another boat come by here in the last few minutes?"

The wake from Packard's engine caught up to them and rocked the two boats. He kept the throttle going enough to keep moving in a circle around the pontoon. The man on board pushed away the blanket and stood up, holding on to the bimini frame for balance. He was shirtless and middle-aged and tubby. "Someone came by a few minutes ago with no lights. I yelled 'Lights!' at him. He went"—he paused for a moment, getting his bearings—"that way."

Packard pushed both throttles forward and sped away from Seth Rogan. "That way" led him through a narrow spot where the land came out to a point, then widened again. The ribbed hull lifted out of the water like a breaching humpback. Packard wasn't familiar with the shape of the lake. In the dark he was all but lost.

He stayed fifty yards from a shoreline that undulated like a crawling snake through a series of small bays. There were few houses, fewer lights. For all he knew, the boat he was looking for was already lashed to a dock, the shooter long gone.

A car went by just beyond where the cattails were particularly thick, giving him a better sense of where he was. He'd reached the far end of the lake. The boat's dual motors struggled with thick weeds in the shallower water.

Packard killed the engine and let the boat drift. In the bow he found life jackets, a fire extinguisher, and a marine flashlight under the front seats.

He sat listening for a moment but couldn't hear much above the sound of his own blood rushing. He hadn't realized how amped he was, how hard his heart was pounding. It wasn't a great idea to chase after someone with a long-range rifle in the dark. He had no backup. No one knew where he was.

He heard another car approaching, this time from the other direction. Headlights swept the cattails and briefly illuminated a boat backed into the weeds, a man at the bow.

Packard triggered the powerful flashlight. "Sheriff's department," he yelled.

The man held up a hand to block the light and cranked his motor with the other. The boat leaped to life suddenly and sped past Packard.

"Shit," he said, dropping the flashlight. At the wheel, he struggled to get the boat started again. The motors revved loudly, then stalled. Packard tried reversing the props, assuming weeds wrapped around the drive shaft were causing the problem. When he jammed the throttle back into forward, the boat lurched ahead and he gunned it, chasing the other boat that now had a good hundred yards on him.

The hull bounced on the waves created by the other boat. He hadn't had a good look at the motor pushing the other guy, but he knew it was no match for Leon's dual 250s. With enough lake ahead of them, he'd catch up.

Remembering the point that narrowed the inlet, he swung wide and pushed the boat faster. The roar of the motors and the speed were incongruous with the late hour and the absolute dark all around. He saw trees near the water but wasn't sure exactly where the point ended.

The other boater apparently did. As Packard slowed down, the other boat shot around him. Packard gunned it again. They were both through the strait and Packard was going the opposite direction of the other boat now. He saw the lights of the pontoon from earlier and came close enough to see the startlingly white breasts of the wife who appeared to be straddling her husband on the pontoon's back bench.

Packard swung around them, pushed up a wall of water, and was back on top of the other boat in less than a minute. He stayed to one side and shined the flashlight at the other guy, who finally slowed and then stopped his boat.

"Kill the motor," Packard instructed, gun drawn. "Put your hands on the back of your head and get down on your knees."

The man did as he was told. He was wearing a black stocking cap and dark clothes. Packard brought his boat close and lashed them together with a ski rope. Something was bothering him about what he was seeing. The boat looked like it was mid-'80s with brown and orange vinyl seats. He saw exposed plywood on the bow decking and ancient green outdoor turf in the bottom. There were two battered Coleman coolers in the back near the 125-horse motor. It didn't look like the boat of an assassin by any stretch of the imagination.

When the man turned toward the light and showed his face, Packard rec-ognized him and put his gun away.

"Walter, what the hell are you doing?"

"Ah, shit. It's you," Walter said, hanging his head. Walter was known to every DNR officer and sheriff's deputy in three counties for his poaching and general troublemaking. He hunted and fished what he wanted, when he wanted, rode his snowmobile and ATV through private property and pro-tected lands, and regarded any and all laws pertaining to the outdoors with contempt.

"Why did you run?"

"Why do you think? I was fishing and not following the rules," Walter said in a mocking voice.

Packard stepped onto Walter's boat and opened his coolers, which were full of walleye. Walter had been using a dragnet to catch them, which was ille-gal, and he was well over the limit. He admitted he had a buddy with a restau-rant who paid him for the fish.

Packard helped him dump the coolers. A lot of the fish were already dead and floated beside the boat. Walter thought that was reason enough to allow him to keep them.

"If you think I'm going to let you keep fish you took illegally and get paid for it, you've lost your mind, Walter."

"Well, goddamn. You wouldn't have caught me if it weren't for that boat. When the hell did the sheriff's department start driving the Rolls Royce of lake boats?"

Packard told him who the boat belonged to and where he'd come from and about the shots fired at Leon's house. "You get shot? Is that why you got blood all over your face?" Walter asked.

"I got hit by glass, not a bullet. Did another boat come by before I showed up?"

"Yup. He was running with no lights. Took the channel through the reeds and went over to the other lake real quiet-like."

Packard didn't know the lake well enough to know a channel connected it to another lake. Walter couldn't tell him anything about the boat or the driver. He said he'd heard him go by a few minutes before Packard came roaring on the scene.

Packard got back on his boat and untied the rope holding them together. "Go home, Walter. And tell your friend with the restaurant that if I come in there and see walleye on the menu, he's gonna have bigger problems than that jukebox that's been out of order for the last year. You get me?"

Walter mumbled his understanding and started his motor. Packard watched him disappear into the dark. In his pocket, his phone buzzed and jumped with more life than the dead walleye floating around him.

Back at Leon Chen's, the place was swarming with deputies and flashing lights. Leon had giant riprap boulders along his shoreline that absorbed the waves as Packard docked the boat. He looked up at where the two of them had been standing and saw the broken window. A deputy was on the deck taking a photo.

Back inside, he found a powder room on the lower level and looked at himself in the mirror. His hair was stiff with dried blood. It was all over his face and neck and had soaked into the collar of his shirt. He could see glass shards when he moved his head under the light.

His friend Sean White Cloud had arrived with the ambulance crew. "Don't touch it," he said. "I'll clean you up."

Packard said he needed to talk to Leon first. The two of them went upstairs. Everyone stared at Packard like he was a movie monster.

"Why is someone outside your house shooting at people inside?" he asked Leon.

Leon Chen looked pale. He had a white-knuckled grip on his whisky glass. "I don't know. It never happened before."

"You make anyone mad enough recently for them to take a shot at you?"

"No. My company does architectural design. It's not a dangerous business."

Packard knew it was his own bias that made him assume the wealthy Chinese man would have enemies. "No business deals gone bad? No angry employees or investors?" Packard pressed.

"I've been here for a week, mostly alone," Leon said and finished his drink. "There were plenty of other opportunities to shoot me when the house wasn't full of people and there wasn't a police officer standing right next to me. They were shooting at you."

Packard rubbed the back of his hand through the blood congealed in his beard. He had a screaming headache. "Get comfortable," he said to everyone who had gathered for the poker game. "No one leaves until I say so."

CHAPTER TEN

PACKARD SKIPPED HIS SWIM the next morning. Lake water didn't seem like the best thing to apply to the lacerations in his face and scalp. He also didn't feel like giving whoever had taken a shot at him another chance to finish the job by floating facedown in open water.

It had been a late night—after midnight before he let everyone go home. The card game never got started again. The chips were put away, the wins and losses recorded. Leon Chen claimed Packard's winnings for himself. There was some grumbling, but no one was able to convincingly argue they were owed their money back just because Packard had forfeited the take he'd won using Chen's money.

It only added to the resentment toward him. He'd taken their money in the game and then ruined the night further by attracting a maniac with a gun. Bill Sandersen at least had the decency to go home before getting shot.

Leon Chen continued to drink, getting visibly drunk as the hours progressed. The rest looked at their phones or wandered back and forth to the buffet. They all wanted to go home, but Packard wouldn't let them leave until they'd all been interviewed by a deputy.

Sean White Cloud had taken him out to the ambulance and picked the biggest pieces of glass from his hide.

"I need to get up and look around," Packard complained. He was still vibrating with adrenaline.

"Keep your ass where it is and don't move," Sean said. He had a bright light strapped to his forehead and wielded a pair of tiny tweezers. "I'm trying to keep this beautiful face of yours from being dotted by little puckered scars."

A deputy stopped by the open back door of the ambulance and told Packard the first bullet had deflected upward after hitting the glass and lodged in one of the overhead beams. The second bullet had punched a hole in the drywall on the ceiling. Packard told the deputy to wait for crime scene to do the recovery of the slugs.

After Sean had cleaned him with diluted peroxide and used skin glue to close up the larger cuts, Packard went out on the deck and watched Shepard and another deputy with flashlights search the yard. A third deputy led the department's K9 along the shore and onto the neighbor's dock. The wind had died down and the lake was black as oil.

Jim Wolf came outside and stood beside him. "Whose Cheerios did you piss in?"

Packard wanted to ignore the question. *Pissing in someone's Cheerios. Who talked like that anymore?* "Usually, I have a pretty good idea," he said as he turned his back on the yard and leaned against the railing. His face itched. He crossed his arms to keep from scratching it. "In this case, I have no clue."

Jim Wolf took out his phone and unlocked the screen. "I got a photo of you all covered in blood when you weren't looking. I'll text it to you. You could use it on your campaign signs. You look like Rambo."

Packard glanced at the screen, then looked away.

Jim Wolf pocketed the phone. "You know, Packard, you're not much of a team player," he said. "You've barely tolerated input from the board while you've been acting sheriff. Your attitude has been noted by the members."

"By the members or by you?" Packard asked.

Jim just smiled. "You're going to have to learn a new song if you win the election. I'll be the closest thing you have to a boss."

"You have no authority over the sheriff's department. The voters of Sandy Lake are the boss of the sheriff."

"Seems at least one of them wants to put a hole in you. Why is that?"

"Could be the company I keep," Packard said, eyeing the distance between them.

Jim stuck his hands in his pockets and hitched up his pants. "Well, good luck to you. If you count me and the shooter, that's at least two people who won't be voting for you. Hope for your sake it's not the sign of larger trend." Jim Wolf stepped through the door with the shattered glass and went down the stairs and went home.

Asshole, Packard thought. Not that he cared that Jim Wolf wasn't voting for him. Nobody was going to vote for him.

He wasn't running.

He worked out in the basement, took Frank for a walk, then ate breakfast and drove back to Leon Chen's house, where Thielen and two deputies were going over things again in the light of day. From the yard, Packard could see a large sheet of plywood had already been secured over the door shattered by the bullets.

Leon and Thielen were in the back courtyard, sitting across from each other on teak patio furniture. Leon stood up to greet Packard. He was dressed much the same as last night, in a white button-down and a sport coat. He was drinking tea from a large mug but didn't look any the worse for wear considering how much he'd had to drink the night before. "I must apologize for the terrible experience you had in my home last night," he said.

"No need to apologize," Packard said. "I apologize for getting your door shot out."

"Yes, very unfortunate. It will cost eight thousand dollars for a new sheet of glass."

Thielen blanched.

"It's special glass," Packard explained.

The three of them chatted for a bit. Leon confirmed again he couldn't think of anyone who would have a reason to try to kill him. He had security cameras around the house, but the yard lights had prevented the cameras from seeing out to the lake. Thielen had reviewed the footage and said the video hadn't captured a boat or a shooter or even a muzzle flash.

Her phone rang then and she stepped away for a minute. While she was gone, Leon said, "I would be happy to make arrangements to pay you your winnings from last night. I assure you it would be a private matter between the two of us."

"Thanks, Leon. I can't accept. It wouldn't be ethical. What you could do if you were so inclined is pay some of that money to Roger Freeman. He's a local dairy farmer. The money Bill Sandersen lost at the game here wasn't his own. It was taken from a shared business account and most of it was Roger's money. It took him a long time to come up with it and only hours for Bill to lose it."

"Hmmm," Leon said. His tone was as noncommittal as the sound he made.

Leon stood and excused himself to do some work. Packard wandered down to the dock. It was cooler and overcast. He watched the clouds move over the mirrored surface of the lake. The sun came out and went away and came out again.

"Hope you're not here to interfere with my investigation," Thielen called as she came across the yard to where he was standing. They'd agreed last night that she'd take the lead on this one since he had his hands full with Bill Sandersen. "Let me see your face," she said.

She grabbed his chin and moved his head to the side. "It's not so bad. Lots of little dark scabs. You're still fuckable."

"Thank god for small favors. Anything new I should know about?" he asked.

"We got the slugs out of the ceiling. First guess is they're .223s. The lab will help confirm. We obviously don't know what he was shooting. My guess is a gust of wind or the boat rocking might have saved your life."

"That eight-thousand-dollar pane of glass turns opaque with a verbal command. Leon had set it to privacy mode right before the shot."

Thielen shook her head in disbelief. "Why do you think you were the target?"

"Leon and I were the only two visible in the window at the time. He insists he's got no enemies, and I've got no reason not to believe him."

"So then why you?"

"I honestly don't know. Bill Sandersen is the only thing on my plate lately. I've been doing mostly sheriff stuff since wrapping up Emmett Burr this summer."

"Maybe it's related to the election," Thielen said.

"The election news is two days old. No one's even announced their candidacy yet."

"Well, Jim Wolf knew you were coming. He knows about the election because it was his decision to have one now that Stan is gone. You're obviously not his first choice for sheriff." Thielen raised an eyebrow.

Packard thought back to his conversation with Jim on the deck the night before. He'd never hidden his dislike for Jim's politics. Last night he'd let Jim know in no uncertain terms that he'd never take orders from him, sheriff or not. "Eh, I don't buy it," Packard said. "If I was running—and I'm not—I think Jim Wolf would relish the opportunity to put up his own candidate and see me lose."

"Not if he's desperate to make sure you're not a factor at all. He might have plans in mind that you know nothing about."

Thielen's phone rang. Packard realized he never explicitly told Jim he wasn't planning to run. Not at the council meeting when the election was announced. Not last night. He'd only told Kelly and Thielen so far. Word wouldn't have gotten back to Jim from either of them.

"That was dispatch," Thielen said. "They just got a call about an unmanned boat floating over in the adjacent lake. Let's go check it out."

The boat was on the other lake that connected to Lake Redwing via the channel Walter had told Packard about the night before.

Dispatch gave Thielen the address of the man who called it in. His name was Chuck Seversen. He and his wife were in their sixties. His wife, Sharon, was the one who noticed the boat floating in the shallow end, the bow plowed into the reeds. Neither of them recognized the boat as belonging to anyone they knew.

Chuck had binoculars that he handed to Packard, who handed them to Thielen since it was her case.

"I could radio for Fisher to meet us at the launch with the boat," she said. Fisher was their rec deputy who spent his time on a boat, an ATV, or a snowmobile, depending on the season.

"Hell, I'll run you over there," Chuck said. "I got a rope. We can haul it back to my dock."

Thielen looked through the binoculars again. "Let's do it," she said.

Chuck's boat was a pontoon. Packard and Thielen put on gloves as Chuck cut the throttle and they drifted toward the reeds. It took a bit of maneuvering to get the abandoned boat turned around, then aligned with the back of Chuck's boat so they could tow it across the lake. Thielen wanted to get it back to the dock before anyone went aboard.

She called in the boat's registration numbers and already had an address by the time the boat was lashed to the dock opposite Chuck's pontoon.

"The owner is Scott Layman. Address is 1880 Blue Heron Lane."

"I know Scott from the lake association meetings. He lives down in the Cities. You can't see his place from here, but I'd say he's eight or ten houses down that way," Chuck said, pointing.

Thielen had two different phone numbers for Scott. He didn't answer the first one. The second one he picked up and confirmed he was at work at his law office in Bloomington, Minnesota. Thielen asked when he'd last been to his cabin.

"Labor Day. We came up on Thursday and left early Monday," he said. Three days ago. He had been up with his wife, her sister and her sister's husband, plus five kids between the two couples ranging from eight to fifteen.

Packard pointed to the key in the ignition. It had a red-and-white fish bobber attached to it.

Thielen told Scott about his drifting boat and asked if he kept a key onboard. "Yes. I know it's stupid, but it's a long walk down to the water, and I can't count how many times I've forgotten to bring the key. There's a spare in the watertight storage spot behind the dash."

She told him his boat was secure at Chuck Seversen's and someone would get it back to his dock. They still had no idea if it was the shooter's boat so she left out those details. If it was covered in fingerprint dust the next time Scott came up, he could ask his questions then.

Chuck went back up to his house while Thielen and Packard stared down at the boat as if it were a body floating in the water. There wasn't much to examine. It was an eighteen-foot Crestliner fishing boat with a 115hp Yamaha. It had beige carpeting throughout and a small trolling motor laid across the bow.

Thielen had retrieved her investigator's kit from her car. She bagged the key from the ignition and the storage compartment cover to take back for fingerprinting. The steering wheel and the throttle handle weren't coming off so she took out the powder and tried to see what she could raise in situ.

Packard stepped aboard and tried to imagine where the shooter took his shot from. Climbing to the bow, which was a flat deck with a hole for another chair, made him feel unstable even with the boat lashed to the dock.

He went to the back again. Maybe the shooter came into the bay, turned his boat around so it was already facing the getaway direction and took his shot from the stern. Depending on the gun, he could have balanced it across the back of the motor for support.

The boat had storage slots cut out of the interior on both the port and starboard sides that extended from the behind the windshield to the motor mount. Packard took out his flashlight and shined it on plastic bottles of bug spray and sunscreen, a pair of sunglasses, an empty grape-soda can. On the other side, he found two oars, a fire extinguisher, and a knotted ski rope.

The color of brass tangled in the ski rope caught his eye.

"I'm getting nothing off the wheel," Thielen said right then. "It looks like it's been wiped, which is suspicious itself."

"Look at this," Packard said. He used the tip of a mechanical pencil to manipulate the blue-and-green braided rope. "Get a bag," he said.

With the tip of the pencil he lifted out a shell casing. It had WIN 223 stamped around the primer.

"I'll be damned," Thielen said.

————————

They didn't find the second shell casing. After some discussion they decided not to take the boat off the water. The idea of combing it for material to DNA-test after a Labor Day weekend when no less than nine people had been in the boat—in addition to the shooter—didn't make sense from a logistics standpoint. There would be too much material to test, it would take months, and they had no suspect DNA to compare the results to.

Thielen took the items collected from the boat and went back to Leon's to wrap things up with the deputies. Packard drove into town. It started raining on the way. He put down the window and inhaled the smell of ozone and wet roads. He kept shifting which hand was on the steering wheel to keep from scratching the maddening itch from the cuts on his face.

Kelly was at her desk looking at the stack of mail that had arrived. She shook her head when she saw him.

"You got shot in the face last night and here you are already the next day?" she said.

"I didn't get shot in the face. I got shot at through a window and cut by the glass. It wasn't that bad." He showed her the side of his head. "The real story is that I got shot in the face and all I get from you are disapproving looks."

"You didn't get shot in the face. So you get what you get," Kelly said. She reached for a piece of paper in her file sorter, then handed it to him on top of his pile of mail. The paper said AFFIDAVIT FOR CANDIDACY at the top.

Packard didn't acknowledge it or her. He moved it aside, looked through the stack of junk mail and law enforcement catalogs, took out two things that looked important, and handed the rest back to her, including the application form. "Recycle," he said.

He found Suresh in the office they had made for him by taking down a wall between a storage closet and a little-used interrogation room. It was full now of computer towers running different operating systems, stacks of laptops, bins full of cords, and hard drives and every kind of USB accessory ever made. County dispatch operators had three huge monitors side by side at their stations, but Suresh had six—three up, three down. All of them showing different content. The thought of all those screens made Packard's head swim. He didn't know where to look.

Suresh was wearing headphones. Packard could hear the faint strains of Indian pop music as Suresh rolled on his chair from his bank of monitors over to a separate laptop and leaned in toward the screen. The top of his bald head was shiny under the fluorescent lights.

Packard knocked loud enough to be heard. Suresh took off his headphones.

"Find anything for me?"

Suresh looked glum. "This is Bill Sandersen's work computer," he said, nodding at the laptop in front of him. "There is so little here, it could almost be new out of the box."

"Do you think it was wiped recently?"

"Oh no. There's plenty of log-in history, just not much else. He did not have a job that required regular use of this computer."

"He was a car salesman," Packard said. "And not a great one, according to his coworkers."

"Maybe if he read an email now and then. In his Outlook he has hundreds of unread emails and less than a dozen going out."

"Could he have trashed things as he worked?"

"Possibly, but there's nothing else here either. No Word documents. No Excel files. Last time Excel program was accessed was eighteen months ago. This is the computer of a man who doesn't use a computer."

Packard imagined Bill pacing the lot and smoking cigarettes out back with the mechanics. Didn't leave a lot of time for computer work.

"Dead end?"

"I did find two things that might be of interest." Suresh slid back over to the bank of monitors and tapped the keyboard. A window opened on the lower-right screen closest to Packard. "In his browser history I found he accessed his benefits website a couple of weeks before he died. He downloaded a report of his annual benefits, health insurance, dental insurance. He has life insurance on both himself and his spouse—one hundred thousand dollars each."

Packard said, "Huh." Out of context it wasn't that interesting. Bill could have just been looking at the rules for his medical coverage, trying to figure out how big his deductible was or what procedures were covered. Having life insurance on your wife wasn't a crime, though it was often incentive for a crime between two people who had fallen out of love. Suresh was right to mention it.

"They're each other's beneficiaries, correct?"

"Wrong," Suresh said. "He's the beneficiary on Carrie's life insurance. Sherri Sandersen is the beneficiary on his life insurance. Secondary is named Wendy Beardsley."

"Sherri is his ex-wife. Wendy is his sister." Packard's wheels were turning. "Can you tell if he was trying to make changes to his benefits?"

"I can't," Suresh said. "This is all just based on the report I found in the downloads folder."

"You said two things. What else?"

"The other thing is he was looking at something on craigslist. The ad is no longer there so I can't tell you what it was. But an hour later he put this address into Google Maps. The two might be related but I don't know for sure."

On the screen above the one Packard was looking at, a browser window flew into place and brought up a satellite view in Google Maps of a house set back from a dirt road and surrounded by trees. Another structure on the property might have been a barn or large shed.

"Property records?" Packard asked, knowing Suresh would already have looked.

"Yes. The property changed hands two years ago to a Robert Whitehouse from Gerald Whitehouse. No record of any police calls to the property. Neither of them has a record."

"Nice work, Suresh. I'll be around for the next few hours if you find anything else. Text me that address, and I'll stop by on my way home and see what I can find out."

It was early evening by the time he was on the road again. Everything cast long purple shadows. His side mirror captured the setting sun as the navigation system directed him to the address Suresh had sent.

Packard took off his sunglasses and mulled over the fact that Bill was examining his work benefits days before he was killed. Packard wasn't a big believer in coincidence. Bill had been up to something. He needed money and had no money. He had insurance on his wife, enough to get a small restaurant up and running. But if the plan was to kill Carrie for the insurance, how did Bill end up the one catching lead? And what to make of the fact that Bill's ex-wife stood to benefit in the event that something happened to him? Packard had a mental image of Bill and his sister wives chasing each other around in a circle, only he had no idea who was doing the chasing and who was trying to get away.

He held the steering wheel with one hand and flipped through his notebook until he came to the business card the HR lady at Sandy Lake Auto had slipped him with her cell phone number and a smiley face on the back. He didn't expect her to be at the dealership this late so he called her cell.

"Katherine, it's Detective Ben Packard from the sheriff's department."

"Hi, Ben. I take it you found my card."

"I did. Thanks for that," Packard said.

"I'm glad you called. What's up?"

"I have a question about the benefits employees get from the dealership."

"Oh…" She sounded disappointed. "What about them?"

"Tell me about the life insurance benefit."

"Just a minute," she said. He heard a pan slide on the stove and then water running for a second. "For employees, we offer a minimum one-hundred-thousand-dollar policy as part of our package. The dealership pays the premium. Employees can go up to five hundred thousand dollars, but they have to pay extra in the form of a payroll deduction and the larger policies also have more eligibility requirements."

"What about spousal coverage?"

"That's extra, regardless. Just a few dollars per check for the one-hundred-thousand-dollar limit."

"Had Bill asked you questions recently about his benefits or changing his benefits?"

"No. It would take a major life event to be eligible to change his benefits.

A marriage, a child being born. Something like that. We do enrollment once a year in November. I haven't even sent the first email about it for this year's."

"Is the life insurance beneficiary something you can change only during enrollment?"

"No. You can change that anytime you want using the website."

"Did he ask you about anything like that recently?"

"He didn't. Like I said, I was pretty short with him. He didn't come around much just to chat. Any questions he had about his benefits he could have answered by going to our benefits website. It's all there."

"That's what it looks like he did. I was just hoping to figure out what he was looking for."

"Sorry I couldn't be more help. Listen, if you haven't eaten, I've made way more beef stew than a single woman can eat on her own. It'll be ready in twenty minutes."

"I appreciate the offer, Katherine. I'm still working, trying to track down the last people to see Bill. I'm on my way out of town to interview someone right now."

"OK. No harm in asking. Have a good night, Detective. Call again if you have any other questions."

He thanked her and let her go.

The nav took him east of town, to a dirt road hemmed in by thick trees on both sides. A left turn onto a long dirt driveway littered with yellow leaves led him back to a clearing with a peeling gray house that was twice as tall as it was wide. The roof shingles were curled and covered in moss. Small trees grew in the gutters. Beside the house were a covered woodpile and a lozenge-shaped propane tank and an old Chevy truck with a camper top.

Packard got out and glanced through the windows of the truck as he went by. He saw fifty-pound sacks of corn under the camper. The cab was filthy with road dust and junk mail and fast-food containers thrown on the passenger-side floorboard. A padded shotgun case stuck up from behind the seat.

He went up the steps to the porch. The wood was soft and flexed under his weight. He opened the screen door and knocked loudly. A pair of crows cawed in the trees. One of them came down and lit on top of the woodpile to get a better look at him.

Packard knocked again. A window in the door showed him a front room that was empty of furniture. Beyond that was a room with a built-in hutch and a dining table with six chairs around it. More chairs were against the wall in front of the windows. A heavy swinging door closed off the kitchen.

He came off the porch and regarded the other building, which was a small barn. White paint on the lee side gave away the color it used to be. Packard crossed the short, scrubby yard to the front of the building where a large sliding door on a rusty track had been slid open wide enough for someone to slip through. Packard took out his flashlight and shined it inside.

One side of the building was divided into stalls. One of them looked to be filled with old kitchen appliances on wooden pallets to keep them off the ground. The furthest stall had blankets draped over whatever had been stacked inside. On the other side, a set of stairs led to the loft above. Daylight leaked through the weathered siding. It smelled like a hundred years of bird shit and hay and motor oil.

In the middle of the room, a trapdoor in the floor stood open. "Anybody here?" Packard asked.

A man came up through the floor then and gave Packard a squinty look, like a troll peeking up from under his bridge. Packard snapped off his light and entered the barn just as the man climbed the rest of the way out of his hole and pulled the door shut with a slam. A cloud of dirt and dust rose in the air.

"What do you want?" the man asked. He looked to be in his late sixties. Feed cap pulled over white hair that escaped over his ears and down his neck. Unshaven with a deeply lined face and a hump in his back.

"I'm with the sheriff's department—" Packard started.

"Well, no shit. I got that much from the uniform. What happened to your face?"

"I got cut by some flying glass. I'm looking for Gerald or Robert."

"I'm Gerald." He positioned himself over the door in the floor as if keeping whatever was down there from getting out.

"I'm wondering if you either of you met a guy out here recently by the name of Bill Sandersen."

"What would he have come out here for?" Gerald asked.

"I was hoping you could tell me. Did you have an ad on craigslist?"

"An ad on what?"

"An ad online. On the internet. Something you were selling?" Packard said.

"My son takes care of all that computer nonsense. He's been trying to get rid of some of this stuff we got out here."

Packard took out his phone and showed Gerald a photo of Bill Sandersen. "He look familiar?"

As Gerald held the phone and looked at it through one eye, Packard noticed a sour, yeasty smell and the faint trace of rot. It was coming from beneath the floor.

"Yeah, he was out here a week or so ago. Came to look at the fryer," Gerald said, nodding at the center stall filled with appliances.

Bill was scouting equipment for the wings and beer restaurant. Packard wandered over to the stall to look at what was stacked there. "Did he buy it?"

"No, sonofabitch had the nerve to call it an antique and tell me I'd misrepresented what I had. I bought the damn thing at an auction for a restaurant that went out of business and used it for twenty years of Friday night fish fries for the Knights of Columbus. It damn well is too a professional fryer."

Packard spotted the fryer sitting on top of a yellow stove. The cloth-covered electric cord dated it to the previous century. It had been a professional fryer a lifetime ago.

"I told him if he didn't like the fryer to take a fuckin' hike. What'd he do? Report me to the police for hurting his feelings?"

"No. Someone shot him in his bed last weekend. I'm retracing his steps in the days leading up to that."

Gerald took off his hat and scratched the top of his head. "Well, goddamn. That's a shame. It sure as hell wasn't me. Buy the fryer or don't buy the fryer. Makes no difference to me. I had no reason to shoot the man."

Packard looked around again. It was another dead end. Bill Sandersen's life moved on a very small track. Even the detours led right back to the main path. Somewhere there was a connection to the shooter. He either hadn't come across it yet or he hadn't recognized it.

"What do you got going on down there?" Packard asked, pointing to the door in floor.

Gerald put his hat back on and picked at something on the back of his arm. "You'll have to come back with a warrant if you want to see what I got down there."

"It smells like… I don't know what," Packard said.

"It smells like none of your business. Get a warrant."

Packard closed the space between them. He tapped the door in the floor with his toe. "Last spring I found a cement-block cage in a man's basement, where he'd murdered women he kidnapped. When I see a guy climbing up out of a rat hole I naturally get curious about what he's doing down there."

"Ah hell. I'm not another Emmett Burr," Gerald said. "That crazy sonofabitch got what was coming to him. There's nobody kidnapped down there. I promise you that. It's my business and it's private."

"All right then. I'll take your word for it," Packard said.

Gerald followed him out of the barn and waited in front as Packard got into the sheriff's SUV. Packard followed the driveway back through the trees and watched in the rearview mirror as Gerald pulled the barn door shut from the inside and went back to whatever he'd been doing in his hidey-hole.

Packard wanted to believe it was nothing, but he wasn't sure he did.

CHAPTER ELEVEN

FRIDAY MORNING. STAN'S FUNERAL.

Kelly's schedule had Packard at the church an hour before things officially started at 11:00 a.m. so everyone speaking could walk through the order of events with the priest.

Marilyn wanted the funeral to be limited to family, close friends, and the staff of the sheriff's department. When she came in with her daughter and granddaughter, it was the first Packard had seen her since she'd called with the news that Stan had died. The death of her husband looked like it had diminished her, like a Russian doll with one of its shells removed. She was wearing a wine-colored blouse with a black sweater. She hugged him tightly, the top of her head under his chin.

All the people who would be speaking or singing stood at the front of the church with the program open as the priest explained what was going to happen. After that, people started taking their seats.

The priest spoke. The choir sang. There was a sermon. A prayer. More singing. Stan's oldest son went up and spoke of his dad as a father and a husband. He'd been strict with his kids, but he gave them the guidance they needed to become successful adults. Packard resisted the urge to look at Patty, Stan's only daughter, who had married rich but was otherwise miserable in her life. One of her kids had gone to rehab. The other one—her son, Sam—had been crushed under his car last spring. She would have given a different speech if anyone had let her speak.

When it was his turn, Packard stood behind the pulpit and talked about Stan Shaw, the public servant—his time in the army and all the high points of Stan's law enforcement career, including his sixteen years as sheriff. He talked about Stan the Sunday school teacher and Catholic marriage counselor.

"Stan had infinite patience when it came to people. Even ones who broke the law. He never treated anyone as anything less than a human being deserving respect. But if you worked around him in the office, you know he had zero patience with everyday modern conveniences."

Kelly laughed. She had read his speech but this part hadn't been in there. She knew where it was going, though.

Packard imitated Stan's gruff voice as best he good. "Kelly! This goddamn computer... Kelly! The goddamn coffee maker won't turn on!"

"His goddamn phone," Kelly said from her seat in the second pew.

"The goddamn riding mower," his son called out.

Marilyn had a hand on her cheek and was laughing and shaking her tear-streaked face.

"Come on, Marilyn, give us another one. You must have heard more than any of us," Packard said.

"He used better language at home," she said. "The sonofabitchin' TV remote drove him nuts."

———————

The church had a banquet room where the family and all the deputies in their uniforms gathered for ham sandwiches and coffee. Packard apologized to the priest for the language and was forgiven.

He was happy to see Shannon Gherlick, Stan's granddaughter, looking tall and healthy. The last time he'd seen her was in the hospital after she'd nearly overdosed on prescription opioids. She'd been the one to tell him everyone in town knew he was gay and thought he was sad and lonely.

"You're looking well," he told her. She was wearing a floral-patterned A-line dress and a light sweater. She had a tattoo that said *Princess* on her neck.

"Thank you. I'm just here for the funeral. My dad is driving me back right after. I'm living in a sober house in the Cities. Studying for my GED and working part time at Target."

"That's great news. I'm thrilled to hear it," he said.

Her dad, Dan, came over then and asked Packard if he'd made any progress on finding out who killed Bill Sandersen.

"Not enough," Packard admitted.

"His wife—wives," Dan corrected himself, "are my cousins."

"I knew that," Packard said. Dan's father, Jack Gherlick, and Sherri and Carrie's father, John Gherlick, were brothers. "Did you guys grow up together?"

Dan made a face and shook his head. "Big family events here and there. My mom and their mom did not get along at all. The girls were hard to like. Especially the younger two."

Packard thought for a second about what he'd just said. "Who are the younger two?"

"Mary is the oldest. Sherri is the middle and Carrie's the youngest."

"I didn't know there were three sisters. I've only met Carrie and Sherri," Packard said. "Mary wasn't married to Bill, too, was she?"

"No." Dan laughed, then looked more serious. "My understanding is she's cut most ties with her mom and sisters. I don't know the whole story, but I remember as kids Sherri and Carrie used to rag on her mercilessly. The two of them were pretty and popular. Mary was plain and bookish. They gave her hell."

"Mary live nearby?"

"She does. You know Gherlick Bead & Craft downtown, across the street from the bank? That's her business."

Packard noticed Thielen trying to catch his attention from across the room. He thanked Dan for the info, told Shannon good luck with her studies, and excused himself.

"What is it?"

"Look at this," Thielen said and handed him her phone. She had a text message with a clickable image and a Facebook link. When he clicked it, it took him to a page titled "Shepard for Sandy Lake Sheriff." The top banner was a photo of Shepard standing beside his patrol car and the sun setting behind the trees on the opposite side of a lake. The way his arm was angled, Packard could tell Shepard had taken the photo with a selfie stick.

Packard shook his head. He looked around the room and noticed a lot of people were staring at their phones right then or just sliding them back into their pockets. Shepard was standing off by himself looking red-faced.

"Either someone fucked up or Shepard has no shame at all," Thielen said under her breath.

"You make it sound like it couldn't be both," Packard said.

———————

People started leaving after an hour. Packard sought out Shepard, who still had the look of a guy who'd farted in church. Why he wasn't the first to sneak out was unclear. It might have had something to do with the plate of dessert bars and red Kool-Aid he was trying to juggle along with his cell phone.

"I saw your site," Packard said.

"My wife..." Shepard said by way of explanation, shaking his head. "The announcement wasn't supposed to be made until next week. She published the page this morning thinking she'd just share it with a couple of friends. It took no time at all for it to get around."

"It's nice you have a lot of interested people."

Shepard stared at Packard like he was waiting for the punch line. He had powdered sugar in his goatee and down the front of his shirt.

"Are you working on a site for your campaign?" he asked.

"I'm not running," Packard said.

Now Shepard really looked like he was being pranked. "What do you mean? You already have the job. It's yours for the asking, practically."

"I'm not asking. And I'm not sure being acting sheriff is much of a leg up. You must think you have a chance if you're throwing your hat in the ring."

"Well, you have the advantage of already having the job. I just think I have more recognition with the voters."

"Can't argue with that," Packard said, sipping his coffee and watching Shepard over the rim of the cup.

Shepard took another bite of lemon bar, then brushed the sugar from the front of his uniform. "You really aren't running?" he asked with his mouth full. "What about the salary bump? That'd be nice, wouldn't it?"

"Believe me when I tell you the winner of the election is going to earn every penny of that salary. I've seen what it takes to be sheriff. It's twenty-four seven. It's politics and council meetings. It's paperwork as far as you can see. It's staff squabbles and unhappy citizens and a constant scramble for money. The salary doesn't begin to compensate for the headache."

Shepard suddenly looked like he was questioning his life choices.

"Who's encouraging you to run?" Packard asked.

"No one. I want to. I mean, I've always thought about it, but I was never going to run against Stan. I heard a few weeks ago there was going to be an election in November. I decided to start getting my campaign together after Stan died."

Jim Wolf had been planning to elect a new sheriff for a while if Shepard knew about it before Stan died. Jim hadn't told Packard about it until the day after Stan died and the day before the board meeting where it was planned to be announced. He probably should have been grateful he'd had that much notice.

"I heard about the election from Jim," Packard said. "Who told you about it?"

"Same," said Shepard. "He's going to help me with my campaign. He's got experience running as a commissioner."

"He's a good one to have in your corner," Packard admitted.

He wished Shepard good luck with his campaign and caught up again with Thielen, who was talking to Marilyn Shaw.

"Benjamin, come by the house tomorrow morning if you're free," Marilyn said just as she was turning away to say goodbye to others hovering nearby. "I need to talk to you, and I have something Stan wanted you to have."

Packard said he'd come by and then asked Thielen what she was doing next. "I have paperwork to catch up on," she said.

"Come with me. Dan told me Carrie and Sherri have another sister. I had no idea. I'm interested in seeing if she has any thoughts on who shot Bill Sandersen."

"Let's go."

Gherlick Bead & Craft was in Sandy Lake's downtown district on the corner of Main and Fourth with an entrance on the side street. Packard and Thielen arrived in separate vehicles, one after the other, and parked in the slanted spots outside. Sandy Lake Commercial State Bank, a two-story red stone building built in the prairie style, was across the street.

Inside the shop was a cacophony of colors and shapes. Packages of beads and stones and crystals and spools of wire hung on the walls. There were rolls of ribbons and fabric and tiny tools and shiny rocks and photo albums and craft scissors and colored paper and bottles of glitter and glue and paint. There were candles and wax and wicks and bottles of scented oil. The air was heavy with the smell of incense. Packard spotted a stick burning next to the register and a small plastic fan blowing the scent around the room.

It all made Packard want to slowly back out the way he'd come.

There were no customers in the store. A tall, robust woman stood in the center of a U-shaped arrangement of jewelry display cabinets. She had dark hair to her shoulders and was wearing a maroon cardigan with a fringed silk scarf wrapped around her neck and piled high on her chest.

She smiled at first, then looked alarmed when she recognized who they were. "You're either looking for a gift for a coworker or you're here about Bill Sandersen."

"It's the latter," Packard said.

Mary Gherlick shook her head. "Give me a minute to put up the out-to-lunch sign. We can chat in the back."

The back was half stock room, half break room. Stacks of boxes, a couch, a small table, a fridge, and a sink. Mary plugged in an electric kettle and made tea for her and Thielen.

Packard watched her from his seat at the table as she moved about the cramped space. There was only the vaguest resemblance to her sisters. He'd have to see all three of them together to know what it was. He imagined that Mary took after their father, as firstborns tended to do in his very unscientific opinion. She was broad-shouldered and had a strong chin. There was something about her that seemed out of place. Maybe it was the big scarf, which he associated with willowy European girls on account of one who had lived in his condo building back in Minneapolis. She'd had a Dutch accent and always kissed both sides of his face when they ran into each other in the common spaces.

Mary sat at the table with him while Thielen perched on the edge of the love seat.

"What would you like to know?" Mary asked as she dunked her tea bag.

"When's the last time you talked to either one of your sisters?" Packard asked.

"I don't talk to my sisters. Or my mother. Not if I can help it," Mary said. "You'd think it would be hard avoiding each other in a town this small, but it's really not. I don't go to bars or casinos where you'll typically find Sherri. Princess Carrie only breathes rarefied air so you'll not often find her mixing with the hoi polloi."

"Did you know Bill Sandersen at all?"

Mary humphed. "I couldn't tell you the first thing about Bill Sandersen other than he must have been two kinds of stupid for marrying not just one but both of my sisters." She gave Packard a deadpan expression as she adjusted her scarf.

"I've noticed your sisters aren't exactly fond of each other either," he said. "What happened with the three of you?"

"I'll tell you what happened. We grew up the children of a narcissist," Mary said and sipped her tea. "Our mother made us compete for her affection, then she competed against us for our father's—she wanted all of it or none of it, depending on her mood."

Packard gave Thielen a look and caught her raised eyebrow as she hid her expression behind her tea mug. He wrote in his notebook.

"Tell me how this impacted your relationship with your sisters," he said.

"She had us battling each other so we'd never form an alliance against her. Carrie and Sherri were happy to play along. A lot of their abuse was directed at me, but they gave it to each other just as good."

Mary went on to describe her pet fish being killed from vodka poured in the tank, dog shit put in the bottom of her book bag so that it was all over her books when she pulled them out in class, rumors that she was known to give blow jobs at rest-stop bathrooms, other rumors that she was a lesbian. Kids made a V with their fingers and stuck their tongue through it or coughed the word *lez* into their fists as they passed her in the hall. Friends abandoned her because the heat was too hot standing next to her.

Mary counted the indignities on her fingers as she repeated them from a well-rehearsed list. Packard imagined her as an awkward teenager, taller than the other girls and probably most of the boys, red-faced and weary from the scorching contempt of her classmates, and unable to find any respite at home because the source of her misery lived under the same roof.

"My mother blamed me for everything wrong with her life. It was while she was pregnant with me that my father's cheating started. That's the story according to her, anyway. Who knows, maybe he was cheating on her the whole time. I was too big and ugly for her to remake in her own image. Sherri was too wild. With Carrie she finally got the baby doll she could shower with gifts and attention and slowly mold into her idealized self."

"What happened between your parents?" Packard asked.

"My mother kept my dad under her thumb until he decided he'd had enough and hung himself in the garage."

Thielen made a sound that was almost a gasp. "I'm sorry. Your dad is part of this town's history. I'd never heard that story about him."

"Mom did a good job of keeping it quiet because it was embarrassing to her," Mary said. She spooned more sugar into her tea and seemed to lose herself for a moment as she stirred the dark water. "He tried it with a clothesline first, but it broke. It was still around his neck when he grabbed a heavy-duty extension cord and finished the job. I think about that second chance a lot and how badly he must have wanted out to step off that chair a second time."

Packard watched Mary's eyes mist up at the memory. "How old were you when that happened?" he asked.

"Sixteen. He was the only shield between my mother and me, not even that good of one because he only said anything at all when she or my sisters were particularly out of line. I still loved him more than anyone else. He did his best to love us back, but mostly he seemed to live in his own headspace. And then he was gone."

Packard pictured the same girl as before, now with a father with enough of his own demons that he couldn't stick around to protect her from the wolves. "That must have been terrible for you."

Mary tapped her wet spoon on the rim of her mug and set it aside. "In some ways it set me free. I tested out of my final year of high school and moved to Duluth when I was eighteen. Worked for a couple of years, then paid for college from my trust fund."

"Why did you come back to Sandy Lake?"

"I met my husband, Jay, in Duluth. He was from Sandy Lake," she said. "He wasn't going to college there. He was visiting a friend who was. We met at a party. He said he knew me from high school. I didn't recognize him because I barely lifted my eyes from the floor while at school. He kept visiting his friend and stopping by the library where I worked. After a while he was coming to visit me."

Packard was surprised to hear she was married. She wasn't wearing a wedding ring. She caught him looking.

"Jay was killed while deer hunting. Shot in the chest. It'll be twenty-eight years in November."

"Accident?" Thielen asked.

Mary shrugged. "No one knows. He was found at the base of the tree underneath his deer stand. He was all by himself. No one came forward. We were supposed to get married the following June. I still refer to him as my husband."

There was enough tragedy hanging over the families of the two Gherlick brothers—John and Jack, the banker and the builder—that Packard was starting to wonder if they'd bulldozed a native burial ground or made a deal with the devil in exchange for all their wealth.

"The two of you moved back here together and he died and you still stayed."

Mary nodded. "We bought a house I loved. Staying in the house made me feel close to him. I started making jewelry to keep busy and that turned into this place."

"Your father owned the bank across the street, right?"

"Yes, for many years. The board agreed to sell it after the 2008 mortgage crisis. It's a Wells Fargo branch now."

"What's it like working in the shadow of the bank your father started?"

"It's a beautiful building. It's on the list of historic state architecture. The

Wells Fargo people haven't changed the inside at all. It's just like it was when I was a kid and my dad would take me to work with him and the tellers would give me Dum-Dums lollipops and Dad would let me draw on the deposit slips with a pen stuck to the table with a chain."

"How's the crafting business?"

"Not great. Even less so when I lock the door all afternoon to talk to the police."

Packard apologized. "Just a few more questions," he said. "You mentioned a trust fund. Same as your sisters."

"Yes. I've done well by investing it. It helps keep this place afloat when the customers don't show up."

"Did you know Sherri had run hers dry?"

"I heard as much. I don't have to talk to my sisters to know what's going on with them. The only thing the crafting community loves more than a hot glue gun is gossip."

"Did Sherri ever come to you and ask for money?"

Mary laughed. "She knows better. She could ring my doorbell engulfed in flames, and I wouldn't so much as squat to piss on her."

Packard nodded, made a couple of notes. "Where were you Saturday night?"

Mary fiddled with her giant scarf again. "I had a booth right here on Main Street all day for the Labor Day festivities. I saw you walking around. I packed up and went home before the band started. I was exhausted. Took a bath and went to bed."

"You live alone?"

"Yes."

"Anyone see or talk to you that night after you left?"

Mary shook her head. "No."

Packard flipped his notebook shut and thanked Mary for her time. She walked them back to the front of the store. Packard stopped at the door. "One more question. Who do you think killed Bill?"

"Carrie," Mary said with no hesitation.

"Why Carrie?"

"'Cause she's a cold, calculating bitch. A narcissist just like our mother. Maybe even worse."

———————

Packard followed Thielen back to the sheriff's department. After she stopped by her desk to check messages and email, she came back to his office and shut the door. "Okay, first things first. What do you think about Shepard running for sheriff?" she asked.

"I think Shepard has as much business being sheriff as he does being a brain surgeon. But if he runs and the people elect him, then the job is his."

"He'll be your boss, you realize."

"He'll be our boss," Packard corrected.

"I can't imagine having to call him my sheriff, standing behind him at a press conference, being deferential…"

"I've never seen you be deferential to anyone," Packard said. "I doubt you'll start with Shepard."

"You know what I mean. Treat him like he deserves respect."

Packard shrugged. It was tempting to tell her about the complaint he was filing against Shepard for violating the code of conduct, but he had to keep his sheriff hat on and not think of Thielen as a friend. Shepard deserved privacy until the issue or the findings became public.

Thielen picked at something on the front of her button-down shirt. She was still dressed for the funeral but had left her jacket at her desk. "You have to run," she said, not looking him in the eye.

Packard turned to his computer. "I don't have to do any such thing."

"What if Shepard runs uncontested? You're just going to hand him the job?"

"If that's the way it works out, then that's how it works out," Packard said.

Thielen let out an exasperated sigh. "Packard, don't be a dumbass."

"I'm not being a dumbass. You know as well as I do how the deck would be stacked against me in an election. Do you think people are going to vote for the native son with decades in the department or the new gay guy in town?"

Thielen wasn't having it. "You thought you had to hide being gay from everyone when you first came to town. Now everyone knows and it hasn't stopped you from doing anything, but you're using it as an excuse not to run in an election. Why not just be yourself and see what happens?"

"I am myself. And my self is getting pretty sick of people telling me I'm making excuses. Why don't you fucking run for sheriff if you're so worried about Shepard taking over?" he shot back.

Thielen opened, closed her mouth. "Yeah, exactly," Packard said. "I'm a detective, same as you. I don't want to be a full-time sheriff any more than you do."

"But you could do the job. You'd be great at it. You've been great at it."

"I've been doing the bare minimum. Doesn't matter. I said I'm not running. I don't want to talk about it anymore. Let's talk about Mary Gherlick instead."

Thielen shook her head. "I walked out of there wanting to donate a month of sessions with my husband so she can work through her anger."

"Maybe she has worked through it. Maybe that was her best self."

"Could be. Besides her trust fund, life has given her a shit sandwich. She's got plenty to be angry about."

"There's something going on with this family that rubs me the wrong way," Packard said. "I don't have a shred of evidence or even a hint of a motive for any of them to kill Bill Sandersen, but it feels like all three of them are guilty."

"Carrie and Sherri I can see," Thielen said. "Why do you put Mary in that group?"

"'Cause she's their sister."

That night, after the dinner dishes had been washed, Packard sat on the couch with his feet up and Frank within belly-scratching range. The details of his conversation with Mary—all his conversations, actually—had been written down, but he often did his best thinking about a case on the couch with a yellow notepad in front of him.

He wrote *Bill* in the middle of the page and circled his name. He wrote *Carrie* and *Sherri* on either side and drew circles around them, an arrow from Bill to Sherri labeled 1 and an arrow to Carrie labeled 2. He wrote Mary's name above Bill's and somewhat further out he wrote *Margaret*, the mother of the three sisters.

He made a circle for Roger Freeman under Bill's name and one for Leon Chen to the right of Roger. He listed the names of everyone else at the poker game the night Bill played and connected them through Chen.

Near the bottom of the page he made a list of the others he'd talked to, including Bill's sister Wendy; Ronnie Winder, who had hooked him up with Leon Chen; Bill's boss and his coworkers. Gerald with the questionably professional deep fryer.

It looked like a small life from this angle. No kids. One friend. Packard drew a $ inside the circles for the three sisters and Leon Chen, then drew an X through Sherri's. He put $ signs next to all the poker players. He added a $ to Margaret, the widowed wife of a banker, then decided to add her husband, John, in a square box even though he'd been dead for thirty-plus years. He added a box for Mary's husband, Jay, killed in the hunting accident.

He wrote *Money* and *Gambling* and *Theft* and *Infidelity* at top of the page. Bill wasn't killed for his money. He didn't have any. The money he lost in the poker game was taken from his shared account with Roger. Roger had an alibi for that night—a weak one but an alibi nonetheless. Packard didn't like Roger for the job at all.

There was something else he wasn't seeing, something acting on this solar system of circles he'd drawn like a rogue planet with a wide-ranging orbit.

The doorbell rang as he was staring at the ceiling with the end of the pen in his mouth. He and Frank both started. Frank barked and ran for the door.

All the blinds were drawn against the night. Packard got up from the couch, skirted the front door, and went into the garage instead. Unexpected visitors were his least favorite thing in the world. He never answered the door without knowing who was on the other side.

The side of the garage extended beyond the front door. Packard had installed another peephole in the garage wall and partially hid it behind a decorative metalwork WELCOME sign Thielen had given him. From there he could see the whole front step without blocking the light coming through the front door peephole and letting someone know exactly where he was standing.

Under the yellow porch light, bombarded by moths, was his neighbor Bert. Packard hit the button for the garage door and came out that way, and Bert came around and said hi and put his hand down with a treat for Frank. Bert always had a treat for Frank. He was wearing khaki pants rolled at the ankles and a flannel jacket. He had a white beard and crinkled eyes behind thick glasses.

"Your face looks like you got into a fight with a cat."

"It was broken glass," Packard said. "It's nothing. It's healing up fine."

"I should've called, but I wanted to talk to you in person."

"'Bout what?" Packard asked.

"Somebody's been driving by here the last couple days like they're looking for you but not really hoping to find you home."

Bert was in his early seventies, a retired juvenile court judge from the Twin Cities who had permanently moved with his wife to their cabin ten years ago. His wife had died before Packard bought the house next door. Bert liked John D. MacDonald paperbacks and whisky on the rocks and putting around the lake on his pontoon with his grandkids. He was home all the time and kept a close eye on everything.

"How so?"

"I've seen a guy drive by the last couple of days. Brake lights come on as soon as he reaches the hedge, like he's slowing down to check out your place. If you thinned that thing out, I could see better what was going on."

This was about the tenth time Bert brought up the row of cardinal dogwoods between their houses. They were overgrown when Packard bought the place, and he'd done nothing to cut them back or thin them out since. There was still so much work to do on the inside of the house that he couldn't be bothered with much outside beyond basic yard maintenance. Also, he didn't exactly mind the separation.

"What was he driving?"

"That's the odd thing. It was a white sedan of some kind the first day. The next day it was a gray SUV. But I'm pretty sure it was the same driver."

"You get a good look at him?"

"No. Just a silhouette of a man. The way he drove, the way he slowed down both times on the other side of the hedge and came driving the other way a couple of minutes later made me think it was the same guy."

The road in front of their houses was dirt. Packard knew the sound of car wheels on a gravel road brought Bert to the window like a curious puppy, so it didn't surprise him that Bert had seen every car that passed their way.

"They didn't pull in the driveway or get out that you know of?"

"Not that I could tell."

Bert's observations didn't strike Packard as that suspicious. People unfamiliar with the area went around the lake looking for a public landing that wasn't there. There were more houses down the road from them. One of them was rental property that brought a steady stream of short-term visitors all year round.

"I appreciate you keeping an eye out. If it looks really suspicious, call it in. Or get a license plate."

"All right then," Bert said. He reached in his pocket for another treat for Frank. "I heard sheriff's going to be on the ballot in November."

"I heard the same."

"You got my vote, Ben. You'll be a great sheriff."

Packard smiled. It was too late for the truth.

They chatted a bit longer, and when Packard didn't offer Bert a beer like he sometimes did, Bert finally said good night and Packard said good night and lowered the garage door and went to bed.

CHAPTER TWELVE

BY SATURDAY MORNING, PACKARD'S face had scabbed over well enough that he felt fine getting back in the lake. The water was noticeably colder than just a few days ago, caught in the battle between the cooler nights and the sunny but shorter days. He'd need the wet suit again before long.

He was planning to take the day off. All the rooms in the house had been newly drywalled, walls and ceilings. As soon as he finished the taping, the plan was to rent a blower from the hardware store and reinsulate the attic. He had bales of compressed insulation in the garage, bought last winter when they went on sale. Running the blower was a two-person job. Thielen's husband had offered to help.

Packard rolled over on his back and finished his last lap with a backstroke. Water coursed over his face as he exhaled like a dolphin. He entertained the idea of calling Marilyn with an excuse for why he couldn't make it even though he told her yesterday at the funeral he'd stop by. Leaving the house was the surest way to get distracted by other things and not make progress on his projects. If he didn't want to spend another winter paying a fortune for heat, he needed to get the insulation in. It should have been done months ago.

Out of the lake, he toweled himself dry while Frank licked at the water he dripped onto the dock. On the way to the sauna, he talked himself out of bailing on Marilyn. He'd promised to be there for whatever she needed, before and after Stan had passed. He couldn't put her off now that she was asking.

———————

The Shaws' house was a brick rambler with green shutters that backed up against undeveloped acres thick with trees five miles outside of town. A decorative split-rail fence ran a short way on either side of the driveway, then ended abruptly.

Something about the Shaws' house struck Packard as different as he pulled up. He'd spent a lot of time here since the sheriff got sick, hours and hours just shooting the shit, watching TV while Stan got smaller and weaker. Now the man who'd hired him and made him acting sheriff was gone. The house, with no memory of its own, felt like it had already forgotten him.

Marilyn was waiting for him with the door open as he got out of the truck. They hugged and he followed her inside.

"I didn't ask yesterday, but I'm going to ask now," Marilyn said. "What happened to your face?"

"Glass from a broken window."

"And what broke the window?" She'd been the wife of a cop more than half her life. She knew what questions to ask.

"A bullet."

They were in the kitchen. Marilyn paused as she poured his coffee. "Oh, Benjamin. Are you okay? Was anyone hurt?"

"He missed. Still trying to figure out who it was and why he took the shot." He gave her a few details about Leon Chen's house and the shot from the boat. She didn't know Leon, but she was familiar with all the expensive houses near where he lived.

They moved to the living room. The hospital bed and all the equipment managing Stan's pain were gone. His recliner was back and Marilyn sat on the edge so her feet would reach the floor.

She thanked him again for speaking at the funeral and he gave Kelly credit for making sure he got all the details right. "I went off script a bit with his swearing. That was part of who Stan was to me. I thought we could all use the laugh."

"It was the best part," Marilyn said. "It didn't burn my ears at all."

They chatted about people Packard had met briefly after the funeral, family members he didn't know, where they were from and how long they were in town. He had the feeling she was working up to something. He had a pretty good guess what it was.

"So...the election," she said finally.

Packard set his coffee cup down and sat back further in the couch. "Yeah, that's going to be something."

"I've heard through the grapevine you're not running."

"Does the grapevine sit at the front desk and love Barry Manilow?"

"Of course she does," Marilyn said.

"Well, the grapevine has a big mouth but she does not lie. That's where I'm at regarding the election. I really don't want to be the sheriff full time. I'm a detective. That's what I enjoy doing."

Marilyn looked disappointed. "Ben, have you stopped to think about why Stan made you acting sheriff?"

"I know I was his second choice. He was in a bit of a bind when Deputy Callahan turned him down."

Ron Callahan was Stan's chief deputy and school liaison. He'd retired shortly after Packard was appointed acting sheriff. A new chief deputy had yet to be appointed. Packard had wanted to leave the decision either up to Stan when he got better or whoever succeeded him permanently.

"Let me stop you there," Marilyn said. "Stan knew Ron wouldn't take the job. He asked him because he had to and he needed to get a formal no from his chief deputy before he could ask who he wanted. It was never in doubt that Ron would be a no. Ron and his wife bought that place in Montana and were count-ing the days until they could move there full time. Also, Ron liked you for the job as well. It was a decision he and Stan made together."

This was all news to Packard. He'd leapfrogged over a lot of people in the department who had more seniority to take the role. Even though he was a full-time member of the department, he'd felt like a scab—an outsider. Stan had warned him that there would be hurt feelings and bruised egos. *They will know unequivocally that this is my decision, but you'll have to stand up for yourself on the day-to-day. I trust you can manage that.*

Packard had initially tried to manage it by giving the impression he wasn't the acting sheriff. He'd put his detective responsibilities first and kept his sher-iff actions and decisions out of sight. He'd resisted moving from his cube into Stan's office. Kelly practically had to bend his arm behind his back and march him through the door.

It had gotten easier with time. He still wasn't comfortable with people calling him Sheriff, but he got used to representing the department and deal-ing with issues that needed a decision maker or a law enforcement voice or a thoughtful opinion. He'd grown into the role. It also helped that people found other things to be pissed off about.

"I appreciate hearing that, Marilyn. I was honored that he asked. I was happy to help him out."

"His mistake was not grooming someone younger for the job. I think he thought he was going to live and win elections forever."

"I think we all thought that."

Marilyn smiled wistfully. "And by the time we knew we were wrong, it was too late. Stan was sick. Ron was retiring and what remained was a bunch of deputies that were too old or too young or too unqualified to move up the chain of command. And then there was you."

Packard didn't know what to say. He drank his coffee.

"You said you were happy to help him out. And you did. But did you ever stop to think that he was helping you?"

"It's not lost on me what a great opportunity I've been given. It'll look good in my file if I—"

"This isn't about your file, Ben. Think about your career. Think about where you want to go from here. Stan said you were the best deputy he'd seen in years. Better than you gave yourself credit for. *He should be doing bigger things than investigating pissant drug dealers and shitbirds committing burglaries. He should be the example others aspire to.*'"

It was funny hearing Stan's words come out of his wife's mouth while she sat in his chair. It felt like a ventriloquism act or a medium channeling a departed spirit.

"It's not that simple. There's an election involved. I'd have to have the support of the majority of voters to get the job. I don't think that's possible. An ideal candidate should have a history with the department and the community. I'm too new here."

"And you're gay," Marilyn said.

Packard struggled to keep his expression neutral. He'd never discussed his private life with Stan or Marilyn. He'd found out last spring—before he started admitting it when asked—that everyone had already concluded he was gay based on scant evidence. 'Everyone' would of course include the sheriff and his wife, but there'd never been an opportunity to confirm it.

"And I'm gay," he said. "I don't have to tell you the politics of this county. It's gotten redder and redder with every election."

"And you think the people here will overlook a highly qualified candidate because of his personal life."

"Don't you?"

"I think we'll never know if we don't give them the option to choose."

———

They talked a bit longer about Stan and the things he loved about being sheriff. He'd seen himself as the champion of everyone who worked for him. He loved promoting the good works of the department and wasn't afraid to shoulder the responsibility when they came up short. He had a wicked memory for names and details about people and their lives. People felt like they knew their sheriff and he knew them.

Packard thought by steering the conversation to Stan, they could move off the election. Marilyn wasn't having it.

"I know you know Howard Shepard is running, after his little fiasco at the funeral. Have you heard who else?"

"No."

"Alan Costas. Does that name ring a bell?"

"Vaguely. Was he a deputy?"

"Yes, let go before your time. He had a personal relationship with a dispatch operator. No problem there, except that he was married at the time," Marilyn said with a disapproving look. "Things ended badly, big surprise, and resulted in the operator quitting her job and moving out of the state. Her final word on the matter was an email sent to Stan with graphic details and photos regarding liaisons she had with Deputy Costas in an interview room and in his patrol car while he was on duty. There was an investigation and Costas was fired."

Packard said, "Hmm." He didn't know what else to say.

"If you don't run, you'll be handing the job to one of those two on a platter. We both know what kind of deputy Howard is. I don't know or remember Alan Costas that well, but he obviously has poor judgment."

"Obviously," Packard agreed.

"I can name ten people right now who will serve on your campaign team," Marilyn said. "I know we can raise the minimal dollars it will take to pay for ads, posters, yard signs. I'll write the check myself. It's not that much. I can also deliver at least twenty people who will write letters to the editor of the *Sandy Lake Gazette* endorsing you if I ask them. This isn't to say it's all going to be easy. Even getting Stan elected again and again was never as easy as it looked. I know it feels like you'll be putting yourself way out there, but I promise you won't be standing alone."

Packard finished his coffee. "I didn't move to Sandy Lake with the intention of being sheriff one day, and I wasn't aware of Stan's thinking when he asked me to fill in for him. All I've ever wanted was to be the best investigator. I don't feel like that's selling myself short. It's what I do."

Marilyn looked like she agreed, but she wasn't giving up. "You can be the best investigator there is, but if you're not the boss, what gets investigated and who investigates isn't up to you, isn't that true?"

Packard shrugged.

"I'm not going to sit here and pretend I know all the ins and outs of being a sheriff and running the department," Marilyn said, "but it seems to me the boss gets to decide what he wants to take an interest in and what he wants to delegate. The boss determines the priorities. The boss hires, fires, and promotes the people he wants working for him. Being sheriff would allow you to…be the boss."

Packard grinned and shook his head. "You're very persuasive, Marilyn. I'll give you that."

"Are you still saying no?"

Packard was worried how much longer this conversation would go if he said no again. That drywall wasn't going to tape itself. "I'm saying I'll think about it."

Marilyn looked disappointed. "There's one more thing we should talk about it."

"What's that?" he asked.

"The real reason why you came back to Sandy Lake."

Packard felt like he'd been caught in a lie he didn't remember telling. "I don't… I came for the job. The deputy job."

"Wait here," Marilyn said.

This meeting had gone from feeling like a social call to being a performance review. He had no doubt Marilyn was used to getting her way when it came to her husband and her family, but he wasn't going to change his mind and run for sheriff just because she wanted him to. Or told him to.

She came back a minute later carrying a white box with a number written on the side. Packard felt himself go cold.

"I can tell by the expression on your face you know exactly what this is," Marilyn said.

He did.

———————

There was something hypnotic about taping and mudding drywall. Packard had music playing but he didn't hear it. There was just the scrape of the knife along the wall and the slap against the hawk. Sunlight moved across the room. He worked through lunch. Frank came in to watch, lost interest after a while, and disappeared through a gap in the hanging plastic.

The white box was never far from Packard's mind.

I can tell by the expression on your face you know exactly what this is.

It was an evidence box from the cold-case storage room. Number 18729.

He'd first gone looking for it last spring. On the shelf where it was supposed to be was an empty space. Kelly controlled access to the storage area and had no record of anyone taking it out. She'd either lied to him about her knowledge of its whereabouts or Stan had used other means to get his hands on it. He was the sheriff. There was no place off-limits to him.

Case 18729 concerned the disappearance of a seventeen-year-old boy who left his family's cabin late at night on a snowmobile almost thirty years ago and was never seen again.

"This was your brother," Marilyn said as she handed him the box.

Packard could only nod mutely as he took it, unsure if the weight he felt was in his hands or in his mind. He set the box on the floor in front of him.

"Older or younger?" Marilyn asked.

Packard had to clear his throat. "Older," he said.

Marilyn went to the kitchen, poured herself another cup of coffee, and then came back.

"Stan knew all this time?" Packard asked.

"For a while," Marilyn said. "I remember him asking not long after you started why the name Packard was familiar. He never asked you?"

"He didn't."

"When those kids went missing last spring, we started talking about others who had never been found. The two women who were buried on Emmett Burr's property. And a boy who had disappeared not long before that. We were in bed one night and Stan suddenly grabbed my hand. 'Packard!' he said. 'The missing boy's last name was Packard.'"

Visits to the cabin Packard's grandfather had built peaked over the summer months, dropped off once the kids went back to school after Labor Day, then revived again over the holidays. During the long Christmas break there was ice-skating and snowmobiling and winter bonfires that threw sparks high into the frozen air. Packard closed his eyes and could smell wet mittens and ginger snap cookies.

It was two nights after Christmas when Nick snuck out of the house. Ben Packard was twelve at the time and the last family member to see Nick alive. He'd caught his brother putting on his coat and boots near the back door after everyone else was asleep.

"I want to go with you," Ben said. "I'm bored and not tired at all."

"Forget it," Nick said. "I'm meeting a friend. We don't need you hanging around."

Ben threatened to wake up their mom and dad. Nick called him a tattle-tale baby. They wrestled at the back door. Ben was a boy, Nick almost a grown man. He yanked his little brother outside and shoved him in the snow in his pajamas so he'd be too cold and too wet to do anything but go inside and change.

Nick took off on a snowmobile and never came home. Divers found the sled three days later in open water after someone spotted a frozen glove near the edge of the ice. It looked like someone had struggled to climb out.

Divers searched underwater for days, and again in the spring. Boats labeled

SHERIFF patrolled the shoreline. The lake was over ten thousand acres and more than one hundred feet deep in spots. Nick's body was never found.

"Stan told me to make sure to give you this box after he passed."

"Did he talk about what was inside? What he found?" Packard asked. He wanted some kind of warning about what was under the lid. He felt like he was staring at a jack-in-the-box that was the tiniest turn of the handle away from exploding in his face.

Marilyn shook her head. "Stan kept the details of his work away from me. He did tell me he remembered the case. He was only a deputy when it happened."

Packard left the Shaws' house without opening the box. Marilyn had made one last request of him as they said their goodbyes by the front door. "Think about what it meant for Stan to pick you. All the things you two never talked about—the secrets you thought you were keeping—he knew. He still picked you, Ben," she said, putting her hand on his chest. "If you could only see what he saw in you, you'd know that you're the best man for this job."

———————————

Packard taped and mudded until his shoulders got too tired to raise his arms above his head. He cleaned up and took a whole chicken from the fridge, cut the backbone out of it, pressed the bird flat, and rubbed it under the skin with butter and lemon and thyme he was growing in a pot on the deck. He put the bird on the grill, skin side down, with a cast-iron pan on top to keep it flat. In the pan he put some butter and olive oil, salt, and a diced potato.

He sat outside as the sun went down and drank a beer and stared at the lake. He still hadn't opened the box Marilyn had given him. There were too many things on his mind already without adding the details of his brother's disappearance to the list. The box could wait.

He thought more about what Marilyn had said about Stan picking him for the job and asked himself why his automatic answer about running in the election was no. And why was it automatic?

It was true that he was a detective first. It was a job he enjoyed doing and was good at. He hadn't moved to Sandy Lake with any thought of what it would mean for his career. There were far more opportunities for advancement on the Minneapolis police force if that's what interested him. He was running from his former life, from the death of Marcus, and the private grief he couldn't share.

The primary reason he and Marcus had had to be so discreet was their careers. Police culture was not known for its welcoming attitude toward those outside of the typical power structure.

That's why he said no so quickly to the idea of running in the election. If he couldn't be a gay cop in a large city, what chance did he have to be a gay sheriff in a rural county?

Did you try being a gay cop in Minneapolis?

No, he hadn't.

So you might have been able to be that, but you were too cowardly to try.

He didn't know about cowardly but—yes, he had decided it was not in his best interest.

Just like you're deciding without even trying that you can't win this election. You could do like Thielen suggested and be yourself and see what happens.

It'd be like tilting at windmills.

The difference is that the hero Don Quixote saw a challenge and ran toward it. You are running away.

Packard flipped the bird over, stirred the potatoes, and grilled a wedge of radicchio that he dressed with olive oil and lemon and pumpkin seeds. He ate at his makeshift dining room table (a piece of plywood across sawhorses) with Frank beside him, patiently waiting for tiny bits of chicken and crispy skin and the chance to lick the plate clean.

After the dishes were washed, Packard moved to the couch and opened a second beer. Frank crawled up and sat beside him. Packard turned the TV on, then turned it off before the satellite could find the signal.

The thing was, he wasn't trying to be a gay cop or a gay sheriff. He wasn't trying to be a gay anything. Sure, last weekend with the drummer whose name he couldn't remember, he'd been gay as hell. But outside of that, he was just a regular guy, just a deputy. If he ran in an election, it wouldn't be as a gay candidate. The people would label him that—no doubt—but not because of anything in his platform or his vision for the department. The trick would be to convince people he was the best candidate, not just the gay one.

A three-way race between him and two verified morons like Shepard and this Deputy Costas, who didn't have the common sense to realize all the ways allowing himself to be recorded having sex in his patrol car could blow up in his face, had the potential to be interesting. Maybe the two of them could split the anybody-but-the-gay-guy vote and he could squeak out a win with enough votes from the people who actually gave a damn about qualifications.

Packard drank the beer and sat with his elbow on the arm of the couch, the beer can on his shoulder. With his ear close to the opening, he could hear the boil of the carbonation. It sounded like the ocean.

The flaw in all of this was that he was only thinking about the day of the vote and the results. There would be weeks of campaigning until then, the idea of which felt like lying naked on a table and letting everyone in the county poke and prod him, look in his mouth, and check him all over for suspicious moles. Marilyn had said he wouldn't be out there alone, but the truth was he would be. And he'd be home alone at the end of every day just like he was now. The decision was his alone. The personal consequences—win or lose—would be his to bear. Alone.

"Frank, what should I do?" he asked the dog beside him.

Frank lifted his head at the sound of his name, then put it on Packard's thigh. He looked undecided.

"You and me both," Packard said as he finished his beer.

CHAPTER THIRTEEN

A WEEK AFTER HER husband had been murdered, Carrie still jumped every time the phone rang. For the first few days, she'd turned her cell phone off and disconnected the kitchen phone and all the extensions in her mother's house. The police knew where to find her if they needed to talk to her. No one else needed to know where she was. The absence of phones felt like a bubble that protected her and hid her. If she couldn't be reached, then the weird stasis she'd built around her couldn't be breached.

Eventually she turned her phone back on but left it muted. She read through her text messages and transcribed voicemails. She was most dreading a call from the sheriff's department. She didn't want to answer any more questions about what happened that night.

When the call finally came, it wasn't what she was expecting. It wasn't Detective Packard, first of all, but another deputy who said he was calling to let her know that her husband's body was back from being autopsied in Saint Paul and she could make the funeral arrangements. He also told her their investigators were done in her house and she could return home. An itemized report of the personal property that had been collected from the home as part of the investigation had been emailed to her.

"If you need a company that has experience with crime-scene cleaning, I can recommend one."

He means blood and brains and the smells a dead body leaves behind.

"Yes, I'll take the number, please."

Carrie called the cleaning company, which turned out to be a husband-and-wife duo whose last name she recognized but whose faces she couldn't conjure over the phone.

"Please take out all the furniture and the carpeting and throw it away," Carrie said. In her memory, most of the blood was on Bill and on the mattress and a little bit on the wall behind him. She still wanted everything gone.

"There'll be an extra dumping fee," the cleaner said.

"I'll pay whatever it costs. Do you know a painter who can repaint the whole room close to what it is currently?"

"Yeah, I can arrange that, too."

"Any personal items in the drawers and in the closets can be boxed and set outside the bedroom. Everything else goes."

"Understood," said the cleaner. He started to talk about his schedule and how many days he thought it might take.

"I don't need the details," Carrie said. She gave him the code to the garage so he could get into the house and said to send her the bill when the job was done.

She had no intention of going back home. She'd been thinking about selling the place even before Bill died. She'd built the house with her first husband, raised their kids there alone after they divorced, and had it remodeled shortly before she married Bill, who had mocked its rustic farmhouse style. "This is a decorator's idea of a farmhouse, not anyone who's actually been on a real farm."

Reclaimed shiplap aside, the house was too big now that the kids were gone. She had kept their rooms the same since they moved out after high school, but they came home infrequently now that they had their own lives. Neither of them had bothered to come see her in the last week. Her son at least called. Her daughter wasn't speaking to her.

Carrie had found comfort staying with her mother in the house where she'd grown up. It was dark and cramped and dated—the opposite of everything she had loved about her house—but it made Carrie feel like she was on solid ground. Nothing changed here, not the electric stove or the old grandfather clock or the blocky dining room set from the '80s. The things in her house felt like they could all blow away in a strong breeze. Her mother's house persisted.

Too bad the same couldn't be said for Margaret's mind. When they went for a walk, Margaret would ask her the name of every person they passed. Nights were the worst. Margaret's doctor called it sundowning. She would get confused when it got dark, sometimes would throw open the door to Carrie's bedroom and turn on the light and ask where the kids were or where her husband, Carrie's father, was.

"Dad's been dead for thirty years, Mom."

"What?"

"He hanged himself in the garage. A long time ago."

"Oh. I think I do remember that."

———

Carrie was watching television by herself after Margaret was asleep the first time the killer called her. The screen on her phone said BLOCKED but she answered anyway. There'd been so many calls lately. She did it without thinking.

"This is Carrie."

"Why didn't you tell the police the truth about what you saw?"

"Who is this?" Carrie asked.

"You know who it is," the man said. "You lied to the police. How come?"

"I don't know what you're talking about."

"It's in the statement from the sheriff's department on their website. 'No physical description of the suspect.' You saw enough of me to give them the basics but you didn't."

She recognized the voice now. He'd been wearing a balaclava like snowmobilers wore in the winter and big plastic safety glasses that obscured the rest of his face. He was average height—taller than her, shorter than Bill.

"I didn't see anything. I only heard the shot."

"Come on, Carrie. We both know that's not true. How are police going to catch your husband's killer if you won't help them?"

Carrie didn't say anything. She felt like she was holding her breath.

"What makes you think I won't come for you next?" the killer asked.

"How did you get this number?"

The phone beeped in her hand.

He was gone.

On the day of Bill's funeral, Carrie drove herself in her mother's 1988 navy-blue Oldsmobile. She'd ordered herself an appropriate black outfit on Amazon in a brand she'd ordered before, which saved her a trip to her own house. Zeinab was on Margaret duty.

Carrie had called Bill's sister Wendy after Bill's body came back from Saint Paul and asked her again to plan the funeral. Carrie promised to cover all the costs if Wendy would only manage all the arrangements with the funeral home.

And the church.

And the obituary.

And the people who wanted to speak and what they were going to say.

She and Wendy stood inside the door and greeted people as they entered. Carrie received their condolences with a sad nod of the head. The whole time she was watching for strangers, looking for a face that matched the voice on the phone. She asked the men she didn't recognize their names and how they knew Bill. *From the casino* was a common answer. *We used to hold court at Bob's*, one guy said. Bob's was a bar downtown.

None of them sounded like the killer.

She was surprised to see Deputy Packard, out of uniform in a black wind-breaker and dress pants. He told her and Wendy he was sorry for their loss. No mention of the murder or the investigation. He took a seat near the back.

Carrie sat in the front row, next to Wendy and Wendy's husband and their kids. Bill's parents were both dead. Roger, Bill's best friend, sat in the pew behind them. The rest of the people there were mostly strangers. Some faces from high school she vaguely recognized, including Bill's boss at the dealership.

On the other side of the church, Sherri was sitting with her girlfriend, the same one who had come to the wedding and ruined the whole thing with their drinking and nonsense. Carrie gave Sherri a dirty look. Sherri returned it.

The service started. Bill's sister went up first and talked about their child-hood and how he'd been a good uncle to her kids. Roger said Bill would do anything for his friends. He talked about Bill helping out at the dairy farm years ago when Roger first moved back to Sandy Lake and was shorthanded, a fact Carrie never knew. He also told a story about the time he put his car in the ditch during the wintertime and racked up daily storage fees because he couldn't afford to pay for the tow, let alone the damage to the car's front end. Bill gave him the money—*Sherri's money*, Carrie thought—to get his car out of hock and fixed.

No one really talked about what was important to Bill, what he lived for. Carrie had no idea what she would have said if she'd had to go up there and memorialize her husband. What she remembered most about their time dating in high school was all the hand jobs (and occasional blow jobs) she gave him until she finally realized her virginity wasn't like a savings bond that increased in value the longer she held on to it. Bill readily cashed it for her the summer before her junior year. He'd already graduated (barely) and ended up dating Sherri behind her back while Carrie was still trying to pass trigonometry. He'd had no real career to speak of. His prime years were spent partying and drink-ing with Sherri until the money ran out. A brief second marriage to his ex-wife's sister was followed by an unexpected and violent death. Not a great story.

Carrie was so lost in her memories that Sherri was already at the altar before Carrie realized what was happening.

Carrie turned to Wendy. "Did you know about this?"

Wendy looked terrified. "No, she didn't say anything to me about speaking."

The pastor looked confused as well. He rose, sat down, half rose again, looking to the front row for an answer. By then, Sherri had the microphone.

"I loved Bill most of my life," she started, leaning all the way into the mic, then pulling back and wiping away hair that had gotten into her mouth. "We got married when we were still practically kids and stayed married for a long time."

Sherri stopped and breathed through her nose. "I loved Bill," she said again. She was definitely drunk, or within walking distance. She was wearing tight black jeans and a purple sweater and was likely on her way to a bar after this to watch the Vikings game.

"You know, his CPAP machine was bullshit." She was talking only to Carrie now. "He bought it used on eBay. It was broken, but it still made noise when he turned it on. He just wanted an excuse to get out of your bed. He said having sex with you was like having a birthday—once a year was enough."

This was too much for the pastor, who finally stood up and gently put his hands on Sherri's shoulders, guiding her away from the mic.

But Sherri wasn't done. She grabbed the mic from the adjustable holder like a singer about to hit the chorus and came around to the front of the lectern. "We were sleeping together this whole time. Did you know that? Ask Deputy Packard. There's *evidence*," she said and pointed toward the back of the church where he was sitting.

Carrie glowered at her sister, who looked pleased with herself but also drawn and bleary from crying. If they were still kids, Carrie would have marched up there, grabbed her by the hair, and rubbed her face into the carpet. She watched as Sherri held the microphone out from the pastor's grabbing hand and sidestepped his reach. "Bill and I still loved each other," she said hurriedly, almost yelling. "Someone is gonna pay for his murder. So help me god, Carrie, if I find out you had anything to do with it, you'll be the next one up here who fits in a can."

Sherri slammed the mic on top of the table holding Bill's ashes in an urn, causing the PA system to squeal. She gave Carrie a look that could start a fire as she came down the steps and kept going right down the aisle and out the door. Kristie gathered up their things from the pew and scurried after her.

Carrie sat there, burning with embarrassment. Wendy was beside her but not there for her. She leaned away from Carrie, reached across her husband, and whispered something to her kids.

The pastor did his best to get things back under control. "Let's all rise and open our hymnals to page 139," he said. A plodding organ played and he and a church lady with a high, warbly voice sang "Great Is Thy Faithfulness" until the rest of the crowd reluctantly joined in.

When the service was over, Carrie stayed in her seat. As much as she wanted to be anywhere but where she was in that moment, there was no way she was going to be the first one out and have to walk down the aisle past everyone gathered. Sherri was the one who had shown her ass. Why should Carrie have to go around with the offering basket and collect all the pitying stares on her behalf?

"I'm not getting up," she said under her breath. Wendy motioned to the pastor, who correctly interpreted her head tilt and flat hand motion and walked down to the first pew after the family's and invited everyone to exit.

Carrie twisted and folded the printed program into a tortured origami until the chatter and shuffle of bodies along wooden pews diminished and the church was empty. She stared at the urn with Bill's ashes and remembered how she felt when Bill came back to her after leaving Sherri. She had told Packard about feeling lonely and Bill making her feel like a high school girl again. That was true. But the best part was taking the only person Sherri had ever loved and claiming him for herself.

The only good thing about the funeral was that there was no reception planned afterward. Wendy's announcement had stated that today would just be a service and that there would be a chance to gather and celebrate Bill's life on a date and at a location to be announced.

Some life, Carrie thought.

When Wendy and her family and the pastor were the last ones in the church, Carrie finally gathered her things, touched her hair, and made her way out.

She handed the pastor a folded check from her purse without comment. To Wendy she said, "Thank you for handling all the arrangements. I'm sorry my sister ruined it for all of us."

Wendy put a hand on her heart, bit her lip, and shook her head. She had nothing left to say. Carrie didn't blame her.

As she made her way down the front steps, Wendy finally found her voice. "What about his ashes?" she asked.

Carrie stopped and looked back. She knew there were ashes in the urn, but she imagined something heavy and wet, a cream of some kind of soup. It made her shudder.

"I can't," she said. She touched the side of her face and shook her head. "I can't…please. You take him," she pleaded.

A red pickup in the far corner of the lot slowly approached as she made her way to the Oldsmobile.

Carrie froze, wondering if it was him. The caller.

It was Detective Packard. He came around so his driver's side was by hers. She put on her sunglasses and stood with the car open. "I'm sure that wasn't exactly the service you had planned," Packard said.

Carrie shook her head and looked down. "You can always count on my sister to shame the family. It's what she does. I'm sorry she dragged your name into it."

"Didn't harm me, but we should talk about the things she said. I'd also like to go over again with you what happened the night Bill was killed."

Carrie found herself scrutinizing Packard's good looks from behind her sunglasses while he talked. He was an attractive man. Gay, according to the rumors. She wondered whether oral sex was as one-sided with gay guys as it had been with her and her two husbands.

"Meet at your house?" Packard asked.

"What was that?"

"I said I'd like to meet at your house and walk through exactly what happened that night. Is there a time we can do that?"

"I feel like my memory is already getting blurry," Carrie said.

"That's why we need to go through it again as soon as possible."

"Tomorrow," Carrie said. "I'll have to arrange for someone to stay with my mother again. Let's plan on 10:00 a.m."

"See you then."

CHAPTER FOURTEEN

CARRIE WANTED TO GET to her house before Detective Packard did. She hadn't planned on bringing Margaret with her, but the home-care service said they were short-staffed. Carrie thought they were punishing her for cutting back their hours.

She drove the Oldsmobile again. The front seat was like a couch covered in dark-blue crushed velvet. "Do you remember buying this car, Mom?"

Margaret shook her head. *No* was her automatic answer to most questions. But then she said, "I wanted a Cadillac, but your father was too cheap."

"Dad was tight with a dollar. That's how you guys got so rich," Carrie said.

"Where is your father?" Margaret asked.

"He's dead, Mom. For a long time."

"Oh."

———

She got her mom settled on the couch with an iPad and a game of solitaire. Dementia might have been eating holes in her brain, but Margaret still knew how to count and play red on black.

In her bedroom, Carrie opened her closet and went to where her coats were hanging and unfastened the hummingbird pin from the lapel of the camel coat she wore in the fall. It was the size of an actual hummingbird, maybe even a bit larger, a rare example of her father's extravagance. The back was solid gold. Carrie turned it in the light and noticed a tiny engraving on an inside edge of the wing.

For Sarah—Love, John

She couldn't recall ever hearing about a Sarah before. "John" might not necessarily have been her father. Maybe he bought the pin in an antique shop and John was the previous owner.

The problem was that hummingbirds were her dad's favorite bird. They'd always had hummingbird feeders at their house. She remembered her dad would mark the first day on the calendar that he saw a hummingbird after putting the feeders back out again once winter was over. He loved hummingbirds and he'd loved this Sarah, whoever she was.

Back in the living room, Carrie sat next to her mother and gently took the iPad from her. She took her mom's hand and put the hummingbird pin in it. "Mom, do you remember this pin?"

Margaret shook her head as she stared at the piece of jewelry cupped in her hands.

"You used to wear it all the time. I remember you wore it on a black fur coat for the longest time."

"Hmmm," Margaret said. "Yes."

"Mom, do you know who Sarah is? Did you or Dad have a friend with the name Sarah?"

"No."

Carrie turned over the pin. Her mother's old eyes would never pick up the engraving, but maybe she would remember the pin had been engraved. "Her name is inscribed on the back on the pin. It says, 'For Sarah—Love, John.' You don't remember who Sarah was?"

Margaret shook her head. She touched her top lip with the tip of her tongue.

Movement out of the corner of Carrie's eye turned out to be Packard pulling into the driveway in an SUV marked SHERIFF. "OK, Mom. Never mind. Play your game again." Carrie handed her mother back the iPad and put the pin in her purse. She went down the stairs to the entryway and got ready to meet Packard.

They sat at the dining room table after he first introduced himself to her mother and shook her hand. Margaret smiled at him and went back to her solitaire game.

"Does it matter to you how much of this your mother hears?" Packard asked, lowering his voice as they took their seats.

"She's not paying attention to us," Carrie said. "Our conversation won't register with her at all."

Packard went on to recap all the leads he had followed since Bill was murdered. "We've examined his phone, his work computer, his email, his truck. Nothing points to a suspect. The closest thing we have to a motive is that he made a large withdrawal from the business account he and Roger set up together and lost it at a poker game."

"He loved going to the casino. I wouldn't go with him."

"This was a private game. I interviewed everyone there that night. No one appears to have a motive to kill your husband."

"What about Roger?"

"Roger was angry about Bill taking the money but not enough to kill his best friend. He's got an alibi for the night of the murder. It's thin, but I don't think it was Roger."

He looked like he was waiting for her to say something else. She didn't know what to say. "What else have you found?"

"You told me Bill got home around midnight that night."

"That's right. He was with Roger."

"That's what he told you, but it wasn't true."

"Where was he?" Carrie asked.

Packard waited for her to figure it out for herself. "He was with Sherri," Carrie said, recalling her sister's outburst at the funeral the day before.

Packard nodded.

"You found out how?"

He told her about the texts on Bill's phone and that Sherri's number was saved under Roger's name and the confusion it had initially caused. "Sherri lied to me about what she was doing that night. She changed her story when I came back and confronted her with the evidence from Bill's phone."

"And this was an ongoing thing between them?" Carrie said.

"Seems so. There's something else you should know if you don't already."

"What's that?"

"Bill had life insurance through work. Sherri is the primary beneficiary. His sister Wendy is listed as the secondary."

Carrie felt her nostrils flare involuntarily as she took in a deep breath. "He didn't get that job until after we were married so that was a very conscious choice he made." She knew Bill had a small policy on her with himself as the beneficiary. That he'd turn around and direct his life insurance to her sister made her blood boil. She crossed her arms and scratched her shoulder to keep from making fists. "Isn't that your motive? Sherri killed Bill for the life insurance."

"I don't know if she knows she's the beneficiary. I haven't talked to her about it. The insurance company won't pay anything out until the investigation is closed. That said, I guess I just don't see it. She had sex with him the night he died. She seemed pretty distraught at the funeral."

"My sister can put on act with the best of them. Did you ever think that maybe that whole show was for your benefit? She wasn't on the program to speak. She saw you sitting in the back. Maybe this was her way of throwing you off her scent."

Packard stuck out his chin and shrugged. "It's possible. I'm not ruling anyone out until I have evidence that leads to the actual killer. She's still on the list. So is Roger."

"Am I on the list?" Carrie asked.

"The spouse is always on the list."

She could tell Packard was watching to see how she would react. She reacted by watching him watch her. It could have been a staring contest to see who would blink first.

"Let's go through what happened that night," Packard said. "Starting with you in bed and hearing Bill come home."

Carrie imagined a lot of women wanted to get Packard alone in their bedroom but probably not like this. She sat on top of the covers on the side she usually slept on. She had a book in her lap to represent the folder of grant applications she'd been reviewing before going to bed. The lamp on the nightstand was on, even though it was the middle of the day.

"Was your bedroom door open or shut?"

"Shut."

He had her walk through what she had heard (the garage door opening, then the interior door opening and closing). Bill hadn't come in her room or talked to her through the door. She heard him in the kitchen, then heard him go downstairs. After that, she stopped paying attention. Eventually she got tired and turned off the light and went to sleep.

"Then what happened?" Packard asked.

"I heard the shot."

"Did you think or know it was a gunshot?"

"No. I thought something large had fallen."

It wasn't a gunshot that woke her up. It was the sliding door in Bill's room, which was right under hers. The door on the track made a vibration that she could feel whenever it opened. She'd always been a light sleeper. She felt the door open and then she heard the hum of his CPAP machine turn off. Despite the late hour, or maybe because of it, the two activities immediately struck her as out of order if Bill was getting out of bed and going outside.

Packard quizzed her about what made her get out of bed and where she was when she first called out to Bill.

"I called to him from right here at the top of the stairs," she said.

She hadn't called him. What made her get out of bed was the same thing that made her take the gun from the nightstand, the same thing that made her move as quietly as possible to the top of the stairs. She'd felt like Bill had been up to something for a while now. He went out a lot, came home late. They'd hardly spoken in the last two weeks. She knew he needed money he didn't have. She had money she wouldn't give him. Their short marriage already felt like it had the shelf life of a loaf of bread.

She stood there for a long time, just listening. She heard whispering and someone moving in the dark down there.

Packard followed behind her as she went downstairs to the lower level. Margaret didn't look up from her iPad as they went by.

It smelled of fresh paint—the work of the cleaners she'd hired—and was darker and cooler than the top level of the house.

"What did you think when you first got to the bottom of the steps?" Packard asked.

At the bottom of the stairs, she noticed right away that the gun safe at the far end of the family room was open and the LED light inside was on. Bill's bedroom was around the corner from where she stood with the gun in her hand, a round in the chamber, and the safety off because she knew her way around a gun.

"I thought…something had fallen. Maybe the drop ceiling in Ryan's old room or something that was hanging on the wall."

Packard said, "If it was loud enough to wake you, did you think it was odd that Bill wasn't up or responding to you when you called him?"

"I thought with his CPAP machine and the amount of beer he can put away when he hangs out with Roger—which I now know he lied about—he could sleep through anything."

"Did you turn on the lights downstairs?"

"Yes."

No.

"Did you go into the family room or the other rooms before going into Bill's?"

"Yes. I did a quick loop through the family room to see if anything had fallen. I looked in Ryan's room, too."

Not true.

"Then you're back at Bill's room. Was his bedroom door closed?"

"Yes."

No.

"Did you knock?"

"Yes. I think so."

She didn't knock. She stood at the bottom of the stairs and listened to two men whispering. The killer said, "Is this all the jewelry?"

Bill said, "That's it."

She heard someone manhandle her jewelry in the box like he was sorting through a bag of marbles.

"There's supposed to be a pin. A hummingbird with rubies and diamonds."

"The fuck are you talking about?" Bill asked.

"The hummingbird. You're the one who told me about it," the killer said.

"No, I didn't... I think she has a pin like that. It's usually on a coat she wears in the wintertime. I didn't tell you it had diamonds and rubies because I didn't know it was made of diamond and rubies."

They argued about the pin and where it was and who should go upstairs and look for it.

"And then what?" Packard asked.

"I opened the door and turned on the light and saw Bill in his bed. And I saw all the blood."

Something struck her then, as she was lying to Packard but remembering the truth. Everything was exactly as she'd suspected when she went downstairs with the gun—Bill and a friend were using a burglary as a cover for her murder. Bill would collect a meager life insurance policy through his work, enough to open his restaurant that sold chicken finger baskets or whatever the hell.

But then why were they arguing about what was in the jewelry box? And how did the killer know more about her jewelry than Bill did?

The cleaners had done exactly what she'd asked. All the furniture was gone and everything Bill had had in his bedroom was packed into five 50-gallon storage containers stacked outside his bedroom door. The carpet and padding had been pulled out, exposing the concrete floor. All the walls had been repainted. The empty closet's bright-white interior made her think of walking in on someone naked.

Packard asked her a bunch of questions about Bill's room and the things she saw when she turned on the lights. Did he say anything? Was he moving? Did you touch him? Did you notice the patio door was open? Did you think he might have shot himself? She gave one-word answers in response. *No. No. No. Yes. No.*

They went out to the family room and stood in front of the gun safe, now as empty as Bill's closet.

"Did you notice if the safe was open?"

"It was closed, from what I remember. I would have noticed if the door was open when I walked through the room."

"And nothing that you know of was taken from the safe."

The answer she had given when asked the first time was "No, nothing." Telling the police about the stolen jewelry seemed to complicate the story unnecessarily. But she also didn't want to get caught in a lie. What if they found the killer and recovered the jewelry? How would she explain that?

"This is the first day I've been back to the house. I didn't think about it at the time, but when Mother and I got here, I checked for my jewelry box at the top of my closet and it wasn't there. Then I remembered I had put it in the safe when Bill and I went to Minneapolis for few days about a month before…all this. Was it in the safe when you emptied it?"

Packard shook his head slowly and wrote something in his notebook. "There was no jewelry box in the safe."

"All the jewelry my mom gave to me was in there. It's quite valuable, some of it."

Packard gave her a hard look she didn't like. He looked back in the direction of Bill's room. "So the killer came in through the patio door, got past a sleeping Bill, and made his way to the safe to steal the jewelry."

"I guess so?" Carrie said like a question.

"We found something in the carpet." Packard took out his phone, scrolled for a bit, then showed her a photo of a three-karat earring from a matching pair that her mother used to wear. "Would this have been in the jewelry box?"

"Yes."

"So he went through the box or juggled it while he was standing here and this earring fell out."

Carrie nodded.

"But he didn't steal any of the guns that were also in the safe."

"I don't know what Bill had in there for guns. I had the one in my nightstand but I don't really like guns."

"I don't know what you had for jewelry, but the eight handguns we took out of there would be worth a lot of money on the street. And probably easier to sell than jewelry."

Carrie didn't say anything. This was why she hadn't wanted to mention the jewelry. There was no taking it back now.

"Was the safe usually kept unlocked?" Packard asked.

"I…don't know. I never had a reason to go into it. It was Bill's idea to keep the jewelry in there. I didn't have a need for it since we got back from Minneapolis so it was just…there."

"So the safe was unlocked or the killer knew the combination."

"Maybe Bill opened it for him," Carrie suggested.

"Then got back in bed under the covers before he was shot?"

"Maybe not," Carrie said.

"Do you think the killer would have had time to shoot Bill, get to the safe, get the jewelry box, dig through it and drop the earring, and get out before you came down the stairs after hearing the gunshot?"

Carrie thought about it. "No, I don't think so."

"So he got past Bill, got the jewelry box, then shot Bill on his way out."

"Yes."

"And you only heard one shot even though he was shot twice."

"I only heard one."

Lie.

"Hmm," Packard said.

———————

They went back upstairs. Carrie's phone rang in her purse as they reached the main floor. Eager for a break from Packard's questions, she took the phone out and left the purse on the couch next to her mother. "Mind if I take this?" she asked Packard.

"Please," he said. He had a seat at the table where they'd been sitting earlier and took out his notebook.

Carrie stepped onto the deck through the sliding door and closed it behind her.

"This is Carrie," she said.

"I know you're with the detective," the killer said.

Carrie went to the end of the patio to try to see around to the front of the house. "How do you know what's going on?" she asked.

"Police scanner. He told dispatch he was at your address."

"What do you want?" Carrie asked.

"Are you telling him the truth this time?"

Carrie went to the edge of the deck and looked out over the pond behind her house. The breeze blew her hair across her face. She would miss this view when she sold the place. The kids had gone ice-skating out there when they were little. Out near the middle somewhere was a sunken paddleboat that had taken on water and left her daughter and a girlfriend swimming for shore.

"I'm telling him I don't know who shot Bill because it's the truth. I don't know who you are. Why don't you tell me so I can tell Detective Packard," Carrie said.

"Care-ree." He said her name like he was singing it. "We both know what happened that night. If you want to keep other people from finding out, I want a million in cash," the killer said.

Carrie had the money. Unlike Sherri, she'd managed her trust fund well, letting the investments grow and not touching the principal. She could pay this guy without creating too big of a hole in her net worth.

"How come you specifically asked Bill about the hummingbird pin?"

The killer waited too long to respond. He was thinking. "It was one of the most valuable pieces. It was where the money was."

"You knew about the pin but Bill didn't."

"He told me about it."

"No, he didn't. Bill knew nothing about my jewelry. Only that I had some and that it was in the gun safe. I heard him say he didn't know about the pin or that it was made from diamonds and rubies. So who told you about the pin?"

"I want a million in cash within ten days. I'll call you back and let you know where to bring the money."

"Here's another idea. You don't get shit and you fuck off. You murdered my husband. Go ahead and tell Packard your lies. Then prove any of it, asshole."

——————

When she came back in the house, Packard was sitting next to her mother on the couch. Her purse was tipped on its side and the contents spilled out. Margaret was holding the hummingbird brooch to her chest.

Carrie felt her icy bravado from the phone call turn to steam and evaporate. The last thing she wanted Packard to know about was the hummingbird pin.

"It's a beautiful pin," Packard said. "May I see it?"

Margaret handed him the pin with a shaky hand. Packard looked at it closely. Turned it over and looked even closer at the back.

"She was going to steal my husband," Margaret said.

"Who was?" Packard asked.

Sarah, Carrie thought.

"The slut he gave this to. She was going to steal my husband so I hit her over the head with the fire poker. John helped me get rid of the body."

CHAPTER FIFTEEN

PACKARD DROVE AWAY FROM Carrie's wondering whether he now had two murders to solve. Carrie had laughed at what Margaret had said and told Packard her mother's grasp on reality was tenuous at best. She said Margaret got confused and thought things she had seen on TV had happened in real life.

Why didn't Packard believe her?

Maybe because he didn't believe a lot of what Carrie had told him about the events that took place the night Bill was killed. Her story didn't add up. She should have heard two shots. Did she sleep through the first one and wake up for the second? The events themselves didn't make sense, especially after the details of the jewelry box being stolen from the safe were added. Why shoot anyone if burglary was the motive? And why take only the jewelry and leave a safe full of handguns that could have easily been sold on the street?

Bill had gotten a defensive hand up. They knew that from the autopsy and the wound from the first shot. But why was he still in bed? Why hadn't he tried to get out? He was still under the covers, which meant he'd confronted the burglar/killer—after he or she came back through his room from stealing the jewelry in the safe—from the warmth of his bed.

It seemed to him Carrie and Bill had an unhappy marriage and had gotten there in a relatively short time. The fact that Bill was screwing his ex-wife for the duration of it spoke for itself. It made Packard wonder how much Carrie knew or suspected. If she was over the whole thing, she stood to come out the other side of this with exactly what she wanted—Bill out of her life.

Provided she didn't get charged with murder.

In the days since the murder, Carrie hadn't bothered to contact anyone about the stolen jewelry. Her excuse was she hadn't realized it was stolen until today. Even so, she hadn't bothered to mention it until asked point-blank while standing in front of the safe from where it had been taken. He practically read on her face the moment she made the decision whether or not to tell him about it.

He left her instructions to get him a list of everything in the jewelry box, photos if she had them. When he asked her if she had any other jewelry in the house that hadn't been stolen, she said no. Everything was taken except the pin in her purse, which was beautiful and looked expensive.

"Why was this pin not with the rest of the jewelry?" he asked as he photographed the front and back of it.

"It was on my coat in the bedroom closet. I just took it off and put it in my purse when we got to the house today."

Hmm.

Which brought him back to Margaret and her confession. The thing that struck him the most was the light in the old woman's eyes, as if she could see directly into the past and the past was lit like a movie screen. That light slowly went out as he tried to ask her more questions about the woman she hit over the head with a fire poker.

"How long ago was this?" he asked.

"Before she was born," Margaret said, meaning Carrie.

"She's talking nonsense," Carrie said.

"Carrie wouldn't even be here if the slut had her way."

"Mom, don't be crude."

"I raised my girls to be better than that," Margaret said. "I told them sluts always get what's coming to them." She made it sound like this was parenting advice worthy of being written down.

He didn't get much else out of her. When Carrie put the iPad back in her lap, the window seemed to close on her lucidity.

Packard took one last look at the pin before handing it back to Carrie. "It's engraved on the back. John was your dad's name, right?"

Carrie nodded.

"Any idea who Sarah is?"

"Never heard of a Sarah before," Carrie said.

Packard drove on, and wondered what he would find if he looked into suspicious deaths or disappearances involving a female named Sarah that predated Carrie's DOB.

He'd gone to Carrie's house from home, and when he got to the office, he found Kelly in a mood that dropped the air pressure in the room. He could feel it in his bones as he approached her desk.

"I have a research assignment for you," he said.

She glared at him without a word and made no move to write anything down. He took a Post-it and a pen from the raised counter in front of her desk and started writing. "I'm looking for a Sarah with some connection to John Gherlick who might have died sometime before April 1979. Maybe eighteen to thirty years old. That's all I got. Can you release the hounds and see what they come back with?"

Packard peeled up the Post-it and held it out for Kelly. She ignored it. He flapped it on the end of his finger. She turned to her monitor and started clicking the mouse. She'd gotten her nails done and had M-I-N-N-E-S-O-T-A spelled across each fingernail with an outline of the state on her right pinkie.

Packard left the note, started to walk away, then came back. "I know why you're pissed."

Kelly didn't look away from her screen.

"I've been ignoring your emails."

"And?" she asked.

"And dodging calls from Marilyn," he said.

"And?"

"And today's the last day to file to run in the election."

Kelly picked up her coffee mug (WILL WORK FOR BARRY MANILOW TICKETS) and gave him a look over the rim as she drank.

"Do you still have the application form?" he asked her.

Without breaking eye contact, she reached down, slid out the file drawer in her desk, and pulled out the paperwork. Packard looked it over. It had been filled out with everything except his signature.

"It says I need to file a petition with one hundred signatures from eligible voters in the county or pay $50."

Kelly reached into her drawer again and pulled out four sheets of paper stapled together with the signatures.

Packard was shocked. "You did this? You know all these people?"

"You think I don't know one hundred people in this county? I know one hundred people in this building," Kelly said.

Packard flipped through the pages. About half the names he knew, half not. A hundred signatures didn't mean a hundred votes. The list was more a testament to Kelly's persuasiveness than to his electability.

"If I wanted to pay the fee instead, can I have $50?"

"You can have my foot in your ass if you don't get upstairs and get those papers filed by 3:00 p.m."

Packard peeled up another Post-it, pretended to lick the end of his pen. "I'm just gonna make a note quick for your annual review…threatened to put her foot in my ass…"

"Just do what I said," Kelly said.

"Fails to understand the department reporting structure…"

Kelly had taken her reading glasses from the top of her head and picked up her phone. She could only use the pad of her pointer finger to type because of her long nails.

"Who are you texting?" he asked.

"Your mom. I'm asking her why you turned out to be such a shit."

"'Called me a shit,'" he pretended to write on his Post-it.

Packard scooped up the papers Kelly had given him. "In all seriousness, thank you, Kelly. I appreciate what you've done for me."

"Go away," she said and kept texting.

He had a text from Thielen that was just a smiley face with star-shaped eyes before he made it back to his desk. He sent her back a skull and a water pistol, which was the only gun emoji in his phone.

One of the conclusions he'd come to while considering his options the last several days was that being a public servant meant being of service when needed. Not on his schedule or per his priorities. You showed up when called, whether it was a missing child, an active shooter, or a natural disaster, no matter the day, date, or time. This election—now and under these conditions—was the call. If he truly wanted to serve in his best capacity, then the time was now.

He certainly wasn't excited about what was to come. He was going to put himself out there to be scrutinized personally and professionally in a way he'd never done before.

His phone rang as he was verifying all the data in the application Kelly had filled out for him. It was Marilyn calling.

"Hi, Marilyn. How are you?... Yeah, you heard right," he said as he put his signature at the bottom. "I'm running for sheriff."

CHAPTER SIXTEEN

THE FIRST MEETING OF the Ben Packard for Sheriff campaign committee took place three days after he filed his papers. Packard offered to host it at his house but was shot down by Thielen. "No offense, but you live in a shipping container with a really nice bathroom."

"It's not that bad," he protested. "You haven't been over in a while. I've made some progress."

"Is there a floor yet?"

"Subfloor."

"We're meeting at my house," Thielen said.

At the meeting were Thielen and her husband, Tim; Susan Wheeler, Packard's cousin and owner/chef of the Sweet Pea restaurant; and Marilyn Shaw. Kelly had sent her regrets via text. She needed to keep the appearance of being a neutral party even though she'd gone above and beyond to help get Packard's name on the ballot.

"We've only got five weeks until the election at this point," Thielen said. They were gathered around the end of her dining room table, looking at a wide-screen monitor attached to her laptop. On the screen she had a calendar with all the days between now and the election date. She'd already filled in some of the coming events.

"The *Sandy Lake Gazette* is hosting a meet-the-candidates forum a week from tonight," Thielen said. "Ray Hanson is moderating."

"Ray Hanson hates my guts," Packard said. Hanson was the paper's publisher.

"You've pushed his buttons quite a bit," Thielen said. Last summer, when Susan's daughter, Jenny, and her boyfriend were missing, Packard had held a press conference and called on everyone with a question except Ray.

"He uses his paper as a bludgeon to get what he wants from people. He's an asshole. Pardon my language, Marilyn."

"Don't apologize. He is an asshole," Marilyn said and sipped the red wine Thielen had served. "The *Gazette* will definitely endorse another candidate so we need to flood it with letters to the editor in support of you. I know Ray still has a say in what to publish, but we can make sure he has plenty to choose from."

"You need to have a vision statement for the department and a handle on the numbers for the forum," Thielen said. "Budgets, crime statistics, population numbers, community health stats, etc. I don't think Shepard or Costas are going to be data-driven candidates. They're going to play up their experience and roots in the community. We've got to make them look as unprepared as possible."

Thielen's husband was going to manage social media. "I've already got a Facebook page set up," Tim said.

"Jenny says you should be making TikToks," Susan said.

"I know what those are, but I have no idea what to do about it," Packard said.

"Short videos," Tim said. "I'll think about how we can do that without being seen as too frivolous. If we can't get Ray Hanson to run letters in support of you, we'll put them on your Facebook page as graphics." He also wanted photos of Packard and Stan Shaw together, any commendations dating back to Packard's days on the Minneapolis police force, and photos from his childhood in Sandy Lake for Throwback Thursday posts.

"I'll be working on endorsements besides my own," Marilyn said. "Stan's former chief deputy, Ron Callahan, will endorse for sure. I also want to be with you at every appearance as a stand-in for Stan. I want everyone to remember who he picked to be sheriff before he died."

"Could be a lot of busy nights," Packard warned.

"I'm not afraid of being busy. I would welcome it. It's too quiet at home."

Thielen reported that they had three thousand dollars donated so far, mostly from their own pockets. "We also got a nice check from Jim Henkel, thanks to Marilyn."

"Jim Henkel?" Packard was shocked. He hadn't had a chance yet to personally meet Henkel, who was the closest thing Sandy Lake had to a hometown celebrity—a best-selling author of science-fiction novels that had sold millions of copies all around the world. Henkel and his wife lived in a huge gingerbread Victorian on Lake Redwing. A bookstore in downtown Sandy Lake sold almost exclusively Jim Henkel titles to his rabid fan base of readers and collectors. Packard remembered his brother Nick had a shelf of Jim's paperbacks when they were kids, books that made their way into Packard's possession after Nick disappeared. He'd read some of them back in the day but hadn't kept up with Henkel's latest titles.

"Jim followed the Emmett Burr story closely. He was impressed with how you handled it," Marilyn said. "I'll be able to get a letter of endorsement from him, no problem."

Thielen said they had enough money to get yard signs and T-shirts made. She'd already come up with a logo that would look great on both. "I'm going to go through the events calendar in the *Gazette* and look for other places for you to show up and be seen at. I'll email it to you tomorrow. Your evening hours are not your own from now until election day," she said.

Despite all the planning and scheduling, Packard felt like they were dancing around a key issue. "How are we going to manage the response to me being gay?" he asked.

Crickets.

Marilyn bit the inside of her cheek and made a motion like she was trying to twist her thumb off. "I could use a glass of water. Anyone else?" She stood and headed for the kitchen.

"Maybe we should spend some time anticipating how it's going to come up," Tim said.

"What are you thinking?" Packard asked.

"I don't think anyone is going to stand up in a public forum and shout 'GAY' like at a witch trial. How much do people know about you from what you've told them, and how much is speculation?"

"I'm not sure I can put numbers around that. I've been honest with people who have asked or needed to know. Not a lot of people have asked," Packard said.

"The other candidates will be oblique about it unless they can find something to use against you," Thielen said. "Is there a revealing Grindr profile we need to worry about?"

"I'm not on Grindr," Packard said.

"Any dick pics or explicit videos going to come out of the woodwork?"

"Absolutely not," Packard swore. "I have not sent photos like that to anyone."

"Are you serious?" Thielen asked. "I have a pic of Tim's dick on my phone right now. Probably more than one."

Tim shrugged. "For the record, I didn't send it to her. She took it herself."

"I have a photo of Sean White Cloud's," Susan chimed in. "I asked for it." Sean White Cloud was an EMT and nursing student half Susan's age who had been putting the blocks to her since her husband had died a couple of years earlier.

Packard imagined all the cock shots flying invisibly through the air at any given moment and wondered if he wasn't too uptight for his own good. Then he remembered he'd just hooked up with a drummer whose name he couldn't remember the next morning and decided he was doing all right for himself.

Marilyn came back from the kitchen with a glass of water, so Packard changed the subject. "I can see Shepard running on the fact that he's a family man. The other guy cheated on his wife with a coworker and ended up getting divorced. I'm not worried about him. Family values and spending his whole life in Sandy Lake is all Shepard's got. He's not a great deputy. It's a matter of public record that he was demoted from patrol captain by Stan five years ago."

Packard didn't mention the most recent disciplinary action he'd taken against Shepard for interfering in his investigation by texting and calling Sherri Sandersen with the news that her ex-husband had been murdered.

He and Shepard had had a private meeting just the day prior to discuss the matter. "We have written rules and regulations for the department," Packard reminded him. "We also have a handbook on conduct principles and disciplinary guidelines. Have you looked up your misconduct to see what the penalty is?"

Shepard shifted in his seat and scratched his goatee. "I haven't."

"The city attorney, acting as the finder of fact, has determined that you interfered with an investigation, which is a level eight violation per Appendix F of the handbook. The mitigated penalty is ninety days suspension. The presumptive penalty is dismissal."

He could tell by the look on Shepard's face that he was surprised by the word *dismissal*.

"Come on. It wasn't that bad. She was a friend. I thought she should know. That's all."

"When you're on duty, your priority is the oath you took as a law enforcement officer. Not your friends. You've been doing this longer than I have, Deputy. Why do I have to explain this to you?"

"I made a mistake. I didn't think about what I was doing," Shepard said. "Or how it would impact your investigation."

"The issue here is that you constantly display behavior inconsistent with a deputy in this department. You've been doing it since Stan Shaw was sheriff, and it hasn't gotten any better since I've been sitting in this chair."

"I've been a deputy for twenty years. I know what I'm doing."

"No, you don't! That's my whole point. You're confusing longevity with competence. How many written reprimands have been added to your file since I've been acting sheriff?"

Shepard had to think about it. "One," he said.

"Two," Packard corrected. "Now this. What would you suggest I do?"

Shepard shrugged but didn't say anything.

Packard waited.

"What do you want me to say?" Shepard asked.

"You really think you have what it takes to be sheriff?"

Shepard had never looked so unsure of anything in his life. "I do."

"So what would you do in my position? You might be sitting where I'm sitting come January. What would you do?"

"I'd give the guy another chance."

"How many more chances?"

"Enough until he improved."

Packard shook his head, disgusted. "Here's the deal. The election complicates things."

"In what way?"

"I filed papers to run."

Shepard looked shocked. And wounded. "You said you weren't running," he whined.

"I've been encouraged by people smarter than me to set my reservations aside." At that moment, Packard couldn't believe he'd spent one second imagining he was just going to hand this job over to Shepard, like it didn't matter to him who was going to be in charge or that there was any downside to giving the reins to Shepard if it turned out he was the only one who wanted the job. What was he thinking?

"So that's three of us now," Shepard said.

Packard opened his desk drawer and took out a stack of folders. "Three candidates with personnel files from the department. I'm releasing these, plus my file from Minneapolis. There's going to be a story in next week's *Sandy Lake Gazette*."

Shepard looked sick. "That's not...."

"What? Fair? Right?" Packard asked. "You think the people don't deserve to know the record of who they're voting for?"

"So what does this have to do with my punishment?"

"I'm releasing your file without this report in it."

"Why would you do that?"

"Because I don't like the optics of me being the acting sheriff, running against you in the election, and firing you a month before the vote."

Blood rushed to Shepard's round face and spotted it like a clown's. "Wait a minute. I'm fired?"

Packard leaned forward and looked Shepard right in the eye. "If you win the election, it's a moot point. You won't be a deputy anymore. You'll be the sheriff. If you lose and I win, I'm going to give you two weeks to submit your resignation in writing and announce the election made you realize it's time to look for a new opportunity. If I don't have your resignation within two weeks of election day, I'll release the city attorney's report and dismiss you for conduct contrary to department guiding principles and standards."

Shepard looked like he was trying to juggle and do math in his head. "What if…the other guy wins?"

"If the other guy wins, you still have to resign or I'll fire you before he's sworn in."

"Packard, I've been—"

"I'm your sheriff," Packard reminded him.

Shepard looked like he'd rather bite off his own tongue than refer to Packard by his title. "Sheriff…I've doing this job for a long time. I should be able to keep my job whether I win the election or not."

"Your years of service don't entitle you to indefinite employment regardless of performance. You'll leave with your full pension and it'll be up to you what people know about why you left. But listen to me, your career as a deputy in the Sandy Lake County Sheriff's Department is over. You're being dismissed."

Shepard was reaching for his phone before he even made it out of Packard's office. Calling Jim Wolf, no doubt. Packard could only imagine how apoplectic the county commissioner would be once he found out that Packard was running and that Shepard was on the verge of being fired.

Packard mentioned none of this to his own campaign team as they wrapped up their meeting. Shepard's performance was still a private personnel matter. He also didn't want them to know that he might have lit a fire under their biggest competition.

CHAPTER SEVENTEEN

CARRIE PUSHED THE BUTTON on the garage door opener and watched sunlight creep across the concrete floor. She'd been in and out of the garage a dozen times since coming to stay with her mother, but this time she was looking for answers about her father. On this morning, it felt like the opening of a tomb.

Inside were things found in every Minnesota lake home garage—a second refrigerator, an aluminum ladder and a canoe hanging on the wall, a snowblower, an orange bucket with ice melt and an old coffee cup in it. She'd left the Olds parked in the driveway yesterday, knowing she'd need the space to work.

Carrie set an Adirondack chair near the garage opening and brought Margaret out so she could keep an eye on her. Even though she was in the sun, Margaret complained about the temperature. "I'll get you a blanket, Mom," Carrie said.

In addition to the normal garage stuff, there were three green filing cabinets against one wall, lined up like soldiers. Carrie had never been curious enough to wonder what they might contain. *Bank stuff*, she'd always assumed, which, maybe for the first time ever, was what she was after.

She hadn't been able to stop thinking about the pin for the last several days. The inscription on the back, the fact that the killer had asked Bill about it specifically, and Margaret's confession all had her wondering why the hummingbird pin—something she, and her mother before her, had worn for years with little comment—had suddenly taken on such significance. If the killer knew about it, knew Carrie had it, then someone must have told him. But who? Who else knew about the pin?

Not Mary. She hadn't been involved in family matters for years. Her taste in jewelry ran toward the ugly, homemade kind.

Sherri was the obvious answer. She'd thrown a fit when she found out Margaret had given all her jewelry to Carrie.

"Half of that should've come to me," she had whined.

Carrie scoffed at the thought. "So you could pawn it and spend the money on chardonnay and cigarettes? Not happening."

Since Sherri had spent all her money, Carrie had noticed a cold, calculating look would come over her sister whenever confronted by something of value. You could see her size up the worth of a thing and question whether its owner was more deserving of possessing it than her. Sherri could have told the killer to make sure he got the hummingbird pin. It was obviously valuable. The size and weight and the number of stones gave that away. But was it more valuable than any other piece? Than all the rest of the jewelry? Carrie felt like they knew something about the pin that she didn't. What was it?

She decided to start by trying to figure out who Sarah was. If her father truly was the stud about town he'd been rumored to be, it made sense he'd find his women from the steady stream of pretty young things that worked at the bank. It was where he met his wife, after all. Margaret was a teller before she married the bank president.

The top drawer of the first cabinet was full of manila folders inside green hanging folders. The paper had swollen and grown heavy over time. The dates were from the early- to mideighties. A lot of the documents looked like they were produced on a typewriter and then mimeographed in purple ink. In the other drawers she found ledgers and three-ring binders and green and white striped printouts folded and sandwiched between cardboard covers. Statements of assets and reports to shareholders and changes to government banking regulations. It was the library of a dead society, indecipherable to the living.

The last cabinet was full of garage odds and ends—a drawer full of old T-shirts to be used as rags, a drawer of Christmas lights wrapped around blocks of wood, a drawer of lawn chemicals and bug sprays and tool lubricants. Not what she was looking for.

Carrie stood with her hands on her hips, blew some hair out of her face, and wondered where else she could look. She knew there was nothing of her father's still in the house. After his suicide, all his clothes had been packed and donated. His office was emptied out and turned into a guest bedroom. Margaret had anything that bore a trace of her husband—photos, artwork he liked, mounted fish, framed certificates—removed from sight and the house completely redecorated. Carrie still associated the caustic smells of fresh paint and new carpet with her father's death.

Above the garage was a lofted space where Carrie thought things were stored, but she had no idea what was up there. A string with a plastic pull on the end dangled from the ceiling and pulled down a folding ladder. Carrie batted at the knob, debating if it was worth going up there. She had a terrible fear of spiders, and if a garage loft where no one had been for thirty years wasn't full of spiders, she didn't know what was.

"Mom, what's up in the loft? Do you remember?"

"What loft?" Margaret asked.

Carrie pointed to the ceiling. "Up there. What's up there?"

"I don't know."

"Did any of Dad's stuff get stored up there?"

"What stuff?"

This was getting her nowhere. "Never mind," Carrie said. She pulled the knob and stepped back as the ladder dropped. She had to unfold the last section so it reached the ground. She looked up. The opening over her head looked like the doorway between day and night.

"Ah jeez," she said. She took her phone out of her back pocket, turned on the flashlight, and climbed the stairs.

———————

Carrie was eleven years old when her dad hung himself in the garage with an orange extension cord. Before her mom found him with thirty inches of air between his feet and the oil-stained concrete, Carrie had regarded her father like the furniture. He took up space and was easy to ignore but was there to collapse into when she wanted something. The times she went to her father were rare because Margaret was the one who treated her like a princess and catered to all of her wants. Even Margaret needed her space sometimes. That's when Carrie would find her father in his office behind a large cherrywood desk or on the deck holding a drink and staring at the lake like a man waiting for something to emerge from the fog: a ship or a swallowing whale.

She remembered her father as tall and handsome, with thick hair just gray at the temples and heavy black-framed glasses. He smoked cigarettes and sometimes a pipe, and his favorite drinks had gin in them and she would smell the juniper and the lemon twist whenever she crawled on his lap. He was a meek man who lived under Margaret's thumb throughout Carrie's childhood. She watched him defer to his wife on all decisions regarding the child raising, the house they lived in, the food they ate, the vacations they took. When Margaret felt like waging war, she made sure the girls knew about their father's past indiscretions, how he slept with whores, and that it was only Margaret's willingness to forgive that kept the family together and the girls from being cast out and living like poor people.

It was more insight into a marriage than a child should have had. Most of it was drowned out by a pink haze of new Barbies and stuffed animals, and, when she got older, clothes and makeup. Occasionally, the hostility between her parents broke into the open and it felt as if they had both summoned the fury of the weather in their battle against each other.

Stop criticizing Mary's looks, Margaret. She's a teenage girl. Look in the mirror if you want to see the ugliest person in the room. In any room.

Don't push me, John. I'll do something terrible. You know I will.

After the suicide, Carrie's feelings were mostly for herself. It was embarrassing to have a father who had so little regard for you, so little interest in your future that he would kill himself. It was selfish and rude.

When her sisters told her about the trust funds he had set up for them and that a trust fund meant she'd be getting money when she was older, she stopped thinking about her father and started imagining the things she would buy for herself when she got her money.

How bad things must have been for him, how awful he felt inside, had never occurred to her.

Plywood sheeting had been put down over the rafters on just the front half of the garage. The back half was open. Seldom-used items like a patio umbrella and leftover pieces of downspout lay across the open space. Carrie went up the steps with just her phone, realized she'd need more light, and came back down and found a flashlight. The second time up the stairs, she spotted the curved impressions left in the wood where her father had looped the extension cord and hung from it with his full weight.

There were fewer spiderwebs than she expected but not none. She had to hunch and step over the struts that angled up to the roof until she reached an open spot where boxes had been stacked years ago. She shined the flashlight across the front of them, looking for markings that would indicate what was inside. Nothing.

She opened the first box, found old dishes, and moved it aside. She found a box of clothes, colors and patterns that brought back flashes from her childhood, and set it aside. There was a box of Christmas knickknacks and a box of candles and random decorations. She found a box of finance and banking magazines, then a box of golf trophies and a large glass award in the shape of a candle flame, engraved with her father's name and Sandy Lake Commercial State Bank. Now she was getting somewhere. This was the stuff from her father's office.

"Mom, what are you doing down there?" Carrie called.

"I'm watching the cars drive by," Margaret said. "Where are you?"

"I'm above you in the storage space. Stay there and we'll have lunch soon."

"Soup?"

"Yes, if you want soup."

In the next box she found file folders, not unlike what she'd found in the file cabinets below. She found empty folders marked WILL and LIFE INSURANCE and CAR TITLE. She found a folder that had clipped newspaper ads from the bank advertising the Christmas savings club and interest rates on home loans (14.5 percent!) and free movie tickets for kids who got straight A's on their report card. At the very bottom, she found a heavy metal box with a key taped to the top. Inside were a revolver wrapped in an oilcloth and an old box of bullets. The gun said Smith & Wesson on one side of the barrel and .44 Magnum on the other. Carrie set it aside.

In another box she found a photo album full of pictures from events her father had attended. She saw a lot of wide lapels on suits and tweed skirts to the calf and high-necked blouses with big bows. None of the photos were labeled. Next was a stack of bank calendars with pictures taken around Sandy Lake for each month. She flipped through a couple, almost discarded the stack until she spotted a photo on the inside back cover that showed the bank employees with a list of their names and titles underneath. She checked the other calendars—all had a staff photo.

Margaret had said her father's affair with the slut had happened before Carrie was born. She sorted through the stack and discarded any for years since she was born. She was left with only three.

In the first one she found what she was looking for. *Sarah Pellak, Bank Teller.* Two other women stood between her and her father, who stood on the end, the whole group standing outside in front of the bank's large windows. Sarah was trim with thick, dark hair pulled back and dangling over one shoulder. Her skirt was a bit shorter than those of the other women, her blouse a bit shinier. In the next year's calendar, her title had changed to customer service manager and she stood on the opposite end of the group from John Gherlick. The distance might have been intended to avoid familiarity, but Carrie found it had the opposite effect. It made them look guilty.

She was so taken with studying their posture and the frozen smiles on their faces that she almost missed the most important detail.

Sarah was wearing the hummingbird pin on the lapel of her jacket.

In the next year's calendar, Sarah Pellak was gone.

Gone or dead?

Carrie had told the detective Margaret's murder confession was nonsense, but she knew it was true the second she heard it. This was the secret that had cowed her father and kept him bound to a woman who pecked away at him like a bird eating suet. Her mother murdered Sarah, then terrorized her father with threats to harm herself or their children afterward.

Don't push me, John. I'll do something terrible. You know I will.

Carrie heard a car pulling into the driveway as she was closing up the boxes. A car door opened and slammed shut. She heard her mother's voice but not what she was saying.

Carrie grabbed the calendars and the metal box with the gun inside and made her way backward down the ladder. She looked over her shoulder and saw a car she didn't recognize and Sherri standing in the driveway, talking to their mother.

"What are you doing here?" Carrie asked as she set her things down and wiped the dust off her pants.

Sherri pulled an envelope from her back pocket and shoved it in Carrie's face. "You lying, fucking bitch."

CHAPTER EIGHTEEN

"I GOT A NAME for you," Kelly said to Packard when he stopped at her desk to get his mail. "Sarah Pellak."

"Who's that?" he asked.

"You asked me to have the gang research a Sarah possibly connected to the bank, possibly dead or missing, possibly before 1979."

"Yes. You found someone."

"We found Sarah Pellak." She handed him a printed PDF of a short newspaper article.

Cass County Sheriff's deputies retrieved a car with a body inside from a roadside drainage pond on Tuesday. Personal items helped identify the driver as Sarah Pellak, formerly of Sandy Lake, recently of Wilbur, Iowa. Cause of death has yet to be determined. Authorities believe the car was in the pond since sometime this winter and only became visible with the spring thaw.

"Where did you find this?" Packard asked.

"The archives of the *Sandy Lake Gazette* are online. They have papers going back to 1952, all digitized and searchable."

"What's the date on it?"

"May 5, 1979."

"You were here in the seventies. Any—"

Kelly picked up a pair of scissors and pointed them at Packard. "I was not working here fifty years ago and I will cut your tongue out."

"I meant in Sandy Lake in the seventies," Packard said, putting his hands up. "This story ring any bells?"

Kelly lowered her weapon. "No. And we don't have any case files going back that far. A lot of things have been purged over the years."

"Any follow-up articles?"

"Not that I could find. I did a Google search and got no hits for a Sarah Pellak."

"What about a connection to the bank? Or John Gherlick?"

"Still looking into that," Kelly said. "Martha Clay is ninety-one years old and still sharp as a tack. She worked at the bank for a long time. I'm going to run the name by her to see if it rings a bell."

"Let me know what you find out."

"Are you ready for the forum tonight?"

"Ready as I'll ever be," Packard said. When Kelly gave him an unhappy look, he said, "I feel good. I'm actually looking forward to it."

His campaign was coming together better than he could have imagined. He had a great team working on his behalf. He and Thielen had spent every free evening working on his platform. She'd grilled him on county data until he could recite facts and figures from memory. He was confident in his knowledge, if nothing else.

"I'm too nervous to show up in person," Kelly said. "I'm going to stream it from home."

"I'm sure you'll text me after and tell me how I did," Packard said.

"I'm sure I'll text you during it if you screw up."

———

The candidate forum was held in the same room where the county commissioners met. Packard and Shepard and Alan Costas sat with an empty chair between each of them at the elevated table at the front of the room. Each had a sign in front of him with his name on it. About forty people filled the chairs where the public sat during the county board meetings, which was thirty-nine more than typically showed up.

As they waited for the meeting to start, Packard was struck by the similarities between the three of them. All white, all male, all with short, nearly military-style, haircuts. Packard had a trim beard and the other two sported goatees. Shepard had at least a decade on the other two. He and Packard were both wearing jackets and ties while Alan Costas had shown up in a shiny light-blue golf shirt, jeans, and white sneakers.

Packard scanned the audience for familiar faces. He spotted Thielen and Tim, and Marilyn Shaw, who gave him a smile and a nod when they made eye contact, and his neighbor, Bert, the retired judge. His cousin Susan had a restaurant to run and wasn't there. Shepard's wife and teenage daughters were there. Jim Wolf was sitting in the back row. He'd probably tied Shepard's tie for him.

At quarter after, Ray Hanson, editor and publisher of the *Sandy Lake Gazette*, stepped up to the podium and thanked everyone for coming. He was in his fifties, balding, and wore large, gold-rimmed glasses that made Packard think of a child molester from an '80s TV movie. Packard didn't think Ray Hanson was an actual child molester, but he did think Hanson was a prick.

Ray Hanson explained how the evening would go—two minutes for each candidate to introduce themselves, then a minute and a half each to answer questions submitted via the *Sandy Lake Gazette* website and also collected from people in the audience. The candidate to answer first would move from question to question.

Alan Costas told the crowd he was a lifelong resident of Sandy Lake. He'd gone to college on an ROTC scholarship, served six years in the army, the last two with the military police. He was currently working as a police officer in

Wilmington, a town in the next county. He'd been in law enforcement almost all of his professional career and thought his military experience had given him the leadership skills necessary to run the sheriff's department.

Shepard introduced his wife and daughters and said he'd been with the sheriff's department for over twenty years, serving in multiple roles. He mentioned he'd already earned his full pension but felt like he had more to give the people of Sandy Lake. Packard tried to keep the hint of a friendly smile on his face through all of it. He hoped it didn't make him look creepy.

When it was his turn, he said, "I have roots in Sandy Lake going back three generations. I don't know if most people know it, but my grandparents had a home on Lake Redwing for many years. My grandfather built the house, they lived there year-round, and I spent almost every summer there. My grandparents are gone now, but the house is still there."

He'd made a conscious choice not to mention his brother during his opening statement. Not many people had made the connection between him and the boy who had drowned nearly thirty years ago. This wasn't the time or the place to strike that match.

"Like the other two candidates, I've been in law enforcement almost my entire career. I moved to Sandy Lake three years ago after being with the Minneapolis Police Department for fourteen years. I was looking for a fresh start in a place that was special to me at one point in my life. Sheriff Shaw hired me to be a detective, and he personally selected me to fill in as acting sheriff when he became too sick to do the job. It's been a privilege to represent him in this role, and I look forward to continuing to do so if elected."

The round-robin questioning began after that. It became clear early on that Costas was out of his league. The army might have taught him to be a leader, but it hadn't done much to prepare him to answer questions in front of a live audience about a job he clearly knew nothing about. His answer to nearly every question started with the phrase, "Well, I've never been a sheriff before…" He was sure he'd be able to come up to speed quickly, and he was looking forward to learning from the community what it was they wanted

from their local law enforcement. Packard stopped paying attention to his
responses after a while.

Shepard wasn't exactly articulate, but he had talking points that he was
able to verbally stumble through, sometimes circularly repeating himself, and
ending with, "So…uh, yeah. That's my answer." Nothing seemed to catch him
entirely off guard.

Packard gave statistics and examples and budget numbers. He talked about
the department's efforts to address the opioid crisis and the percentage of cases
closed successfully. He shared his vision for expanding technology to keep deputies safe and protect the rights of the public. He had a plan to recruit new deputies graduating with law enforcement degrees by showing them what a career
path with the department would look like. A life in Sandy Lake would sell itself.

A question from the audience asked each candidate to address the misconduct documented in their files that had been posted online.

Costas couldn't hide behind his ignorance for this question. He knew very
well why he'd been fired from the sheriff's department. He admitted to the
relationship with the coworker and the poor judgment he exhibited, then tried
to make it sound like getting fired and divorced were examples of him doing
the right thing. "I took responsibility for my actions. It cost me my job and my
marriage. I accepted those consequences," Costas said.

Shepard explained his demotion from patrol sergeant as an issue with time
cards and deputies under his command double-billing for time they were getting paid as courthouse deputies in the next county. He failed to mention that
there were discrepancies in his own time card as well. Packard kept his head
down, his face expressionless.

"I have one reprimand in my file from my years on the force in Minneapolis,"
Packard said when it was his turn. "It was early in my career. We were called to
do a welfare check on a child who hadn't been to school in a long time. This kid
was a foster child, a different race than his foster family. When we got there, we
found an eleven-year-old boy who looked like a five-year-old because he was so
malnourished. He was tied to a bed that had been soiled repeatedly. The other

half of his room had a large dog cage in it, equally filthy, with a barking, snarling pit bull inside. I've seen a lot of terrible things in my time, but that terrified boy and that furious dog still give me nightmares."

Packard paused for a moment. "The mother, if you could call her that, tried to attack our officers with a knife. She was subdued and restrained. The father was under the influence and belligerent. I got him cuffed and out of the house. As I was trying to get him into the car, he spit in my face. I lost my temper. I slammed his head into the doorframe. He got a facial laceration that bled a lot and needed to be treated by EMS, who rightly reported the incident."

Packard didn't look into the audience to see their reactions. He was staring at the floor in front of where Ray Hanson stood and was seeing that boy covered in sores, his bones near the skin like a boiled chicken. With no effort at all he could recall the smell of feces and animals and smoked drugs that had permeated the house.

He'd lost his temper that day, and he didn't regret it one bit.

The hour scheduled for the forum was nearly over. "We have time for one more question," Ray Hanson said and used a knuckle to push up his glasses. "How will you differentiate yourself as a leader from the previous sheriff?"

Packard was first to answer. "In the last year and a half I've applied for and been awarded multiple new grants that the department has been able to spend on equipment and travel for training. I've also instituted a conduct and discipline handbook that's been successfully used in other sheriff's departments around the country to ensure a consistent and fair approach for disciplinary actions." It was the same handbook he was using to justify firing Shepard. He resisted the urge to turn and give the deputy a knowing look.

Costas said he'd been out of the department for a quite a while and didn't know much about Stan Shaw's leadership style but was certain he would figure out his own approach and looked forward to the opportunity to try.

Shepard said, "Stan Shaw taught me everything I know about law enforcement. I don't know I'd do anything different. He was a great sheriff. Maybe one thing I'd do different than the acting sheriff is where I look for new hires. We got a guy from India on a special visa working for us. That's a job I think should have gone to someone from Sandy Lake, or at least a Minnesotan."

Packard couldn't believe what he was hearing. Shepard had never had anything negative to say about Suresh. Nobody did. He was a great colleague who knew more about technology and social media and encryption than all the rest of them put together. He'd had everyone in the department over to his house earlier that summer, including Shepard, for a traditional Indian meal that his wife had spent two days preparing.

"I'd like to respond to that, if I may," Packard said.

Ray Hanson flipped over his papers as if signaling the end of something. "I'm sorry, you've already had your chance to answer the question."

"That job was posted for months—"

"I'm going to stop you there," Hanson said. "We're out of time."

"And I interviewed half a dozen people, none of whom were—" His mic was turned off at that point and Ray Hanson talked over him.

"I want to thank everyone who submitted a question and everyone in attendance. On behalf of the *Sandy Lake Gazette*, good night."

Packard sat in his chair and stared at Ray Hanson as the other two candidates walked off the stage to meet the audience. Hanson wouldn't look at him. Packard watched Shepard hug his wife and shake hands with Jim Wolf, who patted him on the back.

Packard stood up, smoothed his tie, and put on a smile as he was surrounded by supporters on the floor. *Great job, you had the best answers, you did fantastic*, they said. Things he already knew. What he was late to realize was that he'd been bamboozled. He was so used to handling Ray Hanson that he was blind to the fact that this time, he was the one who had been handled. A weekly ad rag sponsoring a meet-the-candidates forum? Not an independent group like the League of Women Voters? A moderator with a bias against him? If the questions came through the *Gazette* website, Ray could have shared them with Jim Wolf and Shepard. They no doubt planted the question at the end and prepared Shepard's answer so it would be the last thing people remembered.

Sounded like a conspiracy, felt like one too, especially when Packard looked over the heads of everyone around him and saw Jim Wolf and Ray Hanson talking to each other in the hallway outside the council room. Jim Wolf caught Packard's eye, touched Ray's arm, and they moved out of his line of sight.

It was dark with an October chill in the air by the time Packard left the county building and came down the front stairs. Standing under a streetlamp in a black skirt and a denim jacket, arms crossed for warmth, and smoking a cigarette was Sherri Sandersen.

"That thing was supposed to be done at seven," she complained.

"People wanted to chat. It took a while to get out," Packard said. "What are you doing here?"

"I'm on my dinner break from the bar. I had a customer drop me off, and now I'm late getting back. Can you give me a ride?"

"Yeah, I'm over here in the red truck."

Sherri finished her cigarette and stepped on it before climbing inside. Packard started the engine and turned on the heat. "What's up?"

Sherri leaned forward and pulled an envelope out of her back pocket that had taken on the curved shape of her ass cheek. "I got this in the mail," she said.

Packard turned on the cab lights. The envelope had Sherri's name and address on it. No return address. The postmark was from Sandy Lake and two days old. As he took the sheet of paper out, he smelled something like sandalwood or patchouli. Scented stationery, he assumed, and not the smell of Sherri's backside.

The letter was written in heavy black ink that had bled through the paper.

Carrie killed Bill. I was there. If the police don't act, you might be next.

"Who do you think sent this?" he asked.

"I don't have any idea," Sherri said.

Packard read the message again, flipped the paper over and examined it closely. "Why send it to you and not to the police?"

Sherri shrugged and pulled on the end of her skirt. "Maybe he's trying to start some shit," she suggested.

"And did you take the bait?"

"What do you mean?"

"Did you show this to Carrie?"

"Yes, I went to the house this afternoon ready to rip her a new asshole," Sherri said.

"What did she say?"

"She accused me of sending it to myself. She thinks because me and Bill were still fucking that we were plotting behind her back. She thinks she was the killer's intended target, but something went south, and that I'm the mastermind behind it all because I'm broke and after her money."

"Are you?"

"No. I'm not. If Bill was plotting against Carrie, I didn't know about it. Swear to God. I don't know anything. You saw me that night. I was a mess."

"Not too much of a mess to have sex with your ex-husband just hours before he was killed."

Sherri rubbed her arms and rolled her eyes. "It wasn't that much work on my part. We were in his truck. I just had to climb on and hold on, if you know what I mean."

"I understand the mechanics of it," Packard said. "What did you say to Carrie after she accused you?"

"I called her a crazy bitch. I said if anyone was plotting to kill anybody, it was her working with someone to kill Bill."

"Why do you think she would want to kill Bill?"

"I was married to Bill for twenty years. My guess is it took Carrie thirty days to realize marrying him was a mistake."

"It's easier to divorce someone than murder them," Packard suggested.

"A divorce would mean she had to admit she was wrong. A divorce would mean she no longer had what I wanted, which was the whole point of marrying him in the first place. Killing him gets rid of him and hurts me. That how she wins."

Packard still didn't know if the accusations volleyed between Carrie and Sherri were slanderous attacks on the enemy or biting insights based on actual personalities. He knew how easy it was to paint an adversary in broad, shocking strokes until they took on a shape that was less than human. Sherri had stolen her sister's high school sweetheart and squandered a fortune. She drank too much, and she'd lied to Packard early on in his investigation. For some reason, under different circumstances, he couldn't help but think he would have been amused by her if he sat at the bar where she worked and listened to her hold court in front of a crowd of regulars. She'd had a wild life so far and lived to tell the tale.

"How did you leave things with Carrie?" he asked.

"I said if I find out she had something to do with Bill's murder, I was coming for her head."

"You have to quit threatening your sister," Packard said. "You did the same thing at the funeral. If something happens to her, I've got you twice on record threatening to kill her. That's going to put you in a bind."

"Carrie's the one lying here. You don't know her like I do," Sherri said. "She'd lie about anything."

Packard thought back to his last meeting with Carrie and the fact she had accused Sherri of almost the identical behavior.

"Figure out who sent the letter and find out what they know," Sherri said.

"I've exhausted almost all the leads," Packard admitted. He'd been hoping for a hit on the jewelry that was stolen from the gun safe. He'd sent the list and photos he'd gotten from Carrie to pawnshops in all the surrounding states. Nothing so far.

"I can't find anyone with a beef against Bill, no one with a motive, no physical or electronic evidence that he was involved in a plot of some kind. As far as witnesses to the shooting, one of them is dead and the other was asleep in another room and claims she didn't see anything."

"I'm telling you she's lying. The letter writer says so, too." Sherri pulled her phone out of her other back pocket to check the time. "Shit. Can you drive and talk at the same time?" she asked. "I need to get back to work before I get fired."

Packard tossed the letter on the dashboard and put the truck in gear. He could drive and talk at the same time but found he didn't know what else to say.

CHAPTER NINETEEN

THE NEXT MORNING, JUST as the sun was coming up, Packard eased himself into the water off the end of his dock and started crawling across the lake. He counted in his head for the first minute or so, going down from 201 by sixes, to help take his mind off the worst of the cold while his body used its own heat to warm the layer of water between him and his wet suit. By the time he made it to the middle of the lake and back, he'd forgotten about the cold and was able to think about other things.

He hadn't bothered telling Thielen or anyone else on his campaign about his conclusion that Jim Wolf, Ray Hanson, and Shepard had colluded on the forum. What did it matter? The forum was over. That Ray Hanson hated his guts was already accounted for in their strategy. That the *Gazette* would endorse Shepard was a given. There were things they could change and things they couldn't. Packard still felt like he could win without the "local media" (if you could call it that) on their side.

He needed to put more of his focus on finding Bill Sandersen's killer. He'd told Sherri he'd exhausted just about all the leads, but that didn't necessarily mean things weren't happening. Sometimes an investigation was like a garden. You needed to let sunlight and water and time do their work. Out of sight, something would germinate and then, suddenly, where there had been nothing but dirt, there would be growth. Packard usually thought of it like a weed. Something to yank on.

The letter was the weed. The letter was evidence of things happening underground that Packard couldn't see.

Before dropping her off at the restaurant, he'd told Sherri to watch her back. "I don't like the part of the letter where it says you might be next. We can't know if it's a threat or a warning. You need to be careful."

Sherri was putting on lipstick and looking at herself in the sun visor mirror. "I'm a tough old bitch. I can take care of myself," she said.

"A tough old bitch is no match for a guy with a gun."

"I'll be careful," Sherri promised.

"If another letter comes, don't open it. Don't carry it around in your back pocket all day. Call me right away."

Sherri said *all right, all right* as she opened the passenger door and slid out on her way back to work.

"And stay away from your sister," Packard said. "Don't get into it with her."

Sherri just smiled and shut the door in his face.

———

After his swim and a shower, Packard sat down again with his yellow notepad and flipped back to the drawing he'd made earlier in the case. It had been four and a half weeks since Bill was shot on the Saturday of Labor Day weekend. It felt like a lot longer. When he realized in the next moment that there was the same amount of time between now and the election, the same four weeks felt like no time at all.

He looked at his drawing. Bill's name was at the center of the page with all his friends, coworkers, wives, poker buddies, and family grouped around him.

Packard had drawn dollar signs earlier and added them to the people connected to Bill with and without money. He added a new box for *Stolen Jewelry*, and he drew a separate box for *Hummingbird Pin*. Up by Margaret and John's names—Carrie, Sherri, and Mary's parents—he added *Sarah* and connected her to John and the hummingbird pin.

Earlier he'd listed *Money, Gambling, Theft*, and *Infidelity* as possible motives. Bill screwing his ex-wife didn't seem like an obvious motive. Sherri didn't have anyone in her life to make jealous, and Carrie seemed surprised by the news that the two of them were still intimate. Packard drew a line through *Infidelity*.

Gambling was a big part of Bill's life, but Packard hadn't been able to uncover anyone with a motive to kill Bill over moneys won or lost. It looked like Bill had tried to gamble his way to a big-enough stake to get his chicken restaurant going with Roger and lost his nut in the process. No one at Leon Chen's poker game had had any interest in Bill after they'd cleaned him out. He was invisible to them. Packard drew a line through *Gambling*.

The theft of the jewelry was information he didn't have when he first made this drawing. The stolen jewelry made this a burglary and a murder. But the killer's access into the house (through the sliding door in Bill's bedroom), the sequence of events (killer goes past Bill in bed, gets the jewelry out of the safe, then kills Bill) and the things not stolen (all of Bill's handguns in the same safe as the jewelry) almost made no sense. In some ways, the theft of the jewelry and Bill's murder felt incongruous, felt like they didn't belong together.

Sherri's letter said Carrie was the killer. Assuming for a minute that was true, what were Carrie's motives? It wasn't for Bill's money. He didn't have any. If she was unhappy in her marriage, why kill him? Why not just divorce him? They had no children. Bill would have had no claim to Carrie's pre-existing assets. At best, he might have been awarded temporary alimony.

Sherri said Carrie had accused her of plotting with Bill to kill her for the insurance money. The plan might have been to kill Carrie and steal the jewelry to make it look like she had walked in on the burglar in the act. Or what if this was really just supposed to be a jewelry theft and the murder was the unplanned event?

Packard scratched his beard and thought of one more thing missing from his sheet: the person who had taken a shot at him from the boat the night he was at Leon Chen's house. Was the same person who shot Bill Sandersen the one who'd tried to shoot him? They were two totally different settings, two totally different guns. There'd been no fingerprints on the casing retrieved from the abandoned boat. Something in Packard's gut told him the two were not connected. Shooting him might slow down the Sandersen investigation but it wouldn't stop it. It would do nothing to eliminate the evidence he'd collected. Maybe someone was using the unsolved Sandersen shooting as cover for their own intentions. Packard wrote *Boat Shooter* in the bottom corner of the page and circled it.

Packard looked at his diagram one last time. There were a lot of dollar signs by a lot of names. Money and the lack of money touched everything Bill had done. In the sequence of events, the first domino seemed to be taking the money out of the account he shared with Roger Freeman. After that was the big game at Leon Chen's. Sometime after that, Roger had confronted Bill about the missing money. Bill had assured him he had a plan to replace it. Then someone came to the house and killed Bill.

There was a plan. Bill had said as much to Roger. If Sherri wasn't in on it with him, who was? Had to be the killer. But if he and Bill were working together, how did Bill end up dead?

Packard tapped his pen beside Roger's name. Roger had been the first one he talked to. He knew more now than he did when they first talked. Packard decided it was time to talk to Roger again.

———————

Back to the dairy farm. He didn't bother calling ahead. Dairy farmers didn't take a lot of vacations from what Packard could tell, and he really didn't want Roger to have time to think about his answers.

The weather had changed a lot in a month. It was the season of long shadows and seeing your breath in the early mornings. Yellow leaves piled in drifts along the dirt driveway and blanketed the lawn in front of the white farmhouse. The smell of cows and cow manure was less strong than he remembered.

Roger must have seen him drive up. He came out of the house in a Carhartt coat and a black T-shirt stretched across his enormous belly and tucked into his jeans. He had yellow egg yolk in the corner of his mouth. Packard caught a whiff of bacon on the air.

"Hope I'm not interrupting your breakfast," he said.

Roger shook his head, repressed a belch, and thumbed the corner of his mouth. "Just finished. You figure out who killed Bill yet?"

"Not yet. I wanted to talk to you again about what else I've learned since day one. You have an office or somewhere we can sit?"

"Follow me," Roger said as he hitched up his pants.

They went to a wood-paneled office with a glass window on one wall that gave a view of the automated milking station. Roger had a laptop, two large-screen monitors, and an iPad on his desk. Ethernet cables snaked up a wall and disappeared into a hole in the drop ceiling. "Looks like you could mine Bitcoins with all this gear," Packard said as he had a seat.

"I wish. Milking cows is the least of what I do. A dairy farmer today has to be an IT manager, a data analyst, a regulatory specialist, a mechanical engineer, and a shit shoveler."

Packard flipped open his notebook and started to summarize the things he'd learned about Bill and those closest to him since he and Roger first met, including that Sherri had been the last one to see him the night he was killed and that five thousand dollars of the money Bill had deposited into their shared account came from his sister Wendy.

Roger looked annoyed by this news. "So more than half the money he put in came from someone else? He didn't tell me that."

Packard told Roger about Leon Chen and his friends cleaning out Bill at a private poker game, about the jewelry that was stolen and the guns that weren't. Roger sat slumped in his chair and stared down at his belly as he took it all in.

"We didn't know about the poker game the last time I was here," Packard said.

"Sure didn't."

"You confronted him about the money withdrawn from your business account about a month before he was killed. That would be early August. You said he told you then not to worry, that he had a plan."

"That's right."

"But that was after the poker game, which was early July. So..."

"So my best friend lied to me," Roger said. He looked wounded.

"You also said the last time we talked that you still trusted him even after he withdrew your money from the shared account."

"I did say that."

"Could he have taken more money out at that point if he wanted to?"

Roger shook his head and straightened up in his chair. "No. I guess I didn't trust the sonofabitch that much. We had agreed withdrawals of ten thousand dollars and under only required one signature. I called the bank and had them change it so all future withdrawals, regardless of the amount, required two signatures."

Packard wrote in his notebook. Something about the numbers confused him.

"You said before he took twenty thousand dollars out of the account."

"Yep."

"Without your signature."

Roger nodded and scratched his beard. "Yeah, I didn't think about that. I just saw the balance was twenty grand less than it should have been."

"So he must have made multiple withdrawals."

"He would have had to."

"Do you have the statement?"

Roger turned to one of his screens and began typing on his keyboard. "They don't mail you paper statements anymore, but I can look it up online. Give me a sec."

Packard went through his notes and reviewed the list of the key dates for the case. He had rough dates for when Roger noticed the money was missing and when he confronted Bill about it. When Packard asked Roger if there was any way to pin an exact date on the day he'd talked to Bill about the missing money, Roger remembered he'd gotten gas on the way to Bill and Carrie's house, so Packard had him look up the date on his credit card statement.

When they were done, he had a new list of dates that made him realize the mistake he'd made.

- First $10,000 withdrawal July 1.

- Poker game at Leon Chen's July 5.

- Second $10,000 withdrawal July 25.

- Roger gets emailed statement Aug 5.

- Roger confronts Bill Aug 6.

- Bill killed Sept 4.

"I screwed up," Packard admitted. "I didn't ask the right questions earlier. When you said he took twenty thousand dollars out of the account, I assumed he lost it all at Leon's, but he only took ten thousand dollars to the game. He didn't withdraw the other ten grand until almost three weeks after the game."

There was silence while they both pondered what that meant.

"Maybe he lost the first ten and got a note from someone for another ten so he could keep playing," Roger suggested.

"Maybe," Packard said. Even if it were true, it didn't make up for the fact that he'd failed to ask both Roger and Leon to confirm how much money was taken and lost and when. "I'll ask Leon for sure. I should have already done that. I made too many assumptions about the money."

"If he didn't lose the other ten thousand at the game..." Roger said.

"Then there's ten grand out there we haven't accounted for."

Roger leaned back in his chair and crossed his arms on top of his belly. "And that's what Bill was talking about when he said he had a plan."

What was the plan?

———————

They talked for a while longer about Bill and who might be in on a plan with him. "I mean...how many fools can one guy con? I thought we had a plan to open a legitimate business. Now I'm thinking it was all just a scheme to get into my wallet."

Packard tried to reassure Roger by telling him about the craigslist ad and Bill's visit to the old man with the deep-fat fryer. "I think he was serious about the restaurant," Packard offered. "What he was scheming was how to get the rest of his share of the money."

Roger thought about it but couldn't give Packard any other names. "Hell, everyone was his buddy when they were drinking at the bar and he and Sherri were flush and picking up the tab. How many of those people he could turn to for help... I can't think of one."

Packard asked Roger if he knew that Bill and Sherri were still sleeping together. "No, not like that. He didn't tell me anything about it. He knows I've always wanted to get married and have my own family, but it hasn't really happened. Too much work, not enough time, even less money. It's a special kind of woman who wants to be with a dairy farmer. I think maybe Bill would have thought he was rubbing things in my face having a wife and still sleeping with the ex-wife when I'm out here sharing a trailer with a Mexican fella."

The last thing Packard showed him was a photo on his phone of the anony- mous letter Sherri got in the mail. "What do you make of this?"

Roger read the note, shook his head a little, and handed Packard back his phone. "Did Carrie kill Bill? I don't know. That's your job to figure out. Would she or could she?" He shrugged and leaned back in his chair. It squealed with his shifting weight. "I think all those Gherlicks are used to getting what they want, regardless of the cost."

"Do you think Carrie wanted Bill dead?"

"I didn't before. But if she knew about him and Sherri—"

"That's just it. I don't think she did," Packard said. "She knows now, but I don't think she knew before he was killed."

"I don't know what to tell you, friend," Roger said. "I'm just a simple dairy farmer."

CHAPTER TWENTY

IT WAS AFTER LUNCH by the time Packard made it back to the station. He called Leon Chen from his desk and was able to quickly confirm that Bill lost ten thousand dollars at the poker game, plus a few hundred dollars in his wallet. No one offered to bankroll him so he could keep playing. "One of the guys said if I took a check from Bill, he would quit the game. He couldn't stand to see the guy lose any more of his money."

"Did you get your window fixed?" Packard asked.

"Not yet. It's custom. Three months to build and ship a new one."

"Anyone try to kill you again since that night?"

"No. I think they were aiming for you," Leon said.

Packard touched the small scar on the side of his face left from the flying glass. "You might be right. Thanks for the info, Leon."

Packard next went to Suresh's office. The digital forensics expert was taking screen grabs from a TikTok video of a guy standing beside an SUV, yelling at someone while lifting up his shirt to show a gun tucked into his waistband. He paused what he was doing when he saw Packard's reflection in the mirror taped to the corner of his monitor.

"I have a question about the Bill Sandersen murder," Packard said. "Did you find any payment apps on his phone? Venmo? PayPal? Anything like that? I'm looking for a ten-thousand-dollar transfer or payment or deposit somewhere."

Suresh rolled in his chair over to another computer and clicked until he brought up a folder with all the data from Bill's cell phone. He had screenshots of all the apps and a spreadsheet listing the name of the app and the log-in ID and password for all of them. He scrolled through the list. "No, nothing like that. He had a Wells Fargo app."

More clicking, more screenshots of Bill's transactions in his checking account going back ninety days. "He had a balance of $1,135 when he died," Suresh said. "I don't see any deposits for $10,000." Bill's shared account with Roger was not linked under the app. It was no excuse for not having confirmed the dates of the two separate withdrawals Bill had made. Packard was still kicking himself over such an obvious oversight. He should have been on top of this $10,000 a long time ago.

"I heard my immigration status was an issue in the candidates' forum," Suresh said as he started clicking windows closed.

"Yeah, I'm sorry you had to hear about that. It was a stupid thing for him to bring up."

"Him… Deputy Shepard, you mean. He said it."

Packard didn't want to slight an employee in front of another. But he could confirm facts. "He did."

"Do you think you will win the election?" Suresh asked. He pulled on the corner of his bushy black mustache and looked concerned.

"I think I have a chance. I'm going from here to the senior center to call bingo and hopefully convince a few of them to vote for me."

"Obviously I cannot vote, but I would vote for you if I could," Suresh said. "My wife and I are very grateful for the opportunity you have given us in Sandy Lake."

Packard put a hand on Suresh's shoulder. "I appreciate that. I'm sorry you got pulled into this. It's not fair to you to be used to score points in an election. It's the ugly side of American politics in action."

"It is just as bad in India," Suresh assured him.

"Regardless of what happens in the election, you have my support and the support of many others in the department. Even Deputy Shepard. He was coached to say what he did, and he did what he was told. Don't worry about it. You're doing a great job."

Suresh nodded and put his headphones back on. Packard went back to his office and called Sherri to ask her if Bill had mentioned anything about the ten grand. After five rings, her voicemail picked up. He texted her to call him the first chance she got.

He called Max and Sharon at Davis's Deep Cleaning. He'd recognized their handiwork the last time he'd been at Carrie's house with her to walk through the events of the night Bill was killed. He got Sharon on the phone. "You guys didn't find ten thousand dollars when you were cleaning up the Bill Sandersen scene, did you?"

"Oh gosh, no," Sharon said. "That would have been in our report. Have you seen it?"

"I haven't yet. I'll find the report and take a look. Thanks, Sharon."

He was running out of people to call. He turned to his computer and made notes in the case file and went through his mail until it was time to change clothes and leave for the senior center.

He got there early because he'd been warned not to be late. "You want to cause a riot, start the bingo game two minutes late and see what happens," the activities director, a woman in her fifties with big owl-shaped glasses, warned him. "They'll burn your house down."

A dozen of his supporters were there in matching PACKARD FOR SHERIFF T-shirts, same as the one he was wearing. He saw Gary Bushwright and Marilyn Shaw and his neighbor, Bert, in the crowd.

His real person on the inside was Olivia McDonald, who he had met last spring and taken for a drive around Sandy Lake in his patrol vehicle, then out to

Gary's when he picked up his dog for the first time. She was waiting for him by the door. She took his arm and pulled him this way and that, introducing him to everyone she knew and whispering gossip about them as they walked away. *Drinks. Four ex-husbands. Grandson is in jail in Fargo.*

Campaigning was teaching Packard new things about himself. On and off the job, when interacting with people he didn't know, he wore the same stoic expression, had the same calm demeanor, and engaged only as much as the situation required. Part of it was about establishing authority and part of it was maintaining a separation between his public and private selves. Lately, out in the community as a candidate for a job rather than the person doing the job, he found he was able to relax, to smile more, to learn about people and their interests in a way that had nothing to do with gathering evidence or establishing facts or solving a crime. He listened and shared his ideas and opened up about himself, and hopefully proved to people he wasn't a robot in a brown uniform that plugged itself into a charging station at night. Campaigning was really just getting to know people and what was important to them.

He wasn't putting it all on the table, not by any means. There were people who knew absolutely nothing about him who asked if he was married or had kids, questions he was happy to answer rather than explain. At a church carnival last week, a trio of ladies had come up to where he was helping to sell raffle tickets for a donated quilt. The ringleader of the bunch asked, "Is it true that you prefer the company of men?"

Packard shrugged, gave them his best smile, and said, "Depends on the man. Am I right?" Two of the old ladies laughed and one looked like she hadn't heard the question or the answer. They all bought raffle tickets and went on their way.

Eventually Packard led Olivia to the chair saved for her by her granddaughter and took his spot at the front of the room with a microphone and a wire cage full of wooden balls. He didn't know any bingo jokes so he tried to think of funny stories from his career in law enforcement. "You'd be surprised how many people are buck naked when the cops show up," he said. "I want to thank you all for choosing to wear clothes today."

Later, he told them about the time he responded to an overturned tanker truck that had spilled milk all over the interstate in Minneapolis. "Do you know what they use to clean up a truck full of spilled milk?" he asked. "A truck full of Oreos."

More groans than laughs on that one.

He called three games, talked a little bit about his priorities for the sheriff's department, then turned things over to the activities director for the blackout round. He took a seat in the back with his own card for the last game.

"We've had vandalism on some of your signs," Gary whispered as he dabbed his card. "Do you want to see?"

He did and he didn't. Gary took out his phone and showed him a photo of half a dozen of his yard signs in the back of a truck. They'd all been marked in heavy black ink to read FUDGE PACKARD FOR SHERIFF

This was more along the lines of what he'd been expecting. Attacks based on his sexuality. Crude and anonymous. The old ladies at the church carnival at least had the guts to ask him about it right to his face. "That's pretty funny. And a good reminder never to run for judge," he said and gave Gary his phone back.

"I grabbed all the ones I could find. We've got extras, honey, so don't worry about it. I'll get new ones out," Gary said.

Packard forgot to mark his card as he thought about someone vandalizing his signs. He felt the slightest leak in the balloon of self-confidence he'd inflated.

His phone vibrated in his pocket, snapping him back to the activities room and the smell of popcorn and ink daubers and arthritis cream. The screen said DISPATCH, so he stood and stepped out of the room.

"Sheriff, we've got a DOA. Subject is female with trauma to the head, no pulse, and cold to the touch. Medical is in route. Deputies are requesting a supervisor."

"What's the address?"

He knew exactly where it was.

CHAPTER TWENTY-ONE

PACKARD LOOKED THROUGH THE sliding glass door into the living room of Sherri Sandersen's condo. She was on her back on the floor near the couch. The blood on the carpet beneath her misshapen head looked like a shadow. She was wearing a white blouse and a black skirt—the same clothes Packard had last seen her in when he dropped her off at work the night before.

He'd come right from the bingo game, a black jacket that said SHERIFF on the back zipped up over his campaign T-shirt. In minutes he'd gone from being energized by the work he'd been doing to get elected to feeling like the whole process was meaningless and tasteless. He was wearing a shirt with his name on it in giant letters, like *Packard* was a product or a slogan. It made him feel like a dancing clown as he stared at the dead face of someone he used to know.

The murder weapon was on the floor next to Sherri—a large stone bowl with three pointed feet, all carved from a single piece of volcanic rock. The words *Cabo San Lucas* were etched on the side. Most people would use a pestle to grind spices or mash guacamole in a molcajete like this. Sherri had used hers as a giant ashtray. Someone else had used it to smash her skull.

"Neighbor spotted her when she peeked through the window," Shepard said.

"What brought the neighbor over?"

"Uh…she said she sometimes got weed from Sherri. She was hoping to get more. She and her boyfriend are going to a concert."

"She just came out and told you that?"

"Yeah, she don't give a shit."

"Anyone see or hear anything?"

"Nothing so far," Shepard said. "She's the end unit. The neighbors next door are out of town. This is an older complex. There's no security cameras. I sent Reynolds around to check for video doorbells. Not a one."

A technician from the hospital came in through the front door wearing shoe covers and black gloves. She checked the temperature on the thermostat next to the bedroom door, then squatted next to the corpse and opened her case. Packard found something else to look at while the technician raised Sherri's shirt, made a small incision in her abdomen, and inserted a probe to check the temperature of her liver.

"Anybody check the restaurant to see what time she left?"

"They closed at eleven and she got a ride home from the bartender. Name is Kristie Capote," Shepard said. "Kristie thinks it was close to midnight when she dropped off Sherri."

Shepard said the front door was unlocked when he tried it after arriving on the scene. He'd checked the body for a pulse, secured the scene, then kept everyone out while dispatch called Packard.

The sun had nearly set. Packard noticed the living room lights were on. "Did you turn the lights on or were they already on?"

"Already on," Shepard said.

"Lights on, still in her work clothes. She was killed early this a.m. if she got home at midnight. I don't need a liver probe to tell me that," Packard said. "No signs of forced entry on the front door or this slider. The killer had a key or the door was unlocked or Sherri knew this person well enough to let them in her house after midnight."

He looked past the body and noticed a box on the dining room table between the couch and the pass-through window to the tiny kitchen. The lid was open, the interior lined in gray fabric. The shape and the color of the box were meaningful to Packard.

"Pretty sure that's the jewelry box that was stolen from the gun safe the night Bill Sandersen was killed." Carrie had provided photos of most of the stolen jewelry but she didn't have a photo of the jewelry box itself. She'd described it in her report as vintage with cut corners and beveled edges, made from green and brown woods, about sixteen inches by twelve inches. The exact size and shape Packard was looking at now.

He thought of Sherri swearing to God in his truck that she wasn't in on any plan of Bill's against Carrie. Now he was looking at the jewelry box stolen during a crime Sherri had claimed to know nothing about. Maybe the missing ten thousand dollars had gone to her after all. Packard had called earlier that morning to ask her about it, but she was already dead.

Packard wanted to talk to Carrie right then. He didn't know if he wanted to make sure she was okay or ask where she was last night.

He and Shepard walked around the side of Sherri's end unit as the crime-scene van was pulling into the lot.

"You owe Suresh an apology for what you said during the candidate forum," Packard said to his deputy.

Shepard dropped his head and examined his belly. "That was just politics. I didn't mean anything by it."

"That doesn't make it okay. It's actually worse, Shepard. You're telling me you don't stand behind the things you say. No conviction. Just noise. You showed disrespect for a member of our team. If you win the election, you can bad-mouth your people in public all you want. You haven't won yet. Apologize to Suresh. I'm not asking you. I'm telling you."

He tried all of the numbers he had for Carrie—her cell, her mom's house, the house where she'd lived with Bill. A cold dread came over him with each unanswered ring.

He kept calling as he drove to Margaret's house on the lake. Outside of the city limits, he turned on his flashers and picked up speed. Carrie's husband had been shot, her sister bludgeoned. He had no idea about what he was rushing toward.

It was dark by the time he pulled into the driveway. The lights were on inside Margaret's house. He saw someone's shadow move behind drawn blinds.

He banged on the door and yelled Carrie's name. She answered wearing a pink turtleneck, with a dish towel over one shoulder. She looked surprised to see him.

"What happened?" she asked.

Packard just stared at her. He was irrationally angry at her for not answering her phone and not being dead.

"Do you want to come in?" she asked.

Packard nodded and she held the door open and he stepped inside. "I tried calling," he said. "All your numbers."

"Mom has been in a state today. Ringing phones just make it worse. The aide and I have struggled with her all day."

"I'm sorry to hear that," Packard said. "I'm afraid my news isn't going to improve things."

He paused, watching for any kind of reaction from Carrie that would give away that she already knew what had happened to her sister. Her expression stayed blank with just a hint of concern.

"Sherri is dead," he said. "Someone killed your sister."

Carrie gave him the look he was getting used to by now. Stunned, mouth slightly open, big eyes that invited him to fill the silence. He waited.

"The same person who killed Bill?"

"We don't know that yet. We're still collecting evidence and trying to piece together what happened."

Carrie put her hands on either side of her nose and shook her head. "I told you, didn't I? I had a feeling she was involved in this somehow. She and Bill mixed with a bad element. I had no idea I was putting myself so close to danger by being married to him."

Packard thought it was curious how Carrie saw herself as the victim when they were now dealing with two dead bodies. "I met with Sherri just hours before she was killed," Packard said. "She showed me a letter she got in the mail from someone accusing you of killing Bill."

Carrie moved further into the house and Packard followed. "I saw the letter," she said over her shoulder. "She came over here earlier in the day and shoved it in my face, like she'd caught me in the act of something."

Packard took out his phone and showed her a picture he'd taken of the jewelry box before leaving Sherri's. "Is this your jewelry box?"

Carrie looked shocked. "Yes! Where did you find it?"

"It's on the dining room table at Sherri's house."

"Of course, it is. Did you find the jewelry, too?"

Packard shook his head.

"Well, I think it's obvious that she had to be behind the phony letter."

"Why would she send herself a phony letter?"

"To deflect attention!" Carrie's tone made it sound like she couldn't understand how she had figured this out and he hadn't. She hung the dish towel on the oven handle, then leaned close to him to look at his phone screen again.

"Sherri told me you told her that you think you were the intended victim the night Bill was killed."

"I think it more every day, now that it's becoming obvious those two were conspiring behind my back," Carrie said.

Packard wasn't sure he'd call Sherri screwing her ex-husband in his truck a conspiracy, but he could see how Carrie might think that was the least of what those two were up to together. Especially now that the jewelry box had been found in Sherri's house.

"I know Bill had life insurance on me through the dealership. It was a benefit that came with the job. If I was killed, he'd get enough money to set up his chicken restaurant, he could get back together with Sherri, and they could go back to their old ways. Drinking and gambling and I don't know what else."

"If that was the plan, it went terribly off the rails seeing as how they're now the dead ones."

"There had to be someone else in on it with them. A third party who turned against them for whatever reason. What other possibility is there?"

Packard could see that she regretted the question as soon as the words were out of her mouth. He answered it for her anyway.

"The other possibility is that you're the third party."

"Then who sent the letter?" Carrie asked. "A fourth party? How many people are at this party? I've got nothing to gain and everything to lose by murdering those two, Detective. I've got no motive."

"Hatred can be a motive," Packard suggested.

Carrie looked at something on her wrist and pulled her sleeve lower. "I didn't hate my sister or my husband. Sherri—both of my sisters, for that matter—have been jealous of me my whole life. I was the baby, the prettiest one, the spoiled one. Bad feelings in this family have always been aimed at me, not the other way around."

"Where were you last night?"

"Here with Mom."

"Your mom isn't the best alibi," Packard informed her.

"You don't need to tell me after the day I've had," Carrie said. "She just gets more and more confused."

"So you didn't leave the house at all last night."

"I didn't," Carrie insisted.

Packard just nodded. Sherri, maybe Carrie too, had been playing him since day one. He didn't like it. He didn't like not knowing who was putting on the bigger act. Carrie was giving him helpful daughter and Minnesota mom, but every once in a while he felt like he was glimpsing something behind her mask.

"If there's still a third party or even a fourth party out there, I want a deputy outside your place to keep an eye on things."

Carrie nodded helpfully. "Of course. I'm more worried about Mom than myself. But why would anyone come after me now? What's to be gained by kill-ing me? Not the life insurance."

"You're assuming this guy is acting rationally."

"I appreciate the protection," Carrie said. "I'll start making arrangements for Sherri. At least I know the protocol now. Same as it was with Bill."

Packard nodded and said good night to the only named suspect he had in the murders of Bill and Sherri Sandersen. He found it interesting that he hadn't told her how Sherri was killed or when or where and Carrie hadn't bothered to ask. She either knew or she didn't care. Still, you couldn't arrest someone for not being curious.

Back in his vehicle, he requested a deputy out to his current location to door-knock around the neighborhood and ask about any late-night traffic from the night before. He'd lied to Carrie about his reasoning for parking a deputy outside her house. It wasn't as much for her protection as it was to keep an eye on her.

CHAPTER TWENTY-TWO

PACKARD'S INTERNAL ALARM WOULDN'T let him sleep much beyond 6:30 a.m., even when that meant he'd had less than five hours of rest. He was too tired to swim so he showered and spent extra time making breakfast. Eggs scrambled with sausage, broccoli, and cheese, topped with chipotle salsa. He'd missed most of his meals yesterday and felt like he could skin and eat a raw rabbit.

Frank watched from his dog bed in the living room, still sulking after being kept in the house all day the day before. A dog door that went out to the garage gave him access to an artificial grass pad he'd been trained to use on the days Packard couldn't get home. Frank had used it, but he wasn't happy about it. Packard didn't blame him. It was undignified.

They went for a long walk after breakfast. Dark clouds brought the sky low. A cold wind blew air that was heavy with moisture. It was the kind of weather that could bring snow without warning, like a crowd turning violent.

Sherri had died from blunt force trauma sometime between midnight and 2:00 a.m. There were no other marks on her body indicating there'd been any kind of struggle. She'd been hit from behind, then again from the front. They took scrapings under her fingernails but didn't have much hope.

He led Frank around to the back of the house and threw the tennis ball for him for another twenty minutes while he made a plan for the day. He still needed to track down the other ten thousand dollars Bill had taken from the shared account with Roger. He and another deputy had done a cursory search of Sherri's condo last night but turned up nothing. No cash. No sign of the stolen jewelry that had once been in the box.

Packard put Frank back in the house and headed for town. He'd been chasing this case for over a month and the questions, not to mention the body count, had only grown. He couldn't help feel like it wouldn't hurt his chances of getting elected if he could come up with a few answers before the first Tuesday in November.

He wanted to retrace all his steps since the earlier days of the case. Talking to Roger again had revealed that there had been two withdrawals from his shared account with Bill, not just one. Proof that it paid to question people again in light of new information.

He drove by MarketFoods on the edge of town, remembered Bill's sister Wendy worked there, and made a hard turn across oncoming traffic. The lot seemed full for a weekday morning, a sure sign of snow in the forecast. Everyone was stocking up.

He went to the service desk where they sold cigarettes and lottery tickets and asked an old woman in a blue smock if Wendy was working. She tilted her head back and to the side. "She's in the bakery."

Packard walked up the sodas and diapers aisle (an odd combination, he always thought) and found Wendy behind a glass case filled with grocery-store doughnuts and cupcakes and loaves of bread. It all had a vaguely artificial look to it, like it had been 3D-printed from sugar and plasticizers.

Wendy looked hopeful at the sight of him, like he might have good news for her, which he told her right away that he didn't. "I told you last time about the money your brother took from the shared account he had with Roger Freeman. There's ten thousand dollars unaccounted for. Did he tell you about buying anything big? Did you notice any large purchases?"

"No and no. We didn't see each other all that often. I doubt that I would have noticed or known anything like that."

"And he didn't pay you back any of the money you invested?"

"He most certainly did not." She looked offended, like he'd just accused her of lying.

"Sorry. I had to ask just to be certain."

"I would tell you anything and everything you want to know, especially if it would help find his killer. The only person I could think of he'd give it to would be Sherri."

"I'm still looking into that possibility," Packard said. He stepped aside and let a woman ask Wendy for six glazed doughnuts. He pondered for a moment whether to tell her that Sherri had been killed but decided it wasn't the time or place to tell her that her former sister-in-law was dead. It would be news soon enough.

"I'm glad to know you're still looking into things," Wendy said as she reached into the case with a piece of waxed paper and grabbed the doughnuts. "I hadn't heard anything for a few weeks. I was worried maybe you had given up."

"I don't give up," Packard assured her.

Winder Watersports was his next stop. Ronnie Winder, with his fine straight hair and wormy mustache, wasn't much help. Packard asked him if he knew of any outstanding gambling debts Bill had or if there were any other games Bill played in outside of the casino. Ronnie didn't know of either.

"I only knew him to play at the casino. He wasn't a guy who was always looking for a game," Ronnie said. "I think Leon Chen was a desperate swing at building back his bank."

"He didn't give you ten thousand dollars to hold for him, did he?"

Ronnie laughed. "Bill wasn't the smartest guy in the world, but he was smarter than that."

Packard flipped his notebook shut, thanked Ronnie.

Ronnie said, "Even though you busted my balls pretty good about Leon's poker game, you've got my vote for sheriff. Anyone who's spent five minutes with Shepard knows that guy has no business being in charge of things."

"I appreciate it, Ronnie. Thank you," Packard said. "If you can think of anything else about Bill I should know, call me."

He made his way across the street to Sandy Lake Auto, where Bill used to work. Stephen, Bill's balding, walrus-looking boss, had someone in his office when Packard arrived so he killed time wandering the lot, peeking through windows, and sitting inside a few of the cars. The temperature felt like it was dropping by the minute. He got behind the wheel of a black Audi A8 L, all leather interior, driver assistance, every bell and whistle imaginable. It was three years old with seventeen thousand miles on it. The window sticker said $69,900.

Not on this salary. Not even on the full sheriff's salary.

He went back inside just as sandy bits of snow started to come down. Stephen's office was empty but the door was open, so Packard went inside and had a seat. Stephen came in a few minutes later, his hands still wet from the bathroom. He waved instead of shaking hands.

"Any news on Bill?"

"Not much," Packard said. "I came back again to see if I could uncover anything I might have missed the first time around."

"What are you thinking?"

"There's ten thousand dollars that I can't account for. I noticed Bill's truck had a Sandy Lake Auto plate mount. I assume he bought it here."

"He did. A few months after he started working here. There's a ninety-day trial period before new hires get full benefits. He bought it with his employee discount and traded in something. I don't remember what."

"How long ago was that?"

"A year, at least."

"Did he finance it through you?"

"We offer financing through a number of banks or credit unions. There's no employee benefit, really, when it comes to financing."

Packard thought for a minute where else Bill could have spent ten thousand dollars in relation to work. Had to be something that would make it worth stealing from his best friend. He doubted Bill had used the money to pump up his health savings account or retirement fund.

"I'd like to talk to the mechanics again. His cigarette buddies," Packard said. He had to flip back though his notebook to find their names. "Ryan and... Paul."

"Ryan is off this week. Took his girlfriend on a cruise. I expect him to come back engaged. Paul's gone. I got two mechanics back there right now trying to do the job of four. I have a new guy scheduled to start next month."

"Paul quit or...?"

"He provided false documentation when we hired him. Katherine was getting things organized for next year's benefits and taxes and couldn't verify his social security number through the online system. He insisted the number was correct, said he'd come back the next day with his actual card. We never saw him again. Calls to the number we had for him went unreturned. He just...vanished."

Packard felt a tingle at the base of his spine, an almost erotic buzz that made him sit taller in his chair.

"I need to talk to Katherine," Packard said.

———

He found her in her cube, same white plastic glasses and pretty face. She wore a long beige cardigan over a white blouse and black leggings. "I saw you wandering the lot out there," she said when he looked over the wall of her cube and said hi. "That Audi is a nice car."

"I was just waiting to talk to Stephen. He was telling me about the mechanic who quit. Paul."

Katherine frowned and leaned to one side as she pulled a foot under her. "If that's his real name."

"Tell me what happened again."

She repeated what Stephen had told him about the invalid social security number. "I thought I had typed it in wrong, but he insisted the number was correct. I asked him to bring in his card if he had it, and he said sure, no problem. And then he was gone. He lost about a week's worth of wages."

"How long did he work here?"

"About nine months."

"I need everything you have on him in your records," Packard said. "Local address, phone numbers, driver's license, date of birth, etc."

Packard was trying to remember details about Paul from their one and only meeting. He was older. Looked like he'd led a rough life. "Do you have a photo of him?"

"Yes. All hourly employees have badges that they use to swipe the time clock. The badges have their photo on them."

"Send me the digital file for his photo if you can." He gave her his card that had his numbers and email on it. It reminded him that she had slyly given him her card the last time he was here, with her personal phone number on the back and the invitation to call. They both let it pass unremarked.

"Remember anything unique about Paul?" Packard asked.

"He had a lot of tattoos," Katherine said. "He had to wear long sleeves because one of them was of a naked lady. Stephen insisted he keep them covered up. The one I remember, though, was on the palm of his hand."

"Dice," Packard said.

"That's it."

"I saw it when he was smoking a cigarette the last time I was here."

"Does all this have something to do with Bill?" Katherine asked.

"I don't know yet."

She promised he'd have everything in his email before he got back to the office. He thanked her and was just out the door and into the cold when he suddenly had another question.

"Me again," he said over the top of her cube. "Did Paul buy a vehicle while he was here?"

"Let me check," Katherine said. She clicked and opened windows and typed something. Eventually she said, "Yes. He bought a truck that we bought as a trade-in from someone else. A Mazda B series that was about fifteen years old."

"What's the date on that?"

"July twenty-ninth."

Packard flipped through his notes. Four days after Bill made the second withdrawal from the shared account.

"Does it say how he paid for it?"

She ran a finger down her screen. "The total to him with this employee discount was eleven thousand five hundred dollars. He paid with ten thousand cash and a bank check for the rest."

Bingo.

A warm feeling washed over Packard. He felt like he was being lowered into a steaming bath of the truth. Katherine looked startled by the grin on his face. "Send me everything you have on him and his truck," Packard said and headed for the door again.

———————

At his desk half an hour later, he studied the color photo of Paul Brewer that Katherine had sent him from the dealership's employee files. Short gray hair, unshaven, shadows under his eyes, and deep lines around his mouth. No smile. He looked guarded, like he didn't like his photo being taken, like he knew already that this would be used against him eventually. It looked like a mug shot.

Katherine had sent along an employment application Paul Brewer had filled out in jagged letters with a lefty lean and a scan of an Iowa driver's license that Packard was fairly confident was fake. He tried calling the phone number listed on the application and got a message that it was no longer in service. The address was in town, practically walking distance from where he was sitting now.

He pulled up the vehicle registration database and found that the truck

Paul had purchased had yet to be registered. It had been more than sixty days, so he was already in violation of the law on that.

He next looked in the federal database of known felons. No match on Paul Brewer with the DOB on his driver's license. He looked for Paul Brewer, no DOB, found several but none that matched his guy. Same with just searching the date of birth.

In a biometric database maintained by the FBI he was able to search for tattoos using keywords. Dice returned a lot of results. Dice on the palm cut it down to just a few. A few clicks and he was staring at his man.

Paul Bowers. Fifty-three years old. Arrested in Kansas City and sentenced in 2003 for aggravated robbery of a liquor store. The owner was armed and fired in self-defense. Paul shot his own gun, but no one was injured. Firearm possession and discharge charges were pled down. Paul served twelve years of an eighteen-year sentence in a Missouri state prison. Packard saw Paul's booking photo and a significantly aged man in his release photo, which didn't look much different than the picture Katherine had sent him.

Now he had a real name, date of birth, and social security number that he could put through every database there was. Paul was granted parole and released to his family in Harmony, Iowa. He maintained a residence there for two years before registering another address with his parole office, this one in Des Moines. He maintained fairly steady employment at quick-lube oil-change places and then as an auto mechanic after getting a two-year technical degree. After a year in Des Moines, he completed the obligations of his parole and was cut loose. Sometime after that, he had shown up in Sandy Lake.

Packard got the number for Paul's first parole officer, the one he was with longer than the one in Des Moines, left a message, and got a return phone call ten minutes later.

"You remember a Paul Bowers? Convicted of armed robbery. Lived in Harmony, Iowa?"

"Oh yeah, Paul wasn't that long ago. What's he done?" The officer's last name as Hutchins. Packard imagined a round, red-faced man, based on the effort it took for Hutchins to breathe between short sentences.

"I don't know," Packard admitted. "Maybe nothing. He's floating on the periphery of a couple of murders we've had. He used a phony name and SSN to get a job. I found him and his tattoos in the database."

"Dice on the palm."

"Exactly. He's in the wind right now. Trying to find out what I can about him."

"Paul was one of those guys. Who went through the motions. To prove he'd been reformed," Hutchins wheezed. "I always got the sense. There was anger at the core of him. That never went away. Know what I mean?"

"I know the type," Packard said.

"You've seen his sheet. He's pulled a trigger before. Wouldn't take much for him to do it again."

"What about his family? Still around?"

"His mother died a while back. About the time he moved to Des Moines, if I remember. His dad went into a home after that. Not sure his current status. I can try to find out for you."

"I'd appreciate that," Packard said.

"I looked up Sandy Lake in the Google," Hutchins said. "You guys got snow up there yet?"

"It's cold and spitting today," Packard said. "Supposed to have a few inches by tomorrow morning."

"I'd love to get up that way and do some ice fishing."

"Let me know if you do," Packard said. "I'll tell you where to go."

The property owner of the address, Paul Brewer, a.k.a. Paul Bowers, listed on his employment application was Phyllis Egan. The house was once a tiny 1950s bungalow. At some point, a two-story addition with all the architectural elegance of a cereal box was added to the back. The whole house was clad in white siding and had fewer windows than it should have.

Phyllis answered the door when he rang the bell. She was the size of a large doll and dressed in four or five layers with a heavy green sweater on top. She kept the storm door closed between them.

Packard introduced himself and told her was looking for Paul Brewer. "I was told this was where he lived."

"Not anymore he doesn't," Phyllis said. "He rented from me for a few months, then moved out."

Packard had expected as much. "Would it be possible to see where he stayed?"

"There's not much to see. It's just a space in the basement," Phyllis said. She looked unhappy about the request. "I didn't charge much for it."

He could tell she was worried he was going to cite her for something—code violations or lack of a rental license. "Phyllis, I'd just like to see where he stayed and ask you a few questions about him. That's all."

"Go around to the side," she said and closed the front door on him.

A minute later, she let him into a tiny entryway with a linoleum floor and two other doors. One went to the house. The other down to the basement. They had to do a dance of doors opening and bodies moving and doors closing before they could both start down a set of stairs covered in cheap carpeting that was fraying at the edges. The basement reeked of cigarette smoke and dampness. The furnace was on, but Packard had a feeling Phyllis probably kept it under sixty degrees during the winter, based on all the layers she was wearing.

The ceiling was low enough that he had to stay hunched over. A forest of floor jacks and four-by-four timbers spanning the overhead floor joists kept the upper floors from falling down on them. He saw whitewashed cement walls fissured with large cracks and stained by seeping moisture.

An old washer and dryer shared a corner at the bottom of the stairs. They went around the furnace and came to a door in a wood-paneled wall. Inside was a small room with the same concrete floor as the rest of the basement. The walls had been painted a terra-cotta orange. Furnishings were a twin bed, a night table, and a blue rocking recliner with a towel tucked around the bottom cushion, probably to hide a rip or a stain. A doorway with no door opened to a bathroom with a toilet and plastic shower insert. All the plumbing was exposed. Packard didn't see any source of ventilation besides a small transom window that looked painted shut.

The low ceiling and thin mattress made Packard feel like he was standing in a prison cell. Maybe to someone who had spent time in an actual prison, like Paul had, it felt like an upgrade. "When did Paul contact you about renting this space?" Packard asked, trying to keep the judgment out of his voice.

Phyllis had to think for a minute and count back on her fingers. "It was March. I let him move in the last week of March but didn't charge him rent until April."

"How would he have found out about it?"

"I have flyers around town. Sometimes I put a little ad in the *Gazette* if I have the funds."

"And when did he move out?"

"Was somewhere in July. After the fourth for sure. One day he was here, the next he was gone. Never saw or heard from him again."

This surprised Packard. He was expecting her to say September since that was when Paul disappeared from his job at the dealership. He'd found somewhere else to live before he quit his job. What that meant for his current whereabouts was an open question. Would he have a reason to stick around for the last month with no job? If so, what was the reason?

Phyllis was looking more forlorn the longer they stood there. She found a tissue in the front pocket of her sweater and wiped her nose.

"Did you spend much time with Paul?"

"Dinner is included with the rent because I can cook for two just as easily as cooking for one. He had to shop and make his own breakfast and lunch. He had full use of the kitchen upstairs. Sometimes he'd sit at the table and we'd have dinner."

"What did you talk about?"

"He asked me a lot of questions about Sandy Lake. How long I'd lived here. My husband was in sales for a long time. Home medical equipment. Life insurance. Liquor sales. He was on the road all the time. We opened a little five-and-dime store downtown that I ran for about a dozen years."

An old memory from Packard's childhood rose to the surface like a trapped air bubble. "Egan's Five and Dime," he said. The words came out almost involuntarily.

Phyllis brightened. "You remember it?"

"I spent summers here as a kid. You had plastic tubs of Bazooka Joe and jawbreakers and taffy by the register. Five cents each," Packard said. He remembered combing the aisles with his two brothers and sister; all the things sealed in plastic with a card at the top that allowed it to hang from a hook. Squirt guns and soap bubbles and rubber balls and coloring books. He remembered fondue sets and candles in glass jars with pictures of saints on them and a mishmash of holiday decorations always on display in a jumble in the back. Nick, his oldest brother, had liked to look at the magazines and wire racks of paperbacks for something he hadn't read before.

And then this: he and his sister, Anne, had gone in once with a plan to steal something. They came out with a pen that wrote in shiny silver ink for her and a package of Big League Chew gum for him. He remembered the guilt eating away at him and the fear that someone was going to ask him where he got the money to buy the gum. He'd put a wad in his mouth and thrown the rest away—the first and only time he'd ever destroyed evidence.

Phyllis said, "The store never made us much money. I had to close it eventually. My husband died of a heart attack at fifty-two. I've been trying to get by on a life insurance policy and his social security for a long time. I told Paul I needed someone who was planning to stay through the winter. He said, 'Oh yeah. I'll be here that long.' Now I've got no renter and no extra money coming in."

The thought of a human being living down here—whether he was a rehabbed felon or a current murder suspect—darkened Packard's mood. That an old woman needed to find someone to live like this to help pay her heating bill hurt him even more.

"What else can you tell me about Paul?"

"I don't know what else to say. He didn't talk about himself much. I think he said he was from Iowa."

"Did he say what brought him to town?"

"Not that I remember. He was working at the used car place. I assumed it was the job."

"Did he have any visitors? Get any mail?"

"None. Neither," Phyllis said.

"Did he leave anything behind when he left?"

"No, he barely had any possessions to begin with. I had to give him sheets for the bed. I think everything he owned fit inside a few boxes that he had in the trunk of his car."

"What kind of car was it?"

"I don't know about cars. It was white. Rusty in spots. Four doors."

He'd moved out before he bought the Mazda truck, which lined up with the dates Packard knew about when Bill had withdrawn the money.

Packard opened the drawer in the nightstand and lifted the mattress. In the bathroom he looked inside the toilet tank. The bowl had a seat but no lid. He noticed that the plunger sitting right beside it was the exact same orangish color as the walls. It was one depressing detail too many.

"You didn't say why you're looking for Paul," Phyllis said, wiping her nose again. "He didn't rob the bank, did he?"

"No, the bank hasn't been robbed. One of his coworkers was—" Packard stopped midsentence. "Why did you ask if he robbed the bank?"

"It just came back to me that he was very curious about the bank downtown. How old was it? Who ran it? When did it become a Wells Fargo? Not the kind of stuff a bank robber would ask but I remember we talked about the bank and the Gherlicks on a couple of different nights. I told him what I know about the Gherlick family since they were the ones to open and run it for a long time. John Gherlick gave me and my husband the loan to open the five-and-dime."

Packard felt gears in his brain slipping as they tried to catch. If Paul had an interest in the bank—a bank owned at one time by the Gherlick family—then his connection to this case wasn't just from working at the same place as Bill Sandersen.

Packard needed to get out of Phyllis's basement suddenly, and it had nothing to do with the smell of cigarettes or the low ceilings. He said, "Phyllis, you've been a big help." He took out his wallet. He had two twenties inside. "My sister and I stole a pen and some gum from your store when we were kids. I'm sorry. I hope this makes up for it."

Phyllis looked stunned by the offer, but she took the money and stuffed it into the pocket of her sweater. "I accept your apology," she said. "I might even vote for you now."

The freezing sleet had tapered off without accumulating or sticking to anything, but it was colder and grayer than earlier. Packard sat in his vehicle in front of Phyllis's house with the heat on while he checked his email and messages.

Hutchins, the parole officer in Iowa, had already gotten back to him. Paul's dad—Arthur Bowers—was alive and living in a nursing home in Van Grove, Iowa. Hutchins had talked to a member of the staff. "She said Arthur still has his marbles and can carry on a conversation about most things. He doesn't get a lot of visitors. Another old man comes to see him sometimes to play cards. She doesn't recall seeing a son or anyone else in the last year or so."

Packard looked up Van Grove, Iowa, on his phone and found it was a seven-hour drive from Sandy Lake. He could call and try to interview the old man over the phone, but he felt the urge to go down there and see him in person. The situation warranted the extra effort. Before today, Bill was the nucleus at the center of all the objects orbiting this case. Since talking to

Katherine and Phyllis, he felt everything shifting to spin around Paul. Who was this guy?

Packard called Thielen. "Can you clear your calendar?"

"Depends on what for," she said.

"I want to drive to Iowa, and I could use the company and a second set of eyes and ears. The Bill Sandersen case feels like it's about to roll over and show its belly."

"When do we leave?"

"In an hour," Packard said.

"You don't have any campaign events tonight, do you?"

"No. I think there's something this weekend."

"OK. Pick me up at the house," Thielen said.

———

It was a three-hour drive just to get to Minneapolis. On the way down, they talked about the campaign and Packard's chances of winning. No one was doing any scientific polling of the Sandy Lake County electorate to find out how they were going to vote for sheriff, so all they had to go on were feelings and tea leaves.

"I think you're going to take it," Thielen said. She wasn't known for being overly optimistic, which made Packard want to believe her. Easier said than done.

"I don't know," he said. "I think it's a toss-up. It shouldn't be. But I think it is."

Thielen was scrolling through her phone in the passenger seat. She'd dressed in track pants and an Adidas hoodie for the ride down. "Too bad it's not going to be decided based purely on how hard Marilyn has worked. If it was, it would be a landslide in your favor."

"I wish she would take it easy," Packard said. "I probably don't know half of what she's been up to."

"You're right, you don't," Thielen said. "Did I tell you she called Ray Hanson and threatened his advertisers?"

"I did not hear about that." The *Gazette* had endorsed Shepard, as expected, but Packard had been happy to see a good number of letters supporting him appear on the editorial page. It probably made Ray feel like he was shitting pine cones to print them.

"She told Ray if she didn't see an equal number of letters in support of you, she'd make four phone calls and wipe out thirty percent of his largest advertisers."

Packard laughed. He could hear the phone call in his head. "It's barely been a month since Stan died. Shouldn't she be taking time for herself?"

"Your campaign is something she's doing for herself. It keeps her busy. Plus she feels like she's fulfilling Stan's last wish. He wanted you to be sheriff. She's trying to make it happen."

"Shepard's got more yard signs than we do." He had a billboard, too, that Packard was sure Jim Wolf was footing the bill for. Wolf had also used his political clout to get Shepard endorsed by their local representative in the Minnesota House. Packard had a hard time believing the woman knew the first thing about Shepard's middling career as a deputy.

"Signs don't mean anything. You can put a sign anywhere," Thielen said.

"He hasn't had any of his signs defaced either."

"I could take care of that if it bothers you," Thielen offered. "Something like...Shitbird for Sheriff. Shepard...Shitbird. Kind of sounds similar."

Packard made a face and shrugged. "Not near as good as Fudge Packard."

"No," Thielen admitted. "Nothing could be as good as that."

Somehow, during seven hours of driving they'd managed to talk about everything but Paul Bowers and the reason for the trip. Thielen did a lot of singing once they were in range of a Twin Cities' easy-listening radio station. She also grilled him more about his online dating habits, which she hadn't had a chance to do since the topic first came up the night they were discussing how being gay might impact his campaign.

"So you don't have a Grindr account."

"I don't. I can't. Do you think I'd want people to see their acting sheriff is horny and looking and only 3.2 miles away?"

"So you've been on it, you're just not on it now."

"I'm familiar with Grindr. I didn't just arrive on this planet," Packard said.

"And you've never sent anyone a picture of your junk?"

"Nope."

"Is it ugly?" Thielen asked.

Packard gave her a look like she was being ridiculous. "What do you think?"

"It's probably fucking perfect."

"It's been well-reviewed," Packard said.

"Of course, it has," Thielen said, sounding annoyed. She scrolled her phone. "I'll show you Tim's if you want to see it. He wouldn't care."

"No thanks."

"It's a good one."

"I'll take your word for it."

They left the clouds and sleet back in Minnesota. Despite the late hour, it was ten degrees warmer when they arrived in Van Grove, Iowa, after 10:00 p.m. and checked into adjoining rooms at the Quality Inn. They had an appointment to meet Arthur Bowers at the nursing home the next morning. There was just enough time for a drink in the hotel bar, before it closed at eleven, to talk about why they'd made the trip.

They sat at the end of the bar and ordered beers, and after the bartender moved away, Packard told Thielen about Paul's phony SSN and how he'd stopped showing up at work a few weeks ago. He told her about the basement bedroom at Phyllis's and how Paul had moved out months before he left his job. He also gave her a rundown of Paul's record and the time he'd done.

"Bill took ten thousand dollars out of a shared account he set up with Roger Freeman to fund the restaurant they wanted to open. Five days later, Paul bought a new truck at the dealership where he and Bill worked, and he paid for it with ten thousand cash. Coincidence?"

"I know how you feel about coincidences," Thielen said, sounding like a long-suffering partner who'd heard it all before. She was drinking an ultra-light beer that made Packard's hazy IPA look like a glass of scrambled eggs.

"So why would Bill pay Paul ten thousand dollars? To do what?" Packard asked.

"To break into his house and steal his wife's jewelry?" Thielen suggested. "Carrie gets the insurance money. Maybe Bill sweet-talks some of it out of her for the restaurant. Paul gets ten thousand to do the job, fences the jewels, keeps part of the take, and gives the rest to Bill. Did you get an estimate on how much it was all worth?"

"It's insured for more than two hundred thousand dollars," Packard said. "Her mother had a taste for the good stuff—big rings, diamonds, gold. Think 1970s banker's wife."

"He's not going to get two hundred for it on the street. Maybe half that. And Paul keeps half of that."

"He's gets fifty grand in exchange for ten grand. And he owes Roger twelve. Not a great return," Packard said.

"What other choice did he have?"

Packard didn't say anything. He drank his beer. It tasted like fermented pineapple and wet sock. He was remembering when he'd talked to Paul and the other mechanic at work. Ryan. Ryan thought Bill was an asshole because he'd insulted his girlfriend. Paul had been the one who put Packard on the scent of the high-stakes poker game. He hadn't known about Leon Chen but he'd known about the game and known that Ronnie Winder would know more.

"If there was a plot, it makes sense now why there's no evidence of the two of them planning it. No phone calls. No text messages. No emails. Totally unnecessary—they planned the whole thing while smoking cigarettes at work."

"Smart," Thielen said.

"But why pull off the job while both Bill and Carrie are home? Why not take your wife out of town and have the guy hit the place then?"

"Might look too suspicious to the cops and the insurance guys. If you're home, you have an excuse to have the safe unlocked. You're in and out of there all the time. All Bill had to do was lie convincingly. He was wearing his CPAP. He took a sleeping pill. He could have slept through the whole thing."

"So how the hell did he end up getting shot?" Packard asked.

"Maybe Paul wanted all the money for himself."

"Hmm," Packard said. It made sense on the surface. But how had the jewelry box ended up at Sherri's?

"Carrie thinks the plan was to murder her and for Bill to collect the life insurance on her. He had a rinky-dink hundred grand policy on her through work."

Thielen had finished her beer. Packard had a third of his left. He felt like he'd been drinking gravy. "Maybe stealing the jewelry was a cover for killing Carrie," Thielen said. "They make it look like she caught a burglar in the act and got killed for being in the wrong place at the wrong time. Paul gets all the money for the jewelry—there's a good chance Bill didn't know the true value of it at all—and Bill gets the insurance money free and clear."

"But again, Bill's the one who gets shot," Packard said. "It's not like Paul took him out as a loose end. If Bill hired Paul to kill his wife, Paul actually has a vested interest in not killing Bill. When the jewelry money runs out, he can come back for more. 'Remember when I killed your wife for you? Would be a shame if anyone found out. The cost to keep me quiet is whatever I say it is.'"

"How do you think the boat shooter fits into all this?"

"I don't think he does, actually."

"So there's a random out there who wants you dead for an unknown reason."

Packard shrugged.

"You need to be more fucking careful."

"I fled all the way to Iowa to hide out in a hotel with you. That's pretty careful," Packard said.

Somewhere out of sight, the bartender turned the already dimmed lights even lower. Thielen turned sideways on her stool to face Packard. "Was it really necessary to drive all this way to talk to the dad? Are you hoping he can lead us to Paul?"

"That's not the main goal. If he does, great. I feel like there's more to the picture that I'm not seeing. Why did Paul move to Sandy Lake, of all the places in the world, after his parole ended? What's the connection? Phyllis said he asked her a lot about the bank and the Gherlicks when he first moved into her place."

"That's interesting. He ends up getting a job working at the same place as the husband of one of the Gherlick girls whose dad founded the bank."

"Exactly."

"Huh," Thielen said. She looked at her phone, then put it in the pocket of her sweatshirt. "Are you gonna finish that beer or save the rest for breakfast?"

Packard took one more drink. "Bad choice. Too hoppy. Too heavy."

"Let's go, lightweight," Thielen said. "I gotta pee."

CHAPTER TWENTY-THREE

THE VAN GROVE WEST Prairie Senior Living Community was a newer two-story building on the edge of town, shaped like a boomerang, with a view of stripped cornfields from the front and the back. Traffic whizzed by on a two-lane highway, and a towering white wind turbine spun slowly in the distance.

A cold breeze tugged at Packard's jacket as he and Thielen got out of the sheriff's SUV, both dressed in business casual instead of their uniforms. They checked in at the front desk. The smell of breakfast sausage and hot maple syrup wafted from an unseen dining room. The lady at the desk told them Arthur Bowers's room was on the second floor. They took a curved staircase from the lobby up to a landing and down a hallway. Packard knocked on the door, and after a minute, a man in a red cardigan and a black turtleneck opened the door and shook their hands and invited them into his tiny apartment.

Arthur was stooped, with big, fleshy ears and large hands. Officer Hutchins, Paul's former parole officer, had told Arthur to expect two detectives from Minnesota and that they wanted to talk to him about Paul. Arthur took a seat in a recliner positioned across from a flat-screen TV while Packard and Thielen sat side by side on a love seat with a sliding glass door behind them. "What happened with my son?" Arthur asked by way of an opening. "What did he do? Is he dead?"

Packard wasn't sure how to answer any of those questions. "Arthur, your son is a person of interest in one, maybe two, murders that have taken place in the county where we're from."

Arthur exhaled and dropped his head as if he was in prayer. He smelled of aftershave and had something in his hair keeping it flat. He reminded Packard of a schoolboy done up special for picture day. "I had hoped he'd learned his lesson in prison."

Packard held up a hand. "Let me be clear, Mr. Bowers. I don't have any evidence that he's guilty of murder. No evidence he was even nearby when they happened. But he has a connection to both victims and now we don't know where he is. He's quit his job and moved from his last known address."

"I don't know where he is either," Arthur said. "It's been oh…almost a year, I think, since we've even talked on the phone. Probably last Christmas."

Packard said, "He used to live near here, correct?"

Arthur nodded. "Des Moines is less than an hour north. He studied automobile repair while he was in jail. He had a job with a car rental company, servicing their fleet."

"What made him move to Minnesota?" Thielen asked.

"I can't tell you, to be honest. Didn't know he was planning it or had done it until he called and told me he was working some place a few hours north of the Twin Cities."

Arthur said Paul had been a good boy for most of his young life. It was in high school when he fell in with the wrong crowd and neither Arthur nor Evelyn could talk to him anymore. "He got caught stealing a car, got caught with stuff stolen from a local business. He spent a few months in a juvenile facility. Eventually he quit school and lived with a friend and they scraped by, but it was never clear how. Drugs probably. He went from job to job in his twenties, always asking his mother and me for money. Then he robbed the liquor store and that didn't go so well for him."

Thielen asked Arthur if he had a phone number or an address for Paul in Minnesota. He said he didn't have either. "He said the number he was calling me from was temporary and not to write it down. Said he'd send me his info once he got more settled, but that still hasn't happened."

Arthur slapped his knees suddenly. "I made coffee. I forgot to offer you any."

Packard and Thielen said they'd both take a cup black. Arthur got to his feet and took down mugs from a cupboard. His tiny kitchen had a fridge and a microwave and a coffeepot. No oven or cooktop.

Packard turned to the row of framed photos on a narrow table right behind the love seat. He saw a photo of Arthur in an army uniform and a black-and-white picture of Evelyn from maybe her late teens or early twenties. There was a wedding photo and a color picture of them from maybe twenty years ago wearing leis and standing under a palm tree.

A photo taken in winter of two young women standing on the front steps outside a white frame house caught Packard's eye. Snow was piled high on either side of the shoveled sidewalk and on the bushes flanking either side of the front door. Both women were wearing long coats with furry collars. One of them was Evelyn, and she was holding a baby in a stocking cap and a winter snowsuit that made his arms and legs stick out like the points of a star. The other woman had her arm around Evelyn and a hold on one of the baby's feet.

Packard picked up the photo, studying the faces of the two women and what they were wearing. He took out his phone and snapped a picture of the photo. Thielen gave him a weird look.

"Tell me about Evelyn," Packard said.

"Well, she died," Arthur said from the kitchenette, as if the last thing that happened to her was the first thing to come to mind. He came back with two coffee mugs, handed one to each of them and went back for his. "She's been gone a couple of years now," he said as he sat again. "We're both retired school teachers. Only reason we could afford a place like this is because we bought long-term care policies back when insurance companies were dumb enough to sell them."

Evelyn had beaten breast cancer about a dozen years earlier and had started showing signs of dementia about the time they found new cancer on her liver. She still had the ability to decide for herself that she didn't want to go through cancer treatment again when she had bigger problems knocking on her door.

"I will say that Paul was here with her a lot at the end," Arthur said.

"Was that out of character for him?" Thielen asked.

"A bit. She kept calling for him. She wanted to see him. Once he finally came and spent some time with her, he ended up coming somewhat regularly. It was supposed to be a break for me as her caregiver, so I wasn't around to hear what they talked about."

"What do you think she wanted to tell him?" Packard asked.

"I wouldn't know. All I know is she told me she had unburdened her soul when it came to Paul. She said she had found peace regarding him."

"How long were you and Evelyn married?"

"Forty-eight years."

Packard took out his notebook and flipped the pages until he found what he was looking for. "Arthur, I want ask you a personal question," he said. "Are you Paul's biological father?"

Arthur Bowers scowled like someone had spit in his face. "For better or worse, I am that boy's father," he said. "He has my last name. I raised him from a small child. He's my son. I won't tolerate anyone saying otherwise."

The mood in the room turned as cold as the wind outside. After a couple more questions, Packard stood and left his card on the coffee table. Arthur followed them to the door. He pushed it shut before Packard could finish thanking him for his time.

"Did you get what you came for?" Thielen asked as they made their way down the curved stairs to the foyer.

"I got exactly what I needed," Packard said.

"Is it enough for an arrest warrant?"

Packard shook his head. "I don't think so. We're going to have to find Paul and press him."

They pushed through the double set of doors back into the October chill. "What did you need me for again?" Thielen asked.

Packard reached in his pocket and tossed her the keys. "To drive us back. I'm tired."

Thielen fumbled but caught the keys. "You asshole," she said.

It was dark by the time they reached Sandy Lake, and they were hungry again after not eating since stopping for lunch at a pizza buffet in Des Moines. Packard dropped Thielen at her place, pulled into the garage at home, then walked over to Bert's to pick up Frank. He stayed long enough to drink a beer with the retired judge.

"Any more weird traffic driving by here lately?" Packard asked. Frank was between his feet, nose raised so Packard could scratch his chest.

"No, it's been quiet," Bert said. "The Hills put their place up for sale. Did you hear that?"

Packard didn't know for sure who the Hills were or which house was theirs. "I didn't. Seems a little late in the season to be doing that."

"That's what I thought. Maybe they wanted one last summer out of it."

Back at home, Packard put food and water out for Frank and made himself an omelet with cheese and onions and a red pepper that had started to wrinkle in the crisper. He ate it standing over the sink. One night away from home was enough to freshen his eyes and make him realize how tired he was of living in a construction zone. He had enough money to get the place livable and to furnish it how he wanted. It was the time he lacked. He cut a piece of the omelet, pulled up a stringy, cheesy bite and had the thought while he chewed that if he won the election in November, it might be a good time to take some of his stockpiled vacation and use it to finish the house before he was sworn in as the new sheriff in January. Who knew what his free time would look like after that?

He opened his laptop and sat on the couch and caught up on the things that needed his immediate attention after being out of pocket for the last day and a half. He could still feel the vibration of the road humming through him after spending sixteen hours in a vehicle. He'd talked to dispatch while Thielen was driving and had them put out a BOLO for Paul Brewer a.k.a. Paul Bowers, including his photo and the information about the truck he'd purchased that had come from Katherine at the dealership. So far, no sightings of him.

Before closing the computer, Packard checked the forecast to see if it had changed any from what they'd heard the whole way home. If anything, it had gotten worse.

It was nine and he could barely keep his eyes open. It was all right because he knew it was going to be an early morning. "Frank, bedtime," he said.

Frank had no objections.

CHAPTER TWENTY-FOUR

NO MATTER THE DATE or the time of day or the day of the week, the first major snowfall of the year produced the same result. The entire population collectively lost their minds, took their hands off the wheel, and drove into the goddamn ditch. Every single year. When he was a cop in Minneapolis, he attributed it to clueless city drivers, but things weren't any better up north.

There were four inches of snow on the ground before sunrise. The calls to 911 started at 4:30 a.m. They had more than twenty incidents requiring assistance by 6:30, and by 8:00 the count was still going up. Every available deputy was responding to accidents, including Packard. There were times when he needed to be a leader, and times when he needed to be in the trenches with his deputies. This was one of those times.

He responded to an elderly couple who were trying to get to their doctor for an appointment. Packard asked if it was the type of appointment that could be rescheduled. They said yes. He let them warm up in his vehicle, then drove them home to await news from the tow company about their car.

Schools were not canceled. He picked up two high school girls, sisters, whose silver Hyundai was nearly on its side in a ditch and drove them to school.

For an hour he was on the scene of a pickup truck pulling a long trailer loaded with wooden sauna kits on their way to customers. The driver had tried to get off the main road but had chosen an off-ramp too steep for his truck, considering the load. Halfway up the hill he lost traction, slid backward, and jackknifed the trailer.

By late afternoon, the main roads had been plowed. Snowblowers spewed oily exhaust and threw arcs of snow into the air. Packard was back in his office, making decisions about who could go home for the day and how many they might need on duty overnight, considering the road conditions.

His cell phone rang with a call from Deputy Reynolds, the new guy with the baby face. "Reynolds. What's up?"

"I've got eyes on your BOLO. It's the vehicle and license plate, at least. Haven't been able to confirm who's driving."

"Nice job, Reynolds. Where are you?"

"On 15 about four miles from town, heading west. We passed each other a ways back. I gave him some distance before swinging around. I'm three hundred yards back. Not sure if he knows he's got a tail. Want me to light him up?"

"No, stay where you are. Let him go where he's going. I'm curious."

Packard put the phone on speaker, grabbed his coat, and headed down the stairs to the sally port where the sheriff's SUV was parked. He listened as Reynolds announced the crossroads as Paul got farther from town. "He's pulling into the lot at the Beaver."

Packard was on the road, waiting to hit the edge of town before stepping on the gas. "Is he going inside? Anyone with him?"

Reynolds was quiet for a minute. "He's out of the truck. He's alone. He's headed inside."

"Stay close by," Packard said. "I'll be there in ten minutes."

———

The Big Beaver was a bar right off the highway with a wide gravel lot and a faux log cabin front that did little to hide the plain steel building behind it. People who couldn't bring themselves to say Big Beaver with a straight face called it the Beaver or the Beave or just BB's. It was a place where you could get a beer, play pull-tabs, order a Heggies pizza, maybe hear a band now and then.

The interior was sided to look like split logs. A pool table sat on either side of the front door with an L-shaped bar coming off a small kitchen to the left. Booths lined the back wall. Half a dozen people sat at the bar, looking at their phones, looking up at the TVs.

A middle-aged couple on the corner had that slumped, spineless look from too much to drink. Packard gave them a nod as he stood between two empty stools. The bartender was a young woman wearing super-short cutoffs and a St. Cloud sweatshirt. Packard ordered a burger basket to go and water to drink while he waited.

Paul was sitting in a booth at the back of the room. He had two glasses of water in front of him and a drink in a plastic cup with a stir straw sticking out of it. Packard had no intention of confronting him inside the bar. Now he was curious to see who Paul was meeting. He took a seat on a barstool, kept one eye on the front door, and waited for his food.

After a few minutes, the intoxicated couple on the corner of the bar covered their beers with coasters and went out a side door to smoke. Paul got up and went to the men's room, just beyond the swinging door to the kitchen. Packard drank his water and chewed the ice and watched the football game. When his food came in a Styrofoam container, he gave the bartender his credit card. She took it and walked around the corner to the register just as Paul came out of the bathroom. Packard kept his eye on the game so Paul wouldn't feel like he was being watched.

A moment later, a blast of cold air came from the side door. Packard looked over his shoulder, expecting the smokers to come back in. Instead, he saw Paul walking fast across the concrete patio.

"Shit," Packard said. "I'll be back for this and my card," he called to the bartender. He paused in between the bar's double set of doors to talk to Reynolds on his radio. "He just got by me. Stay where you are, but be ready in case I need you."

Packard stepped outside. His breath came out in clouds. The snow from earlier had been plowed into mounds to his right. Paul was ten feet from his truck, which was already running thanks to a remote starter.

"Hey, Paul."

Hearing his name didn't make him stop.

"Paul, we need to talk," Packard said. His tone made it clear he wasn't asking.

Paul paused near the driver's door with the key fob in his hand. He was wearing a wool peacoat that you could buy in any military surplus store. A bright-white light high on a pole made shadows in his eye sockets and the hollows of his face. He looked old and gaunt and anxious to get as far away as possible.

"I need to get home, Deputy. I'm in a hurry," he said.

"You just got here. Looked like you were waiting for someone."

"No…I wasn't. I was hungry but then I started not feeling well," Paul said.

"That usually happens after you eat the food here," Packard joked. He drew up to the tailgate as Paul put his hand on the door latch and pulled it open.

"We need to talk about Bill Sandersen," Packard said.

"I already told you everything I know."

"But I've learned a lot of new things since the first time we chatted. About Bill. About you," Packard said. He was watching Paul's hands. His keys were on a circular beaded key ring that looked like a sunburst and had a thin pocket knife hanging from it.

Paul grabbed up his keys, stuffed them in his pocket, and stood with the door open halfway. "Am I under arrest?" he asked.

Packard shook his head. "I just want you to come in and answer some questions for me."

"I'm not answering any more questions if I'm not under arrest," Paul said.

"If I have to get an arrest warrant, I will. If I arrest you, your prior record is going to make things difficult for you."

"I don't know what you're talking about," Paul said. His hands disappeared inside his pockets. Packard rested his hand on the butt of his gun.

"I know who you are, Paul. I know you did twelve years in a Missouri state prison for that liquor store job. Your last name is Bowers, not Brewer."

Paul rushed at him then. Packard was ready for him. He had his weight on his back leg, his front knee slightly bent. The icy asphalt made him slide back about eighteen inches before he found his footing and pushed back. They were in a narrow space between Paul's pickup truck and a Subaru crossover SUV. Room to jab but not bring around a fist.

Paul tried to stomp on his insole and knee him in the groin, both moves Packard was able to deflect. He shoved Paul away from him. Their breath came out in furious clouds. "Don't make this worse on you than it has to be, Paul."

Paul rushed him again, this time going low, his shoulder in Packard's gut, arms wrapped around his waist. He was smaller than Packard but pushed with a strength that defied his size. This time Packard lost his footing and they shot out from between the vehicles. Paul got a foot behind Packard's and they went down to the ground. Paul wrapped his hand around the top of Packard's vest and tried to bang the back of his head on the ground. Packard felt snow on his neck and the frantic scramble of Paul's other hand near his gun.

Packard pushed himself up and head-butted Paul, who turned his own head at the last second and took only a glancing blow. Packard bucked him off. Paul found his footing like a cat, leaped onto the bumper of his truck, reached inside, and came back down swinging a shovel, gripping it just above the blade.

The last thing Packard wanted to do was kill this guy. He had too many questions. He unstrapped his Taser while backing up from the swinging shovel. "Paul, there's no way this ends well for you. Drop the shovel."

Packard saw flashing lights out of the corner of his eye. Paul saw them, too. He changed his grip on the shovel and flung it at Packard, sending it spinning toward him like a lawn mower blade.

Packard put his hand out and knocked the shovel to the ground. Paul was already by the side of his truck. The door was still open. The brake lights flared and then the tires squealed and the black truck lurched over the concrete bumper at the head of the parking spot as Paul tried to drive straight up the incline to the road.

Reynolds was heading for the turn into the lot but saw Paul's truck coming up the hill and went straight for him instead. Paul saw the flashing lights of the cruiser about to intercept him as his tires spun in the new snow that filled the ditch. He cranked the wheel right, then left, found traction at the last second, and lurched onto the road, back end fishtailing, then shot right across both lanes and into the ditch on the other side.

Just like every other driver that day.

Packard heard the crunch of metal as he ran up the hill in the tracks Paul's truck had left. Reynolds was out of his car, gun drawn.

Paul's truck had taken a nosedive into the ditch on the other side of the road. Packard scrambled down to the driver's side door. The back of his head throbbed.

Paul was slumped into a deflating airbag. His nose was bleeding. He was breathing but dazed.

The door made a sound like flexing metal when Packard wrenched it open. He snapped a cuff on Paul's left hand, reached behind him for his other hand and pulled it back for the other cuff.

"Now you're under arrest," Packard said.

CHAPTER TWENTY-FIVE

PAUL BOWERS WAS TAKEN to the hospital to be evaluated for his injuries. He had two black eyes and a bruised sternum from the airbag and the impact of the accident. Nothing severe enough to keep him from being booked into a holding cell for the night.

Packard had no interest in interviewing his suspect right away. He'd been on duty since before dawn. He reheated his burger and fries from BB's, filled out his report, and was home by ten thirty. He sat in the sauna for almost an hour, hoping the heat would loosen everywhere his body felt tight from the fight. After a long shower, he fell into bed and woke up in the same position seven hours later.

The next day, he reviewed the report from the deputies who had overseen the towing of Paul's truck. The list of items from the inventory search of the truck was so unbelievable that Packard had to go to the evidence room and see everything for himself.

He took his time gathering his thoughts and questions. It was after lunch when Paul was escorted in handcuffs to an interview room near the cellblock. He was wearing the same clothes as the night before. Packard set down his yellow legal pad and sat across the table from him. Thielen was sitting in the corner by the door as an observer.

Paul looked like shit. He was the color of an old T-shirt. His black eyes had darkened overnight and there was still blood encrusted inside his nostrils. It had been more than twelve hours since he'd had a cigarette. It was going to be a lot longer until his next.

"I want a lawyer," Paul said as soon as Packard had finished reading him his rights for the second time. "I'm not talking until I get a lawyer."

"You don't have to talk," Packard said as he laid open his binder. "I'm planning on doing most of the talking. I'd advise you to listen so you know what you're looking at once you do get a lawyer."

He started by laying out the charges that had nothing to do with Bill Sandersen. "You're facing second-degree assault charges for trying to take my head off with that shovel. First degree may be on the table because I felt you trying to take my weapon from its holster while we were on the ground. We have statements from half a dozen people inside the Beaver who watched it all happen."

Paul stayed silent.

"First or second degree—I could give a shit because now I've got you for the murder of Bill Sandersen, which is all I care about it. I'd have nothing, by the way, if you'd just consented to the interview. No arrest warrant. No search warrant for your vehicle. I asked you to come in and answer some questions. In response, you committed felony assault on a police officer. You attempted to flee in your vehicle and totaled it in the process. We then had to tow your truck from the scene and inventory all the contents to protect your property and ourselves from being accused of mishandling your property while it was in our possession."

Packard took a piece of paper from his binder and turned it around for Paul to read. "I'm guessing what we found is no surprise to you," Packard said. "I'm going to read this out loud for Detective Thielen's sake. One black zippered Adidas-brand gym bag. Loose inside, various jewelry items: necklaces, rings, earrings, chokers, jeweled brooches. Items match the description of jewelry reported stolen from the Bill Sandersen residence on the night he was murdered. Also inside the bag, a 9mm semiautomatic Glock 19. It has a loaded clip minus two rounds. Bill was shot twice. It will take some time for our forensics people to identify the firearm, but I'd bet my next paycheck this was the same gun used to kill Bill Sandersen."

Paul looked away from the paper in front of him. "I didn't kill Bill," he said.

"You have to understand how hard that is to believe, don't you?" Packard asked. "Considering we found all this in your truck?"

"I didn't kill him," Paul repeated.

"Here's what I think happened," Packard said. He laid out all the evidence he'd collected so far. Bill and Paul met at work. One or the other of them had the idea to stage the break-in. Paul had been stealing stuff his whole life, so this was nothing new for him. He just needed to get paid for his trouble. Compensation came in the form of the truck he'd just totaled, paid for with ten thousand dollars in cash he'd received from Bill, who had taken the money from the business account he shared with Roger Freeman. "The reason I couldn't find any record of you guys planning this—no emails, no texts, no phone calls—is because you were able to do it all at work on your cigarette breaks."

Packard paused and waited to see if Paul wanted to say anything. Paul just stared at him.

"What I don't know for sure is what was the original plan. Was it just to steal the jewelry? Was it to steal the jewelry and all the guns that were in the safe too? Didn't make any sense to me why those were left behind. Or was the burglary just a cover for the real plan to murder Bill's wife, Carrie?"

At the mention of Carrie's name, Packard thought he saw Paul getting ready to say something. His eyes gave away that he was biting back the words.

Packard went on. "I also don't know what made things go tits up between you two. Unless you had one plan with Bill and a separate plan of your own. You knew how much that jewelry was worth. I'm sure you were promised a cut of the take. Maybe you decided you'd rather have it all for yourself. Why split it with Bill when you could just kill him and keep it all for yourself?"

"I didn't kill Bill," is all Paul would say.

"Then there's the matter of motive," Packard said.

"I thought money was the motive," Thielen said from her seat in the corner.

"Money was *a* motive, but it wasn't *the* motive. Was it, Paul?"

Paul looked at him warily, not sure where this was going.

"I tracked down your record by looking up your tattoos in the federal database. The dice on your palm made it easy. Not a lot of people have a tattoo like that. That's how I knew you did twelve years in Missouri. That's how I knew you were from Iowa and that's where you spent your parole years. Thielen and I drove down to Van Grove and talked to your dad."

"You don't have anything better to do than hassle an old man in a nursing home?" Paul asked.

"When I'm looking for a murderer, I have to follow wherever the trail leads. I was trying to find you and find out about you. I was also trying to figure out why a guy who spent his whole life in Iowa except for an extended vacation in a Missouri state prison would just pick up and move to Sandy Lake, Minnesota, of all places. Most people have lived here their whole lives or own a lake home here. I saw the basement room you rented from Phyllis Egan. You don't own a lake home."

Packard opened his binder again and flipped through some of the paper he had in there. "We didn't hassle your dad," he continued. "We talked to him for about an hour. He couldn't answer the question of why you moved to Sandy Lake, but it wasn't a total wasted trip because I saw this photo and suddenly everything became clear."

He took out a printout of the photo he'd taken of the two women in winter coats holding a baby on the front steps of a small house.

"The woman holding you is your mother, Evelyn."

Packard waited while Paul stared at the photo in front of him.

"The woman next to her is her sister. Right?"

Paul gave him a dead look.

"It's a nice photo. Two beautiful women. Cute baby. But what caught my eye is the pin on the other woman's jacket."

Packard pulled out another piece of paper, this time a blurry enlargement of the photo showing just Evelyn's sister. She was wearing a long coat in a large houndstooth check. On the lapel was a pin in the shape of a hummingbird. Even a zoomed-in photo of a photo taken almost fifty years ago couldn't hide the dazzling jewels in the pin.

"I know this pin," Packard said. "It belongs to Bill's wife, Carrie." He took out two more photos—close-ups of the pin he'd photographed at Carrie's house. "It's about the only piece of jewelry she owned that wasn't stolen. It's engraved on the back. It says *For Sarah—Love, John.*"

Packard swept up his printouts, half turned, and handed them back to Thielen. "Carrie was carrying this pin in her purse the day I met her at her house to walk through the events of the night Bill was killed. Her mom found it and offhandedly confessed to murdering the woman it had belonged to. Carrie's mom has dementia, so I'm not sure how much stock we can put into the things she says. I was curious nonetheless. I had my team do some digging to see if they could find a Sarah connected to the area who died forty-plus years ago. This is what we found."

Another piece of paper. This one a printout from the *Sandy Lake Gazette* with the article about the woman found in a car in a drainage pond in Cass Lake County. Paul's lips moved as he read what was in front of him.

"This woman whose body was found was Sarah Pellak. Sarah Pellak was your mother's sister. Only that's not quite right, is it? Your dad said you spent a lot of time with your mom, Evelyn, when she was near the end of her life. I'm guessing she finally told you the truth that she and Arthur weren't your birth parents. Maybe you already knew about Arthur. He and Evelyn were married forty-eight years—you're fifty-three. But I'm sure it was news to you that Evelyn's sister, Sarah, was your real mother, and your father was John Gherlick, the wealthy married man Sarah met working at Sandy Lake Commercial State Bank."

Paul looked furious. "I want my lawyer," he said.

"Evelyn told you about her sister—your mother—and her banker boyfriend who gave her the expensive jewelry and how she died in a car accident coming back from a visit to Sandy Lake. Evelyn was taking care of you while Sarah was out of town and ended up raising you as her own after the accident."

"No," Paul said.

"You decided to come up here and find out more about the family. Maybe the family fortune. You asked around town. Found out there was money still to be had and figured out a way to get close to Bill by getting a job at the same place he worked. You plotted this whole thing together and then you killed Bill so you could keep all the jewelry money for yourself."

"That's not what happened," Paul insisted.

"You're the one who told me about the high-stakes poker game. You played dumb about who hosted it, but you knew exactly where it was. You knew I'd figure it out, you knew I'd end up at Leon Chen's, and you tried to shoot me that night from a boat in the bay."

Paul slapped the table with his hand. "You're a liar," he said. He looked to Thielen. "He's making all this up. I never—"

Packard kept going. "Bill's ex-wife Sherri was mixed up in this somehow. We found the jewelry box that was stolen from Bill's safe in her house. Maybe she was supposed to get a cut, too, or maybe Bill talked too much and she figured out you were the one there that night. Either way, she was a loose end that needed to be taken care of. You brought over the jewelry box so she'd let you in the door and you killed her, too."

Paul turned sideways in his chair and put his head in his hands. "No! I didn't kill her. I didn't do any of these things."

"You killed two people, Paul. You tried to kill me twice. I may not be able to prove all this, but I have the evidence I need to link you to Bill's murder. That's enough to put away a felon for the rest of his life."

"I want my lawyer!" Paul yelled. "I want my lawyer! I want my lawyer!" He yelled it over and over until his face was red and he had spit on his chin. He didn't stop even as Packard signaled for a deputy to take Paul back to his cell.

When he and Thielen were alone in the room, she stood up and gave him back the printouts he'd handed her. "You could have warned me you were gonna go all Hercule Poirot on his ass," she said.

Packard took the papers and stuck them in his binder. "What fun would that have been?"

"Nice job putting it all together."

"Thank you. It's a crazy story but it's the truth."

"Are you charging him?"

"Kelly's pulling together the paperwork."

"Make sure there's a press release and make sure it mentions your name," Thielen said. "It'll be good for the campaign."

CHAPTER TWENTY-SIX

PAUL BOWERS'S ATTORNEY, LISA Washington, worked part time as a public defender for the seventh judicial circuit. She was a partner in the three-lawyer firm her father had started way back when he was a young attorney himself. He was semi-retired now and did little besides basic estate planning and wills anymore. It was Lisa's idea that the firm dedicate a percentage of its hours to public defense.

She met with Packard to find out what Paul had stacked against him. "I'm holding him on the original assault charge right now," Packard told her. "We inventoried his truck and found jewelry stolen from Bill Sandersen's house the night he was murdered. We found a gun and we're trying to determine whether or not it was used in the shooting. He's a felon so the gun is a no-no, regardless. We also matched tire prints taken near Bill's house the day of the murder to the tires on Paul's truck. That all adds up to probable cause for murder one. I'm writing the complaint right now."

"And if he tells me he let someone else borrow his truck?"

"Then I'd like to know who that someone was," Packard said.

Lisa met with Paul for an hour, left for a couple of hours, then came back and met with him again. It was the end of the day when she came into Packard's office. Thielen was with him, telling him about arresting a woman with an out-standing warrant at a local motel.

"I have a sworn statement from my client about what happened the night Bill Sandersen was killed," Lisa said.

"Is he admitting to it?" Packard asked.

"He's admitting to being there that night."

"Did he pull the trigger?"

Lisa nodded. "But that's only half the story, according to him."

"What's the other half?"

"I think you should come down and hear it from him yourself," Lisa said.

Packard looked at Thielen. "Want to stick around for this?"

Thielen nodded. "Absolutely."

"I'll get us a room."

Paul Bowers had been charged and processed and was wearing an orange prison uniform. He still had two black eyes from the airbag in his truck. He winced and held his chest as he sat down at the table. He looked another decade older than his fifty-three years. Packard and Lisa sat across from him. Thielen stood in the corner.

Packard still hadn't seen the sworn statement Lisa was carrying in a manila folder. Once everyone was seated, she said to Paul, "I'm going to tell you again—in the presence of the detectives—that if you tell them what you told me and I turn over this signed statement, there's very little I can do to defend you against the murder charge, regardless of whether the other part of your story can be proven or not."

Paul stared at his hands and rubbed the dice tattoo on his left palm with his other thumb, like he was trying to remove it. "I understand. I'm fucked either way. But I want it on the record exactly what happened that night. What I did and didn't do."

Lisa sighed. "All right. It's your decision," she said.

"First of all, I never took a shot at you," Paul said, pointing at Packard. "Not from a boat or from anywhere else. Where the hell you got that I idea I don't know. I don't know the guy who had the card game. I don't know where he lives. I've got no alibi for that night but I'm telling you it wasn't me. I don't know these lakes around here or where to get a boat or a gun that can fire from a distance. I don't know who shot at you, but it wasn't me."

Packard didn't say anything. *If not Paul, then who?* He pushed the question away so he could focus on the matter at hand.

"Second of all, I didn't kill the sister," Paul said. He stared at Packard, looking for some kind of reaction. Yesterday he wouldn't say anything and didn't want to hear what Packard had to say. Today he was desperate to be believed. Packard also thought it odd that he referred to Sherri as *the sister* and not *the ex-wife* and not by her name.

"How did Sherri get the jewelry box?" Packard asked.

"I left it on the patio table in front of her house with a letter inside."

Packard and Sherri had sat at that table the morning he informed her that Bill had been killed.

"We didn't find any letter," Packard said.

"Whoever killed her took it then," Paul said.

"Did you send her the other letter? The one that blamed her sister for killing Bill?"

Paul nodded. Packard saw Lisa write *first letter?* on the cover of the file folder.

"What did the letter with the jewelry box say?"

"Nothing happened after I sent her the first letter so I figured she needed more proof. I wrote down everything that happened that night—same thing I'm about to tell you—and left her the jewelry box as proof that I was there and knew what I was talking about."

"And what were you expecting to happen?"

"I wanted her to confront Bill's wife. I wanted Carrie to see I had the power to turn everyone against her."

"And why would you do that?"

"Because Carrie is the one who killed Bill."

———————

Paul's story confirmed a lot of things Packard had pieced together on his own. The deathbed confession from Evelyn, Paul's adoptive mother, about who his real mother was. The married banker who sent her away to have her baby. The fact that his mother had died under somewhat tragic circumstances coming home from trying to see the banker. The family name that was still prominent in the town fifty years later.

Gherlick.

Phyllis, who rented him the room, told him all kinds of gossip about the Gherlick family. About John, the wealthy banker who chased anything in a skirt. His long-suffering wife. His suicide. About his three daughters, two of whom shared a husband, well, not shared at the same time, but one after the other. Still. Phyllis had heard Bill had found out his new wife wasn't as free-spending as her sister and that Bill had had to get a job selling cars.

Getting a job at the same place where Bill worked wasn't difficult. Every business in town was shorthanded. Paul's mistake was trying to hide his felony history behind a fake name and social when Stephen Carter was so desperate for mechanics that he probably would have hired Paul if he showed up with a handcuff bracelet still around one wrist.

After getting the job, it was just a matter of getting close to Bill, who wanted nothing more than an audience to listen to him complain about all the ways life was screwing him over. He liked to brag how he and Sherri used to spend money like it would never run out. How Sherri's mother—that old bitch—insisted she divorce Bill before she'd give her daughter an allowance to keep a roof over her head. How his marriage to Carrie, his high school sweetheart, had turned out to be a mistake. If he could just get the money together to start his own business, he could start fresh.

Enter the ex-con who knows a thing or two about insurance fraud and fencing stolen goods. Who will do the job for the right price. Who sees a chance to stick it to the family who had so much given to them for doing nothing but owning a bank. He was a Gherlick as much as they were. Where was his trust fund?

Another thing Evelyn told him about was the hummingbird pin. How it was made with real rubies and diamonds and emeralds. How his mother wore it everywhere she went because it represented how John truly felt about her and how it meant he'd do as he promised and leave his wife to come be with her and their baby. And how the pin was nowhere to be found when his mother's body was pulled out of the drainage pond months after she slid off the road in the middle of winter.

Evelyn thought a sticky-fingered deputy or morgue worker made off with it. But Paul said he found photos in the social pages of the *Sandy Lake Gazette* archives of Margaret Gherlick wearing the exact same pin months and years after his mother had died. When Bill told him his gun safe held all the family jewelry Margaret had given to Carrie, Paul had his eyes on a single prize.

His mother's hummingbird pin.

When it wasn't there the night of the break-in, he and Bill got into an argument about it. It was Bill's first inkling that Paul wasn't just an ex-con willing to do a job.

It was while they were arguing that Carrie walked in on them with a gun in her hand.

Paul sat up straight in his chair and his black eyes got wide, reenacting his surprise in the moment. "Suddenly I had a gun pressed into my spine. 'You motherfuckers must think I'm stupid,' was the first thing she said."

"What did Bill say?" Packard asked.

"He was like, 'Carrie, what the fuck?' And Carrie said, 'What the fuck is right. Whatever you had planned is not going to play out like you thought.'"

Bill tried to convince her that this was about insurance fraud, that the man in the black ski mask rifling through her jewelry while her husband lounged in his bed wasn't there to kill her. The problem was Paul had a gun tucked into the back of his pants.

"Was killing Carrie part of the plan?" Packard asked.

"No, never," Paul said. "Swear to god. The gun was to scare her in case she caught me in the act. It always was supposed to be a straight-up burglary. Empty the safe, including the guns which I didn't get to because I couldn't find the hummingbird pin. He and Carrie would get the insurance money. I'd help him fence everything and he would collect a second time, minus my cut."

"What happened next?"

"It was dark in Bill's room. All the lights were off. They argued back and forth, whispering like someone might hear them. She was certain Bill had hired me to kill her. I told her it was just about the safe. Bill kept telling Carrie to turn on the light so they could talk things out. Carrie said, 'Shut the fuck up, dear' with the same tone of voice you'd use to ask someone to pass the potatoes."

"How did Bill get shot?" Packard asked.

"She told me to reach for my gun. She told me to do it slowly or she would blow a hole through me, reach through it, and rip my nuts off. I did what she said. She told me to point the gun at Bill. When I hesitated, she moved her gun to the base of my skull. She said, 'Someone was supposed to get shot tonight, but it's not going to be me. It's either going to be you or it's going to be Bill. It's your choice.'"

"What did Bill do?"

"He just sat there. I had my gun pointed at him. He said, 'Stop this, Carrie! You got it all wrong.' She started counting to three...and I pulled the trigger."

"He was shot twice," Packard said. "You shot him twice."

"I shot him, grabbed the bag with the jewelry in it, and ran for the door. That's when Carrie said, 'He better not get up.' She still had her gun pointed right at me so I fired again and then I was gone."

Paul took a deep breath like he'd just finished running a race and studied the tabletop in front of him. Nobody said anything for a minute, all of them busy imagining Bill's final moments, all of them trying to decide if Paul was telling the truth. Lisa doodled a spiral in the corner of her file folder and looked at Packard.

"Let's take a break," he said.

———

Packard, Thielen, and Lisa walked down a hallway away from the detention area to the kitchen near the squad room. They all got water from the water cooler. Lisa stood with her folder under her arm and stared at the detectives over the rim of her cup, waiting for someone to say something.

"Is everything he told us in the statement?" Packard asked her.

"More or less. I made a couple of notes, but the story hasn't changed from what he told me."

"Do you believe him?" Thielen asked Packard.

Packard crushed his paper cup and dropped it in the trash. "I hate to admit it but I do."

"Why?"

"He's already admitted to being there. He's admitted to pulling the trigger. I don't see what he gains by implicating Carrie in the crime if she wasn't there," Packard said.

"Seems like he's got a lot of built-up resentment for the Gherlick family. He could be doing it out of spite," Lisa suggested.

"Yeah, he might. But I've also had the feeling that Carrie's done nothing but lie to me since the day Bill was killed. She's claimed to know nothing, seen nothing. She heard one shot, not two. She didn't tell me the jewelry was stolen until I asked her about it. She's offered me nothing this whole time."

"It's one way to keep from getting caught in a lie—claim ignorance of anything and everything, no matter what," Thielen said.

"That's exactly what it's felt like," Packard said.

Thielen refilled her water. "So if Paul didn't kill Sherri, then do you like Carrie for that?"

"Let's just say I wouldn't put it past her," Packard said.

"What do you want to do next?" Thielen asked.

Packard checked the time on his phone. It was almost 6:00 p.m. "I have a few more questions for our friend. Do you still have time?" he asked Lisa.

"I can stay."

"Let's go back in."

———

Once everyone was back in the interview room in their same spots, Packard asked, "Have you had any contact with Carrie since the night Bill was killed?"

Paul nodded. "Two phone calls."

Packard gave a knowing look to Thielen. More information Carrie hadn't bothered to tell anyone.

"What did you say in those phone calls?"

"I told her I wanted money or I was going to start telling people what really happened that night."

"What was her response?"

"Go fuck myself. She said I was the one who pulled the trigger. That there was no evidence anything I said actually happened."

"She's not wrong," Packard said.

"I know, but I figured if I started telling people, raising questions in enough minds, she'd be willing to pay to keep me quiet."

"So you sent Sherri the first letter," Packard said.

Paul nodded.

"And when you didn't get the response you wanted from Carrie, you sent Sherri another letter with more details and the jewelry box."

"Right."

"And it got Sherri killed."

"You can't blame me for her sister being a cold-blooded, narcissist bitch."

Paul's ability to diagnose a woman he barely knew as a narcissist struck

Packard as odd and familiar at the same time. He thought Sherri had used the same word to describe her sister. "Any more contact since the second letter to Sherri?"

"I mailed Carrie another letter. I accused her of killing her sister and asked her if she was going to kill everyone else who found out the truth. I made a list of people close to her—her kids, her ex-husband, the board members where she works."

"Where did you get all these names?" Packard asked.

"Some from Bill. Some from Google."

"Has Carrie ever contacted you?"

"She can't. I call her from a burner with a blocked number."

"You didn't have a phone on you when we arrested you. I had a deputy go through the trash in the men's room and he found a busted phone under all the dirty paper towels. The guts had been ripped out of it. Smashed on the floor, based on bits of solder and circuit board we found. I'm guessing you flushed the rest."

Paul didn't deny it.

"Who were you meeting at the restaurant?"

"No one. The waitress brought two waters by mistake. I told her to leave the extra one, that I'd drink it."

"I don't believe you," Packard said.

Paul shrugged.

Packard switched tactics. "Phyllis said you moved out of her place in July. It's October now. Where have you been staying?"

"Here and there," Paul said, tracing the dice on his palm. "My truck mostly."

"I saw the list of everything that came out of your truck. It didn't look like it contained all your worldly possessions."

"I've been crashing at different places."

"What places?"

"Empty cabins."

Sounded plausible, but for the second time Packard didn't believe what

Paul was saying. There was something he wasn't telling him. More lies by omission. He'd been truthful to his own detriment about certain things. It didn't make sense why he would hold back at this point. What did he have left to hide?

"Tell me what your endgame was here," Packard said. "You killed Bill on Labor Day weekend. You got away with a bunch of jewelry worth a fair amount of money. A month later, you're still in town. Even after walking out on your job, you're still here. You could have been in the wind and long gone by now."

Paul looked at his hands. "I wanted Carrie to pay for her part in all this. She put a fucking gun to my head and ordered me to execute her husband. It was him or me. What would you have done?"

Three people stared back at Paul. None of them would answer his question.

"No one was supposed to get shot that night," he said. "I figured if the law couldn't hold her accountable, then I'd hold her financially responsible. She could pay to keep me quiet."

"And pay and pay and pay," said Thielen from her corner of the room.

Paul sat back in his seat and shrugged. "That's how it usually works," he admitted.

Paul's lawyer left and Packard and Thielen went back to his office. It was dinnertime and Packard could see snowflakes swirling through the lights shining down on the parking lot.

"What are you going to do?" Thielen asked as she opened a can of sparkling cherry lime water that Packard could smell immediately from across the desk.

"I don't know," Packard sighed. "If he's telling the truth, then I've got the trigger man behind bars, but the killer is still running loose. I can pull Carrie's phone records and confirm Paul called her, but not telling us that she got anonymous calls from a blackmailer isn't a crime I can charge her with."

"If you can't get her on Bill's killing—which face it, you can't—then maybe there's something to tie her to Sherri's."

"If she killed Sherri."

"Doesn't seem likely there's a third rogue killer out there. It had to be her or Paul," Thielen said. "If you believe him about Bill, why not Sherri?"

"I do believe him. I just can't figure out why Sherri's dead."

"Maybe Carrie thought Sherri was the one behind the letters," Thielen suggested.

"But Carrie knows Sherri isn't the only one blackmailing her. It's the guy in the ski mask *and* Sherri. Maybe working together. Killing Sherri doesn't take care of the blackmail."

They were both quiet as they thought. The late evening sounds of the department were the ringing of a nearby extension and someone's boots in the hallway.

"If Carrie would kill her own sister, then she must have slipped up somehow," Thielen said. "Said something that made Sherri realize that Carrie knew more about what happened the night Bill was killed than she's let on. It's either that or Carrie uncovered Sherri's involvement—you said the jewelry box was sitting in plain sight at Sherri's house—and killed her in a fit of rage. Either way, Carrie's got to be desperate to know who the man in the mask is. You know who Paul is, she doesn't. Maybe there's a way you can use him to draw her out."

Packard looked up at the ceiling and rubbed his hand against the grain of his beard. "I'm going to go see her this evening. I'll tell her I got a photocopy of the letter Paul sent to her also mailed to me. Tell her I want the original. Press her on why she hasn't reported getting it. I want her to know that I'm looking at her hard and see if that spooks her at all."

"Want me to come with you?"

"No, go home. I'll call you if there's any news."

Packard still had a deputy stationed outside Carrie's house. He got the deputy on the radio on his way there and then pulled alongside his vehicle and talked to him through rolled-down windows. Snow fell in the gap between them and swarmed in Packard's headlights.

"She gone anywhere?"

The deputy said no. "I've seen her in the window a few times today. She came out and got the mail. She's had no visitors besides the home health aide who left about half an hour ago."

"I'm going to talk to her. Why don't you move to the intersection and park to the north. It's the only way out of here. If she sees you're gone, she might try to go somewhere tonight."

"Understood."

Packard put up his window and pulled into Margaret's driveway. An inch of new snow was already on the ground. There were no tracks from the aide's car, which meant she had left before it started snowing.

Packard got out and rang the doorbell. Through the oval glass window in the door he could see lights on in the kitchen and the living room. He waited. No one came to the door. He saw no movement. No shadows. He rang the bell again. Nothing.

He got on the radio to the deputy. "No one's answering. I'm going to go around back. Let me know if you see anything from where you are."

He took out his flashlight and lit the way around the garage. Yesterday's snow had added up to about six inches. Packard hugged the side of the house where the snow hadn't piled as high. When he got to the back, he noticed right away the tracks leading from the house toward the water. Far from the house, the tracks made a hard left and followed the shoreline across the backyards. There were eight houses spread fairly far apart between Margaret's house and the road that went around the other side of the lake.

Packard radioed the deputy again, told him what he was seeing. "Go up to the intersection, make a right, and see if you can find where the tracks come out. I'm guessing she had the health aide pick her up down the road."

"Shit, sorry, Sheriff. I couldn't see the back of the house from here."

"It's not your fault. She's been playing me for a fool this whole time. She got me again."

"I've got the make and license plate of the aide's car. I'll call it in."

"Yeah. Do that, too."

The back door was a slider that opened onto a brick patio. It slid open when Packard tried it. "Anyone home? It's Detective Packard."

Nothing.

He stomped his boots and went down the hall to the bedrooms. Margaret's room had a simple sliding lock on the outside of the door, likely to keep her from wandering in the night if she woke up while Carrie was sleeping. Packard unlocked the door and found Margaret in her bed on her back. She had the slack, sprawled look of the dead or the drugged. Packard checked her pulse. She was breathing, but she didn't react to his touch at all.

In the next bedroom, on top of the made bed he spotted a metal box with its lid flipped open. He knew it was a lockbox for a gun even before he got close enough to see the box of Winchester Super X .44 ammo. The top was open and he could easily count the six missing bullets.

Packard went back out to the living area, looking for anything that would give him an idea of where Carrie might be headed with a gun. He found the letter from Paul on the dining table with the rest of the day's mail. It was on the same light-blue stationery as the letter Sherri had given him. Packard used a pen to flip over the pages and caught the same scent of sandalwood that he remembered from Sherri's letter.

Paul had written:

Carrie,

How could you kill your own sister? She wasn't part of this. Are you going to kill everyone who confronts you about what happened that night? Your kids, Rebecca and Ryan? Your best friend, Laura? The board members of the Gherlick Family Foundation?

For every name he listed, he also listed an address or a phone number, sometimes both. The letter went onto two pages. At the bottom of the second he ended with:

You know what I want. The next letter goes out in two days.

The letter had put Carrie in motion. It had to have been the letter. Packard took a picture of both pages with his phone while thinking about the trouble Carrie had gone to to drug her mother and slog through the snow so she could be picked up out of sight of the deputy. She hadn't gone through all that—or loaded a revolver—to go grocery shopping.

Packard called Carrie's cell phone number and heard it ringing from a bedroom down the hall.

She'd left home without her phone. She had a plan. She didn't need a phone and she didn't want its nosy computer brain tracking and remembering her movements.

What was it about the letter? Where was she going?

Packard went back out through the sliding door, talking on his shoulder mike, getting his people in motion.

CHAPTER TWENTY-SEVEN

CARRIE'S FEET WERE WET and frozen. Even after Zeinab directed the car's heat to the floor, Carrie's shoes refused to thaw. Her winter clothes were still at the other house, so she'd had to lurch a quarter of a mile through snow up to her shins, wearing tennis shoes, in order to get out without being seen by the deputy parked outside.

Zeinab was confused by the request to pick her up at the boat landing, then reluctant. She didn't understand why Miss Carrie couldn't just leave with her. Why would the police care if she went to town?

Carrie went to her purse, took out two hundred dollars, and pressed the bills into Zeinab's hands. "I need your help, Zeinab. I don't need a lot of questions. Can you do this for me?"

"What about your mother? Who will be with her if we're both gone? She might wake up."

She wasn't going to wake up because Carrie had given Margaret an Ambien with the rest of her evening medication. "I'll call the neighbor and ask her to come over," Carrie said. She went down the hall and made a fake phone call loud enough for Zeinab to overhear. "Nancy said she can come over after she gets dinner on the table."

"I can't stay, Ms. Carrie. I have another client."

"I know. Leave now and wait for me at the boat launch. I'll walk down there as soon as Nancy gets here. It'll only be a few minutes."

The truth was there was no Nancy, no neighbor that would be willing to look in on Margaret. The neighbors were either new and didn't know Margaret, or they'd been there a long time and they knew Margaret.

Sitting beside Zeinab in the passenger seat of a car that squealed whenever she turned a corner made Carrie feel like she was being unjustly punished. Packard had absolutely no proof that she had anything to do with Bill or Sherri getting killed. She should be able to come and go as she pleased without being observed by cops, and without having to pay a woman who made fifteen dollars an hour giving baths to old people for a goddamn ride.

Carrie had convinced herself that killing Sherri wasn't her fault.

She had waited for Sherri to get off work, then went to her condo to get another look at the letter Sherri had shown her earlier that day. Something about it bothered her, like the end of a splinter that she could feel with her fingernail but couldn't grab and pull out. She wanted to see the letter again.

It was near midnight and Sherri was in fine form after drinking during her whole shift. She was more annoyed than surprised to see her sister on her doorstep unannounced. "Oh my god. Whaddaya want?" she asked as she turned her back on her sister and untucked her blouse from her skirt.

Carrie followed her inside. It smelled like a burning cigarette and a thousand old cigarettes. Sherri was the only one in the family who had taken up smoking. Carrie thought it was disgusting. Bill had told her he was quitting when they started seeing each other again, but she smelled it on him all the time after they got married. Now she wondered if she had smelled his cigarettes or Sherri's or—

The sight of her mother's jewelry box stopped her in her tracks. It was sitting on Sherri's dining room table, on display like a centerpiece.

"Where the fuck did you get that?" Carrie asked.

"It was on the patio table when I got home from work. I just brought it in. I thought it was from the girl whose car I borrow when I need one. She told me she makes shit and sells it on Etsy, whatever the fuck that is."

"You don't recognize that box?"

Sherri walked over to the couch, where she had a glass of wine and a cigarette burning in a giant stone ashtray. "Never seen it before," she said.

"Do you think I'm an idiot?"

Sherri stared at her, squinting behind the smoke rising from the cigarette pinched in her mouth. "I think you're a selfish bitch and a total cunt," she said. "I wouldn't call you an idiot, though."

"That's Mom's jewelry box. It was stolen the night Bill was killed. How do you now have it if you weren't part of all this?"

"Part of all what?" Sherri asked. She got up, went to the jewelry box, and opened it. No jewelry. Just some folded blue stationery. "Look. Another letter," Sherri sang.

Carrie tried to grab it but wasn't fast enough. "Give me that."

"Get away," Sherri said. "It's obviously for me if it was left with the box on my patio." She held her cigarette in one hand and sidled sideways around the table, trying to keep it between her and Carrie while she read the letter.

Carrie walked over to the couch and sat down with her arms folded. "What does it say?"

"It says you were in the room when Bill was killed. You held a gun on this guy and gave him a choice of shooting Bill or getting a bullet in the back of the head." Carrie couldn't tell by Sherri's tone whether she believed what she was reading or not. "He says the jewelry box is proof that he was there. That he's telling the truth."

"I overheard him asking Bill about Mom's hummingbird pin," Carrie said.

She didn't realize in the moment what she was admitting. All she cared about was Sherri knowing she was on to her.

"What pin?"

"The pin shaped like a hummingbird she always wore. Gold and rubies and diamonds."

Sherri shrugged. "Doesn't ring a bell. I never paid much attention to Mom's jewelry. It was all so gaudy."

"And you still threw a huge fit when she gave it all to me."

"I threw a fit because it was just another example of you getting everything from Mom and me getting nothing. Look around. I could use a little help."

"Maybe if you acted nicer," Carrie suggested.

"Fuck off. Mom only ever had one child she gave a shit about, and it certainly wasn't me." Sherri came over and ashed her cigarette in the giant bowl on the coffee table. "So you were there if you heard them talking about Mom's pin."

"Let me see the letter," Carrie said.

Sherri handed it to her and sat down at the other end of the sectional. Carrie read it quickly. All true. All things she already knew. "I know you're part of this," she said to Sherri when she was done. "The three of you were plotting to kill me for the insurance. Stealing Mom's jewelry was just a cover."

"I know this is hard for you to believe, but not everything is about you, Carrie." Sherri's eyes looked heavy, like she wanted to go to sleep. "The only thing I was involved in was taking Bill's dick a couple of times a month. If he had something planned with this guy, I didn't know a thing about it." She sat up and scooted to the edge of her seat. "What about you? You lied to the police. Why didn't you tell Detective Packard what you heard?"

"What I heard or didn't hear doesn't make any difference," Carrie said. "The guy was wearing a ski mask. I have no idea who he was."

Sherri looked pissed. She leaned over and jabbed out her cigarette. "If you heard them talking, if you saw him shoot Bill, you could at least tell Packard how tall the guy was. His build. Describe the sound of his voice."

"I've been trying to figure out who he is. How he would know about Mom's jewelry. How he got my cell phone number. It had to be you. Now you two are trying to blackmail me."

"It wasn't me! And it's not your job to figure out who he is!" Sherri yelled. "It's Packard's. And he could do it if you told him what you know."

Sherri stared at her sister, mouth open. Carrie recognized this moment from all the times when they were girls, the moment right before one of them launched at the other and grabbed a fistful of hair and started pulling the other's head toward the ground. The goal was to hurt the other one as quickly as possible, make her cry first, and be the one still standing when Margaret came to separate them. Margaret always took the side of the victor.

"I'm calling Packard. I don't care what fucking time it is," Sherri said. She got up and found her phone in her purse, scrolled through its screens with her back to Carrie.

"Don't call Packard. I'll call him myself tomorrow," Carrie said.

"The fuck you will," Sherri said. "Hang on. I got a text from Kristie."

For a moment, Carrie allowed herself to consider what Sherri had said—that there was no conspiracy, that Carrie was wrong about all her assumptions about what happened that night, and that all Bill and his petty-thief friend had wanted was her mother's jewelry.

But what about the argument between Bill and the killer over the hummingbird pin? And why was Sherri still sleeping with Bill if they weren't planning on getting back together eventually? They needed money to do that. The only money Bill had access to was the life insurance he had on her.

It was the only thing that made sense. She wasn't wrong.

Sherri was lying. She would keep lying, keep producing more phony letters with the killer to show to Packard until he turned all his attention to her.

Carrie grabbed the nearest thing at hand—the giant ashtray on the coffee table. Once she was holding it, she realized it was a huge molcajete for making guacamole or salsa. It was heavy and awkward. The outside was rough like volcanic rock, the inside polished smooth. It said Cabo San Lucas around the rim and was just the kind of tacky thing Sherri and Bill would have bought on vacation together.

"Let me talk to Packard," Carrie said, coming up behind Sherri. She held the ashtray by the edge and brought it down on the back of Sherri's head. Ashes and cigarette butts rained down like the insides of a bad firework as Sherri slumped to the floor. She caught herself with one hand, turned and landed on her butt, and tried to crawl backward, but Carrie was right there and she brought the ashtray down again, as hard as she could, on Sherri's forehead. Her sister went flat. Her leg twitched a couple of times and then she was still.

Carrie dropped the ashtray. She grabbed the letter and, after a minute's deliberation, left the jewelry box. It would incriminate Sherri in Bill's killing once the police arrived.

It was almost one in the morning when she closed the door to Sherri's condo and wiped the handle. She'd parked at the opposite end of the complex, far from Sherri's so no one nearby would hear her car start. There were few lights on in any windows.

When she got home, she slept soundly, certain she had done the right thing.

———

Zeinab had a client to see, which was why she had to leave when she did.

"I have to make sure she's taken her medication, check the dressing from her surgery, and make sure she's comfortable for the night," Zeinab said as they pulled into the woman's driveway. "It will take about twenty minutes. You wait, then I go home and you can borrow the car."

She left the car running and the heat on. Carrie had left her phone at home so there was nothing to do but listen to the radio. She started unlacing her shoes, thinking she would dry her feet under the car's heat, then stopped and asked herself: Why wait for Zeinab? She had the car, she had the keys. In twenty minutes, she could be where she needed to go. In another twenty minutes, she could be back.

Carrie laced her shoes and maneuvered herself over the parking brake and into the driver's seat. She debated running up to the house, yelling from the front door her intention and decided against it. Zeinab would understand. And if she didn't, she'd understand hundred dollar bills. Carrie had plenty of those.

———————

She had memorized the route after looking up the address at home, then wiping the browser's memory so there was no record of it on her phone. The houses were far apart on this road and set back in the trees. Carrie slowed and leaned over the steering wheel, watching for numbers on mailboxes until she knew the next house was the right one. She killed the headlights and let the car slow on its own so she wouldn't have to touch the squealing brakes.

The path to the house had been plowed free of snow. Carrie gave the car a little gas as it went up a slight incline through the trees to a two-story house made from naked pine logs held together with heavy lines of white chinking. She saw lights on in the front windows but no one moving inside.

A light on a tall pole behind the house shone down on a two-stall garage topped with snow and a small outbuilding beside it. Carrie let the car roll to a stop and put it in Park near where the plow had piled the snow to one side. She got out and left the car running, the door pushed shut but not latched.

Up the wooden steps to the front porch, trying to be as quiet as possible. She'd decided surprise would work to her advantage in this situation. No knocking. There was a storm door that she eased open, watching the windows to her right for any shadows or changes in the lighting. Carrie paused to take the gun out of her coat pocket. It was so much heavier than her own gun. It felt like carrying a cast-iron skillet by the handle.

The front door opened with the lightest push. Carrie stepped into a living room. She saw no one. There were no overhead lights, just lamps. A maroon couch and a matching love seat sat across from each other, between them a coffee table made from the shellacked stump of a tree. She picked up the odors from a recently cooked meal—grilled meat and broccoli.

She stepped to the side so she could close the door. There was a landing behind the door and a staircase with a railing made of the same pinewood as the rest of the house.

Someone was standing in the dark at the top of the stars. The figure took two steps down, and Carrie found herself staring into the business end of a shotgun.

"I wondered how long it would take you to figure it out," said the voice from the shadows.

CHAPTER TWENTY-EIGHT

ON THE EDGE OF town, Packard pulled into the gravel lot surrounding the new brewery that still wasn't open to the public yet. There was one other car in the lot and faint lights on in the windows. He needed a place to stop so he could concentrate on his laptop and the radio.

The health aide's name was Zeinab Abdi. Packard got her address and phone number from her vehicle registration. Her husband answered and said his wife wasn't home yet. He gave Packard her cell phone number, but she didn't answer when he called. A couple more calls to her employer finally connected him to someone who knew Zeinab's schedule. She was at Margaret Gherlick's for most of her shift, then stopping by to check on Tracy Hickey, who lived alone and was recovering from a recent surgery.

Packard sent a deputy to Tracy's house and found Zeinab there.

"She's pretty upset. She says that Carrie Gherlick took her car. She doesn't know where she was going."

"How long ago was this?"

"She's not sure," the deputy said. "She was in the house for a while and left Carrie alone in the car. She came out after about thirty minutes and the car was gone. Her phone and other personal items are in the car."

Zeinab's phone was inexpensive and didn't have locator software. Packard asked the deputy to give her a ride home.

It started to snow again. Packard looked at the computer to see the calls that had come in to dispatch and who was responding. No sightings of Zeinab's car or Carrie Gherlick. He bit his thumbnail and tried to think where Carrie might be heading. She couldn't know where Paul had been staying. Packard still hadn't gotten a straight answer from him about that. Somewhere out there was a point where she and Paul intersected. Carrie had the point in sight. Packard did not.

Someone knocked on Packard's window, making him start. The man standing in the falling snow had a dark beard and was wearing a gray beanie pushed back.

Packard put his window down.

"It's Kyle," the guy said, reaching his hand through Packard's window to shake.

"From the county commissioners' meeting. You and your cousin requested approval of the license for the brewery."

"Yeah. I just wanted to make sure everything was okay. You've been sitting out here for a while."

"I didn't mean to cause any concern," Packard said. "I've just been trying to keep an eye on everything going on tonight."

Kyle nodded. They talked about the snow and the roads. Kyle had come in to clean the fermentation tank and mill the malt for a beer that would start brewing in the morning. "I'd invite you in to try what's ready but you're on duty."

"Some other time," Packard said. "I'm definitely looking forward to this place being open."

"I've been getting updates about your campaign from Kelly, my aunt. We're not officially opening until the week of Thanksgiving, but I was thinking if you wanted to have an election night gathering here—just your campaign staff—we could definitely host you."

"Thanks for the offer. Let me talk to Kelly. My life is a whole lot easier when I don't make decisions without her approval."

Kyle stood with his hands in his pockets and rocked back on his heels. "I get it. We all try to stay on Auntie Kelly's good side."

"'Auntie Kelly.' I'm going to call her that next time I see her."

"She'll hate that," Kyle warned him.

"Oh, I know," Packard said.

They shook again and Packard put his window up and watched Kyle walk away. The man was disarmingly good-looking. From the dark hair to the scruff to the scar on his lip.

Packard pushed the laptop away, unlocked his phone, and took another look at the photos he'd taken of the letter Paul had sent Carrie. Paul had listed the names and addresses of everyone Carrie was close to. Fairly easy information to come by if Carrie's Facebook account wasn't set to private. The board members could be found on the foundation's website.

Packard thought of the drawing he'd made early in the case with Bill in the center and all the people orbiting him. He'd imagined some unknown force circling all of them, affecting the pull of the objects on each other. Now he knew that force was Paul.

Bill was the one who had gotten himself killed, but what if he wasn't the star at the center of this solar system? What if he put Paul at the center? Packard started to mentally rearrange the circles to surround Paul by his three half sisters, his birth father, Bill…

And then he saw it. All at once, all the pieces. Things he hadn't noticed or hadn't deemed significant suddenly made sense.

There was a name missing from the list Paul had sent to Carrie.

Mary.

Why wouldn't Paul list her? Why wouldn't he go to her next, now that Sherri was out of the picture, unless he knew firsthand that Mary was estranged from her family? Bill might have told him, but the way Carrie and Sherri acted as if Mary didn't even exist made Packard doubt that she was ever a topic of conversation. Mary could have fed Paul all the inside information he needed about the Gherlicks: where her mother lived, family phone numbers, the people closest to Carrie. Mary surely sold stationery in her store and everything that came out of there probably smelled of incense or scented candles. Packard remembered how the strong smell of the store had made him take a step back the day he and Thielen had visited.

If Paul's first stop in town was the bank founded by his father, the very next thing he would have seen—right across the street—was Gherlick Bead & Craft. Packard suddenly remembered watching Paul's hands the night he confronted him outside the Big Beaver. He'd been carrying a beaded key chain. He should have seen it sooner.

Mary would have been a sympathetic ear and an eager participant in figuring out what had happened to Paul's mother, maybe even a willing partner in whatever plot he had to get his share of the family fortune.

It was Mary this whole time. Carrie must have finally figured out the same thing.

Packard called dispatch and requested that a deputy get Paul Bowers near a phone. Then he called the number he had for Mary, hoping he wasn't too late.

CHAPTER TWENTY-NINE

"I'LL PUT MY GUN down if you put yours down," Carrie said to her sister.

Mary came down the stairs, the end of her shotgun never straying from its aim at Carrie. "I think you're going to put yours down regardless," Mary said. "You broke into my house with your gun drawn, which tells me you didn't come here to talk. What I need is a reason not to blow your fucking head off."

Carrie put her gun inside her coat and zipped it to her chin. "There. I put mine away. Can I sit?"

Mary came the rest of the way down the stairs. She was wearing moccasins and jeans and a black sweater that rolled down at the neck. She directed Carrie to the couch with the end of the gun, then sat across from her on the love seat with the shotgun across her lap.

"That turtleneck doesn't do anything to hide your double chin," Carrie said. "It accentuates it. Your wattle just droops on top of the fabric."

Mary shook her head and ran her hand down the barrel of the shotgun. "You can't help yourself, can you? There's never been a word out of your mouth directed toward me that wasn't an insult."

"I thought it was friendly advice," Carrie said.

"You haven't been friendly a day in your life," Mary replied.

WHERE THE DEAD SLEEP

Carrie tried to remember the last time she'd been in the same room as her sister. She'd texted both Sherri and Mary when their mother was diagnosed with dementia. Mary hadn't responded at all. Before that, Carrie and Margaret would make the occasional lap through Mary's store, mostly to look down their noses at the worthless junk she sold. The Gherlick name had long been associated with banking and construction and philanthropy, and then Mary went and put it on a store that sold beads and hot glue. She made tacky jewelry and peddled it in her store and at flea markets and street fairs. Mary was wearing a necklace over her sweater that was an asymmetrical mess of mismatched stones of different sizes. Ugly enough to be her work for sure.

"So who is he?" Carrie asked.

"Who is who?"

"The guy who shot Bill. The one you've been helping all this time."

"I don't know what you're talking about," Mary insisted.

"For god's sake, Mary. I'm talking about the guy whose shoes are beside the door. Whose Sandy Lake Auto coat is hanging on the rack. He worked with Bill. I should have known."

The stationery and the smell of incense were what had brought Carrie to her sister's house. The smell had reminded her of something, but it took a couple of days to place it. It was while looking through a drawer in her mother's desk that she found a similar package of stationery and put two and two together. Margaret's favorite thing to do when they visited Mary's store was to take things without paying. Stationery. Postcards. Candles. "I'm your mother, so I'll be helping myself to this," she'd say as they breezed past Mary and out the door.

Once Carrie recognized the stationery, everything else made sense. Mary had the number to the phone at the house and Carrie's cell phone number. Most of all, Mary would have known that the best way to get at Carrie was to pit her and Sherri against each other and let them fight like cats in a sack.

"Where is he now?"

"He went to town to get groceries. Supposed to snow a lot tonight," Mary said.

"And why is he living here with you? What's your role in this?"

"All I've done is give him a place to stay while he's tried to figure out how not to be framed for a murder you're responsible for."

Carrie rolled her eyes. "He seems less interested in clearing his name than he is in blackmailing me."

"He told me what happened that night. How you came in with your own gun and put it to his head. He wasn't there to murder anybody."

"What was I supposed to do? I found a man in a ski mask discussing the contents of my jewelry box with my husband. It was two against one. I needed to protect myself."

"You saw an opportunity to get rid of Bill and you took it. The only reason you married him was to piss off Sherri. Once you had him, you didn't want him."

"Bill was a piece of shit," Carrie said. She folded her arms across her chest. The gun under her coat felt like a brick. "Putting two bullets in him was doing the world a favor."

"Was killing our sister doing the world a favor, too?"

"Sherri was a miserable alcoholic without a penny to her name. Mom's jewelry box was sitting right there on her table, proving she was part of this plot the two of you cooked up against me. You've both been jealous of me your whole lives. You couldn't stand to see me be happy and successful so you plotted to have me killed during a phony burglary."

Mary's laugh sounded like a bark. "That's the narcissist in you talking. Can you even hear how much you sound like Mom?" She made a witchy, whiny sound with her voice. "'Why is everyone against me when all I've ever done is try to be a good mother to you girls? You don't love me. I should just kill myself.' Remember that? I'm the only one who saw through her bullshit and refused to play along. That's why she hated me so much. One of the reasons, anyway. But you and Sherri would fall all over each other, trying to snap Mom out of her moods and win her approval. You treated me like shit. You treated Dad like shit. And when you were tired of torturing us, you'd rip into each other for Mom's enjoyment. You did the same thing to your kids. That's why your daughter calls me for advice and why she wants you out of her life."

Carrie narrowed her eyes. She didn't know that Mary knew about her strained relationship with Rebecca. She refused to believe her relationship with her daughter was as bad as Mary's was with Margaret.

"Carrie, you weren't at the center of this at all. It was never about you. It was about the jewelry. It was just a burglary. Bill and Paul were going to split the money they made selling it. You were supposed to be asleep in your bed when it happened. There was no plot to kill you. Sherri had nothing to do with it. You're the one who turned this into a double murder."

Carrie shook her head. Mary was lying. Everyone lied when it came to getting what they wanted. "He knew about my jewelry," Carrie said. "I overheard him asking Bill about Mom's hummingbird pin. There was a plot."

"He knew about the pin because it used to belong to his mother. She was a bank teller in the seventies. Her name was Sarah. She had an affair with Dad and got pregnant."

Carrie was stunned. "You're saying he's our brother?"

"We might share the same DNA, but I would say he's no more our brother than any other stranger on the street. He'd have had to share in our miserable childhood to make him one of us."

"It wasn't that miserable," Carrie insisted.

"You would think so," Mary said. "What about my experience? Your total lack of empathy is what makes you Margaret's daughter."

"Mom blurted out the other day—in front of the detective—that she killed Dad's whore. And that Dad helped her get rid of the body."

Mary didn't seem surprised. "Looks like a knack for remorseless killing may be something else you got from Mom."

Carrie ignored the jab.

Mary got up from the couch and went to the kitchen, taking the shotgun with her. She held it just behind the stock and propped on her shoulder as she worked one-handed putting a pod in a Keurig coffee maker and pressing the button. "It would also explain how Mom ended up with a dead woman's pin. Can't you just see her wearing that hummingbird every day in front of Dad so he never forgot what she was capable of?"

When Mary turned her back to get milk from the fridge, Carrie reached under her coat for the gun and shoved it between the couch cushions. The butt stuck up higher than the cushion so she moved over a few inches so she could close her legs around it.

Lights swept the front of the house. Carrie glanced at Mary, then turned to look out the window over her shoulder. A white pickup truck with tinted windows drove past the side of the house. It was snowing harder now. Zeinab's car had an inch of new snow on it since Carrie had left it running.

"Is that him?" she asked.

Mary drank from her coffee mug. Said nothing. She still held the shotgun with one hand against her shoulder.

A minute later a man in a parka with the hood up walked under the window behind Carrie. He had a sack of groceries in each arm. Mary had gone to the kitchen window over the sink to look out.

Carrie reached between her legs for the butt of the gun, slid it from between the cushions and pulled back the hammer with her other hand. She aimed it first at Mary. "Stay right where you are," she said. "Don't move that gun an inch."

Mary froze. She was holding a coffee cup in one hand. The shotgun in her other hand needed two hands to operate. She was a hand short.

They both listened to the sound of footsteps on the front stairs. The man stomped snow from his boots on the porch. When Carrie heard a paper bag rustle and the spring of the storm door, she counted to one, then turned and aimed at the front door.

"*She's got a gun!*" Mary yelled.

Carrie looked behind her just in time to see her sister drop to the floor behind the kitchen counter. She turned back to the door and pulled the trigger on the .44. A baseball-sized hole appeared in the wooden door. She was pulling the hammer back again when a bang shook the back of the house.

A man yelled, "*Police! Drop the gun! Drop the gun!*" A team in black tactical gear poured through the back door and into the kitchen like an oil spill.

Carrie put the gun on the coffee table stump and stood with her hands up as the police approached her with their guns drawn. The one closest to her took her gun and yelled, "*Secure!*" while another reached for her hands and moved them behind her back.

The man in the parka pushed open the front door. Carrie wondered if her brother would look like her. Or her dad. Or her son.

The man pushed back his hood.

It was Packard.

The detective stuck his finger in the fist-sized hole in the front door. "You could have killed somebody," he said.

CHAPTER THIRTY

ELECTION NIGHT.

Packard and about a dozen others were gathered at Hopfenstopfen Brewery. The name was a mouthful, but Kyle and his cousin said they expected everyone to call it HopStop. The interior of the building was all concrete and stainless-steel brewing equipment. At the far end was a long wooden bar with sixteen tap handles and enough high-top tables spread around to seat the busy crowds that were sure to descend on the place next summer. The LCD menus hadn't been connected yet, so the beers on tap were printed on office paper. There were baskets of pretzels and potato chips, and frozen pizzas were coming out of two electric pizza ovens at a regular clip.

Packard, who hadn't wanted a gathering at all, was having a good time in spite of himself. It might have been the beer, or the chance to see his closest friends and family all in one place. Might have been the private tour Kyle had given him earlier through the forest of towering brew tanks. He explained the brewing process and what was in each tank. The floors were wet and the air smelled yeasty and funky. Packard was distracted, trying to recall when he'd smelled something similar recently.

"Does the fermentation process ever smell really bad? Kind of rotten?" he asked.

"It shouldn't smell really bad," Kyle said. "Depends on what you've got brewing."

Packard was remembering the old man with the deep fryer and the underground hidey-hole that he didn't want Packard to see and the smell that came out of it. He told Kyle about the bags of corn in the back of this guy's truck.

"If he was using corn in his mash, then he's making moonshine, not beer. That stuff can smell kind of rank and vomity a few days in," Kyle said.

So the old man had an illegal still down there, not dead bodies. Small relief.

Packard and Kyle went out a side door to the patio area where there were brick rings for firepits and picnic tables and wooden barrels people could stand around. They walked to the far edge of the patio and looked out at a path that led down to the river and a dock for kayaks and canoes. Snow had matted down the wild grass along the banks, and the water in between was black as ink. Come summer, people would be splashing in the shallow river and crawling up the hill in search of beer like castaways from a sinking ship.

"You guys are going to make a million bucks with this place," Packard said. "The beer is great. You couldn't ask for a better location."

"I hope you're right," Kyle said. "We've put every cent we own and a bunch that we owe into it."

They stood side by side, close enough that their shoulders touched. If it were any colder, they would have hurried back inside. Neither of them made a move. Water rolled by silently. Packard thought of the saying about a man never being able to step in the same river twice.

"What's on your mind right now?" Kyle asked, giving him a nudge with his shoulder.

The election, of course. Packard was already talking when he realized he'd failed to recognize the opening he'd just been given. He wanted to kick himself. He was a detective. He was supposed to be better at this. "I'm glad the election is almost over. I'll be fine whatever the outcome. I have a job to do whether I'm a full-time sheriff or back to a full-time detective."

"I think you're going to win. I think your crew in there thinks you're going to win."

"I appreciate the vote of confidence," Packard said.

"I don't think that article made one bit of difference."

The article was a story in the *Sandy Lake Gazette*, penned by Ray Hanson, of course, where Carrie Gherlick accused Packard and the entire sheriff's department of unjustly persecuting her for suspicion of murder (she used a lot of legal-sounding words that didn't entirely make sense) when they already had the confessed killer behind bars. She also claimed there was a general sense among people she knew that crime was up in the county, and she blamed Packard for not doing his job and the county commissioners for not appointing a more experienced person as acting sheriff.

The only reason she was available to give such an interview was because a sympathetic judge granted her bail, given her close connections to the community and her role as the primary caregiver for her mother.

DNA tests came back two weeks later showing skin from Carrie's hand had been abraded by the rough lava-like exterior of the molcajete used to crush Sherri's skull. They also found Sherri's blood on Carrie's shoe and on a blouse that hadn't been laundered in a hamper at her mother's house. Packard and a county attorney went back to the judge with the new evidence and Carrie's bail was revoked. She'd been in jail for the last three days. It was impossible to know if news of her arrest undid any of the damage done by the article. On the plus side, unless Carrie had remembered to mail in her ballot between all her murdering and newspaper posturing, there was one fewer vote for Shepard.

"I think you're right about the article," Packard said. "Most people's minds were made up the second they heard who was running. It's been a waiting game since then."

"I hope it goes your way," Kyle said. "For your sake and Auntie Kelly's. She's not going to be happy working for the other guy."

Packard tried to imagine Shepard giving direction to Kelly. It made him laugh. "He better start training now if he's going to get in the ring with Kelly. She'll drop him on his head six times before he knows what's hit him."

Back inside, Thielen was refreshing the secretary of state's website on her phone every ten seconds. Everyone was all smiles. Packard talked to his cousin Susan and her daughter, Jenny, who'd done her part to rally eighteen-year-old high school seniors to his side. Jenny showed him how close she was to being able to make a fist again after the surgery to fix her hand that was wounded when she'd been shot by Emmett Burr.

Music played from speakers high overhead. Taylor Swift and Alabama Shakes and The War on Drugs. Packard asked Kyle to play some Barry Manilow for Kelly, and a few minutes later "Looks Like We Made It" came down from above like an angel choir on high. Kelly rolled her eyes, then suddenly whipped her head to one side and started lip-synching into her nearly empty beer glass like it was a microphone. People cheered and clapped and sang along. It was a party for a bunch of people who weren't sure they had a reason to party.

Packard got a text on his phone. **Good luck tonight from both of us.** It came with a photo of Roger Freeman, the dairy farmer, and Bill's sister Wendy sitting side by side at an oak dining table. Wendy was holding a file folder that had the words *Business Plan* on the front. Roger was holding a check. Packard had to zoom in to see the check was made out to Roger in the amount of ten thousand dollars and signed by Leon Chen. The memo line said *Reimbursement.*

Packard was happy to see that Leon had returned the money Bill had lost in the poker game at Leon's house. Sure, the first ten grand Bill had taken from the shared account and lost at the game was the money he put into it (most of it actually coming from his sister Wendy). It was different than what Packard understood when he suggested Leon reimburse Roger, but this was one instance where he didn't feel the need to correct the record. Roger and Wendy recouped some of their money, and it didn't cost the very wealthy Leon Chen a thing in the grand scheme of things.

Packard had had a separate conversation with Wendy after Carrie was arrested to let her know what he knew about Bill's life insurance. "Sherri was the primary beneficiary. With her deceased as well, it goes to the secondary beneficiary, which is you."

Wendy didn't know how to react. "It's a terrible way to cash in," she said. "I'd rather have my brother and Sherri still alive than get any amount of money."

"I know you would," Packard said. "But start thinking about what you might do with that money. You could always open the chicken-wing restaurant that Bill was dreaming about. You and Roger both believed in it enough to give him your money. I don't know the economics of owning a restaurant or whether there's enough money to be made to support two families. Maybe there's enough to provide some financial cushion to two families."

From the photo, it looked like Wendy and Roger were going to give it a shot. It was one of the few things about the whole situation involving Bill Sandersen that made Packard feel good.

The night went on.

Packard hung close to Marilyn while they waited. Win or lose, he had a feeling he'd be seeing a lot less of the sheriff's widow after tonight. She'd done everything she could to help him win, just like she'd promised. He was going to miss spending time with her.

Kyle and his cousin Mark kept the beer flowing. Packard limited himself to one. Newly Elected Sheriff Arrested for DUI on Way Home from Election Night Party was a headline Ray Hanson would be all too willing to write. Packard wasn't going to give him the chance.

Thielen came up with her phone in her hand and a tall, skinny pilsner glass in the other. "I'm going to break my thumb or this screen if they don't post the results soon," she said.

"Relax. We'll know soon enough," Packard said.

The Bill Sandersen case was all but wrapped up. The same couldn't be said for Thielen's investigation into the boat shooter. Besides the two slugs and the single shell casing they'd recovered, they had nothing. No suspects, no witnesses, no leads. Whoever had taken the shot at Packard was still out there. Motive unknown.

"Any idea what Shepard was doing tonight?" Thielen asked.

Packard shook his head. He'd actually extended Shepard an invitation to combine their events but gotten no response. They'd managed to keep things civil all the way until the end. Shepard's dig at him during the debate for hiring a foreigner was as low as things went. Packard had never commented on the letters in Shepard's personnel file, and no one from Shepard's side had tried to make the case that a gay sheriff would turn Sandy Lake into a modern-day Sodom, or worse yet, a Midwest Provincetown, nothing but rainbow flags and lesbian-owned pottery studios from here to Canada.

Thielen went to get another beer. She was talking to Kyle and touching her phone every few seconds. Packard saw the results in her face the instant they hit.

He looked over at Kelly who caught his eye, saw his expression, and whipped her phone out of her back pocket like she was drawing a gun.

The hive mind in the room became aware of the news all at once. More people reached for their phones. Thielen came over with hers and showed Packard the screen.

Sandy Lake County Sheriff		
Candidate	Total Votes	Percent
Howard Shepard	9717	47%
Benjamin Packard	8481	41%
Alan Costas	2413	12%

Kyle turned down the music. Packard felt all the eyes in the room on him.

"Listen up, everyone. The results are in. It didn't go our way," he said. "I'm sorry I wasn't able to win this for us. It wasn't due to a lack of effort on any of our parts." He said some more about being proud of the campaign they'd run and about continuing to work on behalf of everyone in the county as a detective. He couldn't really hear himself. He felt Marilyn squeeze his hand. He felt the weight of everyone's disappointment. In his mind, he was seeing the view from where he and Kyle stood earlier and he was thinking of everything waiting for all of them once they left this place, things that the outcome of the election had no bearing on. Family. Friends. The holidays. A long winter. Things that persisted even as they changed

Never the same river twice.

CHAPTER THIRTY-ONE

THAT SAME NIGHT.

Not far away.

The shooter pushed open a sliding glass door dripping with condensation and stepped onto the deck of Jim Wolf's house. It was too hot inside, too many people celebrating. The night air was cold but felt good compared to the sauna building on the other side of the glass.

Jim Wolf stepped out a minute later and slid the door shut behind him. It was just the two of them. They clinked glasses.

"Congrats on your candidate winning," the shooter said.

"If I'd known that fat bastard was going to invite this many people, I never would have had the party here. It's like a herd of cattle in my house."

The shooter smiled and drank. "I wonder how Deputy Packard is feeling right now."

Wolf grunted. "Fuck him. It's nice to see that sonofabitch taken down a notch for once. He was overdue for an ego check. The best part is that Shepard is the one giving it to him."

"I'm sure Shepard will make a fine sheriff."

"Shepard is an idiot," Wolf said. "But he thinks we're friends, and it's nice to have a friend be the head of law enforcement when doing business in this county."

"I can understand how that would be true."

The moon was nearly full and wrapped in a frozen nimbus, the only place colder than Minnesota in the winter.

"I've been meaning to ask you something," Wolf said. There was a chatter in his voice, like the cold was getting to him. "That night at Chen's when someone took a shot at Packard." He waited and stared at the shooter, looking for some recognition of what he was talking about. The shooter stared at him blankly. "That wasn't you, was it?" Wolf finished.

"Are you asking if I tried to kill Packard? Why would I do that?" the shooter asked.

"It's just that…your record. It's part of your record…that you…"

"My record? Are you impugning my record?"

They locked eyes, and the shooter saw the curiosity drain from Wolf's face. "Never mind," he said. "It was a stupid question. Forget it."

Inside the house, a man with the same huge gut, goatee, and pattern baldness as Shepard had the new sheriff in a headlock and was rubbing the top of his head with his forearm. They were both red-faced and laughing. Shepard was sloshing Jack and Coke onto the living room rug.

"Fuck," Wolf said. "I paid thirty grand for that rug. These goddamn morons…"

He went back inside.

The shooter turned to stare at the black lake glittering with moonlight. Shepard winning the election was definitely good news, but it didn't solve every problem. Packard had deeper roots in the area than anyone realized. Wolf would use his influence on Shepard to see that Packard suffered under the new leadership. If that didn't run him off, then at least he'd be too busy to sniff around where he shouldn't.

All else failing, another long-range shot fired out of the dark would take care of Packard.

Next time there'd be no missing.

CHAPTER THIRTY-TWO

MARY GHERLICK PARKED HER truck in the driveway of her mother's house, a place she hadn't been for almost thirty years. The place loomed large in her memory—both in size and setting—but looked smaller in person. She wasn't the type to talk about trauma as if it were a proper noun, but she felt a small wave of nausea as she pushed through the front door without knocking.

Inside, things weren't exactly as they'd been when she was a child, but they were close enough. Her mother was sitting in a recliner in the living room in front of the television. A woman from a company called Home Help was washing dishes. Mary smelled laundry soap and heard the rumble of clothes tumbling in the dryer.

The woman from Home Help said hi and introduced herself as Janet. She was fat and smiley and wearing thick oval glasses that were too small for her face. Mary recognized her from the store and they chatted for a bit about the baby book Janet was making for a friend.

Mary took off her coat and sat on the end of the couch near her mother's chair. "What are you doing here?" Margaret asked.

"Came to see how you're doing," Mary said.

"Where's Carrie?"

"Carrie's in jail, Mom." The last word felt dead in her mouth, like she'd bitten her tongue hard and couldn't feel it. "People have been telling you that for a while now."

"I don't believe it. She was just here this morning."

"No, she wasn't. She's been in jail for two weeks now. She killed Sherri. And Bill."

Margaret made a face like Mary was being ridiculous. She had an iPad in her lap. The screen was dark. She touched it with a shaky, veiny finger, trying to remember how to turn it on.

Janet finished the dishes and pulled sheets from the dryer and took them down the hall to remake Margaret's bed. When she was gone, Mary said, "Mom, Carrie said you killed a woman a long time ago. Her name was Sarah. Dad had given her the hummingbird pin."

Margaret's face was blank while her brain tried to process what she was hearing through her broken neural network. "She was a whore. I saved my marriage from her," Margaret said. "Carrie would have never been born if I hadn't done what I did."

"Yes, that would have been a tragedy," Mary said. "Who else did you kill? Anyone?"

Margaret just stared at her.

"I had a fiancé once upon a time. We were very much in love. He was shot climbing down from his deer stand. I was devastated."

"Why should you have been any happier than the rest of us?" Margaret said. Her finger finally landed on the home button that turned on the iPad. She found the icon for her solitaire game and pushed it.

"Mom, what did you do?"

Margaret was gone, lost in the game.

Mary sat back and dropped her chin to her chest. She'd never believed Jay's death was an accident. Margaret's question didn't amount to a confession, but it was no stretch to think she might have been behind Jay's murder, especially in light of her involvement in the death of Paul's mother.

What happened to Sarah Pellak was the mystery she and Paul had been trying to solve since the day he walked into her store and asked her if she was related to John Gherlick. He told her what he'd learned about the woman who was his actual mother from the woman who had raised him. Mary found the article about Sarah's body being recovered from a car in a drainage ditch. Paul told her about the hummingbird pin John had given to Sarah, which Mary knew from Margaret wearing it all the time. They found grainy photos in the newspaper archives of community events from a time when people used to dress up for luncheons and fundraising dinners and rotary meetings. The president of the bank and his wife were at many of them. They found four photos of Margaret Gherlick wearing the pin, all dated after Sarah Pellak had died.

"It's possible my father had two pins made—one for his mistress and one for his wife," Margaret suggested. She doubted it even as she said it.

Paul wanted the pin. He got a job at Sandy Lake Auto, befriended Bill, and slowly hand-fed him possible solutions to his money problems. Mary knew all about Paul's prison background and didn't really care whether he had motives beyond just getting his mother's pin or not. If he wanted to hock the family jewels and run off with all the money, she figured it was the least he had coming to him as a legitimate heir to John Gherlick.

The night of the burglary, Paul had come home from Bill's truly terrified. After Packard questioned him at work, Paul had decided he'd need money if he was going to truly disappear and hide from any suspicion directed his way regarding Bill's murder. He thought Carrie should be the one to fund it. Mary had money she could have given him, but she didn't feel like she should pick up the tab for her sister being a cold-blooded murderer. Mary told Paul the best way to pressure Carrie was to sic Sherri on her. If Carrie got nervous enough about what Sherri might do with information about Bill's murder, she might be willing to pay.

That Carrie would murder her own sister hadn't occurred to Mary. Now she wondered why she hadn't seen it coming.

She was going to do all she could to help Paul with his trial. She liked the public defender he'd been assigned and had agreed to pay for her and another lawyer to defend Paul. How much they could do when he already had a felony record and the police had a signed statement from him that he'd pulled the trigger on Bill was yet to be seen.

Janet finished the last of her chores and came to the living room while buttoning her coat. "I'm all done for today. I'll see you again in a few days, Mrs. Gherlick," she said.

"My god, you're fat," Margaret said.

"I know, Mrs. Gherlick. You tell me every time I'm here," Janet said. She was smiling, but Mary could see the strain.

"I'm sorry," Mary said. "I'd blame the dementia, but she was horrible even before that."

"You're fat, too," Margaret said to Mary. "Where's Carrie? She's how you're supposed to look. A woman has to maintain her figure."

Margaret got up and gave Janet a hug and a fifty-dollar tip and walked her out. She went to the kitchen and took down the things to make her mother a sandwich. "Mom, this arrangement with you staying in this house is coming to an end. It's not sustainable."

The only reason Mary was there was because the home health service was short-staffed and had notified her that there was a four-hour gap in their coverage for Margaret that day. Seeing as how everyone else who might have looked in on her was dead or in jail, the responsibility fell to Mary.

She put the sandwich on a plate and set it on the table beside Margaret's recliner. "As soon as I get power of attorney transferred from Carrie, you're going to a home. I've already found the perfect place. It's small, run-down, and the staff look miserable."

Margaret was lost in her iPad. Whether she heard a word or not didn't matter. Mary looked around the empty house and realized she was the last one standing out of everyone who used to live here. If surviving this family was a competition, then she was the winner.

It felt far from a victory.

"Eat your sandwich, Mom."

CHAPTER THIRTY-THREE

IT TOOK PACKARD SOME time to realize he wasn't as indifferent to losing as he'd tried to be that night at the brewery. After a few days, he understood the outcome to be a judgment, a rejection of him and the work he'd done, and worse yet, a comparison between him and Shepard as law enforcement professionals where he was the one who came up short. When he thought about it for too long, it made him grind his teeth.

Shepard would be sworn in as sheriff in January. Packard looked at the schedule and put in for time off. A lot of it. Thielen said she'd pick up the slack, which she'd been doing since he was appointed acting sheriff, so no change there. Thielen's attitude about the results was that the world was ending. She saw only doom and misfortune in their future. Quitting wasn't an option, so her plan was to go deep and build a wall of work around her tall enough that she wouldn't be able to see or hear Shepard over it.

And then there was Kelly, who looked like she wanted the world to burn. Packard had a vision of her, asking every eligible voter in Sandy Lake County who they voted for and devising a personal vendetta against every last one responsible for making Howard Shepard her new boss.

Packard spent his work hours making a transition plan and his days off working on his house. It was time to finish things. If work was going to be as bad as Thielen and Kelly had already decided was inevitable, he was going to need a place to retreat and relax at the end of the day. He finished sanding his drywall, painted every room, and got help from Thielen's husband to insulate the attic and put down the luxury vinyl tile floors throughout. The kitchen still needed a lot of work and a lot of money but every other room was brought up to finished quality. He ordered new furniture and resold the used stuff he'd bought when he first moved to Sandy Lake. Frank claimed the corner of the new sectional as his favorite spot.

It snowed a lot in November. Packard kept a fire going in the wood-burning stove he'd put in the living room and organized his vinyl collection into the new stackable storage cubes he'd bought. He made time for books and television. Dave, the drummer from Maneater, texted and said they were playing a winter wedding not far from Sandy Lake. Packard told him to come over afterward, and they spent thirty-six hours twisted together like a pair of snakes. Frank lost his spot in the bed again, and then Dave went home and Packard was grateful for the solitude.

He spent Thanksgiving with Susan and Jenny and drove to Wisconsin for Christmas at his sister's. His brother, Joseph, came from the Twin Cities with his family and both of their parents were there, too—his mom and her turquoise jewelry and his dad with his second wife up from Florida. Everyone got along. The nieces and nephews were getting to the age where they were indifferent to most of the traditions outside of opening presents, and it was primarily his sister Anne's insistence that they should be enjoying each other's goddamn company that kept everyone from staring at their phones for three days. They played games and went snowshoeing and drank brandy slushies. His mom gave people neck massages and told them where in their bodies they were holding onto negative energy because that's who she was now—a crazy lady from Arizona.

Everyone had a stocking with their name on it over the fireplace, including Nick, who had disappeared two days after Christmas twenty-nine years ago. The anniversary went by unremarked. What was there left to say after all this time? Packard could have told them about the box with the case files he'd gotten from Marilyn Shaw but he didn't. He hadn't even opened it yet.

The box had gone into the guest room closet during the campaign and stayed there through the remodel. Packard hadn't forgotten about it. He thought about it a lot, but every time he considered taking it out, he felt like someone was sitting on his chest, and the pressure would make him mentally turn away and think of something else instead.

When he got home from Wisconsin, he decided he'd put it off long enough. Shepard was a week away from being sworn in as the new sheriff of Sandy Lake County. If ever Packard needed a distraction, now was the time.

He put on Wilco's *Sky Blue Sky* album, opened a beer, and brought out the box and set it on the coffee table. Frank watched, disinterested, from his corner on the couch until Packard took off the lid, and then Frank lifted his head because every box was potentially a box of treats. Not this one. Frank lowered his snout onto his single front paw and closed his eyes.

Packard put the lid on the couch beside him and sat back before looking inside. It felt like he'd taken the lid off a coffin and let a ghost out. He drank his beer and scratched his beard. Jeff Tweedy sang about impossible Germany, unlikely Japan.

When he looked inside, he was surprised how little there was—just a black three-ring binder and a brown paper bag. When someone disappeared without a trace, there wasn't a lot of evidence to be collected.

Packard pulled out the staples holding the bag shut and looked inside. It was the black winter glove with red stripes across the back they'd found near the hole in the ice they would eventually pull Nick's snowmobile from.

Packard stared at the glove, waiting for a flood of memories or emotions. Nothing. He didn't remember or recognize it at all. He fought the urge to take the glove out of the bag, to put his hand inside it and press it to his forehead like a psychic trying to divine its secrets. It was the only thing of his brother's he could lay hands on, but it was still evidence. He left it alone.

He took out the binder, set it in his lap, and opened the cover. The very first thing he saw was a plastic sleeve of photos the family had given the police.

Nick's school photo from his junior year. His hair was longer, parted just off center and pushed back in arcs that curved around again near his temples. There were photos from that summer at the cabin of a young Benjamin with Nick and Joseph and Anne wearing wet swimsuits, eating ice cream sandwiches on the front porch, holding sparklers at the end of the driveway. Packard leaned forward, looked closely at Nick, looked closely at himself. He was eleven or twelve in most of these pictures. A boy in every awkward, scrawny sense of the word.

In the inside pocket of the binder was an envelope that said BEN on it. Definitely not part of the original case file. Packard recognized the handwriting. Inside was a letter written in the shaky script of a dying man. A third of the way down on the first page, the ink color changed. Packard could imagine the effort it had taken Stan to put down these words even before he started reading them.

Ben,

It took longer than it should have to connect you to this case. In my defense, it was a long time ago and the drugs I'm on make things awful hazy. I wasn't on the drugs when we first met so that's no excuse. I don't blame you for not bringing it up. There are things a man has the right to keep to himself.

I remember this case. It was two years old when I joined the department as a deputy. The lead investigator felt like they'd had all the answers they were going to get. They found the glove and the sled. No body but Lake Redwing is wide and deep and there are some things the water won't let go.

Bullshit.

I circled back on this every year or so for a few years until it was shelved for good for a lack of new leads. I would check in with your parents and grandparents. Check in with the people who had been interviewed before to see if they had remembered anything new. Paw through the paperwork to see if anything had been missed. You know how it is with cold cases.

There was one guy who would never return my calls. Every year I'd have to hunt him down in person and every year I got the sense he was bracing himself for my return, that he knew he might spend the rest of his life answering questions about the missing Packard boy. His answers never changed. He didn't know anything. Didn't see anything. His kids' answers were the same as their dad's.

You know as well as I do that there are things you know and then there are things you can prove. I had nothing but a gut feeling about this guy. He had no record, no previous encounters with police. We had no evidence to make a case against him.

All of this came back as I read through the file again. I ran a search and found him still alive and still living in MN. I called him, reminded him who I was, and we had a long chat spread out over several phone calls. We talked about getting old and being sick. We're both in bad shape, him possibly worse than me, if you can believe that. We talked about the things that keep us awake at night. We both agreed, looking back, that there were times when we vastly overestimated our ability to imagine a worst-case scenario. There were times when we had no idea how much worse things could get.

We talked about his family and about another family who still didn't know what happened to their boy. I didn't get all the answers but we made a deal. He'd give me a location to search in exchange for protection for his family. Otherwise, he was taking what he knew about your brother to his grave.

You'll be angry at me for this and I don't blame you. I had limited time and limited options, but I thought you would want this above all else.

I'm sorry for what I've done, Sheriff.

Stan

The last page of the letter was driving directions and a crudely drawn map, then latitude and longitude coordinates that Stan could have gotten by looking up the general location on Google Maps.

Packard set aside the letter. In the binder, he turned over the plastic sleeve of photos. The first page behind it was an incident report form.

Blank.

The next page was blank, too.

Packard fanned through a stack of paper two inches thick. Every page blank.

Stan had destroyed the case file. Every word, every detail, every name, every interview. All of it predating computers and backup files and only existing inside this box.

Gone.

Packard didn't know what to feel. He stared at the flames raging inside the wood-burning stove. Stan Shaw's last word ever to him—*Sheriff*—stung like a rebuke in light of the election. He'd failed the man who had done so much for him in that regard. But what Stan had done hurt, too. The importance Packard had assigned to this box—all the details collected about his brother's disappearance, the official record of the worst thing that had happened to his family—was gone. He'd dreaded reading through it, and now he was furious that it had been taken from him.

He called Thielen, his heart pounding. He put on his coat and stepped into his boots while waiting for her to answer.

"I need your help," he said when she picked up. "We need dogs, deputies. The snow is going to be deep in spots so we'll need a plow. And lights."

"Hey, slow down," Thielen said. "What are you talking about?"

"There's a body," Packard said. "It's Nick. It's my brother."

READING GROUP GUIDE

1. Describe why Packard, as an outsider, is at a disadvantage during the investigation.

2. Bill and Sheri have a tumultuous, even unhealthy relationship. Would you characterize what they have as love?

3. Outline the reasons Packard is so reticent to run for sheriff. Why do you think he didn't win?

4. Discuss the three Gherlick sisters: Carrie, Sherri, and Mary. Define their similarities and differences.

5. The Gherlick family is an integral part of Sandy Lake. Consider their legacy. How have they shaped the town?

6. Packard's friends push him to run for sheriff, despite his hesitancy. Which of his qualities make him a good leader? Conversely, which might make leadership a challenge?

7. Consider Paul's role in this story. He never wanted to hurt Bill, though he had no moral quandaries about taking back his dead mother's pin or blackmailing Carrie. Do you think his actions were justified?

8. How much blame should we place on Carrie for Bill's death?

9. Packard ultimately learns the sheriff destroyed all evidence that led to his brother's killer. Why? Do you think it was worth it?

10. The damage Margaret inflicted on her daughters and, peripherally, on Paul is extensive and influences their adult lives beyond measure. In what ways have these characters continued the cycle of abuse or trauma? Do you think there's a way to end it?

A CONVERSATION WITH THE AUTHOR

This is your second book in the series. Did your approach to writing change with this book versus *And There He Kept Her*?

My approach to writing changed dramatically with this book. I spent several years writing *And There He Kept Her*, pantsing my way through the plot, then putting it through an untold number of revisions while incorporating feedback and new ideas as they came. I so overwrote the book that I had to cut 35,000 words to bring it in line with the expected word count for a thriller. I didn't have the luxury of that much time with *Where the Dead Sleep*. For this book, I spent about three months working out the plot, developing characters, and writing background I needed to know but that wasn't necessarily going to make it into the book. Once I started writing, I had a pretty solid first draft eight months later.

In thinking about one narrative thread to connect multiple books in a series (here, it seems to be the disappearance of Packard's brother), how did you go about plotting it? Do you have the details figured out ahead of time, or do your ideas change the more you write?

The truth is that Packard's personal connection to Sandy Lake and the disappearance of his brother came very late while drafting *ATHKH*. I didn't have any answers when I came up with the idea, only that I needed something bad to have happened to the family that kept them away from Sandy Lake until Packard suffered a more current crisis and picked Sandy Lake as a place with good memories and unfinished business. With everything else I wanted to happen in *Where the Dead Sleep*, I knew he wasn't going to get many answers about his brother, and to be honest, I didn't have all the answers. I know some readers will want to strangle me for that ending (sorry!), but I promise all will be revealed in the third book.

This story is a study in moral gray areas; there isn't *one* clear antagonist. Did you have one character in mind as a "bad guy" when you started drafting?

A lot of our entertainment centers on stories of women being stalked, threatened, raped, or murdered by men. *ATHKH* was no different. I wanted to turn that on its head a bit. I was thinking of the three witches in *Macbeth*, harbingers of murder and fate, which led to the idea of the three sisters. In domestic crimes, the spouse is almost always the guilty party. I wondered how it could be the spouse but also not the spouse. What if the person who pulled the trigger wasn't actually the killer?

At a time when the public places more scrutiny on law enforcement, why do you think a character like Ben Packard is important?

I'm not convinced Ben Packard is important in the grand scheme of things. Law enforcement is a fraught topic and not one where my voice as a middle-aged, middle class, able-bodied, housed, white male needs to be the loudest. When the topic comes up, I feel like it's my job to listen and learn. My books aren't meant to be treatises on policing. They aren't meant to absolve or condemn police. I'm just trying to tell entertaining stories about a guy doing his best to do the right thing.

Minnesota seems to be the perfect setting for crime fiction. Why do you think that is?

So many things—extreme weather, diverse settings (cities, farms, harbor towns, remote forests, etc.), a dark Scandinavian sensibility, the legacies of racism and colonialism. All these things provide rich opportunities for chaos and conflict.

What was something that surprised you about becoming a published author?

My everyday existence has not changed at all—I still do my day job, I still write alone in the evenings. Josh the Published Author who occasionally does events and signs books feels like someone separate from me. All the great things that have happened feel like they've happened to someone else, and I'm standing off to the side just marveling and feeling grateful on his behalf. I was hoping this second career would relieve me of certain duties around the house, but that has not panned out. "But I'm a published author" carries no weight around here when it's time to rake leaves or clean bathrooms.

Which books are your favorite to re-read?

Stephen King turned me on to Ohio author Don Robertson when I was young, and I've read several of his novels more than once. Don Robertson taught me about the rhythm of sentences and how the repetition of words and phrases can propel the sound of your writing. I had to unlearn a lot of those things because no one else can write like Don Robertson and get away with it. (I have a novel in the drawer that sounds like me trying to write like Don Robertson, and it is not good.) All of his books are out of print but worth seeking out. *The Greatest Thing Since Sliced Bread* and *Praise the Human Season* are two favorites.

ACKNOWLEDGMENTS

When I wrote the acknowledgments for *And There He Kept Her*, I had no idea what was to come. I thought I would sell a few copies to friends and family, then put my mom to work peddling books out of the trunk of her car. I never imagined thousands of Goodreads ratings, hundreds of Amazon reviews, or all the tags on social media. Thank you to everyone who requested an ARC, bought the book, read the book, reviewed it, posted about it, reported on it, and contacted me to say how much you enjoyed it. Thank you to the booksellers who invited me to their stores and recommended the book to buyers. It was an amazing experience to put my work out there and have it get that kind of response. I'm so grateful.

I feel bad dedicating a book about a terrible family to my mom and dad. It's no reflection on them. We were raised to be curious, kind, and creative. They gave us the freedom to wander far and wide, get lost, get hurt, and find our own paths, all the while knowing we had support at home. Seeing their pride in me for finally accomplishing this dream has been a highlight of the whole experience. My mom recommended *And There He Kept Her* to all her church friends and made a scene at her local Costco when it was on sale there. Thank you if you bought a copy from the crazy lady in Atlanta.

Everyone at Sourcebooks and Poisoned Pen Press has been a dream to work with. My editors, Anna Michels and Jenna Jankowski, let me tell the story I imagined, then asked all the right questions that made it better. Marketing manager Mandy Chahal raised me from a shivering baby bird who was terrified to talk about his book in front of an audience into a yattering, cawing crow who won't shut up about it. Thank you to my agent, Barbara Poelle, for giving me something to crow about.

My writing group partners, Gretchen Anthony and Laska Nygaard, provided the accountability and excellent feedback necessary to keep writing through the low points.

Thank you to Pamela Klinger-Horn for welcoming me into the community of Minnesota authors she champions relentlessly.

Chris—sorry for all the book events I made you go to. Thank you for coming to all the book events I made you go to. I love you.

ABOUT THE AUTHOR

Joshua Moehling is the author of *And There He Kept Her*, an Amazon Editor's Pick and a Barnes & Noble Monthly Mystery/Thriller pick. He works in the medical device industry and lives in Minneapolis.